The Blackguard

The Blue Dragon's Geas
Volume Two

Cheryl Matthynssens

Pat and
Sarah —
Right now you two are
our heros. I promise
when I beat this thing
I will pay it
forward!
[signature]
11-23-15

DEDICATION

This book is dedicated to three of my best friends: Alex Hunt, Rebecca Hunt, and Russell Matthynssens.

Alex was the one who encouraged me not to give up or give in to fear. As my editor, he has pushed me. We have fought, cried and danced together through the success of the first book *Outcast*, and through the writing of this sequel.

Rebecca.., well, she has put up with the two of us. She has played mediator many times so we both would come back to the table. Thank you both so very much. Without either of you, this series would not exist anywhere but in the recesses of my mind.

The third person is Russell Matthynssens. He sits patiently as I read things to him. He gives ideas and feedback when I am stuck. He doesn't complain when the dishes are not done. Living with a writer is a unique experience and those who do are very brave individuals. After all, if they anger us, they die in our next book.

ACKNOWLEDGMENTS

I would like to acknowledge my beta readers, who helped me so much with ideas, editing and general encouragement: C.L. Turner, Ben Harris, Matt Wirth, John Roach, Andrew Murray, and Alayna Barnett.

Prologue

The crack of the whip filled his ears, and fire lanced across his back. He arched in pain as much as his bindings would allow. His eyes focused on the flickering flame of the torch that lit the wine cellar. There were no windows, just three wavering torches that cast mocking shadows on the wall. A film of seawater and sweat stung his eyes and obscured his vision.

The mage focused on the flame again, trying to recall the reasons for his anger. His power was linked to his rage, and if he could stoke the fire of anger high enough, maybe he could find a way out.

The crack of the whip sounded and his body arched. Someone moaned nearby, and it took a moment to realize that the sound had come from him. His entire back felt on fire as the crystal-barbed leather snapped again, leaving trails of welts and blood in its wake.

He forced his thoughts to focus on the lies and betrayals. So many lies had fallen around him, from his own lips. Coming to Silverport was supposed to have been a good thing, a chance to grow into power...

The whip cracked again, and the pain of the new strike across already-damaged skin brought a new level of agony. He screamed against the leather in his mouth. How had he come to be here? How had this happened? The darkness that threatened to claim him finally overpowered the pain of the whip, and he sank into the dark comfort of oblivion.

The Blackguard

Chapter One

The creak of the lumbering wagon and the scrabble of korpen feet drowned out the usual sounds of the night. The evening was still miserably warm, despite the fact that the sun had set behind the hills hours ago. The large beetle-like beasts were content to plod down the road at a pace set for them.

The beauty of the landscape was still visible, the dark rocks outlined in white shimmering moonlight. The scent of korpen waste, dry sagebrush and the warm wind had long since melted into the background of Alador's awareness.

He sat on the wagon seat beside his father, Henrick, in silence. Alador had not uttered a word since the wagon had crawled out of

Smallbrook. His father's presence sank beneath the symphony of words that whirled in his mind: Alone. Abandoned. Unwanted. Their cadences crashed and throbbed with the same rhythm as the swelling in his face.

Alador was drowning in misery and self-pity. It wasn't just the fact that he had been cast out of his village for his crimes; he had also begun to realize just how much his choices regarding Trelmar had impacted everyone he cared about.

He couldn't help but wonder how Mesiande would take the news that he was now dead to her. His heart ached every time his mind touched upon the middlin he loved. She would blame herself, and there was nothing Alador could do to prevent it.

She would think he had abandoned her.

Alador started when his father finally spoke. "We will have to stop here." He said nothing in response, merely giving the slightest of nods to show that he'd heard the mage.

Henrick turned the beasts towards a small grove of trees that nestled next to the river. Alador looked around and realized his father was right; the moon was dropping below the hilltop, and soon they'd have no light by which to travel. It had been dangerous enough even with the moon's soft glow. Of the many creatures that hunted in the night, most were large enough to bring down a man.

Henrick turned the wagon sideways against the slight breeze - to provide a windbreak - before applying the brake. "I will set up camp. You picket the korpen and gather some firewood." His father's tone was authoritative: it was clear he expected no dissent from his son. Henrick stretched and hopped down.

Alador was still so wrapped up in himself that he barely found the energy to respond. He slid off the seat and slumped to the ground dejectedly, feeling every bruise and strain from the fight that morning and from the manhandling of the crowd that had meant to hang him.

With a heavy sigh, he began the task of picketing the large six legged creatures. Korpen had to be picketed away from each other, or they'd tangle unmercifully around each other while they fed through the night. The beasts were far too interested in eating the grass at their feet to move, and Alador was forced to fetch some fruit to lure them: so that he could tie them down with a strong rope and a stake.

He stared at the apples in his hand and saw his sister, Sofie's face, remembering how she would tease and hold them out of reach. He shook himself from the memory and completed his task. Once they were picketed, the docile giant beetles set to munching on the grass around them.

By the time Alador had finished gathering the wood, his father had laid out bed rolls and had a small fire started with loose tinder that was close by. Alador was surprised by how efficiently his father had set up their camp. He'd already set out forks for cooking, a rock ring for the fire, and even a filled water-bucket. With a groan, Alador set the armful of wood where his father could reach it and lowered himself slowly to the ground by the fire.

"Here!" Henrick handed him a small metal tin. "Spread this where you hurt. It will dull the pain; and make sure to use some on that face. You look like some creature from a tale to scare small ones."

Alador grimaced at his father, but set about spreading the strange paste on his bruises, swellings and places that just hurt. He gave a soft sigh of relief as the strange salve began to numb the pain. He worked absently, his mind still on his miserable state. His father let him mope, and Alador wasn't going to complain about the silence.

Once the fire was blazing and a pot of water was set to heat, Henrick added some meat and vegetables. He pulled a pouch from his waist and added a pinch of herbs to the mixture. Alador watched him work for a while, before the dancing fire captured his attention, mesmerizing him.

It was amazing how much a single day could change a man's life. His temper had always gotten him into trouble, and his hatred of Trelmar had never been more prominent than it had been today. Alador could not deny that every fiber of his being had wanted to choke the life out of Trelmar; but even so, that had not been his intent. He'd only planned to beat Trelmar to a bloody pulp for his assault upon Mesiande.

He sighed with despair, realizing that his current circumstances were merely the consequence of his own choices. He had chosen a path that meant death for him. If Henrick had not been there, Alador would have been hanged.

A noise startled him from his reverie and he looked around. It was dark now, a cloudless night, and he could no longer see the moon, though its light still glimmered faintly behind the hills to the west. The summer heat had finally begun to fade leaving the air comfortable again. The smell of his father's soup made Alador's mouth water. He realized he was actually hungry. He hadn't eaten since that morning .

"Wondered how long it would take for you to get there," Henrick said. His tone held a gentle edge of understanding and he winked at his son. He moved to the pot and ladled them each a large bowl.

Alador watched his father and took the offered bowl and spoon gratefully. "Get where?" he asked uncomfortably. He didn't like the fact that his father seemed to see inside him. He knew he'd have to guard what remaining secrets he had very closely.

"To the realization that you would be dead now if not for me. The realization that nothing you do is going to change what has happened," Henrick answered, sitting back against a wagon wheel to eat his soup.

Alador sighed and took a couple bites. "I haven't thanked you… I was so upset. I suppose I do owe you some gratitude," he admitted grudgingly.

"You are welcome. Are you done pouting…?" Henrick asked between bites. The man ate like he was three times his size. "…because we have a lot to discuss."

"For now." Alador forced a small smile. Inside, he still mourned the loss of the one thing that mattered most: Mesiande. Without her, he couldn't see why anything else mattered.

"Good. There are things you need to know. Let us start with the one that is most irritating," Henrick took another bite. "My brother, your uncle, is the Minister of the Mage Council of Silverport, and High Minister of all Lerdenia." Henrick let that fact lie there between them, watching his son.

Alador had still been dwelling on his losses, so it took him a moment to register exactly what his father had just said. "You mean, you're…like the brother of a *king*?" Alador stared at his father in disbelief. He couldn't remember his father ever mentioning anything about family before.

"Oh, let us not go that far. He is… *Minister*." Henrick's words dripped with derision. "They are chosen by a council. He is not a king, though I imagine he likes to think he is. There is no royal blood in Lerdenia. It is by the power of one's magic that rulers are chosen." Henrick let go of his bowl with one hand and held the other out to Alador, as if a magic ball lay within it.

"So he's the most powerful?" Alador asked, still staring at his father. He was looking at the man in a new light.

"So he and others believe. If there are more powerful mages, they are not interested enough in politics and rule to show it," Henrick replied.

"Does that mean you hold a special rank, since you're his brother?" Alador asked, leaning forward with interest

"Again, not how it works. Are people wary because we are related? Yes. After all, the… *capabilities* of one brother might also be found in the other. But each mage must earn his own tier placement in Lerdenia, and each tier only allows a certain number of mages. Therefore one must be bested before another can move up to take his place."

Henrick wrinkled his nose and leaned over to refill his bowl.

"And you are a fifth-tier mage...does that mean you removed people to make it there?" Alador eyed his father warily. "I mean, do you kill them or duel them or what?"

"That depends on the mage being displaced, and the mage doing the displacing." Henrick offered the ladle to Alador, who shook his head. Henrick shrugged in response and settled back against the wheel.

"Have you killed mages to get to your tier, father?" Alador asked slowly.

Henrick stared into his bowl for a moment, as if seeing something unappealing. "Yes," he answered finally. He continued to eat, as if unaware that his answer had raised at least one important issue.

Alador took some time to digest that bit of information. His bowl was only half-empty, but he'd suddenly lost his appetite. He stared at his father instead, trying to fit the image of this casual, gossiping enchanter to the man who would kill for a higher place in the tiers. It was difficult to compare the two. But then, as Alador thought about the way his father had spoken to Velkar when he had claimed Alador for Lerdenia, perhaps he could.

"If every mage must earn their own place in the tiers, but family relations don't matter for placement, why is your brother important to my place in the scheme of things?" Alador finally asked.

Henrick stopped eating and stirred his soup for a long moment. "I wonder... can I trust you? I mean, *really* trust you?" he murmured, apparently speaking more to himself than to Alador. He looked up at his son, studying him intently.

Alador felt as if Henrick was seeing through to his very soul, and squirmed uncomfortably. He spoke to break the tension of silence that built between them. "Of course you can. I mean, you're my father... You saved my life. I... Why do you need to trust me?" Alador asked, suddenly suspicious.

"Your uncle, Luthian, tried to buy a very large bloodstone. It was clear. It seems the trader gave up the name of the miner who sold it." Henrick watched his son with those piercing, soul-watching eyes.

Alador swallowed. "Me?" he asked, his words barely audible over the fire.

"You. Fortunately for you, I had mentioned the son I visit, so Luthian recognized the name and sent for me. Alador, he means to use you. I will have to deliver you to him, or lose the position I have fought for in Silverport. He will treat you like family, but you must be aware and cautious. If he can't have the magic of that stone, he will have the person that does." Henrick leaned forward. "Do you understand what I am telling you?"

The wind gusted, and Alador shivered as the fire flared up in ominous response. He set his bowl on the ground and ran a hand through his hair, lowering his voice as if in fear that another might be listening in. "You're saying I can't trust my uncle," Alador answered softly. "Why would he want me? I can boil water and see well enough to shoot. Not exactly sure how that's impressive."

"That is what you've learned to do on your own, Alador, with no training and with no guidance. If the stone was harvested when you drew it from the ground, I doubt you have even begun to discover the limits of your power and what you can do."

Henrick also set his bowl aside. "Listen to me, son. He will control you or he will kill you. You must let him think that you bow to his every whim until you learn how to harness all your skills. Take what he will teach you, but do not hesitate to seek me out. No one will think it odd that a son should seek out his father, even if he is in The Blackguard."

Alador stared at his father. What kind of life was he entering, that he had to worry about his own uncle? "Who else can I trust?" he asked. He stared at his father, concern written clearly across his face.

Henrick stared back across the fire at Alador. "No one. There is no one in Silverport you can trust." His voice was soft and held an edge of past betrayal, his eyes reflecting pain in the fire's glow.

Alador frowned . In the village, he could trust almost everyone. Sure, there were small feuds and jealousy, or the occasional bully. But in a fight against a common enemy, that bully would fight alongside everyone else. To live in a world where everyone was suspect and where you had to keep your back to the wall was a concept Alador was not familiar with… or eager to experience.

They were both quiet for a time. The river, the crackling fire and the crickets made a relaxing melody. "What is *The Blackguard*?" He finally asked.

"Good question." Henrick pulled a pipe from his belt pouch and loaded it , while Alador placed another small branch into the fire. "Your dear uncle and most beloved minister, Luthian, is forming an elite army of battle mages. You will begin your training in this army, the same as all Half-Daezun who enter Silverport. What you make of yourself from that point will be up to you."

"Half-Daezun… Are all The Blackguard made up of half-Daezun?" Alador was surprised there was a place for half-breeds at all.

Henrick lit the pipe with the burning end of a small stick. "Yes," he answered with a trace of annoyance. "It has been discovered that half-breeds who can cast have greater stamina for battle magic. That is why my brother seeks to create his elite force of battle mages with them." Henrick watched Alador carefully.

Alador frowned. "But no one is at war... Who's he planning on using them against?" "Peacekeeping can't be that hard in such a cut-throat city."

Henrick just stared at him, waiting for his son to put the pieces together. He puffed his pipe, turning his attention to making rings out of the smoke.

"He wants to go to war?" Alador asked watching his father and noting his lack of response.

"Yes, he means to end the peace." A ring of smoke directed at Alador seemed to surround and emphasize Henrick's sardonic tone. "With the Daezun unable to fight back, he can hunt dragons freely. He can control the isle and... well, he can gather more power."

Henrick's snarl of displeasure made his position clear. "The one thing that motivates my brother above all things is power; not slips, nor prestige, but sheer power. He wants to be known throughout history as the single most powerful of all Lerdenian mages..."

He looked directly at Alador. "...no matter what he has to do or whom he has to use to get it."

Alador leaned forward, his eyes widened in genuine alarm. "I can't let him do that!" he declared adamantly. "I can't be part of an army designed to kill my own kin!" He looked around, suddenly wary again that someone might be watching or listening.

"Be at ease, Alador. Breathe, boy." Henrick waved his pipe at him. "I do not intend to let there be a war if I can help it."

Henrick put one hand on his knee and stretched out his other leg. "He is not here, and we are far from Silverport. But if you don't go with me, he will just send out hunters to bring you in or to kill you. He will butcher those you care about to draw you out if he has to. That Mesi you have your heart set on would make a good target. No, my plan is better. You learn what he has to teach; and when the time is right you can return to your people and protect them."

Alador stared at his father, trying to remain calm. He didn't feel calm. How could he, after finding out that his uncle was to all intents and purposes a king who wanted to kill him?

"How am I going to do that?" he asked, his voice trembling. "How can I protect them?" Alador thought of Dorien and his mother; his mind flashed to the sweet sass of his little sister Sofie and to the laughing eyes of his friend Gregor. He bristled at the idea of anyone touching a hair on Mesiande's head. He realized he would do anything to protect her, to protect all of them. "What do I need to do?" he asked with slow determination.

Henrick smiled in triumph. He reached into his pocket and withdrew a small object, which he tossed across the fire. Alador barely caught it, his body protesting the sudden movement of his arm. He looked down to see a piece of clouded bloodstone in his hand.

"You learn to harness what the blue dragon already gave you."

Chapter Two

Alador sat up and looked around. He didn't know what had startled him awake, but his heart was racing. Slowly he stood and scanned the area, picking up the bow he'd laid by his bedroll. He hoped he wouldn't need to use it: his hands were still stiff and his knuckles bruised.

He peered around the wagon, glancing out at the agitated korpen. The sun was not yet up but based on his ability to see, it would be soon. Alador looked over to where his father had been sleeping, but Henrick was gone.

He let his eyes rove in a circle, trying to find the source of his anxiety. There seemed to be nothing moving; but at the same time, the birds were not singing either. He remained watchful until the beasts began to graze once more and the birds began their chirping.

Alador moved to the fire and stoked it back to life. He glanced again at his father's empty bedroll. Where was Henrick? He sat close to it, finding comfort in its heat and light.

He was still uneasy and there was still no sign of Henrick. His father's roll had been slept in and looked to have been casually left. He pulled his bow a bit closer. He could not shake the sense that something had been watching him. He stirred the fire absently, glancing often at the wooded surroundings.

Despite the heat of yesterday, the morning was foggy and damp; he couldn't see the tops of the surrounding hills. The road they traveled followed the river valley, and he could hear water tumbling close by. Alador picked up a pot and headed for the river.

He washed and refilled it, watching the water roll by for a long moment. He was downriver from where he and Mesiande often sat to pass the time. He stuck his hand in the water, as if touching the river here meant he could somehow also touch her. He sighed softly, letting the water trail out of his fingers.

Alador stood, grabbing the pot and headed back to the fire. He thought it was a good morning for tea and considered trying to warm the water magically, but decided that he didn't feel up to the effort. The grief of all he had lost was still a heavy weight and Alador felt like his magic was to blame.

Once the water was heating over the fire, he sat back to watch the flames and consider all that he had learned yesterday. Thinking on his father's challenge, Alador pulled out the small bloodstone Henrick had given him. It had been cloudy the night before, but now it held the same shimmering clearness of the huge stone he'd sold to the trader. His father had taught

21

him the simple skill of pulling the magic from its once murky depths.

He and his father had talked far into the night, covering topics that moved freely as the night wore on. Henrick had answered all of Alador's questions without hesitation. Oddly enough, it was a side to his father he hadn't seen before.

He had learned that the average Lerdenian did not live beyond his sixtieth turn: because of confrontations for placement and power, and because few willingly shared the power they held or the spells they learned. This made The Blackguard unique, as its formation was the first known effort to condense and share magical knowledge.

But even then, its members were only taught spells that would be useful in battle. Spells from inherited power or gained from bloodstones had to be discovered or taught by a mentor. Alador would have an advantage with his two mentors in Luthian and Henrick, but both were more influenced by red dragon magic. Alador had gotten his skills, or at least those that he knew about, from the blue dragon.

The fact he had inherited his father's skill for tapping into magic was evident by the fact that he'd harvested the stone; but he'd shown no indication that he could use fire-based magic.

Alador looked up to see his father crossing the field toward him and released an exhalation of breath. The tension he had been holding on to since he had awoken came hissing out. Henrick was dressed in simple leather pants and a deep blue shirt. His long black hair was pulled back into a tail behind his head, and he was carrying a string of fish, but no pole.

Alador raised an eyebrow as he approached, and got a stick ready for placing them over the fire . "Up early and with breakfast?" Alador asked. "Where's your pole?"

Henrick smiled and handed the fish to Alador. "Oh, you have your skills and I have mine. I do not need a pole." He winked and set about packing and organizing the wagon. Alador went down to the river and cleaned the fish. He had them laid out and cooking by the time his father was satisfied with the wagon.

"While those cook, I think it is time we got in some practice."

Alador rose to his feet, actually excited about the idea of learning to control his magic. He turned with a smile to Henrick who then handed him a sword fashioned from wood, replicating a hand and half with a cruciform hilt.

"A sword?"

"Members of The Blackguard have to be able to wield a sword, and while I know you are good with a bow, I have no idea what skills you have with a blade. So let us test them." Henrick swirled his own wooden sword deftly.

Alador groaned. He'd never been good with a blade and he still felt the aches and pains of yesterday's encounters. He had chosen not to hone that skill, favouring his bow instead - although the Lerdenian eyesight he'd inherited from Henrick had kept him from being very good at that, until recently... While Daezun had knives for close combat, few had skill with a sword.

Alador took a firm grip of the wooden sword. He was fairly sure it was too light for an actual blade, but the balance felt right. "This won't be a fair match... You're going to trounce me soundly," he pointed out with a frown. "Add to that, I am still hurting from yesterday."

"You think your enemy is going to care that you already did battle the day before and don't feel like fighting just now? I assure you he will be ecstatic to learn you are not up to the task." Henrick's sarcasm was cutting. Before Alador could reply, he went on: "Now, let us check your ability to parry. I want you to do nothing for a moment but block my blows." Henrick whipped his own wooden sword about a few times, then saluted Alador with an overdone flourish and began to circle him.

Alador gripped the sword in both hands as he had no shield. He watched his father closely. Dorien had taught him not to watch the eyes, but the shoulders and hips of his opponent. That worked just fine. He knew his father could distract with those mesmerizing eyes, so Alador made sure he didn't look at them.

Henrick nodded with pride to his son and then came in swiftly. Despite what Dorien taught him, Alador missed the feint to his right and his sword ended up in empty air as his father soundly thwacked his left side. He cursed and fell back, eyeing his father.

"First rule, Alador...," Henrick cautioned as the two circled. "Always hold on to your temper. Your enemy is going to want you angry, for if you are angry, you will be wild and careless." He spun and came around with an overhand blow.

Alador grit his teeth and met the attack horizontally, the two swords perpendicular to one another. The impact resounded loudly, the vibration rocketing down the blade and into his hands. He fell back again, letting go with one hand and shaking it out.

Henrick paused and looked at Alador. "I see why you use a bow. Remember, do not block with the edge." His tone was scolding and factual. He moved as if holding a sword were natural to him, even though Alador could not recall ever seeing him with one.

"All right, let us start with some basics." He laid his sword down and moved behind Alador. "First, your feet. You need to stay fluid so you can move quickly. If you are planted, it will allow you to meet a solid blow but prevent an easy pivot."

He helped Alador move his feet to a more suitable position. "You want to face your opponent like this - a little to one side, but not fully sideways or it leaves your back open for him." Henrick demonstrated the position.

"Next, it is better to deflect the blow close to your hand, as long as you do not risk losing it, but only close enough to shove it away from your body. If you deflect with the least amount of energy, you will last longer in a fight. Also, turn the blade slightly: you never want to block with the edge."

Alador listened closely. His father had made clear that his life of safety was over and that survival would depend on what he learned. But far more motivating was that he would take these skills back to the Daezun so that they would be prepared for the day they faced The Blackguard.

He watched as his father scooped his sword back up and headed over to the fire. He turned the fish over, which brought a small smile to Alador's face. Leave it to Henrick to make sure the food didn't burn.

"Now!" Henrick turned back to face his son. "I will attack slowly. I want you to move so you can meet me and just deflect the blow . Don't try to stop it. Don't try to overpower it. Just deflect it."

He began a dance of slow motion blows, striking first right, then left or stabbing. Alador moved his sword to slide the blow away. Every so often, his father would give a tip here and there about how to parry a particular swing.

When at last the smell of perfectly-cooked fish caught his father's attention, Alador's arms felt heavy and his biceps ached. He collapsed gratefully by the fire while his father handed him a stick with two fish neatly skewered on it.

Henrick peeled away the skin with a knife to expose the fresh, warm meat of his breakfast. "It is a good start. We will practise every morning until we reach Silverport."

"I'm sorry we have to go by wagon. I know you could be there tomorrow on a lexital." Alador sighed; he knew he was an inconvenience to his father. He didn't like being a burden.

"Every moment we take irritates Luthian, and that is pleasing in itself." Henrick grinned at his son, and Alador couldn't help but grin back. "Besides, it gives me more time with you before Luthian takes over and buries you in his precious guard."

Alador frowned. He would prefer to stay with his father; but Henrick had made it clear that this would raise suspicion. The more he melded into the Lerdenian society, the safer he would be. "What about practising magic?" He wanted to learn the skills that would help his people defeat any attack his uncle had planned.

"That, you can do as we travel," Henrick offered between bites . "We will start with simple cantrips that any child can learn, and work our way up to things that take a bit more energy and focus."

Alador frowned as he picked at his fish. "How is it that you eat so much and remain so thin?" he asked as he watched his father dig into a second large trout.

Henrick didn't look up from his breakfast. "Magic is very draining on the body, Alador, especially if you regularly maintain any spells. It will drain from the person if there not enough fuel to maintain it. That is why many Lerdenians have white hair: magic is devouring their vitality. I have learned that eating whenever I can minimizes the cost."

"ARE you…?" Alador asked, shrewdly watching his father.

Henrick caught Alador's tone and looked up. His eyes narrowed at his son's intense gaze. "Am I what?"

"Constantly maintaining spells," Alador clarified. "Are you using magic on me?"

Henrick chuckled. "What spells I choose to maintain are none of your business. However, I will give you this: I have not used any spells upon you since we were in the alehouse discussing your find."

Alador's eyes held his relief. He had some fear that even now his father had been manipulating him through the use of magic. It was possible that he could not trust his father either; but the truth was that, without his father, Alador wouldn't last a day in Silverport.

They both finished eating in silence. Afterwards, Henrick finished loading the wagon while Alador coaxed the korpen back into their harness. The two beasts got along, so at least it was an easy task with the smell of fruit in his pocket. Alador gave them both a treat for their good behaviour and then helped his father ensure the fire was truly out. A wildfire in the summer could be deadly to Lerdenia and Daezun alike.

Once they were in the wagon and back on the road, Henrick handed Alador an old tin cup full of dirt from beside their fire. It even had a fish bone in it. He tossed the bone out, then looked in the cup again. "What's this for?" Alador asked curiously.

"We start with a cantrip that should be strengthened by the stone you harvested. Each mage has to find his own method of using small bits of power. Some sing, others hum, some use magic words, and some use motions. The truth is none of this is necessary for simple spells. It is whatever helps you grab onto that feeling of power in the pit of your gut and focuses it through your will. I want you to practise finding that center of power within you and focus it enough to dampen the dirt in the cup."

The wagon slowly jostled and rattled its way up the road. Alador took the cup and stared at it. He imagined the dirt growing damp, but nothing happened. He frowned. He knew the feeling Henrick talked about; he'd felt it when he practised at the river's edge.

But he also had to get angry to draw power... No, that wasn't entirely true. He wasn't angry when he shot a bow and the target seemed to jump to him.

Alador considered the cup carefully and tried to feel for his power. His father said nothing as the wagon lumbered along, letting Alador solve this puzzle for himself.

The trail narrowed and brought them closer to the river, between a cliff face and the riverbank. Alador looked up and saw several large nests belonging to ferath - large birds that sustained themselves and their nests with fish. Their calls were eerie and reminded Alador of tales of ghosts calling in the night.

The sun was shining strongly now, and the day was already warm. The river twisted its way south, shining in the bright light. Alador sighed, remembering his task, and went back to focusing on his cup of dirt.

He couldn't find that pit of magic again. He wiggled his fingers over the cup, but the only thing he felt was embarrassment as Henrick looked over and grinned. He cursed inwardly at the dry cup of dirt.

Frustrated, he looked up at the call of a ferath and thought he saw something in its nest. He focused on the nest as he did targets in the field, and then realized that he had felt that pull within him. The nest appeared closer and glimmered with some piece of metal the ferath had stolen.

Alador looked back down at the cup. He'd felt that magic. He closed his eyes, seeking that feeling again. As he did so, he absent-mindedly ran his finger around the lip of the cup. Slowly, he found a small glimmer of the strange pull. He felt... something - like a string inside him that stretched from his core to his fingers. He focused on it and imagined the dirt becoming wet. He jumped when his father spoke.

"Very good." Henrick lounged with the reins in one hand and his pipe in the other. The wagon still lumbered along the road.

Alador looked down at the cup just as a strange fog dissipated from it; the dirt on top was damp. He grinned triumphantly: he'd done it! He'd pulled magic from his inner core without having to be angry.

Henrick took the cup from him and scooped out the top layer of dampened dirt. "Do it again," he stated softly.

Alador took the cup and frowned at his father. "Why?" he asked. He'd done what he was told, and wanted to learn something more useful than just making dirt wet.

Henrick puffed smoke into a ring before he answered. "Took you too long..."

Alador sighed softly and worked to do it again… and again, and again, continuing this exercise throughout the day. He would dampen the dirt, and his father would scoop out the wet layer.

Whenever Alador complained, his father would state that he was taking too long. Finally, when Alador was at his wits' end, he thrust the cup at Henrick. "You do it then!" The dirt had dampened within seconds this last time. His head was pounding and he truly just wanted to close his eyes.

Henrick took the cup and then just handed it back to Alador. He did not say any words or make any motion, but when Alador looked down at the dirt in the cup, it was bone dry.

Alador looked up at his father in amazement. "How did you do that?"

"Practice, Alador. Could you shoot a bow with any accuracy when you first learned?" Henrick pulled the korpen over to a small widening of the road where the cliff ledge high above cast some shade against the sun, near a patch of grass for the korpen.

Alador was grateful for the stop to stretch his legs, but he realized that he was tired and starving. "Well, no." He understood what his father was saying, though: he had to practise just lining up the arrow before he could even begin to worry about being able to shoot.

"It is a matter of honing your ability to just feel that center of magic whenever you wish. More complicated spells will require more energy. In a battle, you cannot worry about the time it takes you to find that center. You have to be able to touch it without thought. It needs to be as habitual as breathing."

Henrick also hopped down. "Get something to eat. You have been at it for some time, and I need to send a message to my brother."

Alador was about to ask how, but having seen the automatic ease with which his father had dried the cup, he realised he would have the magic needed to send a simple message. He moved around to the back of the wagon, grabbed some cheese and fruit, then walked to the water and sat on a rock to eat.

The mist drifting off the river felt welcome against the summer heat. He looked around, appreciating his surroundings and realizing that he really loved this land. A lump formed in his throat as he also realized he was going to leave it.

Silverport was on the coast, where there would be nothing but fog and rain, where everything would be green and damp. Alador gazed across the sheer cliffs that were streaked with the red of iron, or spattered with white. The white powder that formed at the edges of the river gave more evidence of the minerals here.

He watched as a ferath dived into deeper water and came up with a wiggling fish. Alador smiled, remembering when he and Gregor had tried to shoot the fishing birds right above the shore: so they could get two meals from one arrow. Gregor had won that day. Alador's smile faded, and he sank back into his misery.

Henrick joined him after a few moments, and for a while they sat and watched in silence. Finally, his father spoke, looking off into the distance. "Take water to the korpen, and then I want to show you something."

Alador nodded. He handed the last of the cheese over to his father and went to fetch the trough and bucket. The shape of their heads kept korpen from being able to drink out of round containers, so they used a light, flat trough to water them. It took three buckets before the two korpen returned to feeding on the grass.

Alador put the trough and bucket away and went to join his father, who was still watching the river. Henrick had two mugs and handed Alador one filled with the cold river water. He drank it gratefully, realizing that he was as thirsty as the korpen. He finished off his mug and went back for two more.

When Alador had finished and his mug lay empty, Henrick looked at him. "Fill it with water using magic," he instructed softly. "It will take more effort than dampening the dirt, so you will need to pull harder on that center."

Alador closed his eyes, running his finger around the lip. He pulled hard, imagining the cup filling with water. When he could pull no longer, he looked down. There was water there in the cup, but it wasn't full. He looked at his father, disappointed in himself.

"It takes practice, do not fret. It is good enough for our lesson. Come." Henrick got up off the rock he'd perched on and headed over to the cliff, where he pointed at a tuft of green grass clinging for survival among the red rocks. "Stand here..."

Alador looked at his father, puzzled, but he did as he was instructed. Henrick replaced Alador's cup with his own empty one. "Do it again." He moved a good distance back from Alador.

Alador looked at his father puzzled but obediently closed his eyes. He pulled hard at the center of magic, imagining the cup full of water, his fingering running around the lip. When he could pull no longer, he looked down in the cup. There was water, but a lot less of it. He looked at his father with a frustrated sigh.

"Look down, Alador," Henrick said, pointing to the ground.

Alador looked down. The tuft of grass he stood on was partly dried and brown. He looked at it in confusion, then up to Henrick with alarm. Had he just killed the grass?

"You cannot make something from nothing. Magic pulls from the world around you. Just as it takes the energy from you, it also takes from the world around it. You were able to pull more water by the river because water was before you. Here, the water in the grass was the closest source, outside yourself."

Henrick watched his son closely as he explained this vital lesson. Alador looked up at his father in alarm. "I can hurt people just by pulling for my magic?"

"If you do not focus correctly, if you just pull impulsively or in anger or ignorance, yes. You must learn to focus where the magic pulls from as your skills develop. The reason you were so thirsty is because you have been dampening the cup of dirt from yourself, me, the korpen, and the air around you."

Henrick continued to watch his son with sharp scrutiny. Alador knelt down with sorrow as he touched the blades of dried grass. He had not known he would kill it. He looked up at his father with a glimmer of understanding. "I had no idea," he whispered.

He'd always thought magic was some glamorous power of mystery that some people could just reach out and create. He had no idea that to do so they had to harvest from the world around them. "I could kill someone creating water?"

"Not likely, but with the powers conferred by a blue dragon, you could kill someone by totally dehydrating them," Henrick said bluntly. "It would be a horrid and a frightful death."

He smiled slightly at that thought. "I have only met two mages strong enough to do it; but the cost to them would be great, as well. Killing another with slow, deliberate intent is a warping of the gifts that magic offers. It warps the mage in a manner he cannot repair. You cannot kill another slowly and not twist something within yourself, Alador. Remember this: magic is not without cost, regardless of its wonder and magnificence."

Henrick looked at his son with a seriousness he did not usually exhibit. He walked off, leaving Alador kneeling by that tuft of dead grass.

Alador sat thinking in that same spot for a long while, until he noticed his father waiting for him on the wagon seat. Henrick had a pipe out and looked like he'd been waiting for some time. Alador straightened up with an effort, walked over to the wagon and put the mug behind the seat.

Neither of them said anything. He had been excited at the beginning of the day after he'd pulled the water to dampen the dirt for the first time. Magic had been exciting and wondrous. As his father had made him do the same cantrip over and over again, Alador began to feel it as work, no easier than mining or woodcutting. The realization that magic, though wondrous, required effort had only just occurred to him. The few enchanters and healers he had seen use magic seemed to do so with such ease that he had thought it an innate skill, as Tentret's ability to draw or Dorien's ability to mold metal into his desired object from only a description.

Now, Henrick had taught him that magic was deadly. Alador had known it could be used to kill already; the tales of the Great War he'd grown up hearing made that clear enough. This was different though. Just drawing the energy for magic could be deadly.

Alador wanted to run to Gregor or Mesi and share everything that had happened today; but the thought reminded him once more of his losses. He lapsed once more into sullen thought while he sat, staring at the spiny backs of the korpen as they plodded along. The silence continued until Alador smelled smoke faintly in the air and saw its source in the distance.

He looked over at Henrick in surprise. It hadn't occurred to him that they would pass by any villages. It should have: roads were supposed to connect the villages; but no one had passed them on the road thus far. Not that Alador was complaining... With so few travelers, it was unlikely that word of him or his crime had reached any other village yet.

"That is Oldmeadow. Nice place, for the most part," Henrick mused. "They raise fowl and make a good apple mead. We will stop there for the night." He urged on the korpen a little; they'd slowed until they were barely moving. "Tonight, you are my apprentice. You will go by Al and nothing more. Understood?"

Henrick looked over at him, the warning clear in his eyes. "I do not care to besmirch my good name by giving the impression I am prone to stealing fugitives from the noose."

Alador opened his mouth to argue, but then snapped it shut, swallowing hard and nodding. It wasn't really a lie – Henrick was instructing him – and Alador didn't want to be the one to bring the news that he had killed a man. He thought for a moment. "Anything special I should be doing as an apprentice?"

"Keep your mouth shut and your eyes open. A traveling enchanter is not always welcome and must therefore be responsive to the mood of the village. They should be in a fair mood, however, as last night was the circle." Henrick looked over at Alador.

Alador breath caught at his father's words. Last night should have been his rite of passage, the final step to becoming an adult. Alador had devastated the entire ritual when he'd killed Trelmar. He doubted anyone was in a fair mood at home.

"Understood," he answered quietly. He reminded himself that he hadn't wanted the women in the village to choose him, anyway. But truth to tell: the fact that he'd left before the circle was a weight he couldn't shake. It felt like he'd left something incomplete.

The time spent traveling to the village passed in silence. Alador watched the landscape: the terrain was rugged, with large boulders bigger than the wagon lying on either side of the winding road that crawled along the river bank. Vegetation had been sparse for much of Alador's journey so far, but now the rock cliff curved away from the river and opened up into a beautiful valley.

Trees filled with green apples lined the road, extending outward in long rows. Chickens, ducks and panzets - large birds with long legs, prized for their long purple feathers - wandered freely in the orchards. Alador had seen panzet feathers used sometimes in special dress or ritual clothes, and he knew people ate the bird, but he'd never tasted it.

The birds stood out starkly against the trimmed grass that surrounded the fruit trees. Their clucking and calling filled the air with a discordant, yet magical song. Alador opened his mouth to ask how the villagers kept the grass so short, but closed it when he saw a flock of grey and tan rock sheep, whose tightly-curled fleece could mimic the rocky inclines around them. They often hid from their predators merely by curling up. They didn't camouflage well in the orchard, but Alador doubted they had much to worry about in the way of predators.

Word that a red dragon had attacked Smallbrook had apparently been sent out. It didn't take Alador long to spot the archers on platforms built high in the trees. He imagined that it would be devastating if a fire-breathing dragon attacked Oldmeadow's orchards. He nodded to one of the sentinels who caught his eye and was saluted back curtly. The archer's eyes immediately returned to watch the sky.

As Henrick guided the wagon into the village, Alador looked about in amazement. Other than the fact that Oldmeadow was surrounded by orchards and flocks of birds, it could have easily been mistaken for Smallbrook. The village structure was defined by the same wagon-wheel pattern, with all paths and roads leading to the village center.

Just before the center, Henrick turned the wagon to the right and traveled about the wheel till he came to a large building that could only be the alehouse. Two female middlins came hurrying over as Henrick hopped down, hugging him warmly and offering cheerful greetings. Henrick was half-dragged into the alehouse, leaving Alador by the wagon with his mouth hanging open.

He became irritated that his father would leave him so, then belatedly remembered that he was nothing more than an apprentice. It would be his duty to see the wagon safely parked and the korpen stabled. He asked a nearby villager where Henrick's wagon could be placed for the night, and, once he'd received his curt instructions, set about his tasks.

Only when he'd parked the wagon, stabled and fed the korpen, and seen to laying out their bedrolls beneath the wagon bed, did Alador go into the alehouse. Night was falling by the time he ducked into the smoky, bustling building. Just like in Smallbrook, Henrick was surrounded by adults and elders. Their laughter and genuine joy at Henrick's arrival drew Alador's attention, and he went about finding a seat in the corner so he could closely watch his father.

He could see no sign of spell-casting, nor did he see any use of items, yet the villagers seemed very comfortable in Henrick's company. Alador knew that not all enchanters were this well-received. They often set up their wagon on the edge of town, and anyone who needed an enchantment would come to them.

And now that Alador thought about it, Henrick had not always been so well received. That change had only come about four or five years ago, when people had begun to treat him as more of an honored guest. It was a puzzle Alador couldn't solve. The only solution he could think of was how liberally Henrick let the liquor flow about him,

Normally, a Daezun apprentice would see his master's cup filled or a plate of food delivered, but that was not necessary tonight as Henrick's cup was kept full and his plate of food had arrived just as Alador had entered. He made his way to the bar and met the large scowling keeper at the side. "I would like some ale and a plate of simple fare, sir," Alador ordered casually, not really looking to the alehouse keeper. His eyes were still on Henrick. It came as a shock, then, when Alador was grabbed by the shirt front and jerked across the counter.

"We don't serve no dirty half-breeds in Oldmeadow." The large man's face was inches from Alador's own surprised eyes for a few moments before he tossed Alador back like he was no larger than a small one.

Alador hit the ground hard, knocking over a chair. He sat there stunned with shock. He'd been seen as different in Smallbrook, but he'd never been treated with such bold rudeness. He started to get up, but Henrick's hand pressed down on his shoulder and his boot pinned Alador's thigh in place.

"Now, Now Derent! Surely you are not denying my apprentice some food to take back to our wagon?" Henrick's manner was jovial as he smiled at the keeper. "I mean, I am sure my slips are good enough to cover his meager needs. Why, the lad cannot drink but a pint before he snores the night away. Perhaps if you gave him a true measure of your mead, I could get some sleep tonight, for it would put him soundly under."

Henrick stepped across Alador, leaving him on the floor. "Have a heart for me at the very least?" He slipped a full medure across the bar, his other hand held to his chest.

There was a bit of nervous laughter about them, and Alador still sat stunned on the floor. The keeper slowly relaxed, glancing at Henrick and then the medure. "So he's yours, Henrick? Surely you could pick out a more striking lad or homely woman for your needs?" His eyes roved over Alador like he was some stray rent boy.

Alador shifted uncomfortably at the outright laughter coming from those around him. He realized that the keeper was implying that the two of them were... mating. He felt his anger bubble up as his own father played along with their laughter.

Henrick leaned across the bar and murmured, "Not many take to traveling with an enchanter; beggars can't be choosers, now can they? Besides, the boy has a sweet way with him." Henrick winked at Derent, and when the keeper turned, laughing outright, to fetch a mug of apple mead, Henrick looked back with a glance so threatening that Alador said nothing as he struggled to his feet.

When a plate of food was laid on the bar along with a mug of mead, Henrick picked them up and handed them to Alador. "Go keep my robes warm, boy. When I am ready, I will seek you out."

Alador took the food and mug, his jaw clenched with anger he could barely contain.

He stood glaring for a long moment at Henrick then glanced over to where Derent was pouring out another measure of mead from the large keg. Alador stared at it, imagining the keg overflowing. Henrick followed his gaze, then looked back at his son in warning, but Alador was already channeling his anger.

The bung popped out with the pressure he created, soaking the keeper with spewing apple mead. In the pleasing melody of Derent's curses and nearby patrons' shouts for the keeper to plug the keg up, Alador turned and left with his meal. He smiled slightly with satisfaction as he slipped out of the alehouse.

It was a good hour later before Henrick joined him at the wagon. Alador was working on fletching an arrow when his father appeared out of the darkness and sat down beside him, his face unreadable in the flickering lantern light.

"I am not sure whether I should congratulate you or beat you senseless," Henrick growled. "You could have exposed yourself in a manner that I was not prepared to explain, especially since casual use of magic is not well received in Daezun villages and you well and truly know this." He had apparently decided on the middle ground and taken a tone of scolding.

Alador looked at him. "I would apologize, but the dung heap had it coming." He looked back down at his feathers and decided that he'd done enough for the night. He carefully wrapped them up to slide back into his fletching supplies.

"Be that as it may, Alador, you cannot go casting magic at everything that makes you angry." Henrick sighed with exasperation.

"You let him think that I was…that we were… How could you do that?" The reason for Alador's anger came spilling out. He glared at Henrick with indignation.

"I do not care what some low-minded, village alehouse keeper thinks. I DO care about keeping my skin in one piece and the reputation I have intact. Besides, what do you care what he thinks?" Henrick glanced over in mild amusement. He plucked a blade of grass from beside him and began to chew on it absently.

"I don't know! I just…" Alador growled in frustration. It had a feral edge to it, and he did not miss Henrick's quick glance of interest. "I don't like the idea of people thinking I'm not normal." He stilled his hands to look at his father.

Henrick chuckled. "You are a half-breed and a mage. You are not normal by most Daezun standards, Alador."

"But you scold me for using it. What's the point of having magic if I can't use it?" Alador asked, still packing up. "Besides, it's not like it was obvious. I didn't do anything that couldn't have happened naturally."

Henrick half chortled before he forced a more serious manner. "I will admit it was a trifle amusing. I will also admit that I had a moment of pride: clearly you can improvise when using your power, which is good. However, Alador, magic is a tool that requires energy, and you only have so much to use. Careless use of magic may leave you personally drained when you have a need of it, and it pulls from the environment around you, remember. Magic ages you if you are forced to pull it when you are not rested and fed. Most importantly, it is disrespectful to the gods that grant it to you."

Alador looked at his father in surprise. "I didn't think you believed in the gods." He could never remember his father talking about them.

"I keep my beliefs close to my heart. I do believe in the gods. I believe in the tales of the creation of dragons. I believe that magic is limited and that if it is not managed better, mortals will lose their access to it. I believe that when the last dragon falls, magic will die soon after." Henrick stared off into the darkness. His tone had taken an edge of melancholy.

Alador was quiet for a time, digesting this new side to his father. "Why do you not stand up to the council about what the Lerdenians are doing in the bloodmines?" he asked softly.

"I am one man, Alador. I am patient, and I prefer to move behind the scenes. My hope is that the dragons will put a stop to it, but they do not seem to recognize their trapped kin as true dragons." Henrick spoke as if he were in deep grief.

Alador stared at his father. Henrick's face was unreadable, but there had clearly been emotion in that statement. "Is there a way to make them understand?"

Henrick pulled off his boots before he answered Alador. "If there is, I haven't found it. One or two probably do see, but to take the bloodmines would be to declare war, in a manner of speaking. The dragons are already hunted. I doubt they want a war." Henrick rolled under the wagon and into his bedroll.

Alador threw his bag in the back of the wagon and picked up the lantern. He crawled in from the other side, deep in thought. It seemed to him that, whether dragons liked it or not, they were at war already. As he moved to turn out the light, his father spoke one last time.

"Alador…"

"Yes father?" Alador looked over his shoulder, his hand pausing on the light.

"You ever pull a stunt like that again, and I will personally teach you the meaning of pain." Henrick's statement was casual in its delivery, yet there was no doubting its seriousness.

Alador couldn't help but smile as he answered: "Understood." He turned out the light and lay thinking about these new revelations, long after his father's snores interrupted the peaceful melodies of the night.

Chapter Three

Alador's sleep was restless, his mind was filled with the lessons he'd learned about magic. His heart longed for Mesiande and his family. He wanted the safety of the village. He couldn't find sleep at first; but after a while, the repetitive sounds of the night birds and insects slowly lulled him from his thoughts. The sounds blended and merged and soon became the sound of waves, pulling Alador deep into a dream.

Renamaum was perched on a cliff overlooking the sea. It was windy as he stared out at the endless waves. The normally-placid waters were as agitated today as the dragon's heart; their depths were grey and murky instead of sapphire, and they were crested with foam that was speckled brown from the stirred-up ocean floor. The sea birds sailed on the wind without the need for flapping, and a mortal ship bobbed far out in the distance, trying to stay upright on the angry waters.

He had felt his father's arrival before he heard him: his sire was one of the eldest dragons of *Vesta* and his presence could be sensed from a long distance.

"*A fine day for floating on the sky.*" His father's booming tones carried enough to agitate the birds below them, and his large frame made the rocks tremble as he landed.

Renamaum looked at his father, his anger seething. He could not hide his outrage as he glared at his sire. "*Better one for fighting,*" Renamaum snarled.

The large male lumbered closer to his son. "*You are like a scavenger, so hungry for blood that you do not care if it is your own tail you bite.*" His sire shook his head sadly. "*Why should I send my son to die for mortals that would feast upon his blood?*"

"*Not all mortals believe in such things. Some still honor the past and the way,*" Renamaum reminded his father. His tail swished behind him in agitation, clearing the ground and vegetation. Pebbles flew left and right with each sweep.

"And those mortals are losing their battles. Soon all that will remain are those that break the pact and seek only their own glory." Renamaum's sire looked out at the water.

"Go to Rheagos!" Renamaum beseeched his father, his tone pleading.

"Rheagos rarely involves himself in mortal affairs." His father eyed Renamaum. "Why do you care so much if these mortals destroy themselves or not?"

"I care because I see in them the hope of Vesta. Our minds are not one of creation, but they create such magnificent things. They live such short lives and so live them desperately as if they might miss a single moment. They find wonder where many see the natural way of things." Renamaum spoke with passion. There had to be a way. "Please, Sire, go to Rheagos. He does not have to become involved. Just give those that fight for the old ways and the pact something that will equal the battlefield."

His father stared at him in silence for a long while. The crashing waves below them seemed to match the rhythm of Renamaum's beating heart while he waited, knowing that this was a time of decision.

"I will go on one condition," his father finally announced. "I do not promise success, but I will see our golden cousin if you agree."

"Anything!" Renamaum turned to face his father fully, his heart racing with hope.

"You do not enter the fight." His father's voice was firm, but quiet, and he did not look at Renamaum.

His father's words cut deeply, and Renamaum began to argue. But all things had a cost, even magic, and he knew that. If staying on the fringes and not joining the fight would give the ones called Daezun an edge, then he would agree. "As you desire," Renamaum finally conceded, dropping his head in dejection.

"I know you hold your word and in this I am most pleased to call you son. I will seek this gift and do so avidly, for the healing of my own fledgling's heart." The large blue dragon launched himself into the sky.

Renamaum stood in the wind, watching the waves roll in. The ocean, like his own heart, was relentless in its purpose. He knew deep down that the only way to save magic was to save the mortals that fought to possess it.

He didn't know how he knew, but he knew it as surely as he could see the school of fish skimming the waves below. Deciding he was hungry, Renamaum dove off the cliff, his body angling to hit the water at its deepest point.

Alador woke to the sounds of morning village activity: the chopping of wood, the giddy voices of middlin women, the sounds of the roosters declaring the day. He smiled groggily, glad that his nightmare was finally over, only to groan as he realized he was really under the wagon and not in his bed in Smallbrook. His smile quickly turned into a frown, and his mind went over the dream he'd had last night. As usual, it was like he'd been seeing through the eyes of the dragon. He had felt Renamaum's anger at being denied the ability to fight. He had sensed his hunger when he had seen the fish. Alador sighed softly. These dreams were never really of much use, as far as he could tell, but they were definitely becoming more vivid.

He shifted slightly in his bedroll and got a second reminder he was not in his own bed when a rock dug into his spine. He rolled over to see Henrick staring at him. Alador blinked a couple more times to make sure he wasn't imagining things, but no, there was the face of his handsome father. Henrick's lavender eyes bore into Alador as if seeing through him. "What? I haven't been awake long enough to cause more trouble!" Alador whispered with concern at the strange way his father was staring at him. It was disconcerting.

Henrick searched his face for a moment before answering. "Yes, a proper apprentice would have been up and had me some warm tea and a meal by now," he answered.

Alador groaned realizing his father was right. He should have woken before Henrick if they were going to continue their ruse. He peered out from under the wagon, but it was still very early. "I'll get the fire going and set to heating some water," Alador offered quickly. He moved to roll out from under the wagon, but Henrick stopped him with a hand on his shoulder. His father looked at him for a long moment with an expression of concern.

"Wait. I think there is something..." Henrick trailed off and shook his head. "No, it had best wait till we are on our way." He frowned and let go of Alador.

Alador gave him a puzzled glance, but rolled out from under the wagon and pulled his boots on. He made sure Henrick's were in reach and then set about doing all the things a proper apprentice would be doing; stoking the small fire back to life, putting water on to heat, and laying out some cheese and fruit for their breakfast. Someone had left a bag of apples at the edge of their small encampment. They were early and a little green, but they would make a nice contrast [or 'complement' – your choice!] to the cheese.

While Henrick pulled on his boots, Alador set about the village to find one of the women willing to part with some bread for a trading token. He still had a few left from his night when the traders had visited. By the time he returned, Henrick was digging into the cheese and took the offered bread gratefully. Alador made them both tea and sat back to wait. It wouldn't do for him to take from his "master's" plate, and they were already getting plenty of strange looks as villagers wandered about on their morning tasks. Aside from the fields of apple trees that surrounded the village, Oldmeadow really did seem so much like home.

For a time, Alador spent the morning watching as Henrick saw to the few enhancements the villagers brought to him. It was all simple fare: one villager offered a slip to see his bow given an enchantment of accuracy, while another came asking for something to keep the ground pests from her garden.

One by one, Henrick saw to each of these. The last request, however, came from the head of the circle of elders. Alador watched the exchange with interest. It was getting warmer and the biting insects were out in force; he batted at them absently, but didn't let them distract him from watching. The elder had seemed hesitant to approach Henrick, whose amused posture gave Alador a clue that his father was well aware of that fact.

"Greetings Enchanter Henrick, and may the dragons ever avoid your steps," the man called formally.

'Greetings Elder Caneth; I assure you that dragons stay far from my path," Henrick called back with a lopsided grin.

The elder smiled. "I'm sure they do. I've come, actually, on business of dragons [or 'on dragon business'? – your choice]." Caneth moved to stand in front of Henrick.

Henrick lost his lazy posture, becoming a bit tense as he eyed the elder. "Unusual business to see an enchanter for. A matter of dragons, you say?" He eyed the other man with closer scrutiny, clasping his hands behind his back.

"These are unusual times, wouldn't you agree, Henrick?" Caneth glanced at Alador and back to Henrick.

Not one to be baited, Henrick didn't look at his son. "They are indeed. What can I do for you on this matter of dragons?" He smiled with his usual disarming grin.

Caneth took a breath before answering. "I wish for you to ward the orchards against dragons," he requested formally.

Henrick was quiet for a long time. Shielding his eyes from the rising sun, he peered at the orchards that surrounded the village, then looked back at Caneth. "I fear that I cannot do that," he answered with an unusual edge to his voice. "Why ask for such? You have never been concerned before."

"Cannot, or will not?" Caneth murmured stroking his beard with a frown. "We have heard of a dragon attack on Smallbrook. We cannot afford to lose the trees. This crop is how the village maintains itself with slips for goods through the winter. It must be protected."

"I understand your concern, but what you ask is beyond my skills. I am afraid that I cannot do this. Such a powerful ward would be quite beyond my ability to cast," the mage restated. "But I am rather sure that you will find your crops are safe from fire and acids," he offered in consolation. He dropped his arms again, further relaxing.

"Smallbrook was not safe," Caneth pointed out, clearly disappointed that the enchanter was refusing him.

"True enough. But you have a small advantage over Smallbrook." Henrick grinned slightly, but Alador could see that the smile didn't reach his eyes.

"I fail to see our advantage. If anything, a fire would be more devastating." Caneth was obviously growing upset.

"A truth, yes; however, dragons are rather fond of apples," Henrick offered, his voice softening to ease the mood of the elder. "I do not see them burning such a delicacy. Devouring it perhaps, but never destroying it.

Why not try this as your ward: up on the top of the hill, plant some trees. Keep them watered and fresh as you can and leave the apples there for the dragons. I am sure that soon word would spread to protect Oldmeadow, for here you honor dragons."

Caneth eyed Henrick for a long moment. "Are you sure this would work?" he asked, the tone of his voice colored by doubt.

Henrick shrugged. "There is little in life that is certain, Elder Caneth. Each must do their best in the moment and hope it was [is?] enough. However, I am certain that such a gesture will not go unmissed." Henrick relaxed slightly. "Not to mention it would cost you little for the effort, and you would not be giving slips for a very expensive enchantment." Henrick smiled with more genuine mirth.

Caneth nodded. "I will see it done. Paying for an enchantment didn't sit well with the council, so this plan should make many a good deal happier. I only pray the dragons are patient enough for the trees to grow large enough to bear fruit."

Henrick nodded. "That is the thing about dragons; they are often willing to wait a great deal of time for the smallest of pleasures. Unlike our own races, time is rather on their side."

Alador watched as the two men shook hands and Caneth had moved off before he approached his father. "How do you know so much about dragons?"

"You wouldn't believe me if I told you," Henrick answered, putting away the items he had withdrawn to assist him in his tasks. They'd only earned a meager amount from enchanting, but then, Henrick didn't seem too concerned with slips.

"Try me," Alador stated firmly, standing with his arms crossed and watching his father. Surely nothing his father could say would be any stranger than the events he'd already faced since digging up the stone.

Henrick looked at him for a moment, then grinned. "I made friends with one," he offered.

Alador stared at the mage in disbelief, blinking a few times as the words worked through his head. "I was serious. I mean, what dragon would make friends with a Lerdenian? Do they even talk?" His curiosity overcame his disbelief.

"I told you that you would not believe me. And, just so you know, they can talk in the common tongue if they choose." Henrick put his things in the wagon. "Best go fetch the korpen. It is time we were on our way."

Alador sighed and turned to fetch the korpen. The village was now well into its daily routines, and few bothered to take note of him. He fetched some wormy apples that had fallen from the orchards and used those to entice the korpen to the wagon. The korpen were content in their pen, though, and didn't want to leave. It took Alador a great deal of coaxing to get them moving, and he had to bribe them all the way to the wagon. Even then, Henrick still had to help him get them in the traces.

The entire time, Alador wondered if his father had been serious. It was unheard of for a Lerdenian to "make friends" with a dragon. In the Great War, the dragons that had been willing to fight had done so on the side of the Daezun. Surely, he'd been joking. Yet Alador had to admit that his father often spoke with great authority on the subject, and he spoke as if he knew them well. How else could he know them well unless he'd been telling the truth? Alador shook his head. No, it must have been just another of his father's jokes.

A few of the villagers waved as Henrick and Alador left Oldmeadow. Both men were quiet; the older lit a pipe and sat back with the reins loose in his hand. Once the korpen were moving, they didn't need a lot of guidance other than to pick speed back up. Alador sat staring off into the distance, not really seeing the rows of orchards as he thought about his father's admission. Finally, when he could stand it no longer and they were clear of the orchards, Alador broke the silence.

"Are you really friends with a dragon?" Alador looked over at his father.

Henrick put a hand over his heart. "I swear I am so close to a dragon that there is little of him I do not know and little of me that he does not know."

Alador searched his father's face but could see no mockery or teasing light. "How did this come to be?" he finally asked. It seemed so unlikely.

"He was going to eat me." Henrick grinned and took a puff on his pipe.

"Eat you? Yet you're here, telling me you became friends. What happened?" Alador turned on the wagon seat to look to his father, his face and manner as eager as any small one around the fire waiting for the evening tales.

"I will tell you if you promise me you will not interrupt," Henrick offered with a slight grin.

"I promise," Alador answered quickly.

Henrick seemed to take delight in smoking his pipe and making Alador squirm as he waited. "I was traveling by lexital on my enchanting rounds when the blasted bird took fright. It dumped me off near a lake and then fluttered off and left me stranded. My head had been a bit rattled, so I really did not have the means to call it back or the energy left to use a spell of travel."

Alador immediately wanted to ask about the traveling spell, but remembered at the last moment that he'd promised not to interrupt. He stored the question away for a future discussion. He had no idea that there were spells for traveling.

Henrick puffed on his pipe, blowing a few smoke rings. He gestured about as if a dragon actually stood before him. "As I was pondering my situation, I suddenly found myself consumed with a fear that I cannot begin to explain to you. I can tell you that I stood trembling and looking about when I saw him. There, lounging in the lake as if taking a bath, was a great dragon. He lumbered out to stand before me. I swear to you that every spell I could have uttered to protect myself had flown from my terrified mind; I stood absolutely frozen. My brain seemed to have decided that if I could not move, maybe he wouldn't see me. He opened his great mouth and I waited for that pain of bite or flame, and then…he just spoke." Henrick took a puff from the pipe.

"Spoke? I thought you said he was going to eat you?" Alador eyed his father with a bit of disbelief. He had never imagined his father afraid or weakened. Henrick had always seemed confident and assured, or at least he had the last few years. "Wait, how long ago was this?"

"About four years, and you promised not to interrupt, Alador." Henrick's tone became irritated. Alador snapped his mouth shut and nodded sheepishly, hoping that his father would continue.

"He asked me at that moment to give him one reason why he should not eat me. I can tell you that my mind was racing, and for the life of me I could not think of a very good one, so I croaked out that I was bound to be far too bony and stick in his throat. Emboldened by the throaty laugh he gave, I began to point out that to eat a Lerdenian was to risk all forms of different digestive issues. It was a rather long conversation that we both participated in on all the horrid forms of death one might experience by eating a poisonous, bony Lerdenian." Henrick puffed his pipe. "We have been friends ever since."

"How often do you get to see him?" Alador asked eagerly. "Can I meet him?" He didn't know if he'd have had the courage to stand before a large dragon and declare he would be far too poisonous to eat.

"Doubtful you will meet him, as he is rather reclusive. I only see him when it amuses him," Henrick stated.

"What color was he?" Alador asked excited by the fact that his father knew a dragon. He was far more impressed with this then that his uncle was the High Minister of the Lerdenian people.

"I cannot tell you any more, Alador. I made a promise never to disclose facts about him or where I met him." Henrick looked over. "I am sure you can understand that a dragon's resting area is sacred and the fact I live is a rare feat."

Alador nodded and decided not to press his father for more information. He tried to imagine what it had been like to stand there, discussing one's possible death with a dragon. As they rumbled down the road, Alador just sat and thought about this new information. His father seemed content to puff on his pipe.

They both rode on in a long silence before Henrick spoke. "I think it is now my turn." He looked at his son with the same intensity as he had when Alador had woken that morning.

"Your turn?" Alador swallowed; he had a sneaking suspicion that he wasn't going to like whatever Henrick's turn was.

"Yes. My question from this morning that I decided was better not discussed in Oldmeadow." Henrick turned his pipe upside down in the dusty track and knocked the leaves loose. He looked back at Alador as he stuck his pipe back into a pocket. "How do you know the name 'Rheagos'?" His question was soft.

Alador blinked not sure what his father was talking about. "I don't." He frowned at his father. "Why?"

"You were saying it in your sleep. You begged me to speak to Rheagos." Henrick was now watching his son and not the road they were rattling down.

Alador looked away from his father, still not entirely sure what he was talking about. Then his dream came flooding back, and Alador realized he must have been muttering in his sleep. Inwardly, he cursed. How could he begin to explain? "In truth, I really don't know," he offered. It was the truth. He wasn't totally sure who or what Rheagos was, but he had the idea that he was a reclusive and powerful dragon. "Do you know who he is?"

"Yes," Henrick answered clearly not happy with his son's answer.

"Who is he?" Alador asked carefully.

"You were the one asking me to take you to him. Who do you think he is?" Henrick put his boot up on the board before them and handed the reins to Alador.

Alador took them automatically. He considered the dream, or at least what he could recall of it, very carefully. "I would say an ancient dragon."

Henrick considered Alador's words as if weighing their merit. "You have dreams, don't you?" he asked with a low, even tone, and his eyes not leaving Alador.

Alador felt a strange pressure and refused to look at his father. The place where he found his power now felt something coming from Henrick and it rolled in response. "Don't use magic on me, Father," he warned with a growl. "If you want to know and we're supposed to trust each other, stop using magic to compel me to answer," he continued, venturing out in a guess.

The pressure stopped immediately. "I am sorry. The answer, Alador, is crucial to matters at hand. I need to know the truth."

"Will you kill me when you have it?" Alador asked still not willing to look at Henrick.

"There is a time when I might have, but I have reconsidered," Henrick answered back evenly.

"Why have you reconsidered?" Alador had suspected that his father had weighed the subject of saving him from the noose far too long.

"I have decided that I can trust you. I have decided that you might actually be strong enough to help me outwit your uncle. I have decided that to do so would be far more entertaining than letting my dragon friend eat him." Henrick answered. The words were so blatantly honest that Alador looked at him.

"It would be faster to let your dragon friend eat him," Alador pointed out.

"Perhaps, but then there is the matter of restarting the war, and dealing with the mess and chaos that would be left if a dragon ate the High Minister. It would be far more conducive for his fall to come from within," Henrick stated.

"You trust me with a great deal of information that could see you dead within hours of our arrival in Silverport." Alador eyed his father, trying to figure out what game he was playing.

"Indeed! I figure I am going to have to give you something as deeply dangerous as the information I seek to drag from that little brain of yours." Henrick grinned at his son.

Alador slowly grinned back. Despite his fear and the warning not to do so, he decided to trust his father. "I've been having dreams since the moment I took the bloodstone from the ground. I dream of a great blue dragon and in this last dream, he mentioned Rheagos. I can't be sure it was from the stone, though. I was knocked out when I hit my head, and the healer said that I hit it fairly hard. Why is this important?"

"There are two kinds of bloodstones, Alador. One you know well, and have mined since you were big enough to do so. However, there is a type of bloodstone that is exceedingly rare, a geas stone," Henrick replied slowly. "I do not know of one being found in hundreds of years."

"What's a geas stone?" Alador asked uneasily.

"A geas stone is empowered with all the magic of a dragon, usually an elder dragon, often a flight leader. But in addition to all the power of that dragon, it is imbued with a geas that cannot be denied by the recipient." Henrick stared off into the distance.

The road narrowed and wound back next to the river, and Alador had to pay close attention to the korpen as the wagon barely had a foot on either side. The cliff loomed above them on the right and the river raced by on the left. "What's a geas?" He asked curiously after a long moment of silence.

Henrick considered the question. "Well, a geas is like a promise. One that must be kept. The problem is, in a geas stone, one does not know what that promise is until one stumbles upon it. It is usually formed if the dragon was after something very important to him and, in his death, he declares that geas. Unless one chances upon it, or is present at the dragon's death, there is no way to know. However, if your stone was a geas stone, every choice you make will press you closer to completion of that promise." He looked at Alador. "The reason I suspect yours may have been such a stone is that you have those dreams, and vivid dreams of the dragon imposing the geas often act as signs."

Alador sat on the edge of the seat, his body tense. He gripped the reins tightly, partially as the korpen's tendency to wander needed close attention and partially because his father's words felt true. He knew deep down as Henrick spoke that there was something he had to do. And, just as he had said, Alador had no idea what that 'something' was. "What difference will this make for me?" he asked softly.

"I don't know, Alador. What I do know is that you and I must keep this a secret. You must guard your sleep. You must act as if your uncle is the favored mentor and hang upon his every word. And, you must make it seem as if your power falters until you are ready to resist him. Luthian cannot suspect you have taken a geas stone." Henrick's words were urgent.

"What will he do if he learns about it?" Alador glanced at his father worriedly but quickly returned his eyes to the path.

"He will have no choice: he will kill you," Henrick answered softly.

"Who is Rheagos?" Alador asked after the mage's words sank in. He realized that in the distraction of other conversation, he did not yet know that answer.

Henrick was quiet for a while and Alador was finally able to look at him. Henrick met his gaze and finally nodded. "He is the last dragon created by the gods' hands. He is the elder of all the dragons and the only one I know of with golden scales. To know his name, to hear it spoken from a mortal tongue..." Henrick lapsed silent.

"Yet you know it," Alador pointed out. He failed to see why knowing this name was so important to Henrick. He glanced back at the road, relieved to see it widening back out.

Henrick sighed softly. "Yes, I know it. I had thought never to hear it spoken till you were muttering in your sleep. To hear it from my own son is something I am struggling to fathom."

"Why do you know it?" Alador looked at his father curiously. "Is it because you have a dragon friend?" He eyed Henrick and shifted uneasily in his seat.

Henrick hesitated. "Yes; yes, that is it. I heard my friend speak of it," he muttered.

Alador watched Henrick and, for the first time, knew his father was lying to him. He had been about to challenge his words when a low, deep rumble interrupted him, alarming the korpen. Alador looked up to see huge rocks tumbling down from the cliffs above.

"Rock—" was all Alador could get out before the cliff cascaded down upon them.

Chapter Four

The rain fell with its usual steady drizzle. To those that lived in the trenches, rain was a welcome thing. Most of Silverport's sewage was brought down into the trenches and flushed out into the bay opposite the port. There was a slight angle to the trench to allow for drainage, and a small flow of water had been diverted from the falls in an effort to keep the waste from stagnating. The attempt hadn't been successful; relief from the constant stench only came when it rained. Those who made the trenches their home were so used to it, though, that they usually didn't notice.

Though Silverport was the symbol of the grandness of the Lerdenian people, the trenches were its dark and evil heart. Every city had a trench, but only Silverport, as the Lerdenian capital, had a full six levels above the trench. Most Lerdenian cities only had three.

Regardless, every city had a Trench Lord: a leader of sorts who'd risen from the hierarchy built out of the outcasts, half-breeds, and those without magic that were forced to live in squalor. The Trench Lord would always be someone of strength and intelligence who managed to work his way to the top. Once he had risen,, he was met by the leader of that city to make arrangements. Then, he would be left to rule the trench as he desired, as long as certain city needs were met. If they were not, the ruling mage would see to his immediate removal. There was no retirement from the role of the Trench Lord.

Over time a home had been made for the Trench Lord, just a little above the trench - overlooking it but not quite on the first tier. Its interior was as fine as the High Minister's, though the house was smaller. The Trench Lord skimmed the goods coming into the city, and often had first pick on many of the new arrivals. Despite the house's grandeur, however, no one of the trench welcomed an invitation into its fine marbled halls. Few returned.

Aorun stood at the small balcony that overlooked the port. He preferred this spot as the outcropping for the balcony was technically outside the trench, and for a short while he could enjoy fresh air and the beauty of a fine morning. He sipped his tea laced heavily with smalgut, a bracing alcohol he favored. It was the way he began every day, with a moment of silence before a reign of blood and violence.

A ship had come from one of the port cities across the sea. It would have on it a shipment of silks, wine and other luxuries. Aorun preferred the feel of leather for his own clothes, but he had to admit he loved running his hands across a woman's body when it was clothed in the liquid sheen of silk.

Aorun was a cold man. His muscular figure, deadly swordplay, and cruel nature made sure that most stood well out of his path. He had no mercy or concern for those he ruled over; his pleasure, his pocket, and his power were all that concerned him. He saw those within the trenches as toys for his pleasure and minions in his service, while those above him were little more than spoiled fools that did not deserve respect. Fortunately for Aorun, he didn't have to give it until he stepped above the third tier. Those in the first three tiers considered the Trench Lord as necessary and respected his position. Without his goodwill, certain goods became expensive and difficult to obtain.

He stepped back into the room. His personal office had the typical stone walls of any trench dwelling, but his floor was a beautiful tile work of blues and greens. Aorun's fireplace drafted properly and the room didn't smell of soot the way most trench homes did.

His favorite possession was a beautiful, ornate desk that stood impressively across from the door, its deep, rich color not typical of wood from around the isle. It was clearly intended to draw the eyes of visitors that stepped into the room. Aorun approached his desk and set down his cup, before moving to open the door and beckon his two men inside.

Sordith and Owen had been with him since he'd killed his predecessor. Aorun trusted them both as much as he dare trust anyone, and let no one else close to him. He had others in his employ and protection, but only these two knew most of what Aorun did, and only they were allowed to stand beside him in the trench. Their position meant that both of them slept in the Trench Hall.

"Sordith, since you have a head for numbers and do not mind it, I want you to oversee the collections today. Review the warehouse reports and inform me if you see any discrepancies." Aorun indicated the pile of reports on his desk, his tone one of unquestionable order.

He waited until Sordith gave his usual brief nod. Sordith did not speak overly much, but he had a sharp eye and was good at catching errors in figures. Aorun had some education with numbers, but had to belabor them with difficulty. He was a man of the sword and hated anything that required him to sit behind a desk with paper.

"Owen." Aorun paused, waiting for the man to look to him. "The wench in my bed has little skill and giggles far too much. Deliver the slut to Madam Aerius down at the brothel and make sure you tell the Madam to put the girl into training for at least two weeks before she is offered up to any tiers." Owen nodded and turned to head for Aorun's bedroom. "Oh, and Owen...."

Owen turned back and looked at Aorun. "Yes, m'lord?" he asked. His deep voice usually brought him plenty of his own wenches. His commanding tone was what had made Aorun look him over the first time, when assessing men to move up to his side.

"Feel free to test her yourself, but I found her sorely lacking in any skills." Aorun smiled at his man, knowing that to use the Trench Lord's woman in his bed would be a pleasure he would not have to offer Owen twice.

"As you command, m'lord, so shall it be." Owen grinned wickedly, already unbuckling his sword belt as he walked out the door.

Aorun caught Sordith's disapproving glare at Owen's departing back before Sordith could mask it. "You have got to get rid of that sense of honor of yours, Sordith. While it leads me to trust you with my books, I swear one day you will get yourself carved up for some wench who deserved her lot." He shook his head, chuckling softly.

Sordith had already schooled his face to its usual casual blandness. "They can try," he answered with some arrogance.

Aorun just shook his head. When the door behind Owen shut, his demeanor became more serious. "What time is the stable lord due to visit us?"

Sordith moved forward on that question. "Again I beg you to reconsider helping this man. This army he plans to build…what if it is you they seek to dethrone?" Sordith frowned at Aorun. "I do not like this breeding of people like they are dogs."

"Sordith, most of those sent to the stables are little more than dogs. Look at it this way, if it bothers you so much: those that are accepted and keep their mouths shut are given a chance to leave the sewers. It will help some better their lot."

Sordith leaned onto the desk as Aorun sat down behind it. "Maybe the half-breeds, Aorun. Maybe their lot is better, but Lerdenian women are free. They should not be rounded up as slaves." Sordith spoke with passion; he was one of the few that could speak to Aorun so honestly.

Aorun's eyes hardened as Sordith spoke. "Even if I agreed with you, which as a point of fact I do not, the High Minister himself has commanded that I work with the stable lord. I am not going to be the one who irritates that man. There are few that give me cause for concern, but he is one of them."

"So you are afraid to refuse," Sordith shot back, his anger at such injustice flaring up.

Aorun's temper flashed and he rose up to lean across the desk. His eyes narrowed, and he drew his face within inches of Sordith's. "Say that again," he hissed dangerously to Sordith.

The two stood eye-to-eye for a long moment. The only sound in the room was their breathing and the bells from the ships below the window. Finally, Sordith dropped his gaze a half measure. "I apologize, m'lord, it was not my intent to call you a coward. It is just upsetting that the man I serve, who should be treated with the respect he is due, is treated by the upper tiers as little more than a puppet master." He took a step back from the desk.

Aorun slowly straightened up as well, still clearly angered, even though he held Sordith in high regard. "You have work to do. What time will the man be here?" he growled, crossing his arms.

"In two hours," Sordith replied coldly. "I will see to it that a couple of your men brings those gathered into the receiving room."

"Good. I expect your numbers on my desk at the end of the day," Aorun stated.

Sordith nodded. "Of course, my lord." He turned to set about his duties when Aorun called to him again.

"Sordith. One last thing." Aorun waited until Sordith stopped and turned around to look at him. "I want you at my side while the stable lord is in the hall."

"I have no desire to be anywhere near that business." Sordith's voice was tense.

"Exactly! Which is why you will be. Owen is far too willing offer his services, and it is distracting." Aorun's tone held disgust, but it also left no room for argument.

Sordith took a deep breath. "As you command." He bowed low, then turned on his heel and departed.

Aorun watched him go, shaking his head. He counted on Sordith's honor and skill in areas where Aorun was less proficient. Sordith did kill, but he had this sense of warped justice that sometimes reared up the way it just had. Aorun was fairly sure Sordith had never taken a wench to his bed who hadn't sought it first. The rogue had never even taken advantage of the stable lord's offer to come to the third tier. Sordith lived simply, as was evident by his room; it had what the man needed, all of fine quality, but not much more.

Aorun walked alongside his walls, running his fingers along the inset stone shelves, which were full of treasures from all around the world. He liked looking at new and odd things. From strange books to beautiful pottery, his was a collection of world travels he longed to take, but on which he'd never venture. He sighed softly and wandered back to the balcony to stare out at the ships.

Sordith had called him a coward. In one way, Aorun knew he was. His fear of water would always keep his feet on this isle, locked into a position of power from which there was no escape. It had been his decision to seek the heart of the last Trench Lord, and it wasn't a choice he regretted. But in many ways, Aorun realized he was as much a prisoner of position as a ruling lord. He sighed again and went back to his desk, opening the drawer, and removing a silver flask of smalgut, from which he took a straight shot. Grimacing at the burn, Aorun closed his eyes, letting the alcohol scald its way down and accepting its gentle release of his anxiety.

Sordith joined Aorun at the appointed time. His right hand's face was tightly schooled to hide his displeasure, but Aorun knew that Sordith was still indignant by the stiff bearing of his posture and the way he kept one hand on the hilt of his sword. Unlike Aorun, who wore a sword on his back, Sordith favored two smaller swords at his hips.

Aorun had to admit that if any man were quick enough to best him, it would be Sordith. It was just another reason he kept Sordith close. A man quick enough to kill you had best be on your side; the alternative was to dispose of him, and Sordith's quick mind for business was too valuable to waste. "Still angry about being here?" Aorun asked with amusement.

"Best we not discuss it." Sordith's terse response was confirmation enough. The belated "m'lord" he added was clearly nothing more than deference to Aorun's rank.

"Oh, why is that?" Aorun glanced at Sordith, knowing he was pushing the man's tolerance and anger, but delighting in it nonetheless.

"I like living."

Sordith's cryptic reply was not lost on Aorun, who chortled before opening the door and sweeping into the room. At his entry, those present except his men dropped to a knee. He wandered down the line of those that had been gathered.

There were five half-breeds: three women and two men. There were also several Lerdenian women, some dirty and unkempt. Two were obviously from the plain's farms. All of them were beautiful to look at, despite their fear and their soiled condition after being housed in the kennels. There were also two full-blooded Daezun men, their eyes filled with hatred as they looked at their captor. "Well, here is a surprise," Aorun said. "Where did these two come from?"

One of the men guarding them stepped forward. "We found them on the outer edges of the farms, claiming they were outcasts. Apparently their own people turned them out. Won't say what they did to be thrown out of The Peoples' Lands." The man gave a sharp salute to his chest and stepped back.

Aorun moved before the two, looking at them in consideration. "I do not think the stable lord will be seeking full-blooded Daezun males. I could be wrong, but it is outside the realm of what he usually orders. We will leave them for now and see his reaction. He is going to be disappointed in our numbers this week." Aorun noted that the Daezun men were well secured, and when he noticed the disdainful expression from the one on his left, he kicked him in the face. Aorun didn't care about causing permanent damage; he only looked on as blood spewed from the fallen man's nose. Aorun hated the Daezun, a fact that he did not conceal from any that lived in the trenches. "You will keep your dog faces down until spoken to," he hissed. His eyes moved to the second Daezun, who slowly lowered his gaze, though his fury and hate were evident as it dropped.

He glanced over to where Sordith stood by the door. Aorun's right-hand man didn't seem to see anything in the room, but he noted the white fingers that curled around the hilt of his sword. Aorun was pleased with his restraint. He walked back to Sordith casually. "What do you think of those before us, Sordith?"

"You didn't bring me here for my opinion. You are well aware of that." As if to make his point, Sordith stepped out the doorway to stand guard on the other side.

Aorun grinned but did not follow to rebuke the man; Veaneth, the stable lord, was approaching. Veaneth had two of The Blackguard with him. The half-Daezun looked young, but hard. Their faces held no emotion as they walked a half-step behind the mage.

Aorun bowed only slightly as Veaneth entered. The man was of the third tier, and normally he would not have bowed at all, but the High Minister had commanded Aorun to work with the man. He had no respect for Veaneth, who was soft and held little magic. What little he had was in the way of charms and illusions.

Aorun did not regret his own inability to channel magic; he watched those who had it and it seemed to Aorun that most mages served themselves. Few truly did anything worthwhile with the skills they had, other than to make others with less magic fawn upon them. Aorun had earned respect through steel and action. It seemed far nobler than those who waved magic to stand apart, like this man before him.

Veaneth was balding, and his face was cruel; not like Aorun's hard look, but like someone who enjoyed what he did. Veaneth only acknowledged him with a slight nod. Aorun frowned, but decided to let the slight go. He heard Sordith's soft growl and was glad the man had stepped outside. Perhaps Aorun should have brought Owen, after all…he would keep that in mind for future meetings.

Veaneth moved down the line of bowing Lerdenians and half-breeds, tsking as he went. "This is the best you could find?" He looked over at Aorun, then stopped in front of the two

Daezun and scrutinized them. "These are not half-breeds."

"The specifications for your needs are not like loose stones just lying about to pick up. Yes, those are full Daezun found on our borders. We had never brought Daezun in before, but thought to offer them should they meet your needs." Aorun spoke as if they were bartering silks or art. "I am sure that such a pair would be good for your stables. There certainly a man or two who would pay to degrade them."

Veaneth nodded. He pulled out a strange little stone he used when he assessed the merchandise. As usual, the fleshy mage went down the line one by one, starting with the half breeds. He put the stone in the hands of the first one. It lay mutely in her hand, and she looked up at him, her dark brown eyes filled with confusion. Veaneth shook his head and moved to the second, a solid male with deep sapphire eyes that had a hint of sparkling silver in them. The stone hummed softly in his hand, and he too looked up at Veaneth with confusion.

"I will take this one." Veaneth said, scooping up the stone. A Black Guard grabbed hold of the man and hauled him off to the other side of the room.

Veaneth moved down the line to test each one, taking the two half-breed men, one half-breed woman, and all of the Lerdenians except one very beautiful farm girl. She was fair in face, with golden locks and the silver of power in her eyes, yet Veaneth had not wanted her.

Aorun was surprised at this. "What is wrong with that one?" he asked curiously. "She meets all that you have asked."

"Hips are too narrow," Veaneth said bluntly, approaching and assessing the two Daezun.

"What of these two?" Aorun asked. If the mage didn't take them, he'd send them to the mines or the inner sewers.

"Look at me," Veaneth stated firmly to the two men. Both men forced their gaze up, their Daezun spirit dancing in their eyes.

"They are fresh, and not of the mines?" Veaneth asked, licking his lips as if anticipating a great meal.

"Yes, as I said, we found them at the edges of the farms," Aorun replied, watching Veaneth closely.

"I will take them both," Veaneth answered softly.

Aorun nodded to his two men, who grabbed a Daezun each and half-dragged them over to the others - their feet had been bound, and they couldn't walk themselves. Aorun nodded at his two remaining men, who took the three women out of the room. Aorun followed behind them. He did not know what Veaneth did once he left, but Aorun knew he wanted no part of it. "Take these three down to the brothel and see if Aerius will take them." The three women began to cry, and Aorun was startled to feel a hand on his arm.

"I want the Lerdenian farm girl." Sordith's voice was hard, but his words held respect.

Aorun looked at him with surprise. Sordith had never asked for a woman before, let alone one that was not there by her own choosing. He eyed his man carefully; Sordith's eyes were on the woman, and there was something there in them. Lust, maybe?

Aorun smiled slowly. "About time you became truly one of us." He smacked Sordith on the back. He'd had enough of women who didn't know what they were doing last night. He doubted this lass had much knowledge, given the fresh farm look of her. "She is yours. Go and do what you will."

Sordith looked at Aorun coldly, with hard and calculating eyes. "Anything I want?"

For a moment, Aorun almost felt sorry for the girl. "Of course. I cannot deny one of my best. You may do with her as you please. She is yours. You have my word that none will interfere."

The young woman cast herself at Aorun's feet. "Please, milord. Just let me go home, I beg of you! I will ensure my father gives extra in exchange, beyond the general tax." Her hair was spread at Aorun's feet as she kissed the toes of his boots.

Aorun wrinkled his nose at the obvious groveling. Groveling had never moved him. "Get her out of here before I ruin that beautiful face," he said disdainfully to Sordith.

Sordith grabbed the woman by the arm and started down the hall. The girl was kicking and screaming as she was pulled, and in exasperation, he picked her up and threw her over his shoulder as he strode off.

"Have fun, my friend. I think that one is going to tire you out," Aorun called after him. He laughed outright, his laughter trailing after Sordith and his squirming prize.

It was a good hour before Veaneth and his men reopened the door. Owen had joined Aorun after Sordith left, and both had waited outside - Aorun with far less patience than Owen. The latter seemed content to clean his nails with his knife.

Veaneth came through first. Like every other time, those whom he'd chosen walked single file between the two guards, even the two Daezun. They had a familiar glazed look in their eyes as they filed past. Veaneth stopped beside Aorun as he handed him a purse. "Sorry that took so long. The two Daezun took longer than I usually need. One of them is extremely strong-minded."

Aorun just nodded. He didn't like the look of pleasure on Veaneth's face as he watched the line stroll by; he just wanted the slimy dung-bag out of his house. "It is always my pleasure to serve the council." Aorun bowed, having spoken as expected.

Veaneth nodded and followed the last guard out. Aorun managed to hold his disgust till they were out the front door, and only then did he look at Owen. "I feel dirty. I will be in my rooms taking a bath," he snarled as he bounced the bag in his hand. "This is far too light. Send two squads out and have them look for Daezun too close to our border. He seems to pay better for them."

Aorun turned on his heel and strode to his room. He wanted the sour stench that the mage had left behind washed far away. He could still hear the screams coming down the hall from Sordith's room, but they were replaced suddenly by silence. Good, the man had finally gagged the wench. Aorun reached the solitude of his room, closing the door and leaving the rest of the world behind him.

Chapter Five

Alador's scream of warning was cut off as the cascade of dirt and rocks landed on the wagon. He'd managed to bring a hand up to shield his face, but that wasn't enough to deflect the rock. Lights shattered his vision, as the world became a tumbling mass of rock and dirt. Terror coursed through Alador as he fought to shield himself with his arms.

His last moments of recollection were the wagon tipping over the edge of the road. He was flung from his seat and into the cold, murky depths of the river. The sunlight above the water seemed too far away – How would he make it back to the surface? – And then darkness took him…

Alador could hear water rushing nearby when he awoke, spluttering, and lifted his head slightly to cough water from his lungs. He was lying in the shallows of the river, his body scraping against sharp rocks. Everything hurt. His head pounded like a death drum at a funeral, slow and felt throughout his body.

Despite the warmth of the summer evening, he was freezing. He had no idea where he was or how long he'd been there. He carefully flexed his limbs, relieved when he found that nothing was broken. He forced himself to crawl up onto the rocks farther out of the water until he finally reached a sandy section of the river bar.

Despite being fairly sure nothing was broken, every inch of him screamed like he'd just been beaten by Trelmar again. There had been plenty of times when Alador could have sworn Trelmar and his friends had broken something after one of their beatings, but they'd always been careful just to make sure everything hurt. It was that unpleasant yet familiar level of pain that he suffered now.

Alador flopped down and let the late sun warm him. It hadn't fallen behind the hills yet, but it would soon. It took a while for the memory of the landside to come to him, and when it did, Alador forced himself onto his knees with a groan. Henrick might still be buried, or he might be in the river. He could still be alive.

He looked around, trying to get his bearings. The rockslide must have pushed the wagon over the edge and into the river that hadn't been more than a few feet below them. The problem now was that Alador wasn't familiar with the area, and had no idea how far downstream he'd gone.

Based on the sun's position at the cliff's edge, he'd been out for at least an hour, which only gave him about two hours of usable light left. He patted himself down and noted that he had nothing but his knife, which thankfully hadn't come free of its sheath on his belt.

Alador forced himself to his feet. Based on the direction of the water's flow, he was on the wrong side of the river. Just upstream, however, it looked like the river was calm enough that he'd be able to wade or swim across before it shoved him down to the next rapids. He set off slowly, every muscle protesting. His boots were wet and uncomfortable, but he dared not take them off. He didn't want them to shrink, and the thought of trying to cover the rocky ground barefoot was an unpleasant one.

It took him about a quarter of an hour to work his way up to the head of the still water. He waded out carefully, hoping the river would stay shallow enough for him to wade, rather than swim. Luck was not with him, however, and he was forced to swim a good third of the distance; but finally he stood on the other side, winded and shivering. Why did he feel so cold?

He stood for a moment, hugging himself for warmth. He needed to get dry, and remembered the cantrips he'd worked on the morning before. It took all the willpower he had to focus and find that well within him, but when he did he pinpointed all his thought on being dry. Closing his eyes, he pushed his hands down and out, imagining the water leaving him…

When he opened them again, he was steaming. He frowned: that wasn't really what he needed; but at least it was warmer… He tried again, imagining the water returning to the river as he shoved down his hands and then pushed them to the river. He smiled as the sense of wetness left him, and opened his eyes, only to find that, except for his boots and his belt, he was naked.

"Dammit," he muttered in frustration. Now what was he going to do? Yes, he was dry, but to be naked was to be worse off in the wilderness. Not only that, but his knife had disappeared, as well. He should have just stayed wet. He had to get to Henrick, and he was delaying when time could be precious.

"If you are done playing, we really have work to do before dark." The lazy, amused tones that could only belong to Henrick drew Alador's eyes to the bank above him.

"I was trying to get dry." Alador muttered. His head hurt, his body hurt, and he was standing there, more embarrassed that the spell had failed than that he was without clothing.

"You succeeded," Henrick quipped back with a deep-throated laugh. "You appear quite dry.

"Yes, we are all amused." Alador's anger was evident in his voice. His arms flailed about in frustration at his predicament. "Any suggestions on how I can get them back, and… are you okay?" He frowned up and scrutinized the mage. Henrick seemed whole and completely clean, as if they hadn't just been wiped off the road by dirt and rock.

"Yes, I am "okay". You do not get to the fifth tier without learning a spell or two to protect yourself. Fortunately, you gave me enough warning. As for your more pressing need..." Henrick smirked. His finger went up and down Alador with clear amusement. "If you can take something away, then you can put it back. Its elements are around you. Well maybe; they could have floated down the river." He tapped his cheek in consideration. "I guess you will just have to try."

"How do you suggest I do that?" Alador glared at the smirking man. He needed help, not lessons.

Henrick crossed his arms in clear disappointment as he looked down at Alador. "Do I really have to tell you that?" His tone was one of arrogant condescension. "I would like to think you were a bit smarter than that. I mean, if I give you all the answers, how will you ever truly learn anything?"

Henrick's eyes roved over his naked son. "How will you learn to be creative and to be your own man? Surely your Daezun half did not make you stupid and narrow-minded? I cannot fathom that, as your mother is anything but."

"Don't you ever make that suggestion again!" Alador glared up at Henrick in anger.

"She is my mother, and I still don't know if you used a spell to win her affections in the first place." Alador spat out the accusation he'd sat on for some time.

Henrick uncrossed his arms, tossing them up in frustration. "Well, by the gods, you would think you could be a little more grateful. Spell or not, you exist because I was in her furs that night." He turned his back on his fuming son. "The wagon is about a mile back. I am going to head back and make some dinner. Join me in your current state or stay and figure it out. I really do not care." Henrick disappeared back into the brush.

Alador stared after him, wide-eyed and open-mouthed. As he glared at where his father had disappeared into the bushes, Alador considered his dilemma. He could trek the mile back naked, but he only had one other set of clothes. He thought about what his father had said. What was done could be undone. It seemed to him that dissolving something into its basic parts would be easier than binding them back together, but Alador had been told to try. He doubted, given the depth of their conversation before the rockslide, that his father was lying to him.

He considered what he'd done before, working to recall the thoughts and motions he'd used the second time. Alador wanted his clothes back, but not the water. He decided he would start with just some leggings, which would probably be the easiest; and if he could manage no more than that, at least he would be appropriately covered. He knew that the leggings had been made of linen, and that linen was made from flax. He concentrated on flax and reversed the motion of his hands, then looked down to see flax plants all around him.

Alador sighed softly. It was a start. This time he imagined the flax teased into thread and woven into linen. Sweat beaded down his forehead at the level of his concentration; but after a couple of tries he had managed a length of linen that would serve.

Heartened, he poured all his reserves into a final effort – mentally cutting and stitching the cloth into a finished garment. This time when he looked down, his leggings were on the ground in front of him.

He smiled with triumph and pulled them on. Deciding that he was covered enough and too tired to keep going, Alador began the trek back. He hoped there was a shirt still in the wagon, or whatever was left of it.

By the time Alador arrived, Henrick had already recovered what he could find from the wagon. A fire was burning, and the smell of roasting meat made Alador realise how hungry he was.

Henrick looked over and frowned when Alador approached. Whether it was because of their argument or because he was only wearing leggings, Alador didn't know but felt contrite.

He dug through the things that Henrick had managed to recover and was relieved when he saw his pack. All his slips were in there. He pulled off his boots, now that they were dry, then pulled out his other pair of pants and a shirt and slipped them on.

"Couldn't get your clothes back?" Henrick asked casually, watching him. Amusement danced in his gaze.

"I hurt from head to toe. My head is pounding. I'm glad I could get this much," Alador snapped, not feeling up to his father's sarcasm. He flopped down at the fire. It was getting dark. "How bad is the damage?" Alador decided a change of topic was his wisest course while he sat and held his head.

Henrick sighed. "You really like to focus on the worst of things, don't you?" He poked a piece of wood into the fire beneath the spit of food. "The wagon is destroyed, and one of the korpen was pinned in the traces and drowned. The other is wandering down the road from us, eating contentedly. A third of the supplies are gone, and I lost my enchanting pack." Henrick rattled off his list as he took a piece of meat off the fire and pushed it over to Alador.

"What is this?" Alador asked sniffing it. It looked familiar but smelled strange.

"Fresh korpen," Henrick said. "I reasoned we might as well get one final use out of it."

"Oh." Alador poked at it. It was rare to sacrifice a korpen for food. He'd seen it done in times of difficulty, but they had more worth as beasts of burden if other food was about, particularly since it was difficult to get at the meat beneath their hard exoskeletons.

He forced himself to try it. The meat's juices had set off the hunger in Alador that seemed so much greater since he had found the bloodstone. He ate with fervor after the first couple of bites, and Henrick kept replenishing the stick until Alador was full.

"You must have had to work really hard to get those leggings," Henrick murmured as his son finally shook his head, turning down a fifth piece.

"I told you, my head is pounding," Alador said. "I had to work damn hard to get this far."

Henrick went to one of his own bags and pulled out a small red vial. "How did you do it?" he asked curiously.

With some pride, Alador explained the steps he'd taken. He'd figured it out on his own and was rather pleased with himself. When he was done, Henrick handed him the vial.

"What is this?"

"An elixir that will ease that headache and some of the other bruises." Henrick eyed him for a long moment. "Why did you not just make pants?"

Alador looked at him in frustration. "I couldn't figure out how."

Henrick raised a brow. "I assure you, it is quite easy. Watch." Henrick stood and concentrated for a brief second. Colorful dust swirled around him, then his pants became black and his shirt a deep emerald green. It didn't appear to take Henrick any effort.

"You said magic can't be made from nothing. It has to come from somewhere," Alador pointed out in frustration, frowning. "There's no leather just lying around." He also knew his father was already wearing the clothes, so really he'd only changed the look of them.

"The elements that make them up, Alador. The base elements...," Henrick stated. "Try again. Imagine the sort of clothes you'd like to wear. By the gods, imagine the best you can..." Henrick was challenging him again. "Unless you want to go on looking like a poor village lad, then cast the magic to create some better clothes."

Alador laid down the vial and stood to do as he was directed. He found in his mind's eye the nice clothing he'd seen at larger gatherings. He imagined black leather pants with a silver buckle. In his mind, he saw another man's grey linen shirt and black vest. When Alador had them securely in his mind, he lifted his hands from his sides and up over his head, as if forming them up. In response, Alador felt a strange movement on his skin. He dropped his hands, startled, and opened his eyes. Dust fell around him.

"You almost had it. Why did you stop?" Henrick asked with amusement.

"It felt...odd, like a snake coiling around me," Alador admitted.

Henrick chuckled and shook his head. "I have done it for so long that I will admit I do not even notice. I guess that is an apt description. You are prepared this time. Do it again," he coaxed.

Alador closed his eyes, taking less time to reform the image than before. He focused on the well at his core and pulled his hands palms-up to the sky again. The strange whispering trickle moved over his skin but stopped after a bit. Alador looked down to see the outfit that he'd imagined.

Henrick grinned. "Not my first choice in clothing, but well done." His father clapped his hands together in approval. "Well done my son," he said with pride. "Now, take that potion. It will make you sleep, but when you awaken, the pain will be gone."

Alador grinned back, looking at his clothes with pleasure. It was the first thing he'd felt truly pleased with since they'd left Smallbrook. He picked up the red vial from where it lay and looked at it in his hand. "I suppose this tastes terrible." Alador's smile faded and he grimaced as he uncorked the vial.

"Of course; nothing good for you ever tastes good," Henrick quipped.

Alador wrinkled his nose and upended the vial. True to his father's word, the potion tasted vile, and he coughed a few times as he handed the now-empty vial back. It only took a few moments before Alador's head felt light and swirls of color welled up in his vision. He lay down, and the colors faded into darkness: the potion and exhaustion took hold and drew him under.

Alador's first realization as he awoke was that the ground beneath him was soft and warm, not hard and cold. There were no rocks digging into his side, or bugs biting at his neck.

He smiled and nestled deeper into the bed, then realized that the last thing he remembered was a riverside campfire. He opened his eyes slowly... It took a few moments, as his eyes felt heavy and crusted with sleep.

He looked about, his mouth gaping as his gaze traveled around the room. It was the largest room he'd ever seen. Did the bed have its own roof? He moved stiffly to its edge and looked up.

From the bed's roof hung beautiful drapes made of a material he wasn't familiar with. Alador fingered it curiously, then slowly sat up and looked down at himself in confusion. He was in a white gown. Where was he?

He put his feet over the side of the bed, and a slight Lerdenian man seemed to appear out of nowhere. "Good morning, m'lord. Shall I fetch your breakfast?"

The man had hair the ciolour of gold, and managed to bow three times while he was speaking. His accent was thicker than Henrick's, but what he said could still be understood.

Alador had started when the Lerdenian first spoke, and now he riveted his eyes on him. He realized that the fellow must be a servant and relaxed, but only slightly. Alador was famished, so he nodded mutely; but as the man turned to scurry off, Alador called out for him. "Wait! Where am I?" He eyed the man curiously.

"You are in Master Henrick's home. Where else would his son be?" The man smiled and hurried off.

"Where else, indeed?" Alador muttered. He spotted a pitcher of water and a glass beside the bed. It had refilled the glass three times before the parched feeling in his throat began to abate. How long had he slept? He felt much better, but as he looked down, he realized he did not want to eat in a white linen nightshirt.

He imagined an outfit similar to the one he'd made by the campfire, and found the well of power within himself. Alador was pleased to find that he was successful after the first try this time. His legs were clothed in a heavy brown material, and he wore a deep green shirt that laced up the front from his lower rib cage to his neck.

Alador tied it loosely shut and imagined a pair of comfortable boots. Sure enough, when he opened his eyes, he'd managed to create a pair of shining black boots. He sat down and pulled them on, his stomach rumbling with hunger in response to his spells.

Now suitably attired, he moved away from the bed to inspect his surroundings. The room would have easily housed half of his mother's home, despite the bed on a raised floor in the middle. Everything was white and gold, except for the contrasting blue tapestries by the windows and those hanging from the bed.

He moved to the wide, tall windows that went all the way to the floor and looked out. There was a balcony outside, so he opened the windows and stepped out onto it. The warm summer day still had some of the morning's freshness as Alador took in the view. He blinked in amazement.

Laid out below him were white, shimmering roofs that seemed to spiral out as he looked down, creating tier after tier, all the way down to the plains. There, farms stretched out, almost as far as he could see...

A strange, darkened moat surrounded the city below him, but Alador could see no water in it. The streets sparkled in the sunlight with a dazzling array of light and color. The view took his breath away. It was so foreign to him, but Alador could not deny its beauty.

Beyond the farm-filled plain was a line of trees. He focused on them, and as the line jumped forward, he inhaled sharply. They were the most graceful, spherical trees he had ever seen, all of them dense and deeply green. They didn't even seem to have leaves in their waving green boughs. No wonder his father always returned here: the beauty of this place was undeniable.

Alador spent quite some time assessing the city - the busy streets and the bustling movement of morning activity - before stepping back into the room. From where he now stood he could see that the roof over the bed was limited - no larger than the bed itself. The actual roof was another ten feet above it, giving the room a cool, airy feel.

The wood was gilded with gold leaf, as was the writing table set by the fire. Two doors stood side-by-side in the room; Alador opened them to find another room full of clothing, boots, and robes. As he looked at them, he realized they had all been tailored to his build. Why would mages order clothing when they could just form them with magic?

"Because what is made by magic can be dissolved easily and without much thought by a better mage," a voice said. There was a whispering of magic across Alador's skin, and he found himself nude. "Besides, it is a waste of your power. Remember, magic uses up the mage's energy."

Alador turned to grimace at his father. "How did you know what I was thinking?" he asked, concerned again his father was using magic against him, though he'd felt nothing that time.

"Never play cards in the trenches, son. Your face is as easy to read as a child's book." Henrick grinned. "Your man told me you were awake. I thought I would take you to the dining hall, since I am sure you have questions."

The moment Henrick finished speaking, a multitude of questions flashed through Alador's head. He opened his mouth to start spewing them, but his father held up a hand. "Let us eat and then talk. I suspect if I begin to answer now, I will be chewing my own arm off before we ever find the hall."

Alador nodded back. He began to move to his father when he realized he was still naked. He felt his face flush and went back into the closet. He realized that though there were mage robes – garments the like of which he'd never worn - most of the clothes here were of a cut he was familiar with.

He quickly pulled on a dark brown pair of pants and a deep red shirt. "How did these come to be here? Was I unconscious for that long?" he asked with surprise as he put on a belt.

Henrick leaned against the desk as Alador dressed. "Every year for the last three years, it has been expected that you would come to live here. I made sure the room was readied every time I went to test you," he answered.

Alador was surprised by that admission. He remained silent, pulling on a pair of boots. He had no idea his father had been expecting him to pass so eagerly.

One of the walls had plenty of weapons mounted on it for him to choose from. Alador picked a knife and sheath and secured them to his belt. That was enough for now, and he felt better after arming himself at least partially. He also saw his pack and kicked it with his boot. It was heavy, and the clink of medure made him feel secure that he was not without slips. His bow lay on the small rack above his pack, along with his quiver.

"How did you know I would pass?" Alador asked curiously as he returned from the closet.

"You are my son." Henrick shrugged. "I would expect no less from someone of our bloodline."

'Our bloodline? Is it strong with magic?"

"You do not know? I always thought your mother would tell you," Henrick answered.

"No, she never said anything."

Henrick nodded. "Come, I will explain as we walk." He led Alador out of the room and into a corridor that was no less impressive in its striking walls and marble floors. "Our family has always been blessed with a strong line of magic. Very few of our children have ever failed in their testing, as far back as Lerdenians have had magic," he explained.

"So your line is from the first mages that served the dragons?" Alador asked, not sure if he liked being directly part of that line. He still had no respect for his Lerdenian ancestors' betrayal of their oath to protect the dragons as the dragons had protected them.

"*Our* line," Henrick corrected with a grin. "Sorry Alador, you cannot choose your bloodline. I fear you are as stuck with it as I am. But I will be honest with you: we descend from the great mage himself."

Alador stopped. "The one that took the life of the dragon he was sworn to protect?" Alador's face showed his horror as he realized how little about himself he actually knew. Why had no one told him all this before now?

"Yes. Do not worry, Alador. One does not develop into who they will become just because of the blood that flows in their veins. They also become who they are by the choices they make and the friends they keep."

Henrick turned back to grab ahold of both of Alador's arms gently. He looked with seriousness into his son's eyes. "You have been raised with a gentle heart. I doubt that will change because of who your great grandfather – well, many 'greats' back – was in the past. It does mean, however, that magic flows deeply in our blood, and more so in you if your stone was what I suspect it was." Henrick let him go and resumed his progress down the stately corridor.

Alador stood for a moment, digesting this before following . They emerged into a hallway where a magnificent staircase led to an equally grand floor below. Henrick's home was entirely decorated in variations of white, gold, and peach colors. It made the black robes he wore stand out more, and Alador suspected that the effect was orchestrated. His father looked striking dressed as a mage.

They turned left at the foot of the stairs and entered a sumptuous dining hall, where Alador saw a table that could easily have sat twenty. Only two places were set at one end. "Are all homes in Silverport this…magnificent?" he asked, looking around. He was still in awe.

"The lower the tier, the simpler the dwelling and the more people there are to inhabit it. The higher the tier, the grander the home with fewer people. Odd, is it not, that a home that could house a Daezun village houses just one mage here, his family and his servants?" Henrick sat down and picked up the steaming cup of tea that awaited him.

"Why are there fewer people? - besides the fact that the tiers become smaller as you climb…" Alador asked, slipping into the seat on Henrick's right. He was amazed to see the variety of dishes before him, and waited as his father heaped food on his plate.

"You must pass the mage test to a higher tier. Fewer mages pass, the higher up the tiers you go," Henrick answered, piling his plate high with cheese, bread and sizzling, round cuts of some sort of meat.

Alador considered what his father had told him about Lerdenia during his visits. "You are of the fifth tier. Isn't that the highest one?" he asked. He was making an initially cautious choice from all the different foods. He recognized the eggs, so he made sure he got plenty of those on his plate...

"Tested tiers, yes. The fifth is the highest . But there are two tiers above this. The Council's tier is next, and above that is the High Minister, and the Council Hall." Henrick was apparently in an affable mood , and willing to indulge his son's avid curiosity. He glanced over at Alador, who was now trying the more unfamiliar foods.

"Do we have any other family besides your brother?" Alador liked what he'd tasted so far; the sizzling meat was spicy and left a bit of a bite on his tongue.

Henrick shrugged and finished a mouthful before answering. "If there is, I am unaware of it. Our father died when we were young, and our mother died in the way of the tiers. We returned to the third tier until we were old enough to begin working our own way up."

Alador was trying to understand how this tier system worked. He ate in silence for a while before asking his next question. "So one family can be on different tiers?" he asked.

Henrick nodded. "My brother has always been above me. I prefer it that way. I have managed to stay out of his way."

"You said before that people killed to move up in the tiers; but now you say there are tests. Are those... two separate ways, or is killing part of the test?" Alador asked carefully.

"You can test, but even when you become a tested fourth tier mage, if there is no hall willing or able to receive you, then you must wait. Most prefer not to wait, so they choose a hall to their liking and, if they can, remove the mage that stands in their way. As that mage moves up, the mage below who has tested but did not wish to kill can also move up."

Henrick was trying to explain the system, but it was rather convoluted. "For example, if my brother had chosen to host me when he was a fifth tier mage, I could have lived with him as a fifth tier mage."

Alador tried to imagine life split from brothers and sisters, mother and father. In the villages of the Daezun, family was everything. If your brother or sister did take a home of their own, they were still close, and often one home became a central point for meals and laughter.

He ate as he considered, and his father was content to leave him to his thoughts. As usual, Henrick seemed to eat an enormous amount of food, but his servants must have been accustomed to his appetite, given the amount of food laid out for just two of them.

"Don't people get punished if they kill a mage in their way?"

"Only if they are caught. No one looks too closely, except those that might have a shade of feeling for the one who was killed, and the Council only banishes those stupid enough to get caught red-handed." Henrick took a sip of tea.

Alador stared at his father in disbelief. "How can a society... How can people stand to live somewhere where murder is as common as rain? I'd think it's a world of fear, when anyone might try to kill you for a place of power. How can someone always live in fear?" Alador was deeply perplexed. "Why don't they leave?"

Henrick sat back with his cup of tea as he considered Alador's question. "Not all Lerdenians choose to live in the tiers. Many have farms or other homes outside the cities. They may or may not have or practise skills in magic. Some have potential, but no training..."

He took a cautious sip. "Those who choose to live in Lerdenian cities are usually one of three types. They might have been born here and know no other way to exist. They would be just as astounded to see the villages of the Daezun as you are to see Silverport. What seems perhaps evil to you is seen as normal to them. Evil, like good, is a matter of judgement."

Henrick shrugged. "The Daezun see the Lerdenians as evil because we broke a pact made long before our time, and because we are willing to go to great lengths to harness magic. Yet they hate an entire nation for the practices of the few that progress higher than the third tier."

He stared across the table at his son. "For the most part, while Lerdenians can learn magic, few have a natural disposition to it or are born with innate skills. A country is judged by the actions at the top. Such is the way across the world. Nations are judged by their rulers, and not by those that live within the borders."

Alador listened with fascination, considering his father's words carefully. They had merit. If the Daezun were judged by men such as Trelmar, even Alador could see why the Daezun would be hated.

"What are the other two types?"

"The second type are those who have found no other way to live, and see living in the city as a necessary evil. They live in the trenches or in the first tier. Sometimes they are motivated by slips, and sometimes they are motivated by the need to survive. Both are powerful motivators…"

Henrick stared absently down the length of the table. "The last are motivated by the need for power, for prestige, or recognition. These are the most dangerous: for they will go to any lengths to gain their objectives, and often have little or no conscience to hinder them in their advances." He drained his cup and put it down.

"You live in the fifth tier... Does that mean you fall into the last category?" Alador asked softly. He looked disappointedly at his father.

"That would be the usual assumption. However, I assure you that I live as I do strictly as a necessary evil. You will be in The Blackguard and that will be your necessary evil. We do what we must because we must do it." Henrick pushed his plate away. He was finally finished.

"What is it that we must do?" Alador asked as he spread preserves over a generous portion of bread.

Henrick pulled out his pipe and filled it before answering . "What I must do, I am not ready to share, but it involves staying in my brother's good graces for the time being. Your purpose has yet to be revealed. If your stone was a geas stone, eventually you will realize what it is you must do."

He lit the pipe, and stared at his son through a cloud of comfortable smoke. "The best way to prepare you for what a dragon might have pressed upon you is to ensure that you are capable of fighting. The best way to do that is to put you in The Blackguard – again, your necessary evil." He drew on his pipe and watched Alador with an expression that seemed to indicate his words explained it all.

Alador's stomach heaved at this thought. He set his half-eaten piece of bread down slowly. "What if I refuse whatever it is this dragon pressed upon me?"

He would not kill for a dragon. He would not fight his own people. He would not hurt his village. Alador's mind raced with all of the things he knew he would not do.

"I don't know. I honestly have never known anyone still alive who did not fulfil a geas. It seems to me, therefore, that your options are these: complete the geas, or die."

Henrick puffed out smoke rings casually, as if they were discussing the weather and not Alador's life. "I am sure I have given you much to think about. Why do you not return to your room and write to your little skirt you left behind?"

Alador's heart leapt at the idea of writing to Mesiande, and for a moment he couldn't think of anything else to ask. He missed her so much; and though a lot had happened since he'd fled the village, Alador still pined for her the most of everything he had left behind.

His heart sank as quickly as it had leapt. "When a village takes your name off the book of life, no one can communicate with you. You might as well be dead."

Henrick rolled his eyes. "I am a mage of the fifth tier. You do not think I can get one little letter to your lady love? I am really quite insulted." He drew deeply on his pipe and looked at Alador. "Besides, I never told you to put your name on it."

Alador slowly grinned. He rose from the table, eager to go write a letter to Mesiande. Surely a chance to explain would help him repair much between them; and maybe, once he'd found his feet and was secure in his use of magic, he could send for her. He knew how to farm and so did she. Perhaps they could find a small farm on the edge of Lerdenia, where none would bother them. Hope flared in his eyes.

"One last question…" Alador said. "How did we get here?" He wanted to know before he left to go write to Mesiande. He scooted his chair from the table and looked across at his father.

Henrick looked back with a smile. "It was clear that my plans for a slow trip - so that I could teach you - were foiled by the slide. You were in need of rest and healing, so I simply used a travel spell." He was puffing away as if what he had done had been nothing out of the ordinary.

"Why don't you just use this spell all the time?" Alador asked in amazement. He knew that he'd much rather just be somewhere then ride along behind slow, scrabbling korpen.

Henrick shrugged. "I like to travel, and I hate spending spells I do not have to. It is careless and vain. Besides, flying is usually so much more exhilarating." Henrick rapped his pipe out on his plate. "Now, off with you then. I have some business to attend to. Stay in your rooms until I return. I want you to practise with the wet and dry cantrip when your letter is done."

Henrick's tone held sure dismissal and an end to the conversation. Alador snapped his mouth shut. He was determined that if there really was such a spell, that he would get his father to teach it to him, regardless of whether or not Henrick considered it careless or vain. It meant he could visit Mesiande whenever he wanted to.

"Yes, Father," Alador politely answered, leaving that battle for another day. He left his father at the large dining room table. For now, he would write to Mesiande and explain everything. Maybe she would find it in her heart to forgive him. Maybe, just maybe, she would wait for him.

Chapter Six

Once Alador finished his letter, he set about practising. He didn't have any dirt, so he took a small square of linen he found in the closet and started wetting and drying it. It was getting easier; he almost didn't have to search for that well of power within him anymore. He didn't know what else to call it, and a "well" is what it felt like - this pool at his core.

Alador sat and thought about it for a while, by now bored with his task. He wondered if it had always been there, and he just hadn't noticed before...or had it appeared when he'd taken the bloodstone from the ground? Whatever the case, Alador was very aware of it now, and found it easily. He wondered if all magic was this way: nothing more difficult than imagining something and just... making it happen. He decided not to experiment; but one thought did concern him.

What if he couldn't control it?

Alador had no idea how much time had passed until his father strode through the door without knocking, wearing a formal robe of black with red thread and trim. Henrick did not offer a greeting; he just walked to the closet and pulled out a dark blue robe, trimmed in silver. "Put this on," he ordered, tossing it to Alador.

Alador caught it in surprise. He'd seen his father short with him before, but now Henrick actually seemed angry. There was a deadliness about him that Alador didn't like. "What's wrong?" he asked, holding the robe out with distaste.

"Your uncle has decided we will attend him, now. He has denied my request to allow me more time with you as my son. I suspect that we will part ways today." Henrick moved towards the open windows and stared off into the horizon. "Always at such a frantic pace. Bah!" he snorted out with disdain. "There is never enough time."

Alador turned the robe around. "Do I have to wear this?" he asked as carefully as he could. He didn't want to offend his father, but robes just seemed... unmanly to him.

"It is a status symbol, Alador. It tells all that you are of mage blood and, therefore, accorded a certain level of respect..."

There was steel in Henrick's voice, and he did not turn to face his son. "I will not go before Luth - the High Minister - with my son clothed as a mere farming peasant," he snapped. "I do have *some* standards to uphold. Pull your shirt off and wear the robe. You may keep your britches if you feel more comfortable." His father wasn't asking; he was commanding.

Alador quickly did as he was told. He saw that the robe had belt loops, so he transferred his belt to it, making sure his knife was still secure at his waist. Henrick remained silent, staring out the window.

Alador realized that he'd have no idea what to do if there was to be a parting of their ways. "I wrote the letter," he blurted out, hoping this offer hadn't been withdrawn. He needed to make sure it got to Mesiande before anything else. She had to know how sorry he was and how much he still loved her. He moved to the desk and looked hopefully at his father.

"Yes, let us take care of that first." Henrick pivoted on his heel and strode to the desk. "I will add instructions, should she decide to write you back."

He picked up Alador's quill and with strong strokes wrote an additional note at the foot of the letter. He sanded it and then, before Alador could look at what he had written, rolled it up and shoved it into a silver tube with strange markings on it. "Take this and put it under your pillow. Lie upon the bed and think of your little skirt. Fix her in your mind's eye."

"I wish you would quit calling her that," Alador muttered. He took the tube and examined the markings written on it - strange symbols and lettering he wasn't familiar with. "What language is this?" he asked in amazement, tracing the lines along the tube with a nail.

"Draconic, the language of magic. You will learn it soon enough. Now go see your letter off," Henrick ordered, arms folding with impatience. He nodded to the bed as if time was wasting.

Could it really be that simple, just wishing it to her? Alador went to the bed and slipped the tube under a pillow, then hopped up and stretched out. He sighed gratefully when his father went to stare out the window.

Closing his eyes, he imagined her: her braided hair desperately trying to escape its confinement, her sparkling eyes as she laughed at him; the way she would put her hands on her hips when she was yelling at him for something she'd decided needed a proper scolding. A knife seemed to pierce him as he realized how much he loved her and how much he needed her. The feeling twisted the longing and loss back to the surface of his thoughts.

"That should do it. We need to be off, and there are still other things I need to tell you." Henrick's tone was firm as he turned from the window and headed for the door.

Alador sat up, somewhat startled. He felt beneath his pillow. "It—it's gone!" He moved the pillow to be sure.

Henrick rolled his eyes. "For a man nearly grown, Alador, you are in many ways still such a fledgling."

Alador's eyes flew to his father. "What did you say?"

"I said you are in many ways still a child."
Henrick repeated stopping to look at Alador
with exasperation.

"That isn't what you said." Alador slipped
off the bed. "You said 'fledgling.' Why did you
say 'fledgling'?" He searched his father's face
anxiously.

"I am quite sure that I did not," Henrick
replied with a frown.

"You did!" Alador moved to Henrick,
who now looked confused.

"If I did, what does it matter? A slip of the
tongue…," Henrick said, looking flustered as
well as confused.

"Yes, a slip of the tongue," Alador
murmured, eyeing his father suspiciously. Had
his father's been the voice he'd heard in his
dream? Was Henrick conjuring dream-dragons
to convince his son that that he had some
mission to fulfil – this supposed "geas?"

"I have only heard that term in my dreams,
Henrick," Alador accused.

"Here, you will call me Father," Henrick
ordered tersely. "I most likely heard it from my
friend, the dragon. It was a slip of the tongue
or your imagination. We have more pressing
concerns than a word misspoken."

Alador knew he hadn't misheard the mage.
It made him wonder if he could really trust his
own father. He felt like a pawn in a game he
didn't understand. "What other matters?"
Alador asked, feet planted and arms crossed.

"This is your third tier pass. It must always be on your belt." Henrick held up a silver square with three eyes on one side. He thrust it at Alador, along with a copper one: forcing him to abandon his childish posture.

Alador took the passes reluctantly. The copper square had a large P with a strange dragon-looking mark on one side, and five eyes on the other. "This other is a pass to come to me. It holds my mark: so if you are found anywhere in the fifth tier except en route to or in my home, it will not protect you."

"Protect me from what?" Alador asked as he took them and inspected them curiously, still cautious about his father. He felt a strange tingle in his hands as he held them.

"A mage found above his tier and without a pass is put to death without explanation or trial."

"What if you lose it?" Alador asked worriedly.

"Not recommended," Henrick breathed out, his manner tense and worried.

Henrick's predilection for understatement was irritating. Alador frowned but tied the pass to his belt as directed. He held the other one, curious at his father's choice of mark. "What else?"

Alador eyed his father, unsure sure what to do with the other square. Henrick took it out of his hand and draped it around his neck. Alador stared at his father's forehead as he tucked the pass under the front of his uncertain son's robe. It was cold against his chest.

"Luthian may take many paths today," Henrick muttered quietly, "… and I am not sure which he will choose. His actions are often determined by his mood. He may be authoritative and order you to the guard as is his right as High Minister. He may choose to go the route of doting uncle…"

Henrick turned away from Alador, his voice hard and cold. "Or he may just kill us both. I do not know, Alador. This is a fork in the road which cannot be divined." His shoulders drooped somewhat as if the thought tired him…

Then he braced and turned back to look Alador firmly in the eyes. "Be wary. Speak only when spoken to and do not elaborate. Once you are in The Blackguard, there will be little I can do to protect you. You will be on your own, except when you can slip away to visit."

"What about my things?" Alador asked, worried about his pack and other belongings.

"Your room will be as you left it." Henrick gentled his manner, noting Alador's agitation. "I will keep here what you do not absolutely need. You can come on your first visit and decide what you want to take with you. Once a week, you will be allowed a half day with me. Come when allowed and I will teach you the things that you will need to know and that The Blackguard will not teach."

Henrick frowned as he looked over his son. "You are still too young in thought for this," he muttered sadly, "...but I fear that Luthian will not be deviated from the path he has chosen for you."

"I am nearly a man by right of age, and I passed my ritual to manhood with the Daezun." Alador drew himself up proudly.

Henrick just sighed as if Alador had just proven his father's point. "If I teach you nothing else, I want you to remember these things. A ritual does not make you a man. A man has the strength to face what is thrown at him in life. If he falls or is beaten, he does not complain but gets up and rides in to face the challenge once more."

Henrick grabbed his son by the front of his robe and pulled him close, looking down into his eyes as if trying to plant his very words in Alador's head. "A man does not lose focus, as a child does," he continued. "His purpose is unwavering, and though he may find distraction in a wench or wine, he never loses sight of his end goal. Your mind should be on one thing and one thing only: gaining enough power to be free to live your own purpose and not another man's."

Alador went to speak, but his father held up a finger to Alador's lips. "For once, boy, stop your babble and listen. Gather your scattered thoughts and commit what I am saying to memory: in case I do not walk out of that council chamber."

Alador swallowed hard at the intensity in his father's gaze and tone. He realized that Henrick wasn't showboating or trying to be funny. He could see in his father's eyes that they were headed into real danger; so he nodded.

"You must make your own way. Seek council but hold your tongue. Trust no one and nothing but this." He smacked Alador's head lightly. "I know you are a smart boy, but you are quick to anger and quicker to speak. Learn to hold that anger and that tongue. Look for men who have learned those lessons: for they will have the wisdom you will need."

Henrick tapped his chin, apparently thinking about what other words he needed to speak to his son, while Alador frantically tried to commit what his father said to memory.

"There are rules to magic," he went on. "Remember, nothing comes from nothing. Magic draws on everything around it and most through you. Because of this, consider the consequences of every spell: whence its resources are derived, and what may be the effect on the world around you."

He had so much to teach his son, and so little time. "An example for you: if I use magic to water the apple orchards in Oldmeadow and I do not pay attention, I might very well draw that water from every insect in the orchard. Then there would be no insects to pollinate their blossoms and bring forth fruit."

Henrick looked at Alador, beseeching him to remember. "There are rules to all things in life. Pay attention to them! Only then will you know when it is safe to use magic. Never break a rule without first understanding it, and considering the consequences."

Alador stood, wide-eyed, at this barrage of information, much of which conflicted with itself. "You aren't going to die today. You can teach me these things when I come visit on those half-days you mentioned," Alador said, trying to slow his father down.

"I do not know the outcome of today, Alador, no matter how many times I have cast a spell to see it." Henrick was clearly very ill-at-ease. "Promise me one thing: if my end does come today, find the red dragon that lives high in the mountains, next to a lake of immense size. He will be able to help you, regardless of what may come today. Tell him the man who stuck in his throat sent you."

Henrick eyed Alador with a deep intensity. Alador felt as if something squeezed his chest tightly. "I promise," he managed to whisper to the mage who still stood very close.

There was a long pause, and then Henrick smiled as if nothing had just occurred. He let go of Alador's robe and straightened what his grip had wrinkled. "All right then, let us get this business over with. No time like the present to see where our paths will lead." Henrick's easy tone of voice was back, and he turned and strode out the door.

Alador shook his head and hurried after him. The more answers he received from his father, the more questions he had. If he lived a hundred turns, he didn't doubt that there'd still be unsolved puzzles. His father was truly an enigma.

Letter to Mesiande

Dear Mesi,

Let me begin by telling you how I feel about you. I love you very much. I will always love you, regardless of where I am or what I am doing. You will ever hold my heart.

I am so sorry. You have often told me that my temper would be my undoing, and you were right. I do not have regrets for myself, but for you. I am not there with you now when I should be, and I am sorry I cannot be there. I am sorry that I did not protect you. I am sorry you were hurt because of me. I had been looking for you to tell you that I had come into my power and that I would pass my father's test when I found you. It was never my intent to keep this from you.

The fact that I would have had to leave anyway does not lessen the damage that has been done, or the pain I have caused you. My father says he can get this letter to you by some means, and if you can find it in your heart to forgive me, I hope you will write back. Even if you cannot or do not, I will send you letters to let you know what is happening here. I hope you will pass the news to my brother, Dorien, regardless of your personal feelings for me.

I have already learned a great deal in the short time I have been gone. I sit now in my rooms in Silverport and they are unbelievable. The entire view from my window is unbelievable. You could put the whole of my mother's house in my bedroom. The bed is big enough to sleep three or four. It stands on a raised pedestal on the floor. Everything around me is white, and not like the white of our homes, dulled with dust and time. I mean white as the new-fallen snow.

The city rises up from the ground in levels. Henrick lives near the top of these many tiers so I can see as a bird for miles. The city is the same white. I do not know how they keep it so clean that it sparkles in the sun. I have not seen much, as we only arrived last night. I will be honest: I do not know how we got here.

Yesterday, while traveling through a pass where the road narrows between the cliffs and the river, there was a rock slide. Our wagon was damaged and one of the korpen killed. Yes, I am fine, though I was bruised and battered. I went to sleep after taking a potion to help with the pain and I awoke in this room. My father says he used a travel spell. I think he had me take the potion more so that I would not see how this is done than to heal my pain. I think he knows that if I could find a way, I would be at your side.

I fear, in this regard, that he is right. It is a spell I will endeavor to learn and master. I know magic is not something you are comfortable with, but I hope you will let me share what I learn. However, that is all I will speak of in regards to magic, unless you write back and give me permission.

I did find out something that both distresses me and also makes me curious: my father's brother is the High Minister of Lerdenia. I am not sure how I feel about this. Part of me wants to hate him, but I do not know him. My father seems to hold him in disdain and has begged me not to trust him. I am not sure who to trust right now. I do not fear my father's eyes upon this letter. I think he would find me more the fool to put my trust blindly after what he has told me of the Lerdenian society.

You would not like it, Mesi. Do not ever come here. It is not a place where brother helps brother and family helps village. It is a place where only your own power and prestige matter. They kill one another, vying for position. It is a place of little trust and forgiveness. I have yet to see it myself, but my father's descriptions give me pause. I do not plan to live here any longer than I have to. I do not want to live where I must always guard my back. I should have chosen a god to serve, and now I feel as if I am a place where the gods do not look. How can any god give to a people that harvest from their own creations? How can any god forgive what the people here do?

If you still wish to be my housemate one day, and if you can find it in your heart to forgive me, I will find a place that lies upon the borders of our two people. A place where we can live in peace and where maybe others like me can be welcome. A place where a man is judged by his merit and not the blood that flows within his veins.

I will close for now. I will write as often as my father bids me is safe. I can only hope you can find it in your heart to forgive me and write back. You and Gregor are the only friends I have in the world, and I suspect that will not change while I live in the city of my father.

Forever yours to command and scold,
Alador

Child,

If you want to write back to my son, place your letter in this tube and lay it beneath your pillow. Lie upon your pillow and wish the tube to Alador. When he awakes, he will find it beneath his own. This will be the only time my hand will touch these letters or this tube. The matter now lies between the two of you. Tell no one of the letter or the tube and be careful. The tube is spelled: any that pull a letter from it but yourself will see nothing but blank parchment once the tube has been sealed. It will protect the two of you should you find it in your heart to forgive the boy. Please forgive him, lest his moping be his undoing. I find him quite unpleasant company when he is whining and sighing over all he has lost. I would have been forced to pull him from your side, even had he not given justice to the bully that has haunted you both.

Henrick

Chapter Seven

As father and son traveled through Silverport, making their way up the tiers, Henrick continued to share facts that Alador might need. They began to fill his head in a jumbled mess. Henrick rattled off an amazing list of names, ranks, political leanings and their spheres of magic. Alador was just amazed that his father could fill so little time with so many details. He soon lost track of it all, so he resorted to nodding periodically while looking around.

Alador was more interested in what was happening around them as they climbed the steps to the next tier. Guards dressed in mail armor and blue tabards demanded their passes. Alador's eyes took in the royal blue tabard with the embroidered silver dragon, knowing the dragon represented Lyiu, the Goddess of prosperity and beauty. Given the city, it seemed a fitting standard. Alador stood in his father's wake as Henrick offered his pass. It was marked for the family of council and the guard stepped back and thumped his chest in salute.

The streets they passed through were pristine - no dirt or garbage anywhere. The street on the council tier was lined with beds of flowers that seemed fresh despite the heat of the day. Alador could feel the cool sea breeze along with the warmth of the summer sun . The higher tiers managed to catch the air here, and seemed less encumbered by the scent of too many people in close quarters.

His father was going on about each councilor as they passed the houses on the way to the stairs to the final level. Alador was sure to nod his head at appropriate times. His mind, however, was on Mesiande. Questions rushed over him like: Would she accept his apology? Would she write back? Was she healing? Did she still love him, or hate him?

The myriad of concerns were so deafening that he missed nodding as they reached the bottom of the final set of stairs. Alador suddenly found himself jerked around. "Alador, are you even listening to what I am telling you?" Henrick had stopped moving and was staring at Alador intently. He let go of his son's arm, glaring at him.

Alador was startled by the sudden stop, but still managed to answer. "Yes, Father," he said, flushing.

"What was the last Councilor's name?" Henrick eyed his son with sharp scrutiny.

"Umm I think it was Ellard. Yes, Ellard," Alador offered confidently.

Henrick sighed with exasperation. "That was two houses ago. We are about to be separated at best and your head is in the clouds.

Whatever are you dwelling on now that you cannot pay attention at this crucial time?" Henrick's frustration was visible in his expression. "Do not tell me that wench, or I swear I will set your boots on fire."

Alador mouth dropped, and he stammered as he tried to find a way out of this situation. He was not all that certain that his father wouldn't set his boots on fire. "I... We just sent... I—"

Henrick threw up his arms in vexation. "I give up. You are facing death and you are dreaming about some skirt which may well not even want you now." Henrick turned and stomped up the stairs, clearly put out.

Alador glared at Henrick's back with hurt and anger. "What a horrible thing to say!" he managed to sputter. He noticed one of those blue-clothed guards watching him, and hurried up the stairs after his father.

"Truth hurts, child. Learn that now." Henrick stopped at the top and rang the bell. As expected, a guard opened the door, but this one was dressed in black leather. The leather did not shine in the summer sun the way the previous guards' had. There was no tabard, just a red dragon emblazoned on each pauldron: the symbol of Krona, god of death and destruction.

The overlapping pieces of leather were each buckled in front by darkened steel and embossed leather, but no metal piece shone against the armor; they were all dulled in the same manner. It was a striking uniform, clearly made for those that needed to move silently or in the dark. Alador looked down at the blade at the man's side, but he couldn't tell if the sword was also unpolished, deep as it lay in its sheath.

Henrick showed his pass and the guard waved him through the door at the top of the stairs. Alador stepped through the gate and looked around, once again in amazement. The top of Silverport was a plateau, with another gate some ways off that opened to a narrow land bridge and out to the lands beyond.

Alador was uncertain how far those lands stretched. Henrick caught his attention and motioned to his right. "That is where the council gathers for matters of government. This one," he motioned to the left, "belongs to the ruling High Minister."

The building was massive: Henrick's was a hovel in comparison. Alador thought it could easily house half of his village. "How many people live here?" Alador asked in wonder.

He stared up at the great white building. Green climbing vines wrapped about the four large pillars that held up the overhang protecting the stairs and veranda. The two large doors were made of a dark wood. Statues of dragons were pleasingly spaced along the roof top.

"Well, officially, just my brother. But his staff, guards, and guests of the realm stay here as well." Henrick moved down the wide path to the steps that led up into the huge mansion, and Alador followed at his heels.

The doorman opened one of the double doors for the two mages before him. "The High Minister is expecting you in his private study, Master Henrick." The man bowed low.

Henrick nodded curtly and led the way through the foyer and around the great curving stairway. There was a cold and unfriendly air to the rooms they passed through. There was no laughter here, and the few servants Alador saw looked frightened and concerned as they bustled by.

They entered a marbled hall that was long enough to have several doors leading off it. Henrick's boots tapped as he walked on the marble floors, and for a long moment, Alador felt as if they tapped a swift death drum. His father had said they might die here today. Then, by the gods, what were they doing here? Why didn't they flee? He glanced back at the gate they'd crossed with sudden panic.

"Steady, boy! Don't bolt on me now," Henrick whispered as he came to stop at a large wooden door. The door before them was carved, depicting battles with Daezun and dragon alike. It was intricate and fascinating, and despite Alador's anxiety, he stared at it. "This is stupid," Alador whispered back.

"Yes, matters of politics often are. Remember, speak only when spoken to and keep it short. Whatever you do, hold that temper." Henrick threw open the door before Alador could answer and swept into the room, coming to a stop in the middle. "Ah, Brother, how kind of you to invite us to dinner. As you can see, we barely had the time to clean the dirt of travel from our robes." Henrick swept a low bow before the man behind the desk.

Alador followed Henrick into the room as the latter stood. "May I present my son, Alador, son of Alanis," Henrick announced. Alador bowed low as he'd seen his father demonstrate. It was awkward, but he thought he pulled it off well enough.

Luthian sat behind a massive desk, but stood as Alador was introduced. He clasped his hands together. "So this is my dearest nephew, the next generation of our line."

Alador noticed a hint of relief in his father's eyes. "Doting uncle" it appeared to be. Alador permitted himself a small, complicitous smile, but Henrick had already looked away.

Luthian came around the desk and Alador got his first good look at his uncle. His hair was white as snow, pulled back behind his head, and he was dressed in dark purple robes with gold trim. Luthian was everything Alador had always pictured the great mages to be. All he needed was a gnarled staff to fit the image of every tale Henrick had secretly told Alador as a child.

He couldn't help but stare as the man strode right up to him and pulled him into a great hug. Alador stood in the hug stiffly, uncertain if he should return the embrace or not.

"Careful, Brother, you will scare the boy right back to Daezun ground," Henrick warned. His tone held the sarcasm and humor that Alador was used to, but it lacked the warmth that usually accompanied it.

"Right, I imagine this has all been a bit of a shock." Luthian released Alador and stepped back. "Finding out that you are a mage, leaving your homeland. Where are my manners? Please, come and sit."

Luthian indicated chairs that had been set around a low table. He turned his back to both men, a clear indication he considered them no threat, and led the way across the expansive room. He began pouring wine..

Henrick shrugged at Alador, clearly perplexed by the effusive welcome they'd just received. Nevertheless, he followed Luthian and graciously accepted the glass of wine his brother turned and offered to him. Alador followed and was also handed a glass of wine. He stared at it in wonder, holding it up to peer at its beauty. He'd never seen a goblet made out of glass.

In the village, glass was only used for windows because of how expensive it was. The glass decanter and goblets spoke of great wealth. Even with all his slips, Alador would have never squandered it on something like this. He couldn't imagine the wealth Luthian must have had, to use it so frivolously.

"I hope your journey was without complications." Luthian looked to Henrick and indicated the chairs again.

"There were a few minor incidents and matters that could be called complications," Henrick began as he settled into a chair, smoothing his robes.

Alador flashed his father a look of warning and alarm. Surely he wouldn't tell his uncle about Trelmar's death. He caught his father's eyes, but Henrick seemed to ignore him.

"Oh? I hope nothing too damaging or alarming. I would hate to think you had to steal the boy from his kin." Luthian's eyes raked over Alador, and he found himself shivering. There was something deadly about this man, even when he was being so pleasant.

"In a manner of speaking, I did. Alador killed a middlin and was to be put to death. I weighed our last conversation and decided that your words held wisdom, so I interceded on his behalf with the use of the treaty," Henrick said as if discussing the weather. He toasted his brother with the glass and took a drink, watching Luthian intently.

Alador's heart sank and his eyes dropped to the toes of his boots, his hand trembling as it held the glass. Had his father just ensured a sentence of death for his capital crime? He took a breath to calm himself, imagining for a moment shooting his bow in his own defense, and the center needed to do just that. He was unprepared for his uncle's response.

"Already blooded. Well, I'll be..." Luthian paused, sipping his own wine as he scrutinized Alador. "It would seem you truly are of Guldalian blood." His words were softly spoken.

Alador raised his gaze to the man across from him. "I do not take pride in taking a man's life, especially not one I grew up with." He tried to keep his surprise out of his tone and hoped there was an edge of respect.

His uncle held his gaze for a long time, much as when Alador was caught in his father's, though he felt no pressure against what he come to know as his magic. "Liar," Luthian finally said softly, grinning. While Henrick seemed to be watching Luthian, Alador felt like prey before his uncle's gaze.

Henrick said nothing; he watched the two closely, but held his tongue and sipped his wine. when Alador glanced at him for help, he looked back blandly.

"Respectfully, my lord, I do not know why you would say such a thing. Trelmar was close to my age and we learned many things at each other's side." Alador's heart began to race and he was somewhat afraid to keep looking into his uncle's eyes.

"If you truly were contrite, your words would not be so well rehearsed. There was no emotion behind them. A man who truly kills with remorse holds great guilt when speaking of it. I see no guilt in your eyes, nor hear it in your tone." Luthian sat back, clearly pleased to have read his nephew so easily. He crossed his legs, which made his violet robes seem variegated in shades.

Alador swallowed hard. "I... am not sure what to say then," he stammered out. His uncle was imposing, and seemed much more knowledgeable than he should.

"Come Alador, we are family. Let us have no lies between us. Silverport can be a dangerous place enough, without enmity within families..." There was a hint of a warning there that even Alador did not miss. "Though I must say you are proving more your father's son in every moment. Blooded, AND a liar... Who would have thought such a one could have come from Daezun stock?"

This would have been an insult in any Daezun alehouse, but Luthian sounded proud.

"No lies..." Alador murmured. "The man was worse than korpen dung, and a waste of flesh and space. I'm not sorry he's dead, but I AM sorry for the harm that his death has caused to my village and my kin." His vehemence was unmasked, and Alador's eyes flashed when he glanced back at his uncle.

Henrick spluttered out a mouthful of wine at his son's words. He began coughing and put up a hand to indicate he was all right when Alador looked at him with concern.

"Well... well... Henrick, I take back my remarks about your... *failings*." Luthian shifted his eyes to Henrick as he refilled his wine glass, and suddenly it was as if Alador was no longer sitting with them. "You have outdone yourself in the brief times you have been in contact with this young mage. Truly, I am impressed with my nephew."

Luthian's tone held a sly edge that made Alador's stomach turn. He dropped his eyes to hide his confusion, deciding in that moment that he did not like his uncle. He took a deep drink of the wine, surprised at its smoothness and welcoming its warmth.

His father was still wiping up the wine he had spit out upon his robes. He looked at Luthian clearly trying to regain his composure. Henrick's tone was cautious and neutral, giving no indication of his feelings.

"I am sure, Brother, you will find that the Daezun did most of Alador's training. He is quick to learn, deadly with a bow, and already able to practice simple cantrips." Henrick toasted his brother with his wine. "He is also my son - too quick with his tongue, which means he often has to *eat* his words." Henrick glanced at Alador and the warning in his gaze was clear.

Alador looked in turn at the two men. Both would be judged handsome by any maiden's standards. His uncle had a porcelain quality to him, as if carved from smooth white marble. He had a chiseled face and his eyes, a mixture of lavender and silver, were captivating even to Alador. His father sat in stark contrast, with jet black hair and dark robes that accentuated his swarthier complexion. He was more muscled than Luthian and seemed more at ease in his skin.

Both men, however, shared one factor that Alador could not miss: they both exuded an air of insidious danger that was palpable. His father seemed more lethal to Alador at that moment than he ever had. He doubted that any would be able to stand against these two if they were ever united in their purpose.

"Well then, a good foundation to start with." Luthian set his glass down. He clasped his fingers together, steepling them as he considered Alador. He leaned forward slightly, a calculating smile on his lips. "Let me ask you Alador, what do you want?"

"What do I want with what, Uncle?" Alador asked respectfully. He was being careful and trying to follow his father's advice to stick to the questions posed. That one had seemed rather broad.

"With your life, Alador. What do you want to do with your life?" Luthian's long fingers continued to move together.

Alador's first thought was to live. He swallowed hard. "To return to my people and for them to accept me back; but that seems unachievable - beyond my reach. Therefore I would like to learn to be an enchanter – in order travel amongst them." Alador had thought about this a great deal, and it seemed the easiest way to be close to Mesiande and his family.

Luthian's fingers stopped moving. He tipped his head curiously and frowned. "That is it? Nothing more…" Luthian was clearly searching for a word, "…aspirational?"

Alador smiled at the wine in the glass. He had been twirling it slightly and the wine swirled dangerously close to the top. "I can think of nothing more aspirational than to be able to protect and assist those I care for at home."

Luthian leaned forward and picked up his own glass from the table. "Interesting. Most of those cast out as you have been speak of owning a plot of land, finding adventure or amassing a great deal of wealth. I would remind you, also, that this is your home now. Your people cast you out." Luthian's tone held his contempt for the Daezun.

Alador looked back at his uncle. He felt something cold and dark shift within him as he looked to the High Minister. It was an uneasy feeling and it must have hit his face as well, for he heard his father whisper, "Alador…"

Henrick's hissed warning had no effect as Alador sat his glass down and leaned forward.

"I have enough slips to provide for my simple needs. No one owns the land; it's the gods' gift to all the people of the isle. And I've had enough adventure with fire breathing dragons to last me a lifetime."

He gazed unwaveringly at his uncle. "Why am I here, uncle? If you really saw me as family, I would have had a letter or word from you ere now; yet I've seen nothing all these years. Two can see through lies as easily as one: you didn't give a damn about me till I harvested that stone."

Alador was startled at his own confidence. He could feel his father's gaze on him, the heat of it tangible, even though he didn't break eye contact with his uncle. "You said there should be truth between us," Alador reminded Luthian. He was not going to play these politics his father spoke of; he was going to learn and then distance himself from these cruel people with their hideous way of life. Alador sat back in his chair, his eyes boldly meeting his uncle's.

Luthian chuckled with amusement. "That I did. I fear I may have opened a box that I will want to shut from time to time..." Luthian looked at Henrick. "I like this lad. He has spirit." He winked at his brother with what appeared to be genuine good will.

He looked back at Alador, his tone lighter than what had passed between them just moments before. "Then let us be candid, nephew. Your father and I are well aware of the size of the stone you sold, for the merchant tried to sell it to me. A stone that large holds a great deal of power and someone untrained with that much power could be a threat to himself and even those he might care about. As your uncle, I would see you trained: so that you do not accidentally explode. Also, as High Minister of Lerdenia, I would see you trained so that one day - if needed - you could be called upon to protect the isle."

Luthian gestured towards the windows across the room. "The world across the ocean is filled with war. One day, it may come to our shore or we may need to take it to theirs. Is that enough truth for you, Alador?" There was a hint of sarcasm in Luthian's tone. He toasted Alador with his glass.

Alador weighed his uncle's words. There was truth to what he said. He didn't know how to use whatever power the stone had transfused him with. He would protect the isle if war came to it: if war approached the Lerdenians, it was bound to find the Daezun, as well.

"For now," he conceded.

Alador could feel Henrick's tension and finally looked at him. His father's eyes were filled with reproach, and in that moment Alador hoped he'd be sent to the guard that night. He suspected if he left this room with Henrick, he'd get an ear full all the way home.

The door opened and a man bowed low before his uncle. "Dinner is served whenever it pleases the Minister."

"Come gentlemen, I have quite the dinner and entertainment planned. A few friends and council members are awaiting us." Luthian downed the last of his wine and stood.

Alador did the same and rose. He liked feasts. He hoped the boards, well, tables here, were as well laid as the feasts at home. Alador suddenly realized he was ravenously hungry and nodded. He wasn't concerned about guests; most feasts or gatherings involved a lot of people...

They made their way to the dining room, and Alador's expectations were confounded. There were two long tables with every place taken by someone dressed either as finely or even more splendidly than he and his father. As they entered the room, all conversation stopped and everyone rose almost as one. Alador looked at his father wide-eyed.

"Privilege of power, son: a respect for the position and in some cases for the man." Henrick's words were soft as his uncle had stridden ahead to a table that was raised above the others. Henrick indicated that they should follow him.

"Why is our table away from everyone?" Alador asked curiously.

"Why? So the food at our table is not handled by any but the most trusted, and so that all eyes are drawn to the High Minister and those he chooses to display." There was sarcasm in Henrick's voice. "Alador, you will do better to stop comparing. Lerdenia is as different from the Daezun as an apple is to a prickleberry. They both might bring forth fruit, but neither will ever taste like the other."

Henrick climbed the few steps, and Luthian indicated that he should sit to his left and Alador to his right. Alador didn't like being out of the line of sight of his father, but sat down uncomfortably as instructed. When his uncle sat, the rest of the room sat down as well and the conversation resumed.

"Is it always like this?" he asked his uncle.

"A little intimidating, I imagine, yes?" Luthian put a hand on Alador's shoulder as he leaned towards Alador with an understanding smile. When Alador nodded yes, Luthian continued his answer in a slightly more comforting tone.

"I actually find it rather droll and usually take meals by myself. However, given your arrival and the declaration of another blood kin in the Guldalian line, many wished to lay eyes upon you. Look around the room carefully. Note those who look to you, and how. There are some out there that are gauging if you are someone they can curry favor with, so as to gain my ear. There are others who will hate you just because you have Daezun blood.

There are still others who would kill you just to hurt your father or myself."

Alador surveyed the crowd before him carefully. His uncle's words rang true. There were some amongst those dining whom he felt could scarcely contain their animosity. Others, when they noticed his gaze, smiled or nodded back. "Why do you not put a stop to it?" he asked curiously. "Squabbling and killing hardly seem efficient ways to manage things."

Luthian waved a woman over, and suddenly they were surrounded. Everywhere Alador looked there seemed to be beautiful women about his age leaning across the table. One filled his glass, while another leaned across to place a plate of steaming food in front of him. Her dress, leaning as she was, exposed most of her breasts to him, and he found himself almost not hearing his uncle's answer. Other women attended his father and uncle.

"If they squabble amongst themselves, they are less of a threat to me." Luthian answered smoothly.

Alador found his gaze caught by the most beautiful pair of emerald eyes he had ever seen. As the girl straightened up, she caught his admiring gaze and smiled shyly. He was unable to tear his eyes away as he pressed his point. "Could you not just kill off all the traitors, and then make it a law to stop the killing?" he murmured.

Luthian followed Alador's gaze and smiled. "Yes, you definitely are our kin." He chuckled softly and leaned over to Alador to murmur softly: "You find this one appealing?"

Alador nodded smiling at the girl. "Who wouldn't?"

"You have good taste. She is yours." Luthian sat up and picked up his glass.

"Wait, what? Mine? What do you mean mine?" Alador looked over to his uncle in confusion, back to the woman, and then right back to his uncle.

"You may have her. When you are bored with her, let me know and I will replace her." Luthian did not seem to find this conversation the least bit appalling.

"Have her for…" The realization that his uncle was offering her for his bed filled his face, and the flush of embarrassment must have been written clearly, because his uncle laughed aloud.

"You have had a woman before, yes?" Luthian's voice was louder than Alador would have wished.

"Yes, but how can you just dispose of one like property? What if she doesn't want to… you know." Alador looked at him, clearly upset.

"If she doesn't want to perform the tasks assigned to her, she is welcome to return to the lower tiers from whence she came. Most of these beautiful young women do not have a mage's power, and therefore use those attributes they have to gain a higher place." He watched Alador as he picked up his fork, waving at the women about them. "They are not prisoners, my dear boy. They can come and go as they please." Luthian's voice held a quiet tone of finality, and he began to eat.

Alador looked at the young woman who had served him his plate. She was taller and thinner than the women he was used to, and her dark brown hair was braided and coiled back to hold the rest of the length still as she served. She glanced back, catching his assessing gaze, and smiled shyly again before hurrying off to someone's bidding.

He looked down at his food and saw a wonderful array of vegetables and a large piece of fish. The aroma was amazing, but Alador's appetite had faltered. Henrick asked his uncle a question, and as Alador couldn't hear it over the din of general conversation, it gave him time to reflect on the things he had learned.

He nibbled at the food before him as he watched those below. There were many older men, their hair as white as his uncle's. There were women as well, most dressed in more finery than he had seen on any woman, even on a house-mating day.

There was one man that kept drawing Alador's eyes, because of his lack of embellishments. He was dressed simply and sat without talking to those - presumably his peers - around him. He sipped the wine, but his plate appeared largely untouched. His hair was as golden as harvest wheat. But it was the coldness in his eyes that bothered Alador; it reminded him of the way Trelmar had watched him. His uncle was right. Alador hadn't been here a day, and already he had enemies.

Chapter Eight

Aorun waited for Sordith and Owen in his office, fingering a gilded invitation to the High Minister's dinner. It seemed the man had gone and found himself a nephew. Aorun hated the political dinners he was sometimes given the opportunity to attend, but good information could usually be found there.

Aorun's largest trade item was information. He thought about sending Sordith, but suspected that his right hand was not as forthcoming in his observations as Aorun would like. He dared not send Owen. It would be like letting a flight of lexital into the warehouse: nothing would survive.

The door opened suddenly, and reflexively Aorun's hand went to his blade as Owen sauntered in. He had a black eye and a split lip. Aorun raised a brow as he looked him over. "You had best hope that the other man looks worse." He knew that Owen had a penchant for fighting in the rings for a split of the take.

Owen just grinned in that big easy manner of his. "Dead." It seemed all that needed to be said as he moved to his spot on the wall, leaving the door open. Owen leaned back, arms crossed. "Something important to get you up so early, boss?"

Aorun nodded. "I was looking over reports and found a note that the new merchant up on the second tier refused to pay his protective due. We are going to go pay him a visit."

The man they were going to see was a jeweler who specialized in the enchantments of rings and pendants. If he was expecting to get jewels to his shop, he had to bring them through the trenches to do so. His supply line had just dried up. Aorun knew Owen took joy in the breaking of things: windows, goods, bones. It didn't seem to matter much to his henchman.

Owen grinned. "I love my job." He pulled out his dagger and set to it with a stone as he leaned against the wall.

Sordith walked in at that moment, his cat-like movements as silent as ever. His face held the usual bland expression it had until something displeased him. It was that silence that endeared him to Aorun. If he needed eyes in difficult places, Sordith knew how to see it done. "Have a fun evening?" Aorun teased eyeing his second.

"Very relaxing," Sordith answered, moving to stand beside Aorun. "Interesting to see you ready so early."

Owen grinned at Sordith. "That is what I said."

Aorun just shook his head. "I am not always late to rise." Both of his men just looked at him. "What? I'm not!"

Sordith gave a simple smirk. "Alright, not always. We may discount perhaps one day out of ten." He and Owen laughed uproariously. Owen moved to Sordith and clapped him on the shoulder. "So how was the farm wench last night?"

"She was a bit hysterical at first; but she came around," Sordith replied.

"Good! I want a piece of that," Owen said with a cruel grin.

"Afraid I can't let you do that, Owen," Sordith answered.

"Ah, come on, I always offer to share with you," Owen frowned. The big man wore the expression of a child that had been denied dessert.

"How often do I take you up on that?" Sordith asked levelly.

"Well…um…never, actually." Owen paused and looked at Sordith, puzzled.

"There is a reason for that, Owen. I like my women warm, willing and clean. Let us just say I have more discerning tastes." Sordith grinned at the large man, his tone casual.

"Can I at least look her over?" Owen asked with a frown. He was fairly sure he'd just been insulted, but was struggling to pinpoint exactly how.

"I fear I sent her home," Sordith answered.

Aorun had been following the exchange with a grin to the last, but the smile dropped at the word "home." He felt his face flush with anger as he turned to Sordith. "Sent home?"

"Yes, sent home." Sordith met Aorun's angry gaze evenly.

"Why, by the gods, would you send such a comely lass home?" Aorun's nostrils flared. "She couldn't have been that bad in your bed?"

"I wouldn't know, I didn't press her to it. I sent her home last night." Sordith shrugged.

Aorun raised his gauntleted hand to strike Sordith and was surprised when Sordith caught the arm as he pulled back. Aorun had barely seen him move. They stared eye to eye through their own arms.

"Before you do that, remember that you gave your word that I could do with the girl as I pleased," Sordith whispered softly. His eyes were steel as they met Aorun's.

"That is not what I meant," Aorun growled angrily.

"You did not ask what I wanted, merely gave me leave to do exactly as I willed. I willed to send the girl home with a pouch for her fears and trouble." Sordith had not yet let go of Aorun's hand. Owen stood beside them both, out of harm's way, his hand on his sword hilt. It was clear he had no idea what to do if they came to blows.

"You clearly heard me say I wanted her trained in the brothels." Aorun's eyes danced with anger: he was obviously taking this as a slight.

"While you stand there considering whether or not you will kill me for doing only what you, yourself, allowed me to do, I would have you add to my list of sins that whereas I will help in the trenches anywhere you ask, I will NEVER," Sordith emphasized firmly, "... be a party to kidnapping innocent people from their homes outside of Silverport again. If that is a requirement of my service, kill me now."

Sordith slowly let go of Aorun's hand. "There are enough whores and destitute for you to prey on here. You don't need to ruin the lives of those that actually managed to find a life outside this shite-hole.

Aorun stared at Sordith in disbelief as his second drew his sword. Aorun reacted instantaneously, the hissing of the two swords freeing from sheaths echoing in deadly concert.

"Surely you do not wish to die over some little trollop."

He had no sooner uttered the words than Sordith tossed his sword gently to Owen, who caught it in surprise. Sordith followed it with six daggers that swiftly flew across the room, burying themselves in the half-beam on the far wall. They were neatly lined up and quivering, one below the other. Aorun hadn't even known Sordith carried six daggers.

"I am giving you the opportunity to send me to the gods now. Choose wisely, Aorun, knowing full well that I will not be party to the hunting and selling of free women." Sordith put both his hands out to either side of him. "You and I know that there is no going down for me. I rise or I die. I have no desire to kill you. Therefore, if you cannot accept my terms of service, kill me now."

Owen stepped back. This was between the two of them. His eyes were wide as he stared between the two deadly men. He held Sordith's blade like it was a vile object, out away from his body. He wasn't the only one staring in disbelief; Aorun also stared wide-eyed at Sordith.

"By the gods, man! I knew you had some stupid sense of honor, but this is a bit much. We deal in illicit goods every day!" Aorun waved his sword about them.

"I have no problem stealing the fools in the tiers blind. I do not mind keeping the peace - such as it is - in this foul hole. I do not prey on innocent people trying to earn an honest wage," Sordith stated firmly. He still had his hands out. "I tolerate – barely - the muscling of those that live here. However, it is your realm to lead, not mine."

"What would you do differently to lead this 'realm', this 'hole', as you call it?" Aorun asked. There was a deadly edge to his tone.

"Tell that bastard Veaneth that if he wants Lerdenian woman, he can hire them. We are done. We are not enslavers of our own people."

"I see. Anything else you seem to think I am deficient in?" Aorun asked bitterly, wounded that his second was turning on him.

"Bugger it, Aorun! Ever think that it's not all about you?" Sordith let out an exasperated sigh.

Aorun's answer was swift and honest. "No."

"I'm not saying you need to change anything. I'm saying leave me out of it," Sordith countered. He still held Aorun's gaze without fear.

"That is all you want? - for me to leave you out of any of the trafficking?" Aorun considered that. He really didn't want to lose Sordith. He trusted him for this very reason. The man had principle, and...well, he could manage numbers. Aorun made the decision and slid his sword home. "Done."

"You understand that if I am forced to do so, I will act." Sordith's words held a strange edge of promise.

Aorun waved his hands in dismissal. "Good as done. I have enough other things you can be a party to; and besides, even though he is a bit over-eager, Owen seems to have a taste for it." Aorun turned and walked to his desk. "Pick up your weapons. We have work to do."

Sordith moved to pull his daggers from the beam and slid them all back into their respective sheaths. His eyes met Owen's with a withering look. "You got anything to say?"

Owen snorted. "No, sir. I like this arrangement just fine," he said with a large grin, keeping it even as Sordith glowered at him. "You turn them down and I will just console their broken hearts." Owen paused for a moment and then leaned into Sordith to ask quietly. "You do LIKE women though, don't ya?" Owen handed him back his sword.

Sordith took the sword and slammed it back into its sheath. "Of course I like women. Don't be an idiot." He moved over to Aorun, who still had his back to him.

Owen grinned. "Okay, okay… Just checking." Owen went back to his spot, watching the two cautiously.

Auron was staring at his desk, deep in thought. Maybe it wouldn't hurt him to see what Sordith would do. He would go with them, but Aorun would have him make the demand. Aorun turned and regarded the two.

"As I was telling Owen, that new jewelry merchant on the second tier has refused to pay his dues. I was going to explain to the man how Silverport works, but I have decided, Sordith, that you will do this instead. You say there are better ways to do this then 'muscling,' as you call it." Aorun crossed his arms in challenge. "Let me see how you would handle such a situation."

Sordith eyed Aorun. "I see this as a lose lose situation. If I do well, you will see it as a slight to your methods. If I do poorly, I will have confirmed that your approach is best and you will mock me with it."

Aorun grinned. "True, I would mock you with it." Aorun considered this a moment. "An agreement, then. If your way does not work, I get to mock you with it." Aorun grinned again in playful mischief, as if the confrontation just moments ago hadn't occurred.

He then became more serious, and treated Sordith to an even stare. "But if your way does work, I will agree at least to try what you recommend. I am not unreasonable, Sordith. I know you have a head for numbers, and I am for anything that brings more slips into our coffers."

Sordith considered his offer for a long moment before offering his arm. "Agreed," he said with his usual firmness and lack of emotion.

Aorun clasped his arm as they solidified their agreement. "What is the plan then to get this merchant to cough up his due?"

"You watch, play muscle and let me do all the talking." Sordith's eyes were shrewd, he was clearly already calculating.

Aorun nodded. "When we get there then, the task is yours." Aorun strode out the room and his two men fell in behind him. They made their way through the trench to the first set of stairs to the upper level. The stairs were widest here to accommodate the amount of traffic from tier to tier: services to and from the noble houses, from laundry through food and clothing to any goods you could name...

The guards were not as strict at this level during the day because of the flow of commerce; but matters tightened up at night. Aorun nodded to them and they nodded back, partial to the slips he slipped them regularly. It was good to be in the good graces of the city's guards - especially those willing to look the other way.

The trio entered the second tier with the same ease. They held up their merchant passes as a matter of routine: the guard knew them and waved them through. The three men were silent as they moved through the city. There was always someone in the trenches looking to move up, so when they were out of the manor, they were ever-watchful. People parted to go around them. Aorun liked this display of fearful respect; he didn't mind ruling through fear. Actually, he rather liked it, and failed to see how Sordith would get this jeweler to pay up without it.

They reached the jeweler's shop, and stepped in one after the other. There was no one in the shop at the moment, but soon the curtain parted and an older man stepped through. Owen turned and pulled the curtains closed - a sign that the shop was closed. He then leaned his large frame back against the door to keep anyone from opening it. Aorun moved to the right, hand on his sword, but took the position of the silent enforcer, a role he'd played often when he was not yet Trench Lord. His eyes, however, were on Sordith.

Sordith stepped up to the board that separated him from the jeweler. "Ah, good day... Good day, Master Jespeth. How are you this fine day?" Sordith had a wide smile.

"It *was* a good day, but I suspect my fortunes may have just changed." He eyed Owen and Aorun with distaste.

Sordith followed his gaze and waved in dismissal. "Pay them no mind; they are here for my protection."

"So you say. What can I do for you? I fear you have me at a disadvantage, as you have my name and I do not know yours." Jespeth's eyes came back to Sordith, but he still looked wary. He was a small man with a balding head and daring eyes.

"Ah, my apologies. I am Sordith. I have come to discuss a business matter for the Trench Lord," Sordith answered.

"I already told the last man that I will not be blackmailed and bullied. I will not be paying protection fees to men who do not even live in this... *tier*." Jespeth spat out the last word.

Aorun's hand clenched around the hilt of his sword. He wanted to remove the man's vile head, but he'd promised Sordith he could handle this matter. His soft snort was the only sign of his disapproval, making his displeasure clear in the movement of his right hand.

It was then that Aorun detected a noise behind the curtain to the living quarters of the shop. He gave a casual signal to indicate that they were not alone.

Sordith nodded once to indicate that he'd seen the hand sign. "Well, you see, that is why I am here. Obviously, there has been some sort of misunderstanding. It is not security, exactly, that the fee is levied for. You are being asked to donate... "funds" in order that we might provide you with a priority supply line."

Jespeth went to speak, but Sordith held up his hands. "Pray, let me continue. A man on the second tier in need of good stones to practise his craft has to wait for the third tier merchants to make their purchases before he can view the stones. Yes?"

"Well, yes... But that is the way of things. I wait my turn like any other." Jespeth looked about indignantly.

"I am betting you are from an inland city?" Sordith asked with a slight smile.

"Yes, I know how the tiers work. I am not new to city life." Jespeth clearly looked disgruntled, despite his concern, and eyed the three armed men in his shop.

Sordith nodded. "There is one major difference between Silverport and other inland cities. Goods come into the city in two directions. One – the one you are used to - comes across the tier bridge. However, there is another route, a supply that comes from the sea. Now, *those* particular stones are from all over the world. We only share that supply with merchants and dealers who have paid for the privilege: to ensure they have first access to these rare and exceptional gems."

Aorun watched the subtle change come over the merchant. He was fairly sure that Sordith had secured the man's interest. Sordith, however, chose that moment suddenly to flick his wrist and cut the rope holding up the curtain behind the merchant with a throwing knife. It fell away to reveal the most beautiful woman that Aorun had ever seen.

He stood and stared in absolute amazement. Her hair was long and black. It fell all the way to her hip, even gathered at the side of her neck as it was. It was her eyes, however, that captured his attention. They were the deepest green he had ever seen. The girl froze, staring at the knife just inches above her head.

Jespeth moved between the men and the woman. "This is my daughter, she meant no harm! She helps me with the settings, sometimes..." His eyes darted with concern at the three men. "I assure you, what is said here will not leave this room. Keelee, to the back shop with you."

Aorun spoke even though he'd promised not to. "I think she should stay. You got anyone else back there?" He wanted to keep looking at her. His eyes were undressing her, even though she was behind her father. Her waist would probably fit between his hands. Her breasts seemed ready to spill out the top of her gown. He shifted slightly: to ease the growing pressure in his pants.

Sordith glowered at Aorun, a look meant to quieten a guard. "I think she should stay. I am hoping our business is almost concluded." He, too, eyed the girl with swift appraisal.

"No, no one else is here. Sh-she helps me, that is all," Jespeth sputtered out, clearly uncomfortable with the expressions on the faces of the men who eyed his daughter.

"Yes, well, lovely lass, it doesn't do to spy on your father's customers. Some might take objection." Sordith nodded pleasantly to the young woman as he delivered his deceptively calm warning.

"Yes, sir," she answered, her voice soft and husky. It reminded Auron of silk as it flowed over him and he shivered. "I meant no harm.

Please do not hurt my father for my misplaced curiosity."

"I am not here to hurt anyone." Sordith gave her a wink and turned back to the merchant. "Now, Jespeth, if you were to up the dues previously requested - say by a mere ten slips - I could ensure that an invitation to priority-view-and-purchase is sent to you whenever such stones come in. You could have first pick before they went to the upper tiers, giving you a competitive edge." Sordith smiled at him.

"You really mean I would see them first?" Jespeth licked his lips in anticipation.

"It does seem a fair thing to offer in the circumstances - given you always have to take the leavings of the third tier craftsmen where the land-transported stones are concerned."

Sordith leaned against the board and looked at the man. "I mean, look around us. It is clear you are at disadvantage compared to the third tier shops. I bet you rarely get anything unique." He indicated the shelves that held some unguents and a few trays of common rings and pendants. "It is clear that it isn't your setting work that puts you at a disadvantage." Sordith picked up a ring on a tray to his left, turning it over in his hand. "It is fine craftsmanship that deserves the finest in stones."

He tossed the ring down, causing Jespeth to scramble after it and position it so that it was properly displayed. "Of course, if you would really rather just keep taking their castoffs... I am sure I could convince the Trench Lord to leave you off his rounds." Sordith straightened up. "Yes, that is probably for the best." He turned away as if he had settled the matter.

Aorun raised a brow at the strangled sound the jeweler made, amazed. If this man took the bait, Sordith would have nearly doubled the income from this shop to his own coffers. Surely such a tactic of manipulation would not really work.

Jespeth moved around the end quickly to try to stop Sordith from leaving. "Wait, wait now. Let us not be hasty." Jespeth looked at his daughter, who gave a brief nod, and then smiled broadly at Sordith as he turned back around. "I think what you offer is a fair deal. If we would truly have first pick, then this price would be worth my trouble." Jespeth was now in a hurry to get himself included in this deal. He nodded to his daughter, who skittered off.

Aorun watched the girl disappear into the darkened confines of the shop. Her behind presented just as good a view as her front had been; the draping dress showed her back with defined shoulders and unmarked skin. He was going to have to figure out how to get this one in his bed. Yes, he had to have her. He could think of no woman that could hold a candle to her beauty, and he'd held a lot of women.

Sordith, in the meantime, moved back to the counter and held out his hand. "I will come to fetch you personally when such gems are available. You have my word."

Jespeth shook his hand warmly and, when his daughter returned, handed over a small pouch. "If your previous man had offered to explain this, I would have listened. He just came in demanding the Trench Lord's cut."

"About that… How did you get the man to leave?" Sordith smiled with genuine interest.

"I keep a wand for such occurrences. The man decided a few slips were not worth a bolt of lightning between the shoulder-blades," Jespeth admitted.

"I will keep that in mind, Master Jespeth." Sordith grinned wickedly. "It was good doing business with you." Sordith tossed the pouch to Aorun as he passed him. Aorun caught it deftly and shoved it into his belt pouch, and they both strode from the store. Owen took the time to open the curtains back up before bowing and leaving to join the first two.

"I don't understand. Why did you not just grab him by the throat, put a dagger to it and demand the slips?" Aorun was considering things. He would have wasted no words or time in taking his due.

"I could have done that, and there would have been fewer slips for the trouble. The man's work is good, and this way he doesn't hide his true value, nor is he an enemy. Instead, you are left with a man's goodwill and extra slips in your pocket," Sordith pointed out. The two were walking side by side and Owen had dropped behind to watch Aorun's back. The streets were busy and more than one trench lord had been assassinated in such close confines.

Aorun walked silently, considering Sordith's words. The man was right, though he hated to admit it. His way would have been swift and brutal, but would certainly have made an enemy.

They had walked most of the way back to the first tier steps before he spoke again. "You and I both know he is not going to get first pick," Aorun pointed out.

"Yes, you and I know that. But as he will only see the cargo laid before him, he will never know where it was prior to that. Sometimes, using what a man does not know is as effective as using what he does."

Sordith's words were almost drowned out by the noise of day-to-day traffic: Silverport was busy by day trading in the shops, on the market stalls and around most corners. At night, it was the establishments offering more leisurely pleasures that were frequented - the type of establishments that Aorun owned stakes in.

"I concede. While I find my way to be far more personally satisfying, yours creates more wealth." Aorun's mind went to the dark-haired beauty. "Maybe we can convince him to bring his daughter to dinner," he mused softly.

Sordith rolled his eyes. "We would have more slips if you thought with the other head," he pointed out.

Owen piped up from the back. "But not nearly as much fun!"

Aorun laughed. "Owen has the right of it. Slips are not everything." He clapped Sordith on the back in good will. "A man has to have a little balance in his life. You might consider it."

"I will keep that in mind," Sordith answered with a sigh.

Aorun led them back down into the trenches. He had slipped as far down as he could - to the very end of the first tier. Slowly, he and his two men worked their way through the trenches. His presence served to remind those scraping a living in the trenches that there was a form of order. His men were spread out; it was their job to keep an eye on matters, keep the peace, and ensure that certain considerations were kept in mind.

The largest area Aorun had to maintain control over contained the warehouses. Goods from ships were brought in and sorted according to the tier they were destined for. They were stored in cellars carved out beneath the buildings, which helped keep produce safe and at a moderately cool temperature that was constant through summer and winter.

Each storehouse had a keeper who let Aorun know if anything new or exotic came in. That was how Aorun ensured that those who served him were adequately rewarded. First pick of goods on offer was one favor he could bestow.

Another was the trade of illicit goods frowned upon by the Council. He had a large quantity of meraweed, tambert root and bitterstalk - three much-used herbs in smoking-dens and baths. They were powerful relaxants and mind-altering drugs. Too much tambert root had been known to kill.

Aorun's favorite storehouse was the one for exotic items. There, all things rare or previously unknown were processed. Aorun could spend hours in that place. He personally escorted influential merchants on their tours of that storehouse whenever he could. Not only did it smooth the way for other trades and favors down the line; it also reassured him he hadn't missed anything in the bulging chests or on the well-stocked shelves.

When they'd finished working their way through the storehouses and along the trenches, Aorun sent the two men off in different directions. Sordith was to see to the accounting reports and Owen had to ensure that the gate guards were watching for potential product for Veaneth. Half-Daezun were welcome in the trenches more so now than ever. After all, Aorun had found a market for them.

Aorun had had an invitation to a function in the highest tier. He hadn't been to a high tier function in a long time. Most mages ignored his existence unless they needed something, and he found their self-absorbed conversations about their latest spell or greatest deed sickening.

However, he was interested in clapping eyes on the High Minister's nephew. It would be interesting to see what new blood had been found for this long family line. Traced back to the first Lerdenian stand, the Guldalian bloodline had all but been erased. The two brothers were the last of their kin.

Aorun strode to his rooms with determination. He found a clean pair of black leathers and a fine grey silk shirt. He brushed his long, gold hair back and secured it at the base of his neck. It was a simple outfit, but would stand in stark contrast to all the mage finery he could expect. He would draw the eye of this nephew better than any peacock in the room.

Satisfied, Aorun made sure to slip a knife onto his belt and then one in each boot. He liked his boot knives best: they were solidly weighted and flew with deadly accuracy.

He arrived minutes after the bell had tolled at the High Minister's grand table; but as he had expected, the man himself was not yet present. One of the things he'd learned about Luthian Guldalian was that he liked an entrance. Aorun found a place off to the side where he would not have to interact much. That suited those at his table just fine as they gobbled on and on like a flock of fowl. Arriving when he did he did not suffer the boredom of waiting long: the minister entered with his usual flair for being noticed. The room rose as one to acknowledge him, all eyes on the simply but elegantly robed mage as he worked his way through the room towards his place.

Aorun, however, was eyeing the two gentlemen behind him. The first was Henrick, of whom he was already well acquainted. Henrick was a deadly mage to cross, but one that liked his pleasures. It had been easy to stay in the mage's good graces; but at the same time, Aorun had made no headway in gaining the man's trust or confidence.

His eyes moved to the slightly shorter and younger mage beside Henrick. Aorun studied the blue robes carefully, taking in every aspect of this youth. He stared at the boy's face with dawning realization: this nephew of the High Minister was a damned half-breed! Hatred for the Daezun-tainted 'mudblood' boiled up within him as the room was motioned to sit.

He plopped down at his table and picked up his glass, his eyes on the brown-haired, awestruck, bastard child. There he sat at the high table. He would be accorded privilege and power by accident of birth, while he, Aorun, was only a guest in this room as a necessary evil.

He was full Lerdenian and therefore should have whatever he wanted, whenever and however he wanted it. It was not right that a half-breed got between the legs of an enemy should now be sitting at that high table. Aorun didn't care who his whoring father claimed to be.

Aorun's ire rose still further when he saw the young woman who was fawning over the bastard in his service. It was the woman from the jeweler's shop. If she was serving at Luthian's table, that meant she was one of the chosen attendants and only a step above a brothel wench.

Aorun watched the exchange of uncle and nephew as both eyed the young woman. The High Minister owed Aorun a couple favors; it was time to collect and put a little of that favor beneath him in his bed. He smiled with hunger, watching her move, before turning his attention back to the table.

When he saw the youth assessing those about him, Aorun too let his eyes drift over the other mages in the room. When he looked that way again, their eyes met. Aorun did not smile or look away. He held that man's gaze with all the contempt and hatred for the Daezun that seethed inside of him. This one, he would destroy if he got the chance. He would have to be careful, given the power of those who were his kin; but he hadn't got where he was today without knowing how to be careful.

This nephew was but an untrained youth. Best take him out of the equation before he cut his teeth. Aorun smiled at that thought. Yes... He knew how to pull teeth.

Chapter Nine

Alador felt as if the night would never end. Despite all the splendor and luxury about him and the fact his father had ensured he was properly dressed, Alador felt like an oddity that traveling Mesmers brought into the village for people to pay to look at.

His uncle Luthian had set up a receiving line to present Alador properly. He nodded politely to many women: ugly, old women with flat, white hair; simpering, giggling women with too much paint on their faces; and cold marble visions of beauty. He'd been told so many names that they began to blur together, and too easily he forgot the names of the men that shook his hand. His father stood a little behind him, offering occasional comments and support.

Alador looked up as the next man approached to greet him formally, and blinked in surprise as he met the gaze of the man who'd been coldly staring at him earlier in the evening. Unlike many of the other guests, the man was not in robes; instead he wore black leather pants and a fine grey shirt. Their eyes locked, and Alador swallowed slowly. He'd never seen someone who could move with such deadly grace, and he'd only ever encountered such unveiled hatred in Trelmar. This man looked far more intimidating than Alador's old bully. When Luthian spoke, Alador paid attention: this was a name he would need to know.

"Aorun, may I present my nephew, Alador. Alador, this is Silverport's Trench Lord, Aorun Trevion." Luthian glanced between the two with curiosity.

Aorun took Alador's arm in greeting, "It is a pleasure to meet the latest 'addition' to the Guldalian line; though I had not expected it to be a half-breed bastard."

Aorun's eyes didn't leave Alador's, despite the minister's close presence. Alador bit back the pain as the man's fingers dug into his arm.

"The pleasure is mine… *Sir*," Alador fired right back, "though I had not expected a Lerdernian Lord to be so lacking in manners."

He knew he probably shouldn't have said the words the moment they came from his mouth; but although he was doing everything he could not to show it, this Trench Lord was hurting his arm.

In spite of himself, Henrick laughed outright. "Have a care, Aorun. Alador's potential for power shows every sign of being as great as mine or the High Minister's."

Luthian witnessed the interchange with a strange and satisfied smile. Alador wondered what his uncle was plotting. He could almost see the windmill turning in his eyes.

Aorun's mouth hardened at Alador's quip, and he slowly released the boy's arm. "I will keep that in mind in any future… 'interactions' between us." The man's words held an oily menace that fouled the air around them.

"Oh, I would encourage you to do so," Luthian chimed in smoothly. "Not only does he demonstrate proven potential for power: he embodies Guldalian scruples as well." Luthian's voice held an edge of warning.

Aorun bowed low. "Of course, High Minister. One could expect no less from *any* kin of yours."

Alador watched warily for a moment as the Trench Lord moved away, then turned to see that there was nobody else waiting to be formally introduced. Perhaps it was merely a lull in the line, but he seized his opportunity.

"Uncle, do you think I might withdraw? This is all very exciting, but also tiring. I've heard so many names that my head's spinning." Alador murmured this softly, trying not to insult any that might be in earshot while waiting politely for an invitation to approach. He could tell the proceedings were winding down: some had already taken their leave, though many others were still mingling, perhaps in expectation.

"Of course, my boy, of course. Come along. Let us return to my study and have a few words before you find your bed." Luthian led the way, pausing occasionally to say his goodnights. Clearly he knew everyone's name and tier.

Alador mumbled appropriate goodnights, but his mind was on his father's warning. Henrick had mentioned that his uncle might see them parted this very night, and Alador wasn't ready to be shuffled off to people he didn't know.

Despite Henrick's faults, Alador knew his father, and there was comfort in knowing he was close by. When they finally returned to the study, Alador collapsed gratefully into a chair. "How do you do that?"

"Do what, my dear boy?" Luthian slipped into a chair across from Alador. Fresh glasses, fruit, and wine had been laid out on the table between them.

"Handle so many people in such large gatherings. You seem to know all their names and what they do," Alador explained.

Henrick sat down in the other available chair. "To not know your enemy is too soon to know your death, my son," he chimed in softly.

Luthian nodded, watching Alador. "It has paid me well to learn the names of everyone of influence on every tier. The higher the tier, the more I pay attention, not only for thwarting potential enemies, but also in making sure I have allies, if needed."

Alador couldn't believe anyone would want to live this way. He longed for the safety of Smallbrook, for the comfort of Mesiande's arms and Gregor's teasing comments. And, surprisingly, Alador found he also missed the security and protection his brother Dorien had offered him. He'd never known until the last couple of days how safe Dorien had made him feel. Alador didn't feel ready for any of this.

"What of this Trench Lord? What is he?"

Luthian raised his chin and considered that question carefully. "A necessary evil, but one I would not trust any further than the cast of his own shadow," he admitted. "He keeps the criminal elements somewhat in check, and he is also good at handling my more... clandestine commissions."

"You mean he kills for you," Alador spat out tiredly. "Please don't bother massaging the message for me. I would rather you spoke bluntly."

He didn't want to play this game. He wanted out. He wanted to go home. But he couldn't go home; he'd ruined all that. Alador slumped further into his chair, exhausted and defeated.

Henrick noticed the heightened color in Luthian's face and rose to Alador's defense. "I would remind you, brother, that we did not get a true night's rest. Alador has been faced with many changes in rules, culture, and surroundings. Nothing for him is the same and it has only been one day."

Luthian's eyes roved over Alador coldly yet calculatedly. "Fine. The lad wants bluntness, then bluntness he shall have. Yes, the man kills for me when a direct approach is neither warranted nor wise."

"He does not like me," Alador pointed out. "In fact, there was hate in his eyes." He sighed; the last thing he needed was for someone new to hate him. It was likely that this new enemy would try to sink a knife into him before "the half-breed bastard" had acquired enough power to make it the other way around.

"I am sure there was. If I recall correctly, his mother fought in the Daezun war and died with a Daezun arrow through her heart. He will never forgive them, even though he knows a soldier only does what he must in war," Luthian admitted. "I, for one, hold no ill will toward those who fought; I would expect my people to fight just as hard if we were invaded."

Both Henrick and Alador eyed Luthian suspiciously, but the High Minister managed to keep his face passive and utterly bland. Alador nodded but said no more.

Henrick chose that moment to broach the subject of his son's fate. "I wanted to ask, Luthian, that Alador be allowed a brief further respite before reporting to the Guard. As we both know, the challenge will be rigorous, and I would see him get a full night's rest before we turn his world upside down yet again."

Henrick's request was murmured with an almost lazy indifference. He leaned forward and poured himself a glass of wine, picking up a handful of berries as he spoke.

Luthian eyed Alador for a long moment. "The hour is indeed late and you are right. Alador looks quite exhausted. I guess there is no harm now in waiting until morning." Luthian looked at him curiously. "Unless you wish to report now, Alador."

Alador looked at Luthian with alarm. "Oh no sir!" he answered hurriedly. "I have had enough upheaval for one day. I would honestly prefer some time to settle in."

"Well, unfortunately, I can't have an untrained mage wandering about on the wrong tier. You will have to report by tomorrow afternoon." Luthian's tone left no room for argument.

Alador sighed but nodded. At least he would be in the same bed from which he'd sent his scroll. Perhaps in the morning there would be an answer from Mesiande. He would have to ask Henrick if the scroll case could find him if he slept elsewhere. The familiar wrench of pain cut through him as he thought about her and how she would respond to his letter, and the knife turned as he worried about whether or not she would even write back at all.

"Well then, I had best get him home and tucked into that big bed of his." Henrick looked relieved to have the matter settled. He downed his glass of wine and moved to stand.

"I will have someone see him to a room here, Henrick." Luthian's quiet, even response held an edge of authority.

"He is *my* son, Luthian. Let us have one more night together." Henrick's own tone took on an edge of anger. "I promised his mother I would watch over him."

"I am sure you did. However, he is also my nephew and you have had years to get to know him. I have had a single evening. Run along home, Henrick, and leave him with me." Luthian's tone of voice clearly indicated a dismissal.

Henrick stood, glaring at Luthian. "And if I refuse to leave him in my brother's care...?" he asked in his own dangerous tone.

Alador looked worriedly between them. He needed his father; the last thing he wanted was these two fighting over him. He opened his mouth to speak his own thoughts when Luthian answered.

"Then your brother will leave the room and the High Minister's guards will throw you off the tier," Luthian said, rising to meet Henrick.

Alador jumped up. This couldn't continue. He suspected his father needed little more excuse to try to kill his uncle. The animosity between the two was clearly only held in check by a tentative truce, at best.

"Stop it!" Alador cried. "I'm not some toy for two brothers to fight over. I need to be trained. I need to know what I must know because, whether you meant to or not, you painted a target on my back tonight."

He looked between the two stunned mages angrily. "If you two don't mind, I'm tired and I want a damn bed and I really don't care whose house it's in." His eyes moved to Henrick with a bit more boldness than he would have dared to show to Luthian.

Both Henrick and Luthian stared at Alador in absolute amazement. First, Luthian began to laugh and then finally, although it was a bit forced, so did Henrick. Alador didn't see what was so funny. He'd just yelled at the only kin he had in this city; kin who could probably kill him without a second thought if they chose.

Henrick put up his hands in defeat. "I apologize. As Alador stated, tonight was trying: it was very tiring keeping track of different houses' reactions to my son's presence."

Luthian moved to Alador and clapped him on the back. "You have some nerve, yelling at the High Minister like that, my dear boy. Be careful; in a public forum I would have to respond."

"I wasn't yelling at the High Minister or at Henrick Guldalian of the fifth tier," Alador said bluntly.

"Oh? And just who did you think you were daring to scold?"

"My uncle and my father, who can't decide who has the strongest grip on their new toy," Alador quipped angrily.

Luthian grinned and nodded. "Noted, then." He turned to look at Alador's father. "Henrick, I will send him to you after breakfast to gather his things. Make sure he is at the training compound before the dinner bell. Best he has a chance to settle in before he joins his new comrades at his first meal."

Henrick nodded and looked as if he were turning to leave when Alador spoke. "If my father could go with me to these rooms you spoke of, I would like a moment alone with him before he leaves for the night." Alador forced more respect into his tone.

Luthian grinned. "Of course. I am sure you have questions that a young man would only ask of someone he has learned to trust. I will see you escorted to a room and send for you at breakfast." Luthian moved to the wall and pulled a tasseled cord. It was just a few moments before the door opened.

You rang, sir?" The servant was dressed in a simple black tunic with red trim.

"Take Master Alador to my finest guestroom. I hope all arrangements were made as I requested?" Luthian's tone had a crisp edge with his serving staff.

"Of course High Minister, all is as you commanded." The servant bowed low. "Right this way, gentlemen." He stood to one side of the door as Alador and Henrick moved to exit Luthian's study.

"Oh! Alador...!" Luthian called as they got to the doorway.

Alador turned to look back. "Yes sir?" He was tired and would be glad to escape the constant tension he felt in this room.

"I hope you enjoy what is left of your evening." Luthian held up a glass of wine and toasted him.

Alador nodded, but he was puzzled. Only once the door was closed and they had walked down the hallway a ways, following the servant, did he look to his father and ask, "What was that about?"

"It is Luthian. I have no idea. He could have set in motion one of his "clandestine commissions" for all I know," Henrick snapped, clearly worried on his son's behalf.

"I thought you would be pleased with how tonight went." Alador frowned. "I didn't make any social slip-ups, did I?"

Henrick rubbed his face in frustration and took a deep breath before he looked at Alador. "No, you did me proud in there, though your mouth is going to be the death of one or both of us," he answered.

Alador sighed. "Sorry. He just seems like...a bully. I don't like bullies," he reminded his father.

"He IS a bully, with rank and power to back him up. He is not some mudslinging, overgrown farm boy with little idea how vulnerable he is. If you do not learn to live in this environment, you will not last a month in The Blackguard. I promise you, life is going to get a lot harder before it gets better." Henrick's vicious promise cut deeply.

"Then why did you bring me here? Surely there is somewhere I could have gone where he could not have found me," Alador pointed out, completely forgetting that the silent servant that led them was within earshot.

"Doubtful Alador, very doubtful. I brought you because… I was ordered to." Henrick nodded warningly at the back of the unassuming man before them.

Alador got the point and nodded back, but he was frustrated. He had so many questions, and now they would have to wait; his father was warning him this was not the time or place. He fell silent until they reached the room he was to spend the night in.

The servant opened the door deferentially, as if he were attending to the High Minister himself. "Your room, Master Alador. If you need anything, pull the bell cord by the fireplace."

Alador stepped into the room. It was as large as the one provided to him by his father. There was a bath steaming before the fireplace. Unlike his room at Henrick's house, this one was done in shades of dark blue. There was a thick rug on the floor on which the large bed sat though this bed didn't have curtains. Food was laid out on a sideboard nearby. As usual, his father made a beeline for the food table.

"How do you not gain weight?" Alador asked after nodding to the servant and closing the door.

"I told you, magic uses a great deal of energy," Henrick answered with his mouth full already.

"You haven't cast any spells all night," Alador responded, crossing his arms.

"… that you have seen." Henrick grinned at him mischievously.

Alador couldn't argue with that. His father's ease with magic made his own efforts look like a baby still crawling matched against an adult who could run. "I have a few questions before you go." Alador stated, moving to pick at some cheese on the table.

"I had figured that out for myself, when you asked to speak privately." Henrick seemed to have relaxed now that they were alone.

"Luthian does not seem as horrid as you make him sound," Alador pointed out while nibbling on the cheese.

"A man can wear many masks that create illusions of who he is. Never take such masks at face value. I assure you, Luthian is as deadly as I made him out to be." Henrick eyed his son. "I beg you not to be taken in by his charming manner. He does nothing without having some gain for himself in mind."

Alador nodded. He wasn't going to tell Henrick that he didn't like his uncle, but he had wanted to hear his father's thoughts. "If I don't go home, can the scroll case still find me?" he asked. Truly, that was the largest matter on his mind. Yes, he had enemies again. Yes, he lived in the middle of the cruelest society he could imagine. But if Mesiande still loved him, he could handle that with more ease. He would handle whatever he had to so that he could return to her side one day.

Henrick threw a berry at him. "You are standing in the viper's den and you still think about that little skirt of yours. You had better get your head out of the clouds before it gets removed from your shoulders."

Henrick looked at him with frustration. "All those beautiful women fawning over you tonight and you are worried about one so far away. Just when I think you will do me proud, you make some such statement. The damn scroll case will find you wherever you sleep. I am going home."

Henrick growled this out as he crammed his pockets with sweetmeats. Once finished, he turned to storm out of the room. Alador could only grin at him. "I love you too, Father," he called after him.

"Fat lot of good that will do when you are dead," Henrick called back without looking at him. He slammed the door behind him.

Alador looked at that hot bath. He was tired. He was sore. But he was too tense to sleep. He pulled off the robe first. He didn't understand why men felt the need to dress up to show off their wealth and power. Why did grown men parade around in dresses? He didn't understand the importance of these robes. They seemed hardly fitting for real work, even though they only fell to about mid-calf and didn't interfere with his feet.

Alador stripped down the rest of the way and slipped into the tub with a weary sigh. It was not long before he dozed off; the water was a perfect temperature and the fire generated its own warmth on that side of the tub.

"Would my lord like me to wash his back?" A soft, feminine voice struck through his half-dozing consciousness.

Alador flipped over to his side in a panic, hugging the wall of the tub, and looked up into those beautiful emerald eyes he'd seen at supper. "What are you doing here?" He asked in alarm.

Despite his anxiety, his eyes roved over her of their own accord. She was naked except for a diaphanous, thin silk robe. He could see every achingly pleasing inch of her. His eyes widened, and he moved as tight to the tub wall as he could to hide the erection he'd been powerless to prevent.

"The High Minister bid me warm your bed for the night. He did not want you to be lonely in his house." She smiled at him. "I promise, I will do whatever you wish. It is an honor to have been chosen by the High Minister himself to serve the needs of his nephew." She held up a square of linen and a round of soap. "I can wash your back if you want."

"I… umm… I like the bed as it is. Thank you for your kind offer, but you can go now." Alador strove to look only at her eyes. His heart was racing, never having had to cope with a stunningly attractive, all-but-naked young woman looking right at him totally naked in a tub.

She immediately put her pretty lips into a pout, and her eyes filled with tears. "Have I disappointed you? I' som sorry. Would you prefer I wait in the bed?" There was an edge of panic in the girl's voice.

"I don't need your… 'services' tonight. I'm flattered but… you can go to wherever it is you sleep," he encouraged. What would Mesiande say if she saw this woman in his room dressed in…? He didn't even know what to call the diaphanous gown the woman wore.

"I do not please you?" she asked in a true panic now. "I can do whatever you wish, Milord. Please, do not send me away." She dropped to her knees beside Alador.

"I do not need you to do anything but leave me to my bath." He looked at her in confusion, then realised that was fear on her beautiful face. Alador's features softened in response. "What will happen if I send you away?" he asked softly.

"They will send me back to the trench. The Trench Lord, knowing I have been in the High Minister's service, will send me to the brothel." The girl's eyes were filled with tears as she knelt before him at the side of the tub.

"What is a 'brothel'?" Alador rolled the word over his tongue. He'd never heard the term before.

"A brothel? How can you not know what that is?" She looked at him in surprise, though her emerald eyes were still tearful.

"I am not from here," he reminded her softly, shifting uncomfortably. Women were not allowed in the bath house when men bathed. Yet here he was, talking to one while he was naked.

"It is a place where men pay to use a woman's body for their pleasure," the girl answered. "Sometimes they want to do horrible things, and they are usually disgusting pigs of men." She shuddered. "Please, my lord, do not send me away."

Alador sighed softly: one more reason to hate this place. However, the idea of keeping this woman out of the Trench Lord's hands appealed to him, and he did not want to be the one responsible for whatever it was she was describing. Sex was not exactly frowned upon by his people, as long as a man and woman had both become adults. Though mating was done in the circle, pleasure could be sought from any willing partner. The concept of someone paying for it seemed unfathomable, but everything about this place was twisted.

"All right. You can stay, but you have to do as I say," Alador finally offered.

"Oh, thank you, my Lord." She moved forward to kiss Alador and met his wet hand.

"First rule: no touching. I love another and she would not approve." Alador was quick to set the rules. "What's your name?"

"Keelee." Her face filled with confusion, and she looked at Alador as though he'd lost his mind.

"Well met, Keelee. My name is Alador. I'd prefer you call me that. I'm going to get out of the bath now so if you would please turn around…" He moved his hand as if to scoot her back and turn her.

She gave him a funny look but rose to her feet and turned her back to him. Alador had thought her turning would help him stop looking at her body, but it didn't. She was shapely, with curves that he couldn't help but stare at, even after she turned. Her bottom showed through the thin material, round and firm. As a middlin he'd caught quick glimpses of Daezun women, but nothing had prepared him for this Lerdenian beauty standing before him. Keelee was taller and more gently defined than Daezun woman. Alador coughed, realizing he was staring, and ducked himself under the water to wet his hair. He came up and grabbed a nearby towel to wrap around his middle, hoping to hide his interest, then looked around for his pants.

"Where are my clothes?" Alador asked with concern. His pants weren't the only things missing, none of his clothes were anywhere to be found.

"I did not think you would have need of them in your bed and in my arms, so I sent them to be cleaned. Your other items are over on the bench by the dressing screen." Keelee's voice held panic once again.

Alador gave a frustrated groan. He was in a room with a beautiful woman who was barely clothed. He was naked. He couldn't send her away and condemn her to this brothel...

"Well, of all the...," he trailed off, stepping out of the tub and drying himself. "Do not turn around," he commanded, closing his eyes and concentrating on one of the few spells he'd learned to do. He felt the security of soft linen pants form around him, then he used the towel to finish drying.

"Okay, here is what we'll do. It's a big bed. You sleep on your side, I'll sleep on mine, and if anyone asks, we had a wonderful night. Understood?" Alador was trying not to look at that shapely bottom.

"Yes my lord," she whispered, not turning as she had been told.

"Good then, off to the bed with you." Alador turned away so she could get into the bed and also to hide the fact that he was still aroused. He felt a bit like he was betraying Mesiande…but then again, it was a natural response, and he knew that some things just couldn't be avoided.

Keelee hurried over and got into the bed and sank down beneath the covers. Alador waited to turn around until he was sure she'd settled, then moved to the other side and slipped into the bed, himself. He looked about and realized he hadn't lowered the lanterns. "I forgot to put out the lights." He started to rise when she sat up.

"I can get them." Keelee grinned at him. She held her hand up to her lips and blew softly. Every lantern in the room winked out.

"That's something you'll have to teach me," Alador chuckled, settling back. The only light in the room now was the flicker of the fireplace.

"Then you will keep me?" Keelee's voice brightened.

"Keep you?" He looked over at her in confusion. The light still allowed him to see her beautiful eyes, framed by shimmering hair.

"Yes. The High Minister has commanded that I am yours for as long you desire. Let me… Please keep me, my… Alador, I beg you. Take me from this house." She scooted across to him in the bed and took his hand.

"I'm going to live in some kind of training compound for guardsmen. What would I do with a woman?" Aladar didn't want to abandon this lovely woman, but he didn't want her to think it meant they were housemates.

"I can care for your room. Warm your bed. See to your needs. I promise I will do well. I am skilled in many arts." She kissed his hand fervently.

"Keelee, I love another. I... I do not want anyone but her in my bed," Aladar whispered, though his body was definitely telling him otherwise.

"I promise I will behave. I will do as I am told. Please... take me with you. You do not understand what it is like for me here, and the only other place I have to go is back to the trench." Keelee started to cry. Aladar could feel her tears against the back of his hand.

"What's it like for you here?" he asked with real concern. "My uncle said you were free to return to wherever you came from."

She stiffened and fell silent for a moment, not responding. Then she wept against Aladar's hand, her tears coming with greater sobs.

"It is my uncle, isn't it?" Aladar asked. "My uncle uses your body, whenever and wherever he wishes, like now?"

Keelee remained quiet, merely nodding. Anger flooded through Aladar, and he pulled the young woman against him protectively. "You can come with me," he promised softly.

She cried against his shoulder for some time, and Alador didn't stop her. He couldn't imagine what she must have had to do, but based on her tears, it obviously hadn't been pleasant. He had no idea what he was going to do with her, but the least he could do was offer her some protection.

When at last she stopped crying, Keelee looked up at him. "I am s-sorry. I should not have cried. Thank you so much, my lord. I will be forever grateful."

Alador just pushed her head back down to his shoulder. His response was tense, though not because of Keelee. "Alador! You will call me Alador."

"Yes, Alador," she whispered.

"Go to sleep Keelee," he whispered back. He felt her nod, and he laid back to think about the day. Alador had to learn fast and get out. Otherwise, he had a feeling he was going to want to protect a lot of people, and he was only a half-breed bastard.

Chapter Ten

Alador woke up to the sound of rain falling against the windows, tapping gently against the edges of his awareness. The wind howled furiously, and despite the solid, stone structure of his uncle's home, the draft made the fire flicker. Alador rolled over snuggled into the soft confines of the big bed, until he remembered that there'd been a girl there with him last night. He opened his eyes and looked about. With a sigh of relief, Alador realized Keelee was gone.

He didn't want to explain to Mesiande that by his second night here, he'd already had another woman in his bed. Nothing had happened, but it didn't exactly sound good. At the thought of Mesiande, Alador immediately felt beneath his pillow. His hand touched metal, and he pulled the object out slowly.

In his hand was the scroll tube, just as Henrick had said. She had to have opened it to know how to return it. Alador fingered the top, wanting to remove the letter and yet afraid to do so. He took a deep breath and removed the top, pulling the rolled parchment out and smelling it. It smelled like home – the soft scent of smoke and fields was unmistakable. Alador slowly opened it and began to read.

Alador,

You have no idea how relieved I was to receive your letter. I am not sure how I feel about the tube it came in. You and I both know that I could be cast out for using it. I will brave that to send this to you. I still love you! There is nothing to forgive. You were not responsible for the choices Trelmar made. Please do not blame yourself for what he did.

I am having a harder time with the fact that you killed a man, any man. Dorien says that you didn't mean to. I will be honest, I don't know if I believe him. I was at the river. I think you would have killed him then if I hadn't been there. I am not sure how I feel about this yet. It is all very confusing.

Life in the village hasn't returned to normal. The mating ritual was not held because of the anger in the village. They have never missed the high summer before.

It has caused rumors that you have cursed us all. They are having it next week. I am scared. Everything is different. People do not laugh the way they used to. Dorien rarely leaves the forge. The only ones that seem the same are Gregor and Sofie. They spend a great deal of time together. I bet they are going to be housemates someday.

Your mother cries a great deal. She tries to put on a brave face, but her eyes are often red. Dorien says they are having a hard time making her eat. He says not to write to her as it will make matters worse. I can pass him messages and he will decide what is safe for her to know. Dorien has changed a great deal, as well. He doesn't tease and smile. People give him a wide path now. The day you left, there was a fight. Dorien knocked out six men before he fell before the crowd. Fortunately, you were far enough out of the village I guess.

I don't know how I feel about being housemates. You killed a man. I feel guilty because you killed him to protect me.

I do love you. I will always love you. You cannot return here. The hatred is too great. You say I cannot come there and I will be honest, I don't know that I want to. I am so confused.

I am sorry that you live in such a cold place. I would think that, with such beauty at their hands, the people would be kind. Perhaps there is truth that a beautiful sword may not be the best weapon. Perhaps that is why they could not win the war. They are too busy taking out their own to field a proper battle?

I am sorry this letter rambles. I miss you so much. I don't know what I want. I don't know what to do. Please give me time. Please continue to write. I don't mind you telling me of magic. Knowing you are still there somewhere gives me some comfort even if it is sad, as well.

Mesi ♡

The words on that paper wrenched the very core of him. He had done this to his home. He had ruined the circle. He had caused Dorien to fight his own village brothers. The worst was that Mesiande didn't know if she could forgive him for killing Trelmar.

He caressed her signature and the small heart at the bottom of the page. It was hope. While she'd said she didn't know if she still wanted to be housemates, she hadn't rejected him outright either. He'd been prepared for Mesiande to deny him completely. It almost hurt more to see the confusion and pain in that letter.

Was he being selfish? Should he stop writing her, as Dorien had asked that he not write their mother? His own confusion swelled up and swirled about him. Alador flopped back down on the pillow, clutching the letter to his chest. His thoughts ran through a myriad of questions that competed for his attention.

If Mesiande denied him, what did he have to live for? What purpose could he have, if the only thing he needed was taken from him? Alador's chest physically ached as these questions fought for answers, and the painful realization that Mesiande literally held all his hope and dreams in her hands washed over him.

He didn't know what he'd do with his life if she denied him. He did know that he didn't want to live as his father and uncle - that was not how people should live. It was a cruel and cold society based on privilege, not on genuine care for one's neighbor.

The fear he'd felt yesterday and the shock of the last week finally escaped from his heart, and Alador tried to choke back a sob. He rolled over and, clutching the letter, let his grief well up and sobbed until he was empty, with nothing left to offer. Reality became hazy and faded as visions of dragons filled his mind again, his grief giving in to exhaustion. As the sun rose higher into the sky, Alador slipped back into deep dreams…

Renamaum and Keensight sat on the mountain top, looking down into the valley below. Renamaum had a wing in front of the red dragon to keep him from sweeping off the ledge in rage. Below them, in that dark vale, were eight young dragons. They differed in age and color, but each one had one thing in common: large chains bound them to the ground, winding up over their wings, binding them to their bodies, so that none of them could unfold enough to get a proper thrust off the ground.

"*Do you see him anywhere? I know he is down there,*" Keensight rumbled in the fear and pain that only a father could feel.

"*No. He would have barely hatched, and I do not see any that young, old friend.*" Renamaum eyed the entire valley below them carefully. "*Perhaps in that cave, but it is too small for either you or me to enter. If we wish to save fledglings from this fate, it will have to be done by a creature much smaller than you or I.*" Renamaum eyed the red flight leader with sorrow.

Keensight's mate had been killed in her nest, and the egg she'd nurtured was missing. The broken swords and the dead who'd owned them had been Lerdenian. There was no doubt that the egg had been brought to this place. It was called a bloodmine for the dragon's blood that was spilled every turn until they became too large to handle. Then, they were outright killed and left to fester where they lay.

Renamaum closed his nostrils down; even from this far distance, the smell of blood and death wafted on the wind. He felt for his friend, who'd lost mate and fledgling all at the same time. Though most Lerdenians believed them to be nothing more than magical beasts, the truth was that such losses would stay with a dragon his entire lifetime – and dragons had very long lives.

"I will kill them all. Let us fly down and release our brothers. Let us rise up and burn every last one of them. I want every one of them to die," Keensight snarled in rage. He bellowed his rage into the wind, and the dragons below them answered in a mournful call for help.

"Keensight. I understand your anger, but that is to declare war for all the flights. It is not ours alone to do. Besides, look closer. They have their spears of wood aimed at every dragon. We or they would be dead before we freed the first. We cannot help them alone." Renamaum wanted to console the dragon, but he had no idea how to help with such a grievous loss.

"I will demand a war from the council. I will demand they rise up and lay waste to the humans' spiraling cities and crops. I will see their floating wooden toys sunk into the seas they travel." Keensight rocked back and forth as if he was about to leap into the air, and Renamaum knew he had little time to talk sense to his friend. "They have declared this war, not us!"

"You could do this – that is true. And more of our kin will fall. There is a better way brother, but one that will take time. We find one who can do this work. One who can go into that cave and pull out our eggs and newly hatched. One who can love without constraint and protect without thought. This is what we find." Renamaum pleaded against the red dragon's anger, trying to wedge some bit of logic behind Keensight's rage. "We must lose these brothers to win a war much greater than our own pain."

"This is **my** fledgling you speak of! You want me to sacrifice my fledgling that yours might live? I will not! I will find him, and I will free him if I have to claw my way into that cave." Keensight pushed Renamaum's wing out of the way and dove for the valley below. Renamaum knew Keensight's fight was hopeless. He could do nothing now but watch helplessly

Keensight dove for the first of the spear throwers, his fire rained down with deadly accuracy as his sweeping path took out two of *the wooden constructs. He banked up sharply but before he could turn to make another pass, the sound of releasing war machines filled Renamaum's ears. He keened mournfully as four of the chained dragons were killed before his eyes. Their Lerdenian keepers would rather see their prizes dead than released, their blood draining into the ground.*

Keensight must have realized the fate of the other four: he banked sharply and flew off into the distance. His howl of frustration, of rage and loss, filled the air, and miles around, echoing in the wind as other dragons picked up his cry. It bore the heartfelt grief of a leader losing those he could not bear to sacrifice, the angst of a helpless father, and rage at those who'd stolen all that he held dear.

Renamaum watched him go, and a single tear fell from his great eye. "I am so sorry, my friend," he whispered into the wind. Then he, too, took up the cry as the dragons of the isle sang their sorrowful song for the fallen.

Alador started awake. He was crying into his pillow, but it hadn't been for Mesiande. It had been in response to the dream. He had felt the sacrifice, the pain, and the true loss of the dragons. They were losing their small ones to the Lerdenians; losing them to a small, elite group with the natural capacity to absorb what wasn't theirs. Alador sat up and swung his feet over the bed, resting his elbows on his legs and his face in his hands. He sat that way for some time, trying to make sense of the dream. His face rose slowly as an idea came to him.

Henrick had thought that Alador's bloodstone had been a geas stone – a task imbued into the magic that had to be completed. Alador knew what it was. He knew what he was going to have to do: he had to figure out a way to release the dragons in that vale, as well as the dragons held by egg or newly birthed.

Alador could get into the cave. He could reach the eggs when the dragons could not. That was his purpose. With or without Mesiande, that is what he had to do. Alador had to save the dragons from the vile practices to which they were being subjected.

He looked round and spotted his clothes from last night, neatly laid out nearby. Alador dressed automatically, his thoughts on the dream. He made sure to stuff the metal scroll case in his waistband beneath his robes. He had much to learn if he was going to free dragons – he needed to find a dragon; he couldn't help them if he couldn't talk to them. If he was going to one day liberate the bloodmines, he needed knowledge, power, and an ally. Let the

Lerdenians teach him what they would. He would use it against them. He sat down to lace his boots, considering these matters. It was easier to focus on this than the questions that had led to his grief-stricken state.

This determination faltered slightly when the door opened and his uncle stepped in. Luthian was not wearing robes at the moment, but a simple outfit of black pants and a red shirt. He did not pull it off as well as his father, thanks to his pale skin and white hair, but the man was still a striking figure.

Alador took a deep breath. This city thrived on lies, deception, and manipulation - skills he knew that he didn't have and had to learn fast. He was going to have to fool this man first and foremost. Luthian smiled at Alador as he spoke: "Ah good, you are up. I had a simple lunch laid out for us. I had hoped to eat on the balcony, but the weather is not accommodating."

Alador watched as the eyes swept over him with that assessing gaze. He felt like the man could strip away the layers and see the thoughts that lay beneath. Apparently that feeling was a trait his relatives shared. Alador steeled himself and smiled.

"I feared I may have slept too late. I am ravenous, so you are very kind to have waited for me." He had apparently slept far longer than he had thought. When he had first risen to find the scroll case, it had been morning.

Luthian chuckled. "I sent a firecat to your bed. I knew full well you would rise late. I hope you found her pleasing?"

Alador didn't miss a step knowing any complaint meant harm to Keelee. "I have no complaints, Uncle. My night was quite enjoyable and the girl quite willing." He kept his true thoughts far below as he met his uncle's gaze levelly. He didn't like how easily the lie spilled out of his mouth.

Luthian seemed to have expected no other answer, and didn't press the issue. "Good. I understand you have agreed to let her see to your needs in the future. If you get tired of her, let me know and we will pick another." Luthian opened the door and indicated that Alador should precede him.

Alador slipped past his uncle into the hall, choosing not to point out that there hadn't been much "we" involved in that decision. He needed to keep his uncle happy until he had what he needed to strike out on his own.

He suspected, with all his father's warnings, that Henrick would help him when the time was right. The impulsive part of him wanted to grab the High Minister by the throat and shake him until he stopped such a horrid practice. However, Luthian had many years of magical training on him, trained guards, and... well, the power to have him murdered. He'd blatantly admitted that he had a paid assassin at his command.

The "simple lunch" would have fed a whole family. The servants attending the High Minister were, once more, all beautiful women and the large table was filled with different delicacies. Alador was starving, and was soon devouring the food piled high on his plate.

He noticed that Luthian didn't eat with the same intensity as his father. Surely both men used similar amounts of power, yet his father retained his color and youthful appearance while the High Minister seemed drained.

Neither spoke for a time, both taking in the posture of the other. Eventually, it was Luthian who casually broke the ice as he spread butter on a piece of bread. "I am curious. What has your father told you of me?" He took a large bite and sat chewing as he waited for Alador to answer.

Alador had expected this question, and set his fork down for a moment as he considered what to say. "Well, he said that you were a powerful mage. That you were High Minister and that the two of you don't always see eye to eye," he offered. Fairly harmless information.

"That is all your father had to say?" Luthian looked a little insulted as he set his bread on the plate. His lips twitched in irritation.

"Really, I didn't know you even existed until we were on our way here," Alador admitted. "My mother didn't really like him talking much about Lerdenia to me. I think they both thought I was never going to pass my tests. Well, my mother hoped I wouldn't."

Alador spoke the truth, and it felt easier to look his uncle in the eye. "I have thought about what you asked, about what I wanted."

Luthian picked up a steaming cup of tea and sat back, cradling it in his hands. "If you tell me you wish to go home, I will be quite disappointed," he mused with a wry smile.

"No, I want to be a powerful mage. I want to learn all I can. I want you to teach me. My father… well, he's all right, but he doesn't seem too interested in me knowing much beyond the basics. I'd hoped that after what you said last night, you didn't feel the same way."

Alador had to take a sip of his tea at that one. He thought last evening that he didn't want to be embroiled in Lerdenian politics, but that had changed with the realization that he knew what it was he had to do. He felt centered and just a bit more confident. .

Luthian looked very pleased. "Well then, you can spend your half-day with me." Luthian sat back, like a mouser who'd just eaten well. "I will see to the lessons that your Black Guard instructors will not be allowed to teach you."

"May I request that I have a half-day with each of you?" Alador looked into his cup. "It's the only thing I ask, Uncle. You have both set upon me like dogs with a bone, but you both have things I need to know.

Father seems to have little interest in how things work here, or moving any further up the tiers; but he is my father and he knows things about life I still need to learn - things that, having lived in Lerdenia all your life, you might not be able to avail me of. He moves between both worlds – I want to learn how to do that. I want to be able to walk on Daezun ground, in time, with as much ease as I want to walk on Lerdenian ground."

Alador sat the cup back down and looked at his uncle. "I have decided that the time of gnashing my teeth at what's been lost and bemoaning my fate is over. There is much to do and I don't want to waste any time." It was easier to state this now that the dream had brought some sense of focus to his current situation, rather than what he'd lost.

Luthian looked at Alador in surprise. "It would be far from the norm to grant you two half days...," he mused, stroking his face. He set his cup down with the other hand and considered his nephew's request.

"Surely the High Minister can afford to grant this one small privilege." Alador pressed at his uncle's vanity. "I mean, I have no doubt that your blessings upon their endeavors carry a great deal of weight. There's no greater mage in all Lerdenia, is that not so?"

Luthian's chin rose slightly. "Do not play on my vanity, boy, to get what you want," he said firmly, his irritation at the ploy clearly written on his face. "But no, you are right, there is not." He grinned slowly at Alador. "I will see it done. However, if I get any word that you are not diligent in your studies, you will have to choose between us."

Alador pushed his plate away, having eaten his fill. "I assure you, Uncle, my lack of diligence will be the last thing you need to worry about."

They spent the rest of that morning speaking on several topics, before a servant guided Alador back to Henrick's house. He didn't go in right away, however, choosing to sit on the steps and look out at the horizon for a while.

Alador didn't mind terribly much that it was raining, and the house offered a little shelter. Luthian had seemed willing to answer most of what Alador asked, but he had the sense that his uncle was biding his time. There was something Luthian wanted from Alador, as much as Alador wanted something from his uncle. It had been a dance that his uncle had been playing all his life, and one Alador had to learn fast. He was fairly sure he'd managed to escape without revealing how he really felt about this place, his uncle or these people.

Alador frowned at his own thoughts and shook his head. He could not judge the Lerdenians by these upper tiers. He suspected that the farmers and miners were not much different from his own people. It was not fair to judge an entire populace by the actions of the privileged – Henrick had made that point, yet Alador knew this as surely as he knew the back of his hand.

No half-breed could grow up without a keen awareness that too many people passed judgment without really knowing someone. People were only too ready to judge, not by what they knew and experienced but by what they'd been told. If all they had to go on was other people's fiction, with no means or initiative to question, then it became fact.

Alador finally rose to his feet. He had things to tell Henrick. He was going to trust him with everything; he'd either die or have an ally. Either way, he was the only one Alador knew that knew a dragon, and Alador had to talk to a dragon.

He hoped they could talk. In his dreams, Alador always understood them, so he was fairly certain that they could. He knocked on the door. The same man who'd been there when Alador woke up yesterday opened the door after only a short pause.

"Ah, Master Henrick has been expecting you. Come, come! Let us get you next to a dry fire." The man hurriedly led Alador through the house. It was so much smaller than the High Minister's, but to Alador, it still felt far too big. Why did one man need so much space? It seemed like Lerdenians spent their slips just to show that they had them to spend.

Henrick was waiting for him in the library. Luthian's room had been full of books, but Henrick's library went beyond even that. Shelves and specially-made cupboards for scrolls lined the walls from floor to ceiling. The rich, warm wood was a perfect frame to the vast array of leather-bound tomes.

Alador stared wide-eyed, as he looked around. Books were a rare treasure amongst the Daezun; to see shelves of them so high that there was a ladder to reach the higher shelves made Alador's heart pound with excitement. He'd held maybe three real books his entire life. He slowly turned in a circle, staring in amazement. In contrast to the rest of the house, this room was rich in warm tones and was clearly where Henrick spent most of his time.

"It is good to see you in one piece." Henrick put his pipe down and moved over to Alador, clasping him on both arms. He looked over Alador, first left, then right. "Don't seem too much worse for wear." He smiled down at Alador as if they hadn't parted with harsh words only last night.

"I survived. How much time do we have before I need to report to the compound of The Blackguard?" Alador grinned back, but his tone held urgency. He didn't have time to waste on idle pleasantries.

"About an hour or so. Are you in that much of a hurry to find yourself in the clutches of a taskmaster? You realize that this will be no easy training. Luthian sees to it that they are better trained than even the Home Guard." Henrick frowned as he spoke of his brother and eyed Alador suspiciously as he slowly let him go.

Alador considered how to approach this. He'd been sharing more and more with his father, but he had decided to give him his full trust. If he couldn't trust Henrick, he was going to fail anyway; he had nothing to lose.

"No, we need to talk. Can we sit?" Alador looked over at the fire. Though it was summer, the rain storm made for cooler weather, and he liked the warmth of a fire. Henrick always seemed to be close to one.

"Of course, of course. You are wet." Henrick led Alador to the fire and settled into a leather-covered chair. "What is amiss, my dear boy?"

Alador, on the other hand, moved to the fireplace and placed his hands on the mantle, looking down at the dancing flames. "I think I know what my geas is," he said softly, staring into the fire.

There was a long silence from the man at his side. "Dare I ask?" Henrick's tone was gentle, and the usual humorous or sarcastic edge had dropped. He reached over and poured a drink from a decanter on the small table between them. Alador could hear the soft sounds of the stopper.

"I saw what they do to the dragons in the bloodmine. I was there with the blue dragon when he could not stop his friend from trying to rescue his egg. I have been very protective of small ones since I found the stone. I need to find a way to stop the bloodmines. They torture the dragons chained there. They take their eggs and treat them as animals for slaughter, not as the noble beasts they are, and definitely not as the icons of the gods they were intended to be."

Alador turned and looked at his father and there was true pain in his voice and eyes. "I know this is what I am meant to do. I have to save the fledglings."

Henrick had been half way to taking a drink, but his glass just hovered there, his eyes large as he looked at Alador. "Tell me, do you know the dragon's name?" He was staring at Alador as he slowly rose to his feet.

"Why would their names matter?" Alador asked. His father's reaction had him puzzled.

"Humor me. They... You know both their names?" Henrick stood up and joined him next to the fire.

"Yes. The blue dragon is named Renamaum, and the red one is Keensight. I think that might be just a nickname though…it doesn't seem like a very regal name," Alador mused in afterthought. He jumped when his father's glass hit the floor and shattered. "Are you all right?" he asked, moving to clean up the glass.

Henrick waved him off. "The servants will get it," he muttered. "Tell me your vision. Please, tell me all of it." Henrick placed a hand on Alador's arm, stepping over the shattered glass. "I will see if I can help confirm that that is your geas."

Henrick's dramatic reaction had been startling, but Alador did as requested, sharing the vision with as much detail as he could recall. He even shared the thoughts of the dragon he'd felt combined into. After he finished, Henrick remained silent for a long time. Finally, Alador moved to him and touched the hand that still clutched his own arm with concern.

"Father…?" Henrick looked at him, tears in his eyes. Alador stared at him in consternation – he'd never seen his father cry. "What's wrong?"

"The red dragon you saw is the same one that decided I did not need to be eaten. The one I told you of on our trip here. He…"

Henrick took a deep breath and turned away from Alador to return to his chair. "He told me a similar version of this tale. If it helps at all, he did manage to free his son. He waited until they went to bring him out of the cave and, with the help of some flight mates, was able to snatch him from them. It was not without additional loss of both fledglings and flight mates."

Henrick sank into a chair and took a deep breath. "You are most likely right. This is probably your geas. It seems like the type of noble thing one would impress at death. If your dragon was there, he likely feared for his own eggs and fledglings."

Alador nodded. He had already figured this much out as he had pieced together all the differing visions since he'd harvested the stone. "Father, what is a 'dragonsworn'? It was in one of the dreams and I feel somehow that it is important."

"A dragonsworn is a mortal who has been given the powers of all the flights. There have only been two in history - it is rare for the dragons to agree on one who is worthy enough to possess such magic. All the flights must believe that the mortal is of a good heart and has the best interests of both mortals and dragons in mind. Let us be honest Alador, such men are rare, if they ever even really existed."

Henrick moved away carefully from the glass and indicated that Alador should sit down. He seemed to be regaining his composure. "The blue dragon was going to find one such. He wanted to find such a man…but he never got to see it done. It's sad. I think all the isle needs such a man – maybe he could end the feud between the Daezun and the Lerdenians."

Alador sank into his own chair. Henrick must have been very attached to this dragon of his. That it turned out to be Keensight was concerning. "I think it was Keensight who attacked the village." Alador looked over at

Henrick. "If it was, why would he do that? Do you know?"

"I do not. I suspect it had to do with the blue dragon. Despite their differences, Keensight told me that he and Renamaum were close. If the Daezun had unearthed his friend and he knew where he'd fallen, it is possible he sought to punish them for that desecration." Henrick sighed. "My dragon friend is rather impulsive."

"I shot your friend." Alador swallowed hard. "I shot him because the blue dragon told me where to shoot."

"Yes, a rather unfortunate issue there. My son shot my best friend." Henrick smirked a bit at that. "Even stranger that his good friend told you how to repel him. Perhaps there is more to you than this geas you are under." Henrick mused. "Yes, maybe much, much more..."

Alador let out an exasperated sigh. "More? Don't I have enough to worry about? What more could there possibly be?" Alador put his hands out, gesturing. "I just now came to terms with the fact I have to save a bunch of highly-guarded dragons and find a way to stop bloodmining altogether. Don't you think that's enough?" Alador put his face in his hands as if to wipe the burden from his mind.

"Yes, perhaps you are right - one thing at a time. Regardless of what could or couldn't be, you have to answer the call of the geas. It will not let you do otherwise." Henrick nodded slowly, coming to terms with what Alador had shared.

"Yes, but now I have a bigger problem." Alador rubbed his face with both of his hands in a bit of angst at the complexity of all this.

"A bigger problem than a geas? What could be a bigger problem?" Henrick looked at Alador with surprise.

"I can't do this without help. I need you and, well, I'd thought to ask one other to help me but that seems unlikely now. I'm not sure how to get this done." Alador let out his breath in another sigh and stared into the fire, watching it flicker and then surge up almost prophetically.

"Whose help do you need and why is it a problem?" Henrick asked, puzzled. "I mean I understand you needing my help. It would give me great pleasure to see Luthian's face when he realizes his nephew has destroyed his most profitable endeavor."

"I need Keensight's advice, and..." Alador looked at his father evenly. "I shot him in the throat."

Chapter Eleven

Aorun stood at the window looking out to the balcony and watched the rain slowly taper off. The harbor was nearly entirely obscured by a foggy haze, and he could barely see the ships. He'd been trying to assuage the intense hatred he continued to feel about the bastard nephew, but even treating the wench in his bed harshly last night had done nothing to calm him.

He was still focused on the fact that a half-breed was being afforded privileges that Aorun had to kill to obtain, privileges he'd fought for every inch of the way. Mostly likely, if the bastard were left unchecked, he would have privileges that Aorun could never aspire to. His hatred for all Daezun focused on this new foe, as if everything he hated about the Daezun were rolled up in that one half-breed.

He'd spent the morning sieving through the sources he had access to so he could determine what leverage he could use. He now knew that the young man's name was Alador, and that he was the son of Henrick by some Daezun woman from Smallbrook. The boy had only recently passed his testing and knew little of magic and its ways. He had arrived in Silverport only two days ago and knew almost nothing of the city's ways either.

It wasn't much to go on, but it was something. The most important fact Aorun had ascertained was that the half-breed was destined for The Blackguard. Aorun had two men in The Blackguard. He'd sent for whichever one could attend him first, though he had directions for them both. In The Blackguard, the training was intense, and the punishment for error often severe. It wouldn't be that difficult to arrange some kind of fatal accident.

There was a knock at the door, but Aorun didn't turn from the window. "Come!" he directed firmly. The door opened and Owen sauntered in, not bothering to close it.

"I think you will have to go to the High Minister's house yourself if you want that woman," he drawled out, plopping down on a chair in front of Aorun's desk and kicking his muddied feet up on the fine red surface.

Aorun didn't turn from the harbor, but his answer expressed his disbelief. "Surely the chamberlain did not deny my request after all that he owes me? Unless…" Aorun finally turned. "Is she in Luthian's bed?" It would figure: the man had discerning tastes.

Owen laid his hands behind his head, closing his eyes as he spoke. "Nope…! It seems he gave the wench to some relative of his - a nephew or something." The rain off Owen's cloak dripped on to Aorun's floor, creating a growing pool on the fine tile.

Aorun flooded with rage. Luthian only had one nephew. He'd given the woman Aorun wanted for his own to the bastard whelp. He walked over and, without any warning, kicked the chair Owen was lazing in, tipping it over backwards.

Owen scrambled backwards before rolling up to his feet. "By the Gods, what did you do that for?" he growled, his hand reflexively going for his weapon.

"Draw it. I dare you," Aorun snarled. "You are in the Trench Lord's office, telling him news he does not wish to hear as if it is a mere misstep, and you are dripping on my floor and dirtying my desk."

A soft drawl from the door interrupted Aorun and Owen. "I hope you do not intend to waste a perfectly good man, just because he was the bearer of bad news." Sordith leaned against the door post. "I am not sure what that news was, but short of learning that Owen is sleeping with your mother and your sister, you both might want to stand down."

He smirked at the two. It was clear from his lack of concern that Owen had placed himself in similar situations in the past.

"Stay out of this, Sordith!" Aorun wanted to kill someone right now, and right now Owen was standing in front of him.

"Afraid I can't do that." Sordith straightened up and put his hands out in a gesture of offering. "How about I drag him out of here and kick his arse for you while you meet with that guardsman you summoned?" he suggested evenly.

Aorun's eyes riveted to him, and the anger in them seethed with such intensity that Sordith dropped his lazy smile. The last man to draw that much anger out of Aorun had been left on a beetle hill. The flesh-eating beetles had taken their time, and Sordith could think of a hundred more pleasing ways to die.

"Yes, get him out of here and bring me that guard!" Aorun snarled. He went to the desk and plopped down angrily. He grabbed his flask, speaking as he uncapped it. "And later Owen, after I go to bed for the night, this floor gets mopped: by you, you disrespectful son of a…" Aorun drowned the rest of his words with his flask while Sordith ushered Owen swiftly out the door.

The door opened only a few minutes later, and a Black Guard strode inside. He smacked his arm over his chest in salute to the Trench Lord. "You sent for me, sir?"

Aorun would have liked the man if he weren't soiled with Daezun blood. He was smart, used few words, and got the job done. He kept his ears and eyes open, so there was little going on within the High Minister's elite force that he did not know. "Yes, Jayson, I have a job for you." He indicated the man could sit but smiled when he didn't move. There had been improvements in his man that living in The Blackguard had made almost second nature.

"I am listening. I take it the usual number of slips is involved?" Jayson's glance at Aorun was calculating. Aorun could respect that: if he was going to ask a man to kill someone, he'd best be willing to settle up.

"Of course...." He smiled. "There is a new half-breed coming into the guard today. His name is Alador: a privileged bastard of the Guldalian line. I want his life to be hell. Should the opportunity arise where you can take him out and have it look like an accident, take it. I may decide to kill him outright soon enough; but for now I would rather not risk anyone's placement. I do, however, want a full report of his allies and where he goes. I will be putting one of my lieutenants on him for his half days."

"Surely one new recruit is no cause for undue alarm, milord?" Jayson eyed the Trench Lord curiously.

Aorun snarled at those words, causing the guard to take a step back reflexively. "First, do not question me! Secondly, do not underestimate him. The Guldalian line is renowned for their powerful mages. Last, I have my reasons that have nothing, absolutely nothing, to do with alarm."

"Yes, sir!" Jayson snapped at Aorun's tone with a reflexive response. "Make the man's life hell. Kill him if I can get away with it. Anything else?"

Aorun thought for a long moment. "He will have a body servant - a beautiful one with emerald eyes. I want you to get close to her. Be her confidant if you can: her protector and friend. Do not touch her. I plan to take her from the little dog; she is for me. However, I need to know her fears, her weaknesses and where she goes, as well. She will have her own half day when he is off on his. I want to know what she does with it. Perhaps offer to escort her on her errands and such."

Jayson smiled. "You are ordering me to spend time with a beautiful woman? I believe that is the best order you have ever given me."

Aorun looked at him pointedly. "Look, befriend, but do not touch," he reaffirmed with a deadly tone.

"Yes, milord." Jayson's face resumed its bland expression.

Aorun stared at him for a long moment. He was pretty damned sure if the half-breed standing before him got a chance, he was going to touch. Perhaps the beautiful little whore would not be willing to share beyond her duties. He decided that, truthfully, he didn't give a damn. "Any questions?"

"No milord. I will pass this about where appropriate. I will need some brothel passes. I think as far as making things difficult, those will go a long way." Jayson smiled as he calculated how to torture the new guardsman.

Aorun reached into his desk and found a pouch. He pulled out his personal markers and gave Jayson ten of them. "Let me know if you need more," he stated.

Jayson slipped them into his pouch. "Will do. Then, with your permission, I will make my own visit and get back to the cave."

Aorun nodded. "Show yourself out. You know the way." He leaned back in his chair, the departing guard already dismissed from his mind: so lost in his thoughts that he didn't hear the door close.

He was furious that the girl was out of his reach again. Aorun couldn't explain it, but there was something about her, something he had to possess. He wanted to own her, have those eyes beg him for *his* attention. Mostly, he didn't want this Alador to have her.

He stood and went to the wall to look at the map of the isle. It took him some time to find this Smallbrook, but it far too deep into Daezun lands to consider removing Alador's family. Besides, he'd learned that most half-breeds were outcasts, so it was possible that it was more hurtful to leave them alive.

Aorun tapped the map considering, tracing the borderlands with a finger. His mother had served in the Home Guard. Gifted with the powers of a bronze dragon, she had been fascinating to him. She could touch a rock and turn it into a toy. Her ability to shift a stone to any shape she wanted had led to life on the fourth tier.

Many thought Aorun was raised in the trenches, but this wasn't the case; he'd known privilege and luxury. He reached over to a nearby shelf where he'd placed a small stone dragon, which had always reminded him of the ones she would make for him. Aorun ran a finger over the back of it before slowly setting it down.

Not for want of trying, Aorun had never been able to bring a spark to a testing stone. His mother had tried it many times a year once Aorun was old enough to be considered for training. He'd tried so hard for her, to see that look of approval in her eyes, but all he had earned was a look of love and pity. He knew she'd been disappointed that her son could draw no power from the magic in a bloodstone. He simply had no innate ability to draw magic.

Aorun didn't know anything of his father. His mother had only said he was a powerful mage on the fifth tier. He had scrutinized every such mage but could find none that bore a likeness to himself, and she'd never mentioned a name, nor had his parents conjoined their households. Any time Aorun had asked, his mother would usually change the topic. To this day, his sire remained a mystery. A hated one – he had not stepped forward after her death – but perhaps he had died first, and Aorun was truly an orphan.

His mother had been called to duty near the end of the war. The Daezun, always good at mining, had taken to living underground and building traps beneath the very ground that the Lerdenian army had to cross. Bronze mages were capable of detecting these holdings, traps and tunnels. His mother had promised Aorun that she would return, but she never did.

One day, he had awakened to find all the servants were gone. He remembered that sense of panic searching through the house and finding a man from the High Council waiting for him at the breakfast table. The man explained that Aorun's mother was dead and that the house was no longer his to live in.

He'd tested Aorun, but as usual, Aorun had been unable to bring a spark to the stone, despite the fear he'd felt. The grief had been overwhelming, but even without it Aorun doubted he could have found that spark. He'd tried so many times before that day. He still continued to try with a small bloodstone he'd purchased, but he had never been able to absorb its gifts.

The man had given Aorun a small sack of silver and told him he had four hours to gather what he needed and to move elsewhere: in with another relative, down to the trenches, out of the capital; it didn't matter to the man. There had been no concern that Aorun was still just a boy. The fact that he had no gifts for magic apparently discounted his worth as a citizen in the official's eyes.

Aorun knew of no family, and even a rapid search of his mother's desk and room had revealed no clues to his heritage. Aorun shook his head to let go of his feelings of abandonment, wandering back to his own desk. He had sworn then that he would kill any Daezun that crossed his path and, for a time, had kept that promise. As far as he was concerned, they were the ones that had condemned him to a life in the trenches.

Aorun sat down at the desk and grabbed his flask, shaking it angrily as he remembered he'd just drained it. He sighed and caressed the silver etchings of the sea remembering those first few years, having entered the trench with nothing more than a pair of backpacks.

There were no open homes in the trenches; families protected them viciously. Aorun had found a small indent in the rock wall and claimed it for his own. He hadn't realized how spoiled and helpless he really was until a group of boys barely older than he had beaten him senseless, taken everything he'd had, and left him for dead.

That was the day he had met Wieta, a little old woman wizened with too many years, hunched slightly with age. She had taken him to a small cave inside the mines, which had become his home for many years. She had saved him so she could get some help. Wieta had been different: sharp in manner and tone, smart but rarely kind. She had been fair, though. She had taught Aorun how to steal and how to hold a blade. When he was beyond her skills, Wieta found him a tutor. All she asked in return is that he helped her remain fed and fetched her water. It had been more than a fair trade. He'd continued to care for her even after joining the Trench Lord's men.

One day he'd gone to take her food and found that she'd passed over to the Gods. Aorun had seen Wieta properly buried and moved on. He'd never loved her, but he had been grateful. Without her, he probably never would have survived the trench.

Aorun threw his flask angrily, wincing as it crashed into a vase on the shelf across from him. Both tumbled to the floor with a jarring clatter as discordant as his stormy emotions. It was not right that someone could be given everything in life just because he could use magic! It discounted all the merit and skill of the man in other areas of his life.

Professionally skilled craftsmen were relegated to the second tier if they were limited to only simple magic. If someone had no magic at all, he made his living on the first tier. Many of those that lived in the trenches were allowed out during the day and were hired on for work in those three tiers. Some even aspired to service in the upper tiers, but they were always forced to return to the trench at night if they had no magic, and if their employer did not allow them to live in the servants' quarters of their home.

It was a system that Aorun hated, and he'd often found ways to undermine it, until he became Trench Lord. The Trench Lord was a part of the system. He had thought, as he worked his way up, that he could change things: create more equality for the Lerdenian people; but it hadn't taken him long to realize that he'd had far more power to make changes as a nameless man in the Trench Lord's service.

Now, if any of his men crossed the lines, it was Aorun who paid the price. If any hint of rebellion or subterfuge against the mages were detected, it was Aorun they would hang out before everyone so others would take note of and learn that even a Trench Lord had lines he could not cross.

Aorun got up and stared at the harbor, watching the great masts sway in the gently-moving water. He would gladly have signed on as a mere hand, had he not been terrified of Wieta's foretelling. She'd been something of a fortune teller. Aorun had never been able to figure out if she had a true gift or just got lucky enough to keep others seeking her services. Either way, it was how she earned her meager supply of slips.

Wieta had told him over and over what she'd seen for him, and Aorun had it memorized. He whispered it softly to himself:

"The sea shall rise up in a bond of betrayal and rip all that you have gained from your hand. From your blood, dragons will rise up free and hungry. Your death will unite brothers that shall one day seize the thrones of the Gods."

He hadn't, and didn't, know what Wieta had meant, but he'd believed her. If he kept his feet on solid ground, then the sea could not claim him. Aorun frowned out at the water. He could not go beyond this isle without risking losing all he had acquired or his very life. He could, however, deny this half-breed what should have been Aorun's by birth.

He was a full Lerdenian. He had risen up by his own hand, brain, and skill. He suddenly hoped Jayson didn't find a way to arrange an accident. Aorun wanted to kill this Alador himself. He wanted to take him below to the room he used when he needed information and spend a very, very long time with him there.

Chapter Twelve

They both sat in silence, absorbing Alador's revelations. It was Henrick who once again broke the silence with a long, drawn out sigh. "You want to make an ally out of the dragon that you shot?"

"It's the only dragon that I know of that someone knows how to reach out to and actually speak with. I don't suppose you know two?" Alador looked at him hopefully. "Like, did he ever introduce you to a friend?"

"No, I do *not* know two." Henrick sighed. "You realize he will probably eat you." He leaned back in his chair and crossed his arms.

"Well then, I'll have to convince him that eating me isn't in his best interest," Alador said. "I'm not ready yet. Maybe one or both of us will find another dragon in the meantime, one that might not be quite as irritated with me." Though Alador's words shared his hope, the only other dragons he'd ever seen had been a long ways off.

"Yes, because I make it a routine to convince dragons not to eat me," Henrick shot back with a frown, his voice thick with sarcasm. There was a moment of silence, and he sighed again. "Do you know how lucky I was to walk away from that encounter?"

"Father, I have to find a dragon. Without the dragons as an ally, they might think I mean to hurt their fledglings when I go to close this mine," Alador said with a frown.

"How are you going to do that? If it was easily done, do you not think that the dragons would have already done it?" Henrick pointed out, disgruntled. "It seems to me that if it were a matter of just attacking it, the issue would have been settled long ago. They are not weak creatures."

"I don't know yet. What I do know is that a direct attack obviously won't work; so however I do it is going to have to be well orchestrated." Alador's thoughts were racing. "It has to be subtle, or an army will be waiting," he pointed out; "…and it'll need the cooperation of the dragons."

Alador sat back. "Can you ask your dragon friend a question for me before he decides to hate me?"

Henrick smirked. "I can try. What would you have me ask?"

"I need to know if a blue dragon named Pruatra still lives. If she does, maybe I could reach out to her instead," Alador mused. "She was Renamaum's mate."

"I can ask, but he will want to know why I want to know." Henrick pointed out, eyeing his son.

Alador hadn't considered that. After a moment, he answered, "Tell him the truth. The one that harvested Renamaum's stone is asking for her. Maybe it will make him curious enough to overcome his own hate."

Henrick nodded. "Brave move. I hope you do not mind, but I think that I will leave out that it is my son for the time being." Henrick grinned at Alador. "I rather like living," he stated simply.

Alador laughed at that. "A wise thought, I think." He grinned over at his father. "I'm going to go write a letter to Mesiande, and then we can go turn me over to this Black Guard. I've arranged for uncle to allow me two half-days so I can learn from you both."

Henrick looked surprised. "How did you manage that one?"

"I learn quickly. He wants something from me - something specific, I think. As long as he thinks I hold him in confidence, he's rather accommodating. I'm going to try to use that as long as I can."

Alador rose to his feet. "I know I have much to learn, and I'm willing to learn what I can from him as long as it's available. Dorien taught me once that there is no better way of winning than to watch your enemy work: for that is your opportunity to discover how to best him."

"I have always liked Dorien," Henrick mused softly. "I will be ready to go when you have your things gathered. I will meet you in the front hall when you are ready." He did not rise with his son; instead, he stood and stared at the fire.

"I won't be long," Alador promised and turned sharply to head out the door. He found the way back to his own room with minimal difficulty.

Alador wrote out a letter to Mesiande, hoping she would understand his meaning. He rolled it up and placed it in the tube, then laid it under his pillow and concentrated on her for a time...

He was swept away as the memories of Mesiande washed over him painfully: her braided hair always threatening to escape its twisted confines, her soft, rounded body pressed closed to him, the sparkle in her eyes as she teased him, and the scolding in her voice when she stood at the archery range, hands on those perfect, small hips, scolding his form.

Alador's heart ached with every tender memory. There was a good chance he would never be able to hold her again. He knew that she would be trained for the circle in another's arms. All these things melded into the memory that was his Mesiande, his love, his heart. He couldn't imagine any other taking her place in his soul.

When he could stand it no longer, Alador checked under the pillow: the tube was gone. He caressed the dent where he'd placed it, then sighed softly and left the bed, moving around the room. He stored things he wanted to keep safe and only loaded the backpack with a few changes of clothes, some writing materials, and a handful of slips.

He changed into a simple shirt of undyed linen, then eyed the weapons on the wall and took down a sword, testing it. It was weighted well and fit his hand. Alador also saw his bow and smiled, taking it from the rack. Thanks to his father, it hadn't been lost in the rockslide.

He strapped the sword around his waist. The last thing he took was a boot knife, which he slipped into place down the sheath that was prepared on the outside of his right leg. Alador stood before the mirror. He hardly looked formidable, but it would have to do.

He joined Henrick in the hall, hoping he hadn't kept his father waiting long. Henrick's hair was slicked back, and he was dressed impressively in a deep red shirt, a black vest, and matching britches. His boots were black as well, and had a deep rich shine. At his belt was a short sword, and though the handle looked decorative, Alador doubted the blade was. He was learning not to judge his father by how he presented himself.

They didn't speak as they went through the fifth tier to the stairs down. It had stopped raining and the summer sun was beginning to dry the stone streets. The air was oppressive and close, much like in the bathing house at home.

Silverport's population increased as they descended. The fourth tier had many mages socializing or busily making their way on errands. Small inns and taverns were irregularly spaced throughout the tier, and there were still a few shops here and there.

One shop had a bloodstone sign in front of it, and Alador stopped grabbing his father's arm. "Can we go in here for a moment? I want to see something." Alador nodded to the shop.

Henrick noted the sign and nodded. "Just do not cause a ruckus; we do not have that much grace."

Alador nodded and stepped inside. The shop had little to recommend it as he entered. There were bloodstone unguents and pouches of powdered bloodstone on the shelves, most likely something herbalists sought, Alador decided as he moved toward the counter. The shopkeeper came bustling forward, eyes darting over their weapons and Henrick's demeanor and bowed low.

"Good day milords, good day. How may I assist two fine and honored men this day?" His hair was fiery red, his eyes a strange dark jade color. His clothing spoke of money, but it was of simple design. He rubbed his hands together, taking in the men before him.

"I was hoping to see your assortment of bloodstones, maybe five stone weight?" Alador asked. Henrick looked at Alador curiously.

"Yes sir, yes sir. Let me fetch that tray." The man hurried off and soon came back with a large array of stones. "This is my finest selection close to that weight."

Alador went through the small stones carefully. He picked one up, then another and soon was sorting the tray. There were many stones that, while cloudy to show they had not been harvested, were almost pink in color rather than red.

"You know your stones," the man said, watching Alador with sharp eyes.

"Yes, I have much experience with them," Alador murmured. "How much are these over here?"

"They are all in the one slip range, sir." The shopkeeper smiled wide. "Small enough for jewelry enchantments."

"So you cheat your customers?" Alador eyes narrowed, but he kept his tone casual as he looked the shopkeeper up and down.

The man's face reddened. "I most certainly do not." He puffed up with indignation.

Alador waved his hand over the lighter stones. "These are harvested from living dragons and likely to be light on the magic they should hold." He moved his hand over the dark red ones. "These are from deceased dragons and will hold more of the true power of their magic. You're lucky that more of your customers don't know this." Alador leaned across the board between them. "Some might kill a man for selling them a diluted stone as quickly as they might kill over diluted wine." His voice was low and cold.

Despite the warning Henrick had given Alador, he stood slightly back from his son with his arms crossed, his smirking smile a testament to his thoughts. He made no move to interfere or interrupt. Meanwhile, Alador's eyes were locked on the shopkeeper, who swallowed noticeably.

"I buy my stones from one vendor. I assure you sir, I do not know what you mean by 'diluted'." The shopkeeper eyed the lighter stones with concern, and his eyes moved to dart about the shelves, as well.

"I want the name of your supplier then; he should be educated on the varying quality of his merchandise."

"I get them through one of the Trench Lord's warehouses," the man murmured, picking up a lighter stone.

"I see." Alador straightened up. "Do not charge equal fees for these stones. They might as well be fake." He pulled two slips from the bag and scooped up two of the nicer stones from the true stone side. "If I hear that you have been, I will personally see to it that my uncle hears of your theft from the mages of the upper tiers."

"Your uncle?" The man looked at Alador worriedly.

"Yes, I'm sure you've heard of him. Luthian Guldalian?" Alador asked as he shoved the two stones into his pack. His voice held just the right amount of controlled condescension.

"You are the High Minister's nephew?" the man squeaked.

"Indeed I am. Best keep my words in mind," Alador snapped as he spun on his heel and headed for the door. Even as he stormed out the door, he could hear the shopkeeper begging for forgiveness. He didn't pause to give it credence. He was angry that the Trench Lord was a part of his uncle's vile practice. Not surprised, but still indignant.

"You did hear me say not to cause a ruckus, yes?" Henrick mused as he strode to catch up with Alador.

"I didn't punch him, did I?" Alador pointed out as he moved down the tier.

"Apparently we have a different definition of what exactly a ruckus is," Henrick said with a wry smile. "Before you walk us to the end of the tier, take the next right for the stairs down."

They dropped down to the next tier. The streets were filled here. This tier was plainly where most trading took place. There were carts with vendors and shops on almost every street front, crowded together. The mass of bodies felt pressing; Alador had never seen so many people in one place. Henrick took the lead through the crowded tier to the far end.

Here, the tier ended in a cave cleaving into the cliff. Men in The Blackguard uniform stood to either side with a standard flying above them: a red dragon on a black background, fluttering in the sea breeze. The city had been left behind, and the harbor stretched out below them.

Alador stared at the large-masted ships as he stood at the barrier meant to keep people from falling to the rocks below. "I have heard of ships, but I've never seen one with my own eyes," he whispered. Beyond the breakwater was the ocean, and soon he was captivated by the view. "Or the ocean..."

"The ocean is a wide expanse. It takes the fleet many days to just cross to the nearest isle." Henrick moved beside him.

"Have you ever sailed it?" Alador asked. The ships looked massive, the men moving about their decks barely more than small bugs.

"I have crossed it a couple times." Henrick admitted. "The people are as different in look and manner as the Daezun are from the Lerdenians. Many lands are unoccupied. Perhaps one day, we will travel together to see the world."

"Do foreign ships ever come here?" Alador asked curiously.

"Not often. The Lerdenian fleet is better equipped for such crossings. I am sure that, over time, more will come as other nations learn to accomplish long voyages," Henrick offered. "Alador, we have delayed enough. It is time for us to deliver you to the High Master."

Alador nodded. He took a deep breath of the clean sea air, and one last look at the birds flying about the harbor. He suddenly felt like he was giving up his freedom. He glanced over at the great hole in the cliff that seemed ready to swallow him, and hefted his pack. "Let's get it over with," Alador murmured, heading for the opening.

The two guards made no move to stop him. He guessed that he was either expected or that they just let half-breeds in. He and Henrick moved deeper into the darkness, where the air became cooler despite the torches that lit the cave.

They came to a man who sat with his feet propped up on a desk, half-dozing. He sat up suddenly at the sound of footsteps. "Good day. How may The Blackguard be of assistance?"

Henrick stepped forward. "My son has come to enlist," he said firmly.

The man assessed Alador, taking in his shorter and bulkier build. He nodded and picked up a quill. "Name…?"

Alador moved to stand beside his father. "Alador. Alador Guldalian." The name felt strange on his tongue.

The man's eyes shot up. "The High Minister's nephew. We've been expecting you. If you'll grab your things, I'll take you to the

High Master." He jumped up and walked to the door, opening with a flourish. "After you..."

Alador walked through the door, feeling somewhat nervous. He had no idea what to expect, but he was surprised when Henrick was stopped at the door.

"Sorry, Milord. No family is allowed past the door. He will return to you on his half day if he wishes; but for now, only members of the council and The Blackguard are allowed within." The guard had an arm between Henrick and the doorway.

Alador met Henrick's eyes and swallowed hard. His father nodded with a look of reassurance. "I will see you soon, then," Henrick said simply; and, before he'd even turned away, the guardsman had shut the door between them.

"Right then, this way." The guardsman's tone was now tinged with sarcasm. His obliging manner had disappeared the moment the door closed.

The cave had been transformed inside. The walls were squared of the same stone that much of the city had been built from, and the many twists and turns had Alador thoroughly lost. There was light along the way from strange glowing rocks, and the white walls reflected their glow softly.

The guard didn't stop, though they passed a lot of other people all wearing the same leather gear. There was laughter and boisterous voices in those halls, giving away the mixed genders and the equality within this elite group. Finally, the guard opened a door where two men waited on either side.

"Master Guldalian, as you requested, High Master." The guard pushed Alador through the door and shut it behind him. Alador stumbled into the room, blinking at the sudden change of light.

He straightened quickly. The room was bright, with a window that overlooked the distant sea. The man behind the desk looked up at Alador. He didn't look like a half-breed; in fact, Alador thought he looked fully Daezun. He was short like his kin and had the same mundane shade of brown hair. His, however, was long and pulled back, and his face showed the ravages of time and weather. The two men assessed each other.

"Sit down, Master Guldalian." The High Master indicated a chair across from him.

Alador set his pack, quiver and bow against the chair and sat down, taking in his surroundings. They were practical: a shelf of books, a table covered with maps, and a desk. Other than that, there was little in the room. "I prefer Alador," he said quietly as his eyes came back to the High Master, who'd pulled over a page of parchment.

"After this interview, it will be guardsman, so I really don't care what you prefer." The man wet his quill and looked up at Alador. "What is your sphere of magic?"

"Sphere of magic?" Alador asked, not understanding the question.

"Yes, what type of magic can you cast? Natural spells, fire-based, or maybe ice-based?" The High Master seemed to speak with disdain.

"Oh, water," Alador said when he realized what the man sought.

"Water? That's rare. We only have a few in the entire compound, one or two out on assignment. That'll be useful." The High Master wrote something down. "How much teaching have you had?"

"Just a short while. I only recently found out I was even a mage." Alador admitted. "It was only two weeks ago that I was planning a house for a future housemate." It had actually been less than that. It was amazing how much had happened in the last week; Alador had a hard time fathoming that as he sat there and thought about it.

The High Master looked up with a bit of sympathy. "Just now cast out, then?"

Alador swallowed hard and looked down. "Yes, sir," he said softly. Maybe he would like it here. The people here would at least know what it felt like to be cast out by their kin... well, those who'd grown up under Daezun teachings would.

"What experience have you had with weapons?" The High Master continued to press, though his manner seemed less harsh, and he eyed Alador a bit more warmly.

"I'm a dead shot with my bow, but I've barely touched a sword," Alador admitted. "I was a miner by trade and have skills with a pick, but more as a tool than a weapon," he added as an afterthought. Maybe they would have uses for miners and he wouldn't have to stand guard as the men at the final tier had been doing. It did not seem the least bit interesting or pleasant to stand there all day in the hot sun. It was more humid here by the sea then Alador was used to, and that armor didn't look like it reflected heat in any capacity.

"Most of those brought in are at least fair with a bow, and few solid with a sword." The man made a few more notes and Alador remained quiet. "It's a fair life in The Blackguard. The High Minister expects diligence and hard work, but in exchange, we're well-paid and well-accommodated. I know it's not what you're used to, but it shouldn't take you long to adjust. We will keep you too busy to fret about home," the High Master promised.

His tone became harder as he continued. "However, you will get no favoritism because your uncle is our benefactor. If anything, you will be pushed harder. Your uncle has made it clear you are not to receive any special privileges other than an extra half-day for his own tutelage. You will start at the bottom like everyone else and you will work your way up. Am I clear?" The High Master snapped his question in what was clearly his usual manner.

Alador responded without thinking, used to such authority from elders. "Yes, sir," he answered with a blink of surprise.

"Good, I will have the man outside show you to your room." The High Master got up and strode around the desk.

Alador swiftly gathered his things and followed the man to the door. The High Master swung it open and handed a slip of paper to one of the men beside the door. "See the man settled in."

Unlike most Daezun, this guard had red hair, and his face was freckled. His eyes were the color of burnished bronze. He saluted the High Master. "See right to it, sir." He beckoned Alador to follow him and strode hurriedly down the hall.

When they got to the first turn, he took a left and led the way down a long corridor with many doors. He took a stairwell down and led Alador into a great hall filled with tables and benches. It was quiet in the room, but the smell of food wafted to his nose. His guide paused here and seemed to relax somewhat. "This is where we eat. They feed us well enough. The name's Flame, by the way." The man with the hair to match his name stuck out his hand.

Alador shifted his bow and clasped the man's arm. "Alador." He looked about. "How many people live here?"

"Two hundred so far, but the High Minister's said he plans it to house a thousand men and women." Flame drew himself up a bit. "Right proud we are - to be part of his elite force."

Alador did not point out he was being trained to kill his cousins: he didn't know whom he could trust, and Flame seemed to be happy here. He could understand that, to some degree. If he hadn't had his father to lead and guide him, Alador was uncertain where he would have gone or what he would have done if he'd ever been cast out on his own. There were stories of half-breeds being thrown out before they could reach their first circle. As they moved through the large dining hall, Alador took advantage of Flame's openness.

"How long have you been here?" he asked. They crossed the hall and into another carved corridor. He tried to take in the route Flame was leading him; usually Alador was pretty good at not getting lost, but he wasn't used to being so far underground. He'd preferred bloodstone mining, which rarely took him very deep. Here, the walls felt too close, and he eyed the rock ceiling a little warily.

"Oh, I've been here about a year. I am battlemage now, orange squad." Flame turned right as he moved down the hall.

"What does that mean?" Alador asked curiously.

"Well, see, it works like this: you start out as a guardsman. Means you don't know shite when you start. You work your way up to battle mage. That means you have a basic mastery of your talents for battle. Then you're put in a squad based on your sphere of magic. I'm fire based, what about you?" Flame paused to look at Alador in front of a narrow door. He checked his paper and then looked back at Alador.

There was silence for a moment. "Oh, water," Alador replied, realizing he'd been asked a question. "I don't know a lot, but I know it's water."

"See, that will put you in one of the blue spheres. Each company will be made up of at least one of each of the spheres." Flame grinned widely at him. "Red spheres are the largest and the healing sphere is the smallest. It's made up those that can heal and purify." Flame swung open the door. "This one is yours."

Alador blinked. "How do you know one door from the other?"

Flame pointed to the frame around the door. On it, a wave symbol and the number eight had been carved. He held up the paper. "Water sphere and room eight."

"I am going to get so lost in here..." Alador murmured as he moved into the room.

He'd expected, being in the army or military unit, that he would be a room with a lot of other men. The stories of war he'd heard always had men around camps and such, all together in one place. So he was surprised to see a simple room and that it had a fairly large bed, bigger than Alador's had been in Smallbrook.

He focused his attention swiftly to the room and away from thoughts of home. A wardrobe stood on the far wall beside a weapon rack. There was a desk with quill and parchment, along with a few books. "This is mine? I thought the High Master said no special treatment."

"All the rooms look like this. Plus, your first books to learn spells and how to harness your sphere are there on the desk. Trust me, you'll be grateful for the privacy soon enough. Everyone always just wants to fall into bed when they get started. Someone will be around to take you to get fitted…" - he gestured to his own black leather – "…and then take you to dinner. I'm sure I'll see you about."

Alador turned to ask him another question, but the door was already shut: Flame had closed it abruptly and quietly, and he was alone. He sighed softly and settled his bow and quiver into the rack, along with his sword. He just shoved his backpack onto the floor of the wardrobe: he would unpack later; it wasn't like he'd brought much with him.

There was one small door that led into a small room with a hole in the floor for bodily needs. He shut the door quickly, the odor in the room was strong and unappealing. Alador flopped down onto the bed, expecting it to be hard, and was surprised at how soft it was. At least his new life would have some comforts.

Once again Alador tried not to think of home, focusing his thoughts on everything he'd learned in the last few days. He felt like he'd lived months in the last week. However, he couldn't prevent his mind from straying to the words he'd penned to Mesi.

Mesi,

I want to tell you that I am sorry I killed Trelmar. I know that is probably what you hoped I would say, but I have never lied to you. I am not sorry he is dead. What he did was beyond redemption. I am very sorry that it had such an effect on the villagers, my family, and life in the village. I have so much to tell you and there is not a day yet that I have not missed your sweet smile, your tender touch, or even your scolding.

I am not surprised to hear about Gregor and Sophie. There were signs before I left that Gregor was smitten with her. I find it hard to accept that my best friend likes my sister; it seems like there should be something wrong with that. However, I know he will take good care of her, so I guess it will be okay.

There are some things I need to share. I had been trying to figure out how to tell someone before everything went awry. Since I pulled the bloodstone out of the ground, I have been having dreams. They are hard to explain because they are very vivid, like I lived them myself. Henrick has explained there are stones that are very large and hold all the power of the dragon along with something he called a geas. Basically, a geas is some task the dragon needed completing or that was important, and that task is stuck in the bloodstone, too. I think my bloodstone was this type of stone. It turns out that I took the magic from that stone.

Last night there was a new dream. I think I am supposed to free the dragons. The Lerdenians have this horrible practice where they capture dragon eggs and hatch them, then they keep the new babies to use later for bleeding. I got to see some of the stones created this way. They are much paler, and I doubt they have as much magic in them if taken from a living dragon. It is a horrible practice, and one I think the dragon who lived before my stone had planned to stop. I do not know how I am going to do that yet. If the dream is still accurate, these young dragons are very well guarded. The vale I saw them in looked remote. I don't know when or how, but someday, I know I have to go and least try to free them

I am writing this quickly at the moment because Henrick is waiting for me to take me to The Blackguard. My uncle Luthian, the High Minister, has this special unit of half-breeds like me. It is here that I will learn to use what magic I have and, I guess, how to fight in an army. I plan to go and learn everything I can as I will need to know such things if I am ever going to save those dragons. I am not sure how often I will be able to write. I have no idea of what life within this place will be. I know I get a half-day each week with Henrick, so at the worst, I will write on those half days.

Please let Dorien know that I am still well. I understand his request that I do not write to Maman, but I do need his help with something. The Lerdenians use this really large machine, kind of like a giant bow. It fires an arrow that would leave a solid hole big enough for a fist through a man. Will you find out if he has any idea what that is called? I saw it in the last dream and I think it was also what killed the dragon we mined.

I miss you so much. I miss our talks by the river. I miss shooting with you and Gregor. I miss being in trouble and laughing and teasing. It is strange when you are far away from someone you love, the things you miss most are the things you would have said you did not like.

I miss the way your nose scrunches up when you do not like something. I like the way you laugh when I mess up something. I miss the way you stomp your foot, all angry. I love you Mesiande. No dragon or his quest is ever going to stop that. One day I will come for you and we will be together. I don't know how yet. But unless you tell me that you do not want me there, I will be at your first circle.

Forever yours to command and scold,
Alador

Chapter Thirteen

Alador had almost drifted to sleep when a timid knock on the door drew his attention. He jumped up and swung it open, expecting to see another member of The Blackguard in some capacity. When he saw Keelee with her arms full, he just stared at her for a moment.

"Umm…what are you doing here?" Alador asked. He looked out quickly, and seeing no one else in the hall, dragged her into the room and shut the door. "Seriously Keelee, how did you even get in here?" She obviously was carrying her belongings with her.

Keelee looked extremely pleased with herself. "You said I could come with you," she reminded him. Then her expression changed, her large, emerald eyes widening in alarm. "You didn't just say it to keep me quiet, did you?" Her tone shifted to a whisper as she shifted her belongings in her arms.

"I meant like in the servants' quarters," Alador replied. "I mean, it's a large complex, I'm sure they have servants' quarters…" He looked around at the small room. "Where would you even sleep?"

"I told them I was your body servant, and that means they expect me to sleep with you."

Keelee leaned over and her belongings spilled on to the bed.

"Why did you tell them that?" Alador asked in horror. "I mean, they already think I'm expecting privileges for being the High Minister's nephew. What could they possibly have thought of me bringing a body servant? What does that even mean? Well..." he stammered, "besides the obvious... umm..." Alador glanced at the bed.

Keelee looked a little offended as she turned to look at him. "They will think you are a damned lucky man, and treat you a little better because you are affluent enough to have a body servant," she pointed out imperiously. "Unless you don't think I am pretty enough?" She bit her lip, looking hurt now, and glanced up at Alador through her lashes while brushing the floor lightly with her foot.

"No! No. You're very pretty. I'm not saying that. I just... Keelee," Alador sighed, shaking his head. "I told you. I love another," he pointed out in frustration.

"What does that have to do with me being your body servant?" Keelee looked at him in confusion.

"Well," Alador ran a hand through his hair. "Daezun don't have body servants," he finally replied.

"You are half Lerdenian," she fired back. Her hands were on her hips, the same way Mesiande used to stand when she was angry.

Keelee's face melted slowly into a pretty pout. "Besides, I am here and if you send me away I will have to go to the trenches and you said I could stay with you." She batted those long lashes as she looked up at him.

Before Alador could answer her, there was a knock on the door. He opened it with a bit of exasperation to see another man in the same armor. This man was as different from Flame as night from day: he had black hair and eyes that were gray and hard, though they softened slightly when he saw Keelee standing behind Alador.

"Was sent to take you to the armor smith. Glad to see you're settling in already. Afternoon, ma'am." The guard nodded to Keelee.

Alador nodded and looked back at Keelee who had a satisfied smile on her face. "We are not done discussing this," he shot back at her before stepping out.

"I will..." Keelee began.

Alador shut the door firmly behind him before taking a better look at this man who'd been sent to get him. There was something unsettling about his eyes: the strange way in which their gray color shimmered...

"Not here a day and already having trouble with your woman?" The guard asked solemnly as he led him down the hall.

Alador opened his mouth to explain that she wasn't his, but realized he didn't know what risk Keelee would be in if he did. He didn't understand how things worked well enough to say anything much. "A bit of a disagreement on duties and expectations," he offered with a half-smile. That in itself was true.

"You're lucky. Most have to sweet-talk a woman in the guard or visit the trench to meet their needs. It can get cold in here at night in the winter..." There wasn't much emotion in Jon's tone or manner as he led Alador down the many turns and passages. "At least it's nice this time of year. Name's Jon…," he added, almost as an afterthought.

"Alador," Alador offered back, sighing as they made another turn: he was already lost. "How big is this place?" he asked, awed and confused by the many twists and turns.

"Not that big; just feels like it in the dim light and all the cross-passages," Jon answered. He stopped at the corner and pointed to marks just above their heads on the wall where arrows had been carved at the corner above a set of symbols that lined up. "These are in one of the books on your desk. It helps you navigate, though eventually you'll just know the way."

Alador nodded. Like the symbol on the door, some were easy to decipher. The symbol for the dining hall was easy as was one for weapons. "I will definitely make a point of learning those first," he answered.

Jon nodded and led him on down the hall to the armory. The armor smith turned out to be a woman. Her glance was steady and scrutinizing, reminding Alador of the elder Luciesa from his village.

"This is the new lad?" she asked Jon as she walked over to Alador. Her gaze moved over him slowly, the way a farmer inspected korpen.

"Yup. All yours, Aneta. Just let one of us in the practice-ring know when you're done, and we'll help him find the dining hall." Jon saluted her smartly and left the two of them alone.

Alador eyed Aneta as she moved around him with a frown, as if she didn't like what she saw. "Out of shape. Lean in the waist, though. Shouldn't be too difficult." She clicked her tongue in disapproval.

"I am not out of shape," Alador protested.

"Tell me that in four days and I will buy you an ale." Aneta chuckled. She patted his butt with appreciation. "Least this part of you is good."

"Hey!" He jumped forward.

"Stand still. I need to take some measurements." She left to get a string and a slate, then came back to measure Alador. Apparently she was intent to leave no part of him unmeasured, and spent far more time on the inside of his leg than he was comfortable with. She 'accidentally' brushed his manhood with her hand more than once; but when he moved in protest, she reminded him that he'd be living in that armor and would thank her later when it fit properly.

When all the measuring was finally over, she led him across the hall to the weapon smith, which Alador found more to his liking. The forge fire made the room warmer than the other areas he had been. It was interesting to see how it had been vented so it wouldn't fill up with smoke. It reminded Alador of the forge at home, and he took a moment to force down the lump that rose in his throat.

The weapon smith just pointed him to a rack of weapons, where Alador looked amongst the dull-bladed swords until he found one that felt good in his hands. Its hilt was simple, unlike some, and fit well in his grasp. The balance was good, too, and Alador could wield it smoothly. The weapon smith just nodded and tossed him a second blade. He barely caught it with his off-hand.

"What's this for?"

"Practice sword." The man nodded for him to go through the door and went back to hammering on a blade near his forge. He was so obviously not the social type that Alador left him to his work without another word, stepping through the door to find himself outside.

He blinked in surprise as his eyes adjusted to the fading light. He stood, surrounded by cliff walls, in a small oasis where large rings had been set out and trees provided shade. The space was full of men and women talking and practising swordplay or archery, everywhere he looked.

Jon must have been watching out for him: he approached soon after Alador emerged. "There you are. That took longer than normal: Aneta must have liked you." He nodded at Alador. "You saw the weapon smith, as well. Come, I'll take you back to your room to drop those off and then we can be off to dinner. When your armor is delivered, you'll get a proper sheath and belt to go with that."

Alador nodded, still a little overwhelmed. He nodded in greeting to those he noticed staring , then quickly followed Jon through a different doorway. He looked for markings but saw none on this door. He thought about asking about it, but decided to keep quiet - he didn't want to sound stupid.

As they made their way through the halls back to Alador's room, he eyed each turn, noting the passages Jon chose by the symbols on the corners. "What happens now?" he asked as they reached his room. Keelee wasn't there, though she'd clearly moved in, given how tidy everything was. He set his weapons on the rack and walked back to the door.

"We eat dinner. You have tonight to study, and tomorrow you'll enter the first level of training." Jon moved off back the way Alador knew led to the dining hall. "You'll probably have a schedule waiting for you on your desk by the time dinner's over."

"What does that usually entail?" Alador asked. Part of him was excited to be learning magic and swordplay, but part of him was terrified of the changes he knew he'd have to make.

"Well, my schedule had exercises to build strength and endurance in the first half of the morning, then lessons on battle magic till the mid-day meal. After eating, I had an hour to study, then went to archery practice. Another class on survival magic after that; then I reported to where you found me to spend the rest of the day in sword training."

Jon moved swiftly down the hall as a bell rang, apparently signaling the meal. "It hasn't changed too much, though now I have classes in battle tactics and leadership as well."

"What sphere of magic do you control? Or is it rude to ask?" Alador had to move fast to keep up.

"I'm a death mage," Jon said simply.

"A death mage? " Alador eyed him carefully. "That's the power of Dethera, right?"

"Yes," Jon answered. "I can control corrosive elements, and I have some power with poison, but I don't know how much use that is. I'm told that it could be really useful in battle, though that would mean sneaking into enemy encampments."

Jon said this matter-of-factly, and Alador got the distinct impression that the thought did not appeal to the man who was leading him down the hall. "My last phase of training will be on infiltrating such encampments."

Alador was quiet as they walked. A part of him pitied Jon. He could imagine what harm such a mage would do to Daezun food supplies, water and weapons. A non-magical army would need this man killed immediately.

"If you no longer wish to associate with me, I'd understand." Jon's tone was terse and his back became stiff.

"Why would I not want to associate with you? You can't help the sphere of magic you were given by the gods, or the dragons. However, that happens..." Alador frowned, realized he was falling behind and picked up his pace.

Jon stopped and turned to stare at Alador. "I think you're the first person ever to say that." His expression was doubtful. "Do you mean it?" He seemed intent on finding some joke or hidden meaning in Alador's words or face.

They had stopped at the edge of a hall where Alador could see a large number of people moving to another doorway - likely the dining hall, as he could smell fresh bread. "Why wouldn't I mean it? You can't help what kind of magic you have, can you?" Alador peered at Jon curiously.

"You're an odd man, Alador. Be careful: such openness may earn you enemies." Jon slowly smiled. "But I'll have your back; that'll go a ways for you. There aren't many that keen on earning the anger of a death mage."

"I'm used to having enemies," Alador sighed, wishing that wasn't the truth. First Trelmar and his friends back in Smallbrook, now this Trench Lord who apparently hated him the moment he saw him. What difference would a few more on the list make? "I could use a friend." Alador offered Jon his arm.

Jon looked at him for a long moment. "I don't have friends," he said, leaving Alador with his arm out.

"I don't either here. How about we both make a first one?" Alador left his arm out.

Jon took it slowly with a grin, squeezing it firmly. "Done." He let go and led him into the hall, showing Alador where to get a tray. As they moved down the line, food was heaped onto his tray. It all looked and smelled delicious.

"How is it that we're fed so well?" Alador asked curiously as they moved to find a table off from others. Everyone seemed to give them a wide berth. Alador had no idea if that was because of Jon, him, or a combination of both.

"We don't get much in the way of trade slips, so they make up for it in other ways. The food is good. We have training and a home. For a lot of people, this is a big step up from life in the trench or out on the land as a half-breed. We have acceptance and purpose here.

"Doesn't it bother you that they might be training us to fight our own kin?" Alador looked around. A few here looked fully Daezun or fully Lerdenian, but most had traits from both races.

"If our own 'kin' had truly cared about us, they would not have cast us out. And remember, not everyone here is Daezun-born. Some are Lerdenian-born, so they don't have Daezun kin the way you and I do - did," Jon answered softly. "Some hate their Daezun blood because it's denied them much in life. Regardless of skill or power, a half-breed can't rise above the third tier."

"What were you cast out for?" Alador asked following Jon's lead and keeping his voice low.

"Same as most: being dirtied with magic. I don't know why they let Lerdenians into their beds if they don't want the children born from such a mating." Jon's tone was bitter.

"It's strange, yet my mother is totally smitten with my father," Alador admitted. "She's like a middlin whenever he comes around. I always wondered if he used magic on her."

"My sire never came around. I never met him. Apparently he's some trader that my mother took a fancy to. Something to do with his purple eyes."

Alador took the time to look around the now very noisy room. It was filled with laughter and camaraderie, much like a village feast. Men and women were on equal footing here; in fact, some of the women looked far deadlier than the men sitting next to them.

"Do they hold the circle here?" Alador asked curiously.

Jon shrugged. "No need. Women in The Guard don't bear small ones - they take some potion to prevent it. And remember, some are Lerdenian-born; they know nothing of the circle ritual. I think many would find it odd, in fact. Why not take to your bed who you want, when you want to?"

Alador nodded. It was not like the Daezun only shared their beds during ritual; that was just a time of procreation, an assurance that there would always be people in the village who were strong and born at a time that was the least taxing.

Both men went on comparing tales of their villages and life within them while finishing their dinner. Neither spoke of kin: the topic seemed just as painful for Jon as it was for Alador. After they'd eaten their fill, Jon took Alador back to his room.

"I'll see you on the practice fields tomorrow," he said before moving off.

Alador opened the door to see Keelee waiting on his bed. She was barely wearing anything at all, and he looked away. "Keelee, cover yourself up," he snapped. His talk of home had only deepened how much he missed Smallbrook and the villagers. The girl on his bed did nothing to appease his homesickness.

Keelee looked hurt but grabbed a wrapper close by and shrugged herself into it. "I'm sorry," she whispered with a slight pout.

"Don't be. Just… I told you, it's not going to be like that. I need to study. If you must be here, find something quiet to do."

Alador sat down at the desk and began to look at the books. He found the one about rules and life in The Blackguard and swiftly found the page that explained the markings.

Keelee moved to his side and picked up another of his books. "I'll just read for a bit," she said, doing nothing to hide the pouting in her voice. Alador just nodded and didn't look up ; he was more interested in learning how to fit in and get around...

He spent a long time reading. When he next looked up, he saw that Keelee had fallen asleep on the bed, the book on her chest. He got up and carefully took the book from her hands. She was, indeed, quite beautiful lying there, fast asleep.

He sighed softly. He should feel lucky, not cursed, that such a beautiful woman had attached herself to him. He knew that any other guardsman would likely jump at the chance to switch places with him. He laid the book on the desk, finally noting she had been looking at basic spells. He really didn't care. If she could learn enough to move herself up through the tiers, then more power to her.

He removed his boots and stripped down to just his britches. He tried to move into the bed without waking her, but that was impossible as she was on the covers. Her eyes fluttered open, their emerald depths mesmerizing.

His breath caught as he gazed into them, and he felt a lurch in the pit of his stomach. "Come on, off the covers," he murmured softly. "I hear I'm in for a hard day tomorrow and it's best I get some sleep."

He realized that the light was too bright to sleep with, and peered at the stones that lit the room. Each of them sat on black pieces of cloth, probably meant for snuffing them. He covered all but one of them and sure enough, the light didn't show through the cloth. He left one shining in case he needed to get up and see to any personal needs.

Meanwhile, Keelee had removed her wrapper and slipped beneath the covers. As soon as Alador joined her in the bed and was settled, she moved to lay her head on his chest. He started to push her away, but realized her body was cold, and having her gentle touch was soothing, somehow. Alador pulled her tight against him and closed his eyes to find sleep.

He'd almost found it when he first felt Keelee's hands untying his pants. "Keelee…" He whispered. "Stop." He looked down at her just as she glanced up at him. The pale glimmer of light was just enough to show the need flickering in her eyes. Alador swallowed hard as he gazed into her eyes and, without thinking, moved a lock of ebon hair from her face.

"Give me just a short time and if you still want me to stop, I promise I will," Keelee whispered back, her large emerald eyes locked on his. His breath caught at the vision of beauty framed in a curtain of shimmering hair, and he found that he couldn't look away. His heart began to pound in his chest.

"Keelee, I love another." He groaned as her fingers touched him. His body was betraying him even at the grazing touch of her fingers on the lacings of his pants. He could feel her breasts pressed against his chest, acutely aware of the hard nipples against his skin even through the gown.

"I am not asking for your love, Alador. I am asking for your warmth and comfort," she whispered as she slid down his body. She trailed hot kisses down his chest and he tangled his hands into her hair. He'd intended to pull Keelee back up when her mouth sank down around him. His eyes flew open in surprise and an immediate moan of pleasure escaped his lips.

Though Alador's fingers clutched tightly in her hair, he did not stop her.

Chapter Fourteen

Renamaum sat on a cliff top overlooking the sea. Under the waves below him was the cave he had grown to know so well. He inhaled deeply: the rich air was filled with the scent of sea spray and kelp.

His eyes followed the gulls that drifted on the air without the need to beat their wings. The fog had lifted and the pale blue of the sky stood in deep contrast with the dark green water, cut with lines of white foam.

Renamaum's time as a fledgling came to an end today. Last evening his sire had told him that it was time for him to find his own way. His dam had laid a new clutch earlier in the month. The two eggs now lay in the pool where he himself had hatched. He'd spent a great deal of time playing in that pool...

His nostrils flared with emotion and steam heaved from his depths, boiling up into the cool air. Renamaum felt mature enough to leave his nest — he'd often been away for days at a time - but there was something very different about having his father tell him that it was time to set out for good.

He *understood why the request had come at this time: there were tales of dragons slaying their younger siblings out of jealousy. Renamaum didn't feel jealous of the new eggs; yet some part of him felt as if his heart was being ripped free.*

He could hear the resounding snap of his father's wings as he came sailing in on the coastal winds, but didn't turn to look at him. He dipped his large head in respect as the ground shifted with his father's landing and swallowed the lump in his throat as his father shook the water from his wings.

Renamaum knew they weren't parting for a lifetime — he was just leaving the cave — yet a piece of him felt like they would never meet again. For a brief moment, Renamaum wondered if this was what fear felt like. He'd heard the word before, but had no idea what it meant. Was this lump in his throat fear? Was he fearful of leaving the safety of his father's shadow and his mother's comforting nuzzles?

"It is not the end, son, but a beginning."

The deep rumble of his father's voice snapped Renamaum' out of his reverie, and he turned his head to meet his father's gaze, swallowing hard. "It does not feel like a beginning," he confessed.

"All things turn and, in that turning, some things end so that others may begin."

Renamaum snorted in frustration. "Must you always talk in riddles? Can you not speak to me without convoluted sayings and soothsayer visions?"

His father chuckled, the deep rumble vibrating the rocks beneath him. Though Renamaum was fully grown, his father was easily a third larger. Barnacles clung to his scales, covering him in dark clusters - a testament to his preference for sleeping on the ocean floor - that made him look far more threatening. It amazed Renamuam that his father could still take flight, and wondered if he used magic to get his large form off the ground.

"Words have power, my son. Words can cut to the heart and soothe the deepest hurts. They can be puzzles that have you pondering for days. I prefer to cast my spells of words in ways that make others think. It is a fault, I fear, that has come with age."

The massive, blue sea-dragon stretched in the morning sun. "We have far to fly. Words can be spoken when we rest." Before

Renamaum could answer, his father thrust off the ground and over the cliff, dropping only a few feet before catching an updraft and, using his powerful wings, began to climb into the sky.

Renamaum sighed. He had no idea where they were going. His father had said this would be his last lesson: the most important one. He jumped into the air, rather more agilely than his sire, and beat his wings to catch him. Long flights exhilarated him. His father had taught him how best to use the winds to bear him up and speed him on his way...

Father and son flew high: the rounding of the land made the distance shorter at great heights, and they climbed to find a wind headed in the same direction; flying was so much more efficient in thinner air with the wind at your back. The land fell away and they set out over the great sea.

Renamaum had never flown so far. He and his father flew past the small isle where many bronze and red dragons had taken roost; they flew down the coast of the great land where most of the flights had migrated so many turns ago. They stopped only once for water and food, but there wasn't much in the way of speaking. Renamaum knew better than to ask where they were headed, and he could think of nothing else to say. This last lesson was the main thing on his mind.

What could he learn that required such a great flight?

Many hours later, his father swirled down toward a small island that only came into sight as they descended. Renamaum peered at it curiously as they circled downwards; there didn't seem to be anything spectacular about it: just a rocky mountain rising up from the ocean floor.

Red, glistening streams of lava were spilling down its sides, steaming in violent hisses of protest as they fell into the ocean. Renamaum's father came to rest on the edge of this active cauldron of water and boiling rock. The rock was warm with the surrounding heat but solid enough.

Renamaum landed roughly, tired from the great distance they'd flown. He looked around, seeing nothing that would have drawn his father to this spot. Perhaps his father was tired and only meant to rest here.

"Your final lesson, my son. You have done me proud. I have dreamed of the day I would lead you here." His father puffed steam wearily from his nostrils.

"What lesson? This is but new land boiling up and into the sea." Renamaum glanced around. There was no sign of life here, not even small seabirds.

"Yes: through these great breaches in the earth, the Gods permit the decay of their former works: that new life may spring forth. It is not why you are here. Close your eyes, my son; listen with your heart. Here may be found the Gods' greatwst gifts to our kind..."

His father was speaking in riddles again. Renamaum looked around curiously, but saw nothing that he could call a gift. There was no great treasure to start a lair, no female waiting for his call. What gift could the gods have left when they'd deserted dragonkind upon their making?

Renamaum sighed and closed his eyes, reaching out with other senses. He flared his nostrils and then shut them swiftly: the sulfurous smell of the burning rock was too strong for comfort. He listened to the gurgling of molten lava, the hissing of steam, and the snaps of rock breaking and cooling around them.

He sat searching for some time before he felt it — a strange tingling deep within him where he reached for his magic. Renamaum focused on that and felt a call to his very blood. His heart began to race, and the call grew stronger with every pound, pulling him further within himself.

Renamaum's eyes flew open as a rumble of need raced through his veins, a rush so exhilarating that he cast about for the source. "What is that?" he growled out, searching about for this pulsing magic.

"It is a gift. It is the pool of magic placed where only dragons can go and where only dragons can sense it. It is a place to heal, to renew, and to take on your final gifts of power." His father smiled at his son's reaction.

"Final gifts?" Renamaum looked at his father in surprise. He knew all the spells his father had taught him well.

"You will see, and you will understand. Find the pool, Renamaum, and receive your birthright." His father lay down on the flat ground where he'd chosen to land.

Renamaum closed his eyes again, searching for the pull; then he took to the sky. The boiling depths below him made the winds unstable, dropping and gusting at random. He had to be careful as he searched, making his way lower into the crater. Pockets of boiling rock and steaming pools dotted the crater. Renamaum scoured the ground, looking for the pool his father spoke of so fervently.

And there it was, lying right in the center. It shimmered in the evening sun, reflecting all the colors around it. This pool was not like those around it; it did not boil and froth. The surrounding ground was not rock, but sparkling red sand...

Renamaum flapped his way down carefully, unsure of its stability. He put one talon to the ground, testing the solid nature of the stone and the warmth of the ground. Finding it not uncomfortable, he landed and lumbered to the pool, catching his reflection staring back at him. He reached out with a talon and broke the mirror-like surface, wondering how it was so smooth with all the shifting and heaving of the ground around it.

The simple touch of that water to his talon sent a shiver all the way to the end of his webbed tail. Renamaum didn't know what he was supposed to do now that he had found the pool; so he sat back on his haunches and stared at it.

It wasn't large enough to swim in, and it could hardly be safe to drink, given his surroundings. He did not look to his father for help: this was his lesson, and he had to learn it *on his own. It was supposed to be a gift from the Gods. If this was true, then each God had put something into it.*

Renamaum puzzled it out for a long time before reaching his head down and taking a deep mouthful. Power surged through him at its touch, but Renamaum was positive he wasn't supposed to swallow; he called for the power of heat and, when the water was hot enough, blew it up into the air in a cone of steam. The steam rained down around him in a warm shower of magic-filled drops.

Renamaum's head suddenly filled with pain, and he cried out. He tried to move out of the steam, but he couldn't make his limbs work. As his vision swam, Renamaum became certain that he'd failed his test, failed his father...

His heart lurched more at this failure than at his own imminent death. He staggered forward, falling onto his underbelly. His head pounded with his fear and thudded to the ground. Darkness claimed his sight, and he lay gasping what he thought were the last breaths her would ever take.

However, after a few long minutes, Renamaum's breathing eased, and he realized he no longer heard the sounds of shifting rocks and hissing steam. The scents had changed to those of a cool spring evening, rich with the nectar of flowers. He slowly opened one eye, then raised his head, looking about him in disbelief.

He was lying in a green field now, a blanket of stars glittering above him. Renamaum forced his large body back up onto his feet and looked around for his father or for some clue that would tell him where he was. It was then that he saw them: globes of light slowly moving toward him from all directions. He swung around with concern, watching them come, and growled out a warning.

Eight shimmering balls of light slowly circled him, radiating power so intense Renamaum knew that no magic he had would ever compare. When the shimmering figures of light finally stilled, they swirled into the form of eight dragons, each a different color. Had he died? Was this where dragons who died laid their hearts in their final flight?

His eyes traveled the silent circle, shifting uncomfortably. Suddenly, he knew. All his life he'd wondered about the Gods that had supposedly created him Now the great Beings that had created the wondrous world he traveled were around him. He bowed as low as he could, keeping his eyes locked on his own talons.

A great voice sounded in Renamaum's head. "All is well, child of Hamaseic. You are safe in this circle." He was not sure if he'd heard the words, or just felt them. "Look upon me."

Renamaum slowly raised his head to look into the kind eyes of a great gold dragon that could only be Oessyn. His eyes locked with those of the great beast before him, and he could find no words . His father had let him fly to Council once, and he remembered seeing Rheagos in that council cavern – it had been the only gold dragon Renamaum had ever seen before this. His gaze was now transfixed by this golden God.

"You will bring about the salvation of your kind, child of Hamaseic. Though you will not see the fruits of your labor, your path is one of great importance." Again, Renamaum felt the words resounding in the depths of his very soul.

"What must I do, O Great Lord Oessyn?" Renamaum managed to keep the tremble out of his voice. He now knew what fear felt like.

"You must only be who you are, child. Within you is the blood of a hero and the heart of your people. In time, your very essence will

repay the promises of your making. Your fledglings will know peace upon your land," Oessyn declared.

"So I will not live to see this pact restored?" he asked. It was hard to like that thought in any way. At least he knew he would live long enough to have fledglings.

"It is not your path," Oessyn agreed. He stepped forward and put his talon over Renamaum's, making the young dragon flinch in preparation. *"My gift to you is long life within death."*

He stepped back, and the great silver dragon, Lyiu, stepped forward. Her scales were the brightest Renamaum had ever seen; most silver dragons kept their scales dull so they wouldn't draw the attention of hunters. *"My gift is the seeing of beauty in all things: for there is ugliness in many; yet within each is a pearl if you but seek it."*

Renamaum nodded his thanks, overwhelmed by the magic swirling within him. It was dizzyingly powerful, like spiraling down in freefall.

The white dragon, Ninet, was next. Her talon was cold, like a frozen lake. *"My gift is vision in the dead of night. May you ever find your way, even when hope seems lost. May you find your voice when you most have need of it."*

Renamaum wondered if his father had gotten his weird way of speaking in riddles from this circle of Gods around him. He had no idea why they gave him such gifts, or exactly what their meaning was. He suspected they meant more than they said; in fact, he could feel something forming deep within him that he didn't understand.

Hamaseic, the great sea dragon, stepped forward. Renamaum was also fairly sure that the gods weren't really dragons. Perhaps this was a form they felt he would understand.

"You are truly the son of your father and it pleases me greatly to know this path was given to one of mine. I give to you the bounties of the sea: that you may never hunger and always find the treasures that you seek." Hamaseic nuzzled Renamaum before stepping back.

Rian came next, a bronze dragon smaller than the others. "My gift is safety: a cave no mortal may find, where your fledglings and mate will never be under threat." Rian smiled. "Every fledgling should grow in safety. That the mortals betrayed our gifts and stole and steal your fledglings is a crime for which they will face a reckoning upon their passing."

Reistaire, a green dragon only slightly larger than Rian, came in close as the bronze backed away. She did not touch his talon but laid her muzzle against his. "My gift is the awesome power to forgive. May you nurture those about you and end the hate that rises amongst them. Hate has destroyed, destroys so many of mine. Wars ravage the natural beauty of my creations. Nurture healing and love, so that war will never be your first option."

Krona waited until Reistaire withdrew. Renamaum watched him cautiously. His best friend, Keensight, was a red dragon, but they were not the most congenial of the flights: known to be quick-tempered and ravaging in their fury. "My gift is anger. You will need it to find what you seek. Only in the face of injustice will your anger find root and bring you to your purpose."

Krona backed away.

Renamaum looked at Krona, sure that he'd just been cursed. How was anger a gift? His eyes moved to the last dragon, who remained still. The long, wiry, black dragon eyed him back with cold hate. "I bring this child no gift. His path runs counter both to my design and to my wish," the Black Dragon hissed angrily.

Oessyn turned majestically to it. "You agreed to abide by the majority vote in Council. If you renege on that, you will face our wrath. You will 'gift' him to this path, as we agreed," Oessyn commanded harshly.

Renamaum's eyes widened with alarm. "I am content if she has no wish to, Great Father," he murmured. The Gods in dragon shape ignored Renamaum. Time lengthened while they stared each other down.

The Black's eyes dropped and she growled out. "It is against my judgement and my will, but I will do as was agreed," she snarled. She stepped forward, slapping her smaller claw down over Renamaum's, her talons biting into the top of his forepaw. "My gift is a swift death when your dying comes, that you may not suffer." She leaned in closer and whispered, "Your death will be by the hand of him – a mortal – you seek to save."

Renamaum growled in response, not caring she was a goddess. "Then you had best be sure that mortal hand is not set in my sight: for if it be, I will deliver HIM to your keeping, not him me."

Dethera slowly withdrew her claw, its withdrawal more painful than its vicious thrust. Hamaseic laughed, and Oessyn nodded as he spoke.

"We have chosen well. May the wind always carry you high in your flight." Their business was concluded, and Renamaum was dismissed. All eight dragons threw back their heads, and their conjoined howl sent a sword of sound through the centre of Renamaum's brain. He closed his eyes and buried his head between his great paws, trying to drown out the pain.

When at last the noise ceased, Renamaum opened them again. He was lying on the red sand within the great cauldron and the smell of sulfur filled his nostrils. He didn't move for a while, gathering his wits. His spells would be greater now, he knew; the power of the pool coursed through his veins, strengthening him.

Finally he clambered to his feet and kicked up off the sand to return to his father. He would need help to delve deeper into the meaning of what he'd heard. But when he flew up out of the great mouth of steam and smoke, his sire was gone. The ledge was empty. His father had left him to learn his final, momentous lesson on his own.

He landed skittering across the shale. Renamaum reared his great head back, and let out a ferocious roar of triumph... and of sorrow.

Chapter Fifteen

Alador rose from the depths of his dream to someone calling his name and rocking his body back and forth. The haze of the howling dragon intermingled with a decidedly feminine and distinctly irritating call. He batted at whoever was shaking him, hoping she would go away until her words finally got through to him. His eyes opened with alarm.

"Alador! Alador…you are going to be late. You slept through the breakfast bell already." Keelee had him by the arm and was attempting to pull him from the bed.

Alador sat up, trying to shake free of his dream. He could still smell sulfur in the air, and his body tingled with magic. He realized that the room was full of a haze of fog. "What's going on?" he managed to rasp out. Despite the haze in the room, he felt parched.

"I don't know. I came in from breakfast and finding out where things are, and the room was like this. I thought you would get up with the breakfast bell. I have laid out your clothes since your armor is not here yet. Quick, you are going to be late for your first class." Keelee held up a fresh shirt for him.

Alador realized he was naked; a flush of emotion and confusion rushed over him. What had he done? He realized by the panicked look on Keelee's face that he didn't have time to dwell on last night or why the room was full of a watery haze. Alador jumped out of the bed, much to Keelee's apparent relief, and began throwing on clothes as she handed them over. He quickly grabbed a belt and his practice sword, slipping it into its sheath. While he was tying up his boots, Keelee put a couple of books together at his desk.

"Your first lesson is on general magic. I have everything here you'll need till lunch." She handed him a pouch with the books and a parchment. "That is your schedule. Hurry, the late bell will ring in a minute!" Keelee practically pushed him out the door. "You do not want punishment on your first day."

Alador didn't know what punishment being late would merit, but he was caught up in the urgency of Keelee's voice and let her push him outside. He glanced at the paper and was glad he'd taken the time to memorize the symbols.

He scurried down the hall, cursing as he had to stop to check the symbols at the different passages. A bell began to sound just as Alador made it through the arch of his first classroom, and he slid onto a bench in the back as the bell continued to ring. He looked around: about thirty others were in the room, some armored and some not. Their instructor came in through a side door and Alador breathed a sigh of relief, knowing that he'd made it to a seat just in time not to be noticed.

The instructor was a small man and looked to be fully Lerdenian. He had kind green eyes and a soft spoken manner, but Alador noted that everyone paid close attention to him despite that seemingly gentle demeanour. He had been in enough classes as a small one to know that such respect was usually earned. He eyed the small mage – whose name was Master Arborn – with curiosity, wondering what the others knew that he didn't.

Alador's first lesson was on sending: a kind of magic he'd use in battle to send information to a single source in the command tent. Each squad would learn whom they would send to through a chain of communication. It provided organization on the battlefield.

It was easier said than done, though. The message had to be short and concise, quick and directed. Any wavering of thought on the sender's part and the spell would drop off into nothing. Because most of the men here had had more training than he had, they got the hang of it pretty quickly. Alador struggled to master the technique.

Finally, the instructor gave him a small metal cone to speak into and told him to picture another person at the other end of the cone. While the cone was small, the mental picture finally allowed Alador to begin sending one word messages. His head pounded with the effort, and he was relieved when the bell rang, ending the class. He quickly made some notes in the book of blank pages that Keelee had added to the pouch and headed to his next class.

No one really spoke as they left, and Alador wondered if they had as much of a headache as he did. He didn't really understand why his head hurt so much, but he was thankful for the dim light. He quickly found his next class and stepped into a room with a large pool in the middle. There were only seven of them there when the bell rang, and Alador could tell that they all knew each other. He nodded when someone waved to him from the other side of the pool.

"Welcome to blue school," the woman called across the pool, "where you will learn to hate water as you never have before." A couple of others chuckled. "My name is Ness." She began pointing around the circle. "This is Rason, Chel, Aldta, Chrisanne, Sante and Cwena. Master Thor'el will be along shortly. He's a fun sort. So what's your name?"

The words came out in a flurry. Ness was a Daezun-looking woman with the typical brown braided locks. Her eyes, however, were a strange light purple. Alador was beginning to see a pattern – it seemed like everyone he'd met who could use magic had strange eyes.

His were silver. Did the magic alter a small one's forming at birth? He knew that magic could change the person who used it, like the way his uncle's hair had been bleached white. He wondered if perhaps that alteration started at birth.

"Nice to meet you." Alador smiled at them despite his headache. "My name is Alador," he murmured, setting his bag on a bench along the side.

"Well met, Alador. How long have you known you were a mage?" Cwena was also more Daezun in appearance, though her hair was the color of soft wheat. She was thinner and her voice had a more musical lilt to it.

Alador felt rather bland in comparison to those he stood with as he moved closer to the pool. "I guess I've suspected for a few months, but really known? - only about three weeks." He frowned at the pool of water, remembering the day at the bathhouse when he'd heated the water in his anger and fear, scalding the bullies that had nearly drowned him. Of course, when that had happened, Alador hadn't realized he'd been the cause.

Rason nodded. "Most of us here are fairly new. This is only my second week. Ness there is about to be assigned to a squad. It takes some getting used to, but you'll get the hang of it. It is not so bad as long as you do what you are told." Rason looked far more Lerdenian than the others, his graceful figure clothed in dark blue robes. His black hair was pulled back, and Alador could see streaks of white through it.

"My bo…" Alador paused considering what he should call Keelee, "…friend said there were punishments for… transgressions, but I didn't have time to ask what sort of transgressions, or what sort of punishments…" Alador blinked as everyone suddenly looked down, apparently ignoring his question.

"I am sure you will find that out soon enough, Alador," said a firm voice behind him. He turned to see a man of advanced years grinning broadly.

He was clearly an elder of Daezun birth. His sparkling eyes reminded Alador of Dorien, though he was much older: they seemed to hold that same genuine joy of life. His build was larger than most he had seen in the caves. He, too, was dressed in robes of blue, though they were paler than Rason's.

"Greetings, Elder Thor'el." Alador said with a respectful bow, giving his teacher the title he would have had in the Daezun village he missed so much.

Ah, not broken of village life yet, I see. Sad to know that that will soon be lost." The mage tsked as he came to the pool. "Today, most of you will be learning to part water. Sometimes the quickest way to escape is through water, and swimming takes too long. Ness, take Alador to the table and teach him to change liquids."

Ness nodded and beckoned Alador around the pool. He would have much rather learned to part water, but he supposed he'd be better off starting small. He glanced with longing at the pool before joining Ness at a table where liquid-filled containers were lined up.

She sat a chalice of water on the table before them. "This spell is most useful to ensure the enemy has not poisoned your water supply. While most of us could never manage a whole pond or lake, we can nullify any substances in our own water barrels."

She smiled at him. "It's also helpful if you need another form of liquid, like oil, or if you're sick of water and want wine or juice. Chrisanna over there took all the alcohol out of the barrels at a red sphere party once. Basically, they were left with barrels of juice and water. They were... a little upset , but we thought it was hilarious."

Alador grinned. "I once made a keg pop its bung. It was quite enjoyable watching the blustering innkeeper trying to plug it up."

Ness grinned back and continued her teaching. "You have to know the taste of what you are trying to create. You have to be able to recall that taste in your mouth to make it happen. Which means to make lamp oil, for example, you have to have tasted it."

Alador wrinkled his nose at that thought, but nodded, for it made sense. Magic seemed to be tied mainly to one's senses and the ability to draw forth that power to match the memories. While he knew this was not the whole story, there seemed to be a large correlation - at least in simple spells. "Can you make poisons this way?" he asked curiously, eying the goblet of water.

"You can, but it's dangerous. You have to remember the taste, so you'd risk the fate of the poison you tasted. Some mages have worked on this alongside a white mage who can nullify the effects of the poison quickly. Personally, I just like the idea that if I'm sick of water, I can drink anything I've tasted before."

Ness smiled at him, picking up the chalice and swirling her finger through it. The water changed into a dark rose color. "My favorite wine. Here, taste." She took a small sip to show him it was safe.

Alador took the chalice curiously and took a small sip. It was a strange combination of spice, apple, prickleberry, and something he couldn't make out, but it tasted good. "I see why you like it." He smiled at Ness, who returned the smile.

"You try it now. Think of something you know the taste of – it has to be liquid – and run your finger through the water." She nodded to the chalice and crossed her arms, waiting.

Alador frowned. He mostly drank tea, water, and prickleberry juice; he rarely wasted trading slips on drink. He stared at the cup and just decided to go with prickleberry juice. The thought reminded him of Sofie and Gregor, and then he thought of Mesiande as he ran his finger through the water sadly. He looked down to see it had changed color. It was clear again. Prickleberry juice was not clear like water. He took a small sip and wrinkled his nose in surprise. It tasted like salt.

Ness stared at the cup. "What is it?" she asked curiously, not willing to try it after his reaction to the taste.

"I don't know. It tastes like salt," Alador said with confusion.

Ness put a finger in the water and then put it in her mouth. "It does." She watched him and he squirmed a bit under the intensity of her gaze. She leaned into him. "What were you thinking of when you put your finger in the water?"

Alador thought for a moment. "Well, I was thinking of this juice from home, but then I started thinking of home," he admitted.

"Are you sad when you think of home?" She looked at him and then to the others around the practice pool before turning back to him.

Alador nodded as a small lump of emotion formed in his throat. "I don't know any liquids that taste like salt. I don't know what happened," he muttered.

"I know what happened." Ness put a reassuring hand on his arm. "That's the taste of your tears," she explained. She gave him a minute to absorb that, watching him stare at the cup. "Okay, we'll try again, but the thing about magic, Alador, is that you can't be distracted. You ever shoot a bow?"

Alador nodded yes. "I am a dead shot,"

"Then you have practised shooting with distractions. You know that no matter what's going on around you, the only thing that matters is the target, right?"

Alador nodded starting to get where she was going. He didn't tell her that the reason he was a dead shot was that, for some reason, the target loomed to him. He didn't know if that was common, and he didn't want to set himself apart from everyone on his first day.

"Good. Magic is the same way. No matter what's going on around you, when you chose a spell to use, that must be your only focus. In time, you'll find some spells require little mental effort – they're almost automatic – but others will need your full concentration.

That's why a battle mage is at his weakest when he's in the middle of casting a spell – he might not sense the approach of an enemy, or even if he does, he might not be able to stop casting. Some spells have more dangerous results if half-completed than when they're finished." She took on the tone of a teacher, and he could tell she'd practised this more than her fair share of times.

Alador nodded in response, still holding the chalice of salt water. "I see your point: if you lose focus on a target, the arrow will veer," he agreed, looking down at the chalice in his hand.

"Correct! Try again, and this time keep your focus," Ness commanded.

He refocused on the cup, using the same skills that Henrick had insisted on when he was practising the water cantrip. This time when he opened his eyes, the cup looked right, and it tasted like a fine prickleberry juice.

Ness took it from him and tasted it. "Oh, that is good. I've never had that." She took another drink and rolled it around her mouth. Alador could tell she was memorizing its feel and taste for future use.

Ness spent the next two hours making Alador turn that cup into as many liquids as he could imagine. She made him taste oil and other items that were liquid-based, such as a simple broth for when food could not be found.

She always seemed to have an entirely new set of liquids after Alador had gone through all the cups. She even taught him how to turn it to blood, though he could think of no good reason for that particular lesson. Ness seemed quite proud that she could do so. He didn't comment.

The bell rang, and Alador looked at his schedule. It was time to eat. The group beckoned him to come with them, and he grabbed his stuff and joined them. He was ravenous, having missed breakfast. He felt like something was gnawing at his stomach, like he hadn't eaten in weeks.

He'd been warned that magic was draining, and right now he was feeling it. Between the headache and the gnawing hunger, Alador was glad for the break. The group jostled and teased all the way to the dining hall. Alador fell to the back, content just to be with them.

They all went through the line for a tray of food. Alador made sure his was heaped. As he made his way to sit with his class, he saw Jon off by himself. Before Alador could choose which way to go, Flame appeared at his elbow. "Well, there you are! How are you adjusting to life on the dark side?" he teased. Flame's name matched his personality just as well as it matched the vibrancy of his hair.

Alador stood with a full tray and looked past Flame to Jon, but Jon was already leaving. He nodded to Alador on his way out, but before Alador could call after him. Flame had grasped his elbow and was drawing him towards another table. There sat a group of men and women that seemed just as gregarious as the man who guided him.

"Hey all, this is Alador, the one I was telling you about." Flame pushed Alador down into a chair.

The table of faces staring at him made Alador uncomfortable. Once again he found himself longing for the days when no one wanted him around. "Hello," he managed politely. As they all bellowed their welcomes, he managed to get in a few bites of food. He could not believe how hungry he was.

Flame plopped his tray down and slide in beside him. "So...there's this rumor that a body servant came with you." He grinned. "Is it true?" The women at the table groaned in response, but the men grinned and eyed Alador with the same interest in his answer that Flame seemed to have. Flame just nodded at them with a boyish grin.

"I... yes, I guess it's true." Alador flushed ; he'd been of the mindset to just tolerate Keelee's presence until he could find another solution; but last night was bound to have created complications...

Another man who looked a little older than Flame grinned wickedly. "I don't suppose you'd share?" He tried to look the picture of congenial innocence and failed horribly. One of the women hit him in the arm and laughter erupted around the table.

Alador growled out in response. "She is not property." He stabbed at another piece of meat and shoved it into his mouth. "Her body is her own to gift or share where she pleases," he managed to growl out as he chewed. The laughter at the table stilled as they realized he was serious.

Flame eyed him thoughtfully. "You're gonna have a lot of people ask you that, Alador. You might need some help watching out for her. I'd be happy to offer my services." Flame's tone oozed sincerity and commitment.

"Ha! He's the one you have to worry about," another woman quipped, bringing laughter back to the table.

Flame rolled his eyes and threw a piece of bread at her. The woman caught it with a laugh and popped it in her mouth as Flame turned back to Alador.

"I heard she's one of the most beautiful body servants in the caves. If that's true, well it wouldn't hurt for her to have some friends of yours watching out for her. Some are less concerned about the personal feelings of a servant than you are."

Alador looked at him for a long moment. "I hadn't thought about that." He shoved more food in, knowing he had lessons in swordplay all afternoon till dinner.

Flame nodded. "Would you consider introducing me? I mean, I swear upon my maman's head that I will never lay a hand on her – not unless she offers herself to me." Flame put his hand in the air as if taking an oath.

"Careful Alador." One of the women at the table grinned at him. "He didn't just get that name because of his hair. He has a way with the ladies; in his wake lies a trail of broken, flamed-out hearts."

Flame looked wounded and placed a hand over his heart in mock pain. "It is not my fault they all start talking about settling down and having small ones."

"No, it's not; but is it *their* fault that you find another, the moment you creep from each bed?" she fired back. The whole table broke out in laughter.

"Hey, a man needs to taste the full menu before he settles on his favorite dish." Flame drew his chin up with playful arrogance. There was a consensus of groans at the table.

"I believe what I hear them saying is that even if you were to find a favored dish, you'd still keep tasting." Alador grinned at Flame.

"I have yet to find a favored dish," Flame defended. "I mean, there have been some worth a second bite, but if they start planning a menu, I'm gone. Members of The Blackguard really don't have that option – we move around too much. Besides, I don't want a passel of small ones." Flame looked truly put out at that thought.

Alador could not help but grin. In some ways, Flame reminded him a little of Gregor. "I will introduce her. After that, whatever happens, or doesn't happen, is up to her. I will swear to you, though, that if you touch her without her permission, there will be trouble between us." Alador motioned between himself and Flame with his fork to clarify which 'us' he was referring to.

"I understand. I don't take to men forcing themselves where they are not wanted," Flame agreed. "After dinner then…?" He looked at Alador hopefully.

Alador nodded. "After dinner. Now let me eat something before we have to go."

Flame patted him on the back and set to work on his own tray of food. The conversation at the table turned to classes for the rest of the day and gossip about who was sneaking into whose rooms at night. Alador listened, but his thoughts drifted to last night.

Maybe if Keelee could find someone else wanting a body slave, he wouldn't have to worry about repeats of last night. He'd promised Mesiande to be her housemate, and though he hadn't broken any vows in spending his night in the arms of another, a part of him felt like he'd betrayed her.

When everyone started moving to put up trays, Alador did as well. He suspected it would take some time to adapt to the rhythm of life here. Every village had a tempo that it danced to, and this was, in its own way, a village. It just happened to have been built in a cave, which was a little unnerving; but still. Alador made his way out to the practice ground, glad to be outside again.

It wasn't raining for the moment, and the sun shone, the plants glistening with the remnants of yesterday's storm. He and the other students were given time to adjust to the brighter light before being called to practice. Flame helped direct Alador to the beginner lessons before moving off on his own. Apparently, half of those residing in the caves practised swordplay in the morning and the other half in the evening. There were circles of guards in black leather everywhere.

He made his way to the beginners' circle and was paired up with another guardsman that had just arrived. Well, guardswoman was more accurate. She didn't speak to Alador when they were tasked together, neither did the instructor introduce Alador. He figured that the instructor was overseeing so many pairs that niceties weren't really important. They were tasked with practising cuts and parries, taking turns being offensive and defensive.

Alador found he was much better at parrying than he was at making the different types of cuts. He favored horizontal cuts, so the woman across from him soon learned to parry him easily. Alador did get praised on his ability to stay on the balls of his feet and pivot, though, and on his good stance.

When at last the bell rang for the day's end, Alador was exhausted. He now knew exactly what the armor smith had meant when she said he was out of shape. His arms and thighs hurt horribly, along with all the places without armor where he had been hit, having missed a parry.

Alador sat for a time, just catching his breath. His partner moved off to dinner, her motions just as slow and tired as his. It had been a good workout. His headache had diminished some after his last meal, but it still ached dully.

He looked around... This particular practice yard was fenced with a stone wall to give it definition. The inside portion was hard dirt, and here and there it was darkened by the spill of blood from minor mishaps. He got up to move out the practice yard when a man with cold eyes and a hard face stepped into his path. Alador immediately sensed that this man was looking for trouble.

"So, you are the spoiled Guldalian bastard," the brown-haired man said, spitting after the last word to emphasize his contempt.

"I apologize if I've offended you somehow, but I don't think we've been introduced." Alador was not armored and even practice blades could do harm if there was intent not forgetting that everyone here knew something about magic.

"How about you and I get a little extra practice in before we go to dinner? I find myself in need of a taste of privileged blood." The man drew his sword casually.

Alador held up his hands. "I don't want a fight." He eyed the man who'd clearly come with the intent to do him harm. Despite his words, Alador moved to square himself against this threat.

The man's lips curled up into a mocking sneer. "Too bad." He let out a small cry as he lunged toward Alador.

Alador dove out of the way at the last moment, the tip of the man's blade whistling by his ear. Freezing in a moment of panic, he barely managed to get his blade from his sheath in time to block the block the wide arc toward his chest with the flat of his own blade. Alador pushed up against the blade, stumbling backwards as he tried to recover from such a vulnerable position.

The man gave a low chuckle as he circled his blade through the air, making it sing in its movement. "Seems the spoiled bastard has a bit of fight in him after all!" Alador managed to find balance on the balls of his feet, giving note that the blade the man wielded was razor sharp and not a practice blade.

His eyes went wide, watching the blade like it was a viper. Fear pumped through Alador's veins, and his heart raced. He knew the man intended to kill him.

The man lunged at him once again. Sudden adrenaline lent Alador strength, and parries and blocks came hard and fast. He had no magic for an offensive spell; he back-peddled, trying to put some distance between him and his assailant. It was to no avail and he had the sickening realisation that death was staring him in the face.

He glanced around frantically. He was about to be slain, and had no idea what he'd done to this man. Why was no one stopping this? Why had no one noticed? Alador's breathing was labored, and the wicked grin on his opponent's face made it clear that the man was toying with him.

The blows of their blades were wearing down what little strength Alador had left. He felt the stone wall at his back, its sharp edge biting as he fell against it. His terror began to build as the man waved his sword in a testing arc, forcing Alador to follow its lethal point. His assailant's mocking grin confirmed how little effort he had spent on besting him.

The man tensed as if to come in for his final attempt, and Alador's sword point snapped up despite the burning fire in his arms. He closed his eyes as if that would somehow shield him from this powerful final blow, but the sharp impact of steel on steel didn't come.

Instead, Alador heard the sound of a blade being dropped on the ground. His eyes snapped open and he dropped back into a defensive position, his sword arm trembling. His assailant was staggering back with his hands to his throat, gasping; his sword lying uselessly in the dirt. What trick was this?

Alador spotted Jon at that moment. The death mage stood calmly, a hand before him, pointed at Alador's attacker. "Enough Maxis. This mage is under my protection. I suggest you pass that on to your little pack. I assure you that any harm that comes to him I will return tenfold."

Alador stood up, wide-eyed. His sword weighed a ton, and the cold sweat on his palms had made it difficult to grasp. The swordsman before him still clutched his throat, gasping for breath. Slowly he slipped to his knees...

Alador looked at Jon with real alarm. "Jon stop! You're killing him!" Alador's sword wavered in his hand: he didn't know what would happen if he stopped Jon from doing... whatever he was doing.

"Why not? He was going to kill you," Jon snarled out. He didn't move, only continued to focus on the man on his knees, this Maxis...

"Please Jon. I don't need someone's death on my hands my first day here," Alador wheezed out, hard-pressed to catch his own breath. His leg pulsed with pain and he realized he was wounded; he glanced down to see blood running down his leg.

"You are kinder than I, Alador." Jon's voice was cold as he let go of whatever he was doing and the man fell forward, gasping raggedly for air. Jon walked forward and kicked Maxis' blade out of reach. "Stay down, or I will kill you, right now," he hissed.

He beckoned Alador to move out of the ring, keeping an eye on his would-be killer. Before turning on his heel to follow Alador, he snarled down at the man: "Tell your boss to do his own dirty work, and tell him he'll have me to deal with whenever he's ready to try."

Chapter Sixteen

The sun was setting, casting an orange light over Alador as he limped into the caverns. He remained silent for the moment; it took all of his concentration just to keep moving. His body was screaming in pain, and his leg burned – Alador noticed that his pants were soaked with his own blood, now dripping into his boot.

Jon quickly caught up to him and matched step as he looked Alador over. "I am taking you to the healers," he stated in the solemn tone he seemed to favor. He offered his arm, which Alador leaned on gratefully.

"I would rather go to my room… Keelee can bandage it. It's not deep. The fewer who know about this, the better," Alador answered, his voice as shaky as his body.

"Are you certain? You could just say that you were injured in practice. Such things do happen," Jon pointed out.

Alador sighed. "I've only been here a day. I would really rather keep my head down." He added a soft mutter to himself: "…not that that strategy seems to be working."

Between Keelee, his uncle, and now this new danger in the shape of Maxis, it was almost as bad as it had been in the village with Trelmar and his cronies. Now that fear was no longer pumping adrenaline into his system the realization of how close he'd come to death filled his thoughts. His heart pounded in the same way it had when the elder declared that he would be hanged for Trelmar's murder.

"As you wish." Jon led Alador through the quiet halls to his room. No one else dallied around the halls – everyone was off to dinner. Alador's wound and his exhaustion forced them to move slowly.

Keelee wasn't there when they entered the room. Alador sighed softly: of course she was elsewhere the one time he needed her. He limped to a chair and slid into it, trying not to jar the wound in his legs. Alador obviously needed that armor if he was going to have to worry about someone actually trying to kill him. The wound wasn't bleeding heavily, at least; but it was still bleeding...

Jon didn't speak as he moved to Alador's wardrobe. He frowned at the amount of women's clothing within it, glancing at Alador with a look that spoke volumes. Alador's expression turned sheepish, and he shook his head. Jon pushed aside the dresses and rummaged about until he found and withdrew a small box.

"What's that?" Alador asked curiously, wondering how Jon even knew what he was looking for when it was Alador's wardrobe he was searching through.

"Healing kit," Jon stated. "Drop your pants and let's get that wound bound up."

Alador was in too much pain to point out that he wasn't wearing anything under his pants – he'd dressed swiftly and hadn't bothered with leggings. He slid out of them, knowing he'd need to change anyway. Jon put a salve over the open slit in his upper thigh that burned but seemed to slow the bleeding, then quickly wrapped and tied linen over it. When he was done, Alador pulled on another pair of loose linen pants. Neither spoke, just seeing to what needed to be done. When at last Alador was dressed, he turned to Jon.

"You told this Maxis to tell his boss to see to his own dirty work. That means you know who he works for... Who is it?" Alador looked at Jon, who was putting the healing supplies neatly back into the box.

Jon slowly closed the box before turning to look at Alador, the silence between them palpable as he decided how much he was willing to disclose. "I'm curious to know what you did to anger him. Maxis has been known to do the Trench Lord's dirty work."

"Oh." Alador slowly sat on his bed. "I don't know, to be honest. I met him at a dinner my uncle held when I arrived. When we were introduced, it was clear he already hated me before we ever even spoke."

"You are going to have to be careful, Alador. Only your uncle himself would be a greater enemy in Silverport." Jon frowned, considering. "I won't be able to watch out for you except in the practice fields. I know Maxis has at least four accomplices he holds close, but whether they would take action or work for Aorun, I don't know." Jon's tone was even and thoughtful.

"Great - only been here a day and already I have to watch my back." Alador sighed.

"Don't think you're unique Alador. Every one of us has to watch our backs – most of us just have to watch out for your uncle." Jon's voice was solemn as he delivered this news.

Part of Alador wanted to dispute that. He wanted his bloodline to stand for something honourable, but he knew that Jon was telling the truth, if what his father had told him was anything to go by. Would he always be cursed by others for the blood that ran in his veins? "Sorry."

"A man once told me that you can't help the sphere of magic you were given by the Gods, or by the dragons. I would say this is also true of your bloodline. The apple doesn't always fall close to the tree. Sometimes fate carries it far away," Jon offered.

Alador smiled slowly. "A wise man that fellow must have been."

Jon gave a half smile back. "That remains to be seen. He seems to be courting death."

Alador chuckled and shook his head. "I don't know about you, but I'm starved." He still felt exhausted, but he was less unsteady now.

Jon nodded to his weapons rack. "You might want to carry a more potent blade when you aren't in practice, just in case."

Alador paused for a long moment. He would have preferred his bow, but it wasn't very useful or practical in the close confines of the caves. He sighed and switched weapons, sliding the sharper blade into his sheath. "Okay, let's go find some food."

"You seem rather driven by food." Jon led the way out of Alador's room.

"My father tells me that so many Lerdenians are ghostly and white because they don't provide enough energy to their bodies, and that you can minimize the damage if you eat a lot. I really don't want to end up all pale and with white hair," Alador pointed out.

"I haven't heard that. We've been told that power is fueled by a core of magic within us and the elements around us." Jon glanced at Alador curiously.

"Well, I tend to believe my father. His hair is as black as night and he looks far younger and healthier than my uncle." Alador shrugged. "Besides, it makes a good excuse to eat. I kind of like food."

Jon smirked slightly and led the way into the dining room. The two of them got trays and Jon, after considering a moment, added a second scoop as he led the way through the line. Alador just smiled and followed him. The two set about eating, not speaking much: they were comfortable enough in each other's company not to need to foster conversation. Jon had apparently withdrawn as deep into himself as Alador had into his own thoughts about his first day and near death.

Both were startled out of their concentrated eating by the sudden, boisterous appearance of Flame. "Well, you obviously don't mind breaking the mould on your first day." He nodded to Jon. "I mean, most people don't make friends right off with a black mage. No offense, Jon."

Jon nodded back. "None taken. I would have to care about what you think to take offense." He looked up and met Flame's gaze with deadpan seriousness.

Alador bit back the laughter that boiled up within him, both at Jon's comment and the look on Flame's face. Flame was clearly still digesting that remark.

"Thanks... I guess." Flame smirked at Jon before moving back to his original purpose. "You took forever to come to dinner. You promised to introduce me to Keelee tonight," he reminded Alador with boyish excitement.

Alador nodded. "I had to stop by my room before coming to the hall. She wasn't there, probably finding her own meal wherever she does that. I'm about done; meet me at the entrance to the hall in a few minutes. I have something to ask Jon here first."

Flame looked at Jon curiously, but then nodded. "Of course. I'll grab a pint and wait for you at the table nearest the entrance." He sauntered off.

"Is he always so cheerful?" Alador asked Jon, while watching Flame say hi and shaking hands as he walked through the hall.

"He's well-liked and generous," Jon answered in his strange, solemn monotone. "I don't trust him."

"Because he's well-liked, or because he's generous?" Alador looked back at Jon.

Jon picked up his mug, answering just before he took a drink. "Both." He sat the mug back down and spoke again. "What did you need to ask?"

Alador decided that Jon might be just a bit paranoid – just because someone had slips and was nice didn't mean he shouldn't like them. "I don't have any spells to protect myself. How can I study ahead?" Alador asked. "I need something till my sword skills are faster and stronger."

"Got your sphere spell book?" Jon asked.

"No, I left it in the room when we were bandaging my wound." Alador stated finishing the last bite on his tray and mopping up the juice with a piece of bread.

"The first section contains simple spells, easy for your sphere. The second part has the more useful and defensive spells, and the third section has your offensive spells," Jon said.

Alador knew which section he would be studying tonight. "Thank you. I'd best get Flame introduced to Keelee before he bursts at the seams." He picked up his tray. "I didn't thank you for... well, for saving my life." He eyed Jon with serious gratitude.

Jon just shrugged. "I've heard that's what friends do."

Alador peered at Jon for a long moment. "Then I guess I chose my friends wisely," he answered softly.

Jon looked up at him in all seriousness. "Some of them." He stood and walked off, tossing his tray in a nearby bin on his way out, leaving Alador to wonder what that meant. Alador moved around the table and put his own tray away. He scanned the room, but couldn't find Maxis anywhere, though he did feel a few eyes on him as he moved from the table he'd shared with Jon to the table where Flame waited.

Flame drained the rest of his flagon and then hopped up. "Now, let's go meet this fair damsel that everyone is talking about!"

Alador sighed. "Why do I get the feeling that you wouldn't be speaking to me if it weren't for Keelee?"

"Because it'd be half true. Not many out there would be willing to risk angering someone whose dinner mate is a black mage." Flame shrugged. "However, I did meet you first and, well, curiosity sometimes overrides healthy fear." Flame nudged him with an elbow and Alador winced. "Ah, sorry. I forget what first day in the fields is like sometimes."

Flame's happiness was contagious, despite Alador's determination not be cheered up, and he smiled. "What are so you curious about?"

Flame considered Alador's question. "Well, a lot of things, but let me just narrow that down to you. How did you afford a body servant? Did you buy her, or did your family give her to you? Does that mean you're rich? Is she as pretty as everyone says?" Flame walked backwards, looking at Alador as they walked down the hall.

"You're like a small one looking for sweets, you know that?" Alador reached out and jerked Flame to the side when he almost walked back into two women.

Flame just waved at them, causing the two to giggle, and kept walking backwards. "Yes, I know that. I'm told that a lot. And really, if what I hear is true, Keelee amounts to a sweet, right? Come on, tell me!" Flame clasped his hands together in a begging gesture.

Alador just chuckled. "You'll have to see for yourself," he said. "I don't judge such matters. I find her fair enough."

"What about in your bed, is she just fair enough?"

Alador's face darkened at that question, eyes narrowing. He stopped walking.

Flame stopped too. "Oops, too far. I got it, you're one of those guys who don't kiss and tell. I'm good with that." Flame gave him a guilty look, like a small one caught in mischief.

Alador just sighed. "My private affairs are just that Flame – private. Understood?" He began striding down the passage once more.

"Completely!" Flame acknowledged. He turned and fell into step with Alador.

"So is the question 'are you rich?' in the category of private affairs?" Flame asked with a bit more caution.

"I don't have to worry about slips," Alador conceded, "but that isn't because of my family. I earned my own way." Alador frowned at that. He wondered what happened to the trader he'd sold his stone to.

If he ever saw him, he was going to have to pay him back somehow. In truth, he'd been the one to steal from the man rather than the other way around, though he hadn't known at the time that he'd already taken the power from the stone. He felt a slight twinge of guilt.

"Right. Man of his own means. Are you in trade?" Flame asked curiously.

"No, I used to be a miner," Alador replied.

"Did you find a mine of medure?" Flame eyed him. That was every miner's dream.

"Something like that," Alador offered. It was a half-truth, but he didn't feel like sharing more. They reached the door and Alador opened it.

Keelee was there and turned when they entered, rushing to Alador and throwing herself into his arms. "Are you all right? I found your bloody clothes…I was so worried!" She pulled away and looked him over quickly, her face showing genuine concern.

Alador was forced to catch her as her arms went around his neck. "I'm fine, it was a flesh wound; easily cleaned up but left more blood than damage."

Flame stood nearby, staring open-mouthed at Keelee. Alador set Keelee down; she was looking particularly attractive at the moment. Her hair was brushed out, not braided, and it shone in the pale stone light. Her dress was a blue and green that matched her eyes, its bodice offering a fine view of her womanly attributes. In fact, Alador was not quite sure how her breasts were staying in that bodice – they looked ready to spring out.

"Keelee, may I present Flame. He begged me for an introduction, and since he's been kind since I arrived, I thought I'd humor him. That and, well, to be honest, I don't think he would have left me alone until I'd introduced you."

Keelee's eyes moved to Flame, who bowed low. "It is a pleasure to lay eyes on such a jewel of Silverport. The setting you're in hardly fits the beauty it graces."

Keelee blushed a bit. "Thank you, sir." She looked worriedly at Alador. "Are you gifting me?" she whispered to Alador, her eyes and tone panicked.

"No, Keelee, I will never gift you. As I've told others, your body is yours and you will decide who you choose to share it with, not I," Alador answered just as softly.

Flame slapped Alador on the back. "I can vouch for that – I heard him tell someone that myself." Alador winced in pain and groaned. "Gods, sorry man," Flame apologized immediately.

Keelee looked between them in surprise. "Oh," was the only word she managed.

Alador looked at Keelee and felt a moment of pleasure. He wondered how long it had been since she could choose her own path. "Keelee, I'd like a bath. If you two could direct me to somewhere I can bathe in private, then perhaps you and Flame could chat a while while I soak these aches. Flame suggested it wouldn't hurt for you to have more than just me to turn to if there's a problem - that is if you take to one another."

Flame looked at Alador. "Well, the baths themselves are public – lots of people use them. I know a couple of private pools, but they'll be cold."

Alador didn't mention he could heat them. "I would value privacy over heat right now. I have a lot to think about and could really just use some time alone." He didn't want to go into what he needed to think about, and apparently the look on his face was enough to deter questions.

Keelee immediately set to gathering up items. She emptied his pouch of books and put in a towel, soap and a change of clothing. Alador knew he probably reeked of sweat. His headache was still a dull pound – it wasn't distracting, but he was still aware of it. His eyes on Keelee scurrying about, he asked Flame: "Did your head hurt after spell practice?"

"Yup! Around my third day into classes, I asked about that. Master Tylorus told me that our magic is like a muscle and our brain is the focus of its use; so it's a lot like the rest of our body: unused to such exercise."

"It'll stop in a week or two, but if it gets too bad, the healers have a potion you can take to ease it," Flame answered with unusual seriousness. "I so remember that headache." He put a hand to his forehead and looked at Alador with real sympathy.

Keelee handed the bag to Alador and Flame, then turned to lead them out. It wasn't actually that far from his rooms, and the turns were simple. There was a crevice at the back of the hall that didn't look completely finished.

Flame slipped through it, revealing an actual cave not made by mortal hands. "I found this once just wandering. I come here sometimes when I want to be alone, too." He offered a hand to help Keelee through.

Keelee looked at the dirt and shook her head. "I will just stay out here. Maybe while Alador bathes we could take a walk in the practice field: I need some fresh air." She touched the stone at the side of the entry, then rubbed her fingers together.

Flame did not need a second bidding. "Enjoy, Alador. I'll bring her back to your room soon." He slipped back out the crevice and took Keelee's arm. "Right this way, milady. I would be proud to offer you a summer stroll under the stars." Flame gestured dramatically toward the roof of the cavern as if the stars were already overhead.

Alador rolled his eyes. He had no doubt Keelee would tell him if Flame got out of hand, but he believed Flame would keep his promise. He slipped through the crevice and looked around.

The cave was about the height of two men at its tallest point. The pool looked deep, but exactly how deep it was, he couldn't tell through its glass-like stillness. No running water contributed to it. Alador stared into the pool curiously. On one side, there was a ledge that looked just deep enough to sit on.

He stripped down and put a toe in the water – it was cold, but not uncomfortably so. He unwrapped the linen on his leg to find that, while it was bloodied, the wound had already fully closed. What ointment had Jon put on it? Alador slipped into the water, shuddering at the chill. Though it felt good in more ways than one, he noticed that his headache's pounding worsened almost immediately.

Alador sighed and concentrated on the pool, only intensifying the headache. He pressed through the pain, his fingers stirring it as he focused on heating the water. He no longer needed to find anger now that he knew what his magic felt like, but it still took some time – given how tired he was and how deep the pool. He laid his head back on the dry edge to soak away the day's hurts and bruises. After a time, the headache slowly eased its resounding throb.

It was the first time all day Alador had been able to think. The lessons had excited him. He'd always wanted to learn magic and only the potential loss of Mesiande had stilled that desire. Now that he had come to accept his separation from Mesiande – at least somewhat – his desire to learn all that could be learned had returned.

On top of that, Alador was still fairly certain that his geas was to save the dragon fledglings being placed into slavery, and he'd need magic to do that. He wasn't sure how he would know when he had finished whatever Renamaum had saddled him with, but he was fairly sure this was it.

The fact that the Trench Lord, Aorun, had sent someone to kill him was puzzling. Alador had no idea what he could have done to the man to earn such hatred. Surely it couldn't be just because he was half-Daezun.

Everyone here was of mixed blood in some capacity. He doubted that was the sole reason he'd been singled out; but it was a puzzle he was too tired to solve, and there were too few facts to help decipher the problem.

Alador finally let his mind go to the one thing he had been determined not to think about all day. Last night, he'd bedded Keelee. Just the thought sent a wrenching knife through his heart. He knew that if Mesiande had sought another from the circle, he would be devastated. By the gods, he would be devastated if she were to choose someone other than him, even if he were there at the circle. How could he have let Keelee continue? He should have stopped her.

Alador groaned as he realized how much like his father he really was. He had lied and avoided truths. He had used Keelee. The fact that she had offered herself freely didn't matter. He'd felt nothing for her but the relief of his body's needs and the common comfort of another caring soul. Is that how Henrick felt for his mother? Was she just an outlet for his needs and a tender hand?

Alador ducked under the water in confusion. He knew he could not cast Keelee out, not after she'd shared her fear of the trenches. Maybe she would take a liking to Flame or someone else here and would be willing to let Alador gift her to him.

He wouldn't do so against her will. He also knew that she was skilled and, in moments of weakness, having a beautiful woman in your bed with such skills was like putting sweets before a small one and telling them not to eat them.

Alador reached over the side and grabbed the soap and towel, looking at the pouch she had prepared. He could not deny that there were benefits to having a body servant. Having someone to lay out your things, seeing to your every need was something a man could get used to.

Keelee was just doing the work she was paid to do. Yes, that was it. Alador could look at it that way. She was not his love. She was not his desire. She was his servant and as such, his to command.

Having resolved this in his mind and numbed his heart to the consequences, Alador finished bathing with a slightly lighter spirit. He kept the water warm and comfortable and laid back to soak away the day's bruises.

Deep down, he knew that what he was thinking wasn't right, but it was a compromise he was willing to make. It was just comfort, nothing more. Besides, he was protecting her from both the Trench Lord and his uncle.

In another realm, Dethera, Goddess of the Night, smiled in cold satisfaction.

Chapter Seventeen

Aorun strode through the door pulling off his cloak and snapping it once to break loose the inevitable dust from the mines before hanging it on its peg. The new shaft he'd had to inspect hadn't produced more than a small vein of medure. The white stone used to make buildings in Silverport and other cities continued to be cut and removed in transportable sizes. A stone mage would easily be able to shape the pieces into proper form to work with.

Of all the mages, stone mages had some of the most profitable skills. Aorun had a couple of third-tier stone mages on his payroll. But he hadn't been looking for the stone that was Silverport's namesake; he had hoped that his men would unearth something more valuable in the new shaft.

The poor showing of medure had only caused Aorun's mood to slip further, and he'd already been on edge ever since the dinner at the High Minister's palace. On top of that, the numbers had been off when he'd gone over his reports with Sordith earlier: the shipments were down, and they'd lost one ship in a storm. Aorun was not looking forward to delivering that report to the High Minister. It seemed like nothing was going right that damned day.

Aorun sank behind his desk and thought back to the words that had passed between him and Sordith earlier. Sordith had pointed out that Aorun was losing focus. It was true: he wanted that woman, and he wanted that half-breed dead; but he didn't think it was impacting his decisions or his strength of command. The trenches still leapt to his will; its inhabitants still paid their fees as was required.

The connection between Aorun's loss of slips and his loss of focus was nothing more than a coincidence. The audacity of Sordith's accusation was clear. Aorun laid his head in his hands, trying to sort his thoughts. Perhaps he'd had a little too much to drink today.

There was a sharp rap at the door, bringing Aorun's head up. "Enter."

The half-breed, Maxis, came in through the door and strode before Aorun's desk, saluting smartly before the Trench Lord. "I have come to make my report on the man, Alador."

"He's dead already?" Aorun looked surprised. He'd thought the man weak, but not that weak.

"I made an attempt, but a complication arose and I thought I should make my report before going any further." Maxis' lip curled, and Aorun wasn't sure why; but he knew it wasn't good.

"It has been three days. How can it have got complicated in only three blasted days?"

Aorun stood and strode around his desk. He leaned back against it and folded his arms, staring Maxis down. The man looked almost entirely Daezun. Aorun couldn't stand him, of course, but he had some skill with magic and was a prime candidate for The Blackguard. He liked his women, ale, and slips – it made him easy to control and quick to do Aorun's bidding.

"I attempted to remove him as directed; I had him cornered like a cowed whelp when a black mage rose to his defense." Maxis would have said more, but the Trench Lord had put up his hand.

"SORDITH! OWEN! GET YOUR CARCASSES IN HERE!" Aorun hollered loudly! As usual, Sordith quietly emerged from apparently nowhere, his soft footfalls completely silent as he stepped through the doorway. Owen was not nearly as quiet, his weapons rattling as he sauntered through after him. He had a leg of fowl in his hand and was gnawing at it as he entered the room.

Aorun turned his attention back to the young man before him, pinching the bridge of his nose in frustration and closing his eyes. "Let me get this straight. You took this Alador on face-to-face. You failed to kill him and it was fairly obvious you were acting on my behalf?"

He dropped his hand back to his side and looked past Maxis.

Maxis frowned. "I didn't announce the fact that I was working for you, m'lord." He didn't see Aorun make eye contact with Sordith or hear the man slide up behind him. "I thought to remove him swiftly. I assure you that it was an excellent opportunity to remove him."

"What exactly were my instructions?" Aorun asked with a deadly tone.

"To see that he had an accident or mishap. Accidents in practice happen all the time." Maxis looked up at the Trench Lord, his tone a trifle arrogant.

"How often is a first-week trainee matched with one about to be assigned?" Aorun was fairly sure they didn't set new members into a ring with a honed blade.

Maxis' face lost its confident grin as the implication of Aorun's question sank in. "Uhh, well, I hadn't planned on anyone knowing who'd been on the other end of the blade." Maxis' expression made it clear that he hadn't considered that eventuality.

"Do you think me stupid?" Aorun asked softly. He'd had a horrible day and before him was the epitome of all the day's wrongs. His eyes traveled over the guardsman with an assessment of his stance.

"No m'lord. I think you must be quite intelligent to have attained the position of Trench Lord...," Maxis stammered.

"Let me tell you what I think happened. I think that you didn't want to bother with something a bit more intelligent and conniving. I think you wanted the credit for the swift kill to earn favor with me, but you miscalculated: either on the strength of his charm or of his arm." Aorun had not moved from his position against the red, gleaming desk. "Am I right Maxis?"

"It wasn't quite like that. I mean, I just found him there all alone." Maxis voice now held an edge of panic.

"But he wasn't alone. This... death mage was with him. How did you fail to notice a death mage, Maxis?" Aorun asked with deadly calm. "I will tell you how. You got arrogant and complacent, and sauntered in, exposing your identity and that of your employer to my enemy and to a death mage. So what should I do with you now?"

"Let me kill him. I will kill him for you before the day is out," Maxis promised urgently.

Aorun gave a small nod to Sordith who nodded back. "See, there is a slight problem with that. If he is killed now, then whispers of my involvement will ensue, and the High Minster will cast an accusing gaze in my direction. I cannot allow that to happen."

Aorun stroked his chin and then gave a small, malicious smile. "No, there is only one thing to do."

"Anything, m'lord. Speak it and I will see it done," Maxis swore, dropping to one knee.

"Ohhh, I know you will." Aorun smiled down at the guardsman as Sordith brought the sap down hard from behind him. Aorun hadn't had any fun for some time and was looking forward to this. "Take him below and string him up. I don't have a lot of time before dinner, so just the upper half today."

Sordith grabbed one upper arm, waiting for Owen, who'd finished his leg of fowl and went to toss the bone aside before realizing where he was. Looking around, he finally shoved it into his belt and grabbed Maxis' other arm, and the two men pulled him from the room.

Aorun moved around his desk and pulled open the drawer. He withdrew his bottle and took a deep pull before hiding it in the depths of the desk again. He enjoyed killing men, and he especially enjoyed doing it slowly. There was something about their screams that brought a rush of excitement.

Aorun usually took himself off to Aueris' place after he was done. There were a couple women there that had tough constitutions and could handle it rough. Maybe today would end on a slightly better note.

By the time he'd wandered down into the cellars below, Sordith and Owen had already almost finished stringing the man up. Aorun was careful to ensure that those with magic skills were gagged and hung with special metal gloves.

Binding them carefully seemed to minimize the number and type of spells they could cast – Aorun had only seen a few fourth and fifth tier mages have any proficiency without focal movements and words. He helped them anchor the man's feet to the floor, and the three of them stretched Maxis up so that his body was taut. "Leave us."

Owen nodded with disappointment and lumbered out the door. He didn't need to be told twice since the incident with the rain water. Sordith, however, paused at the door. "You sure about this? He is well-placed, and has friends…." Sordith eyed Aorun with concern.

"You heard him; he was seen. Either he has earned the ire of a death mage or will soon be brought before his command. I cannot have my connection to this business confirmed. If he acted so incautiously in this instance, I would hazard a guess that he has boasted about his extra slips, and where they came from." Aorun eyed the hanging man with clear distaste.

"I just need to hear you say that it's his failure and not his… ethnicity that brings him to this end," Sordith sighed softly, his copper eyes fixing on the Trench Lord.

Aorun did not look at Sordith. "Let us just say that his ethnicity makes this pleasure all the sweeter. I wish it were Alador I had hanging here. To hear his screams would be such wondrous music to my ears. To watch the High Minister's bastard nephew dance before my blades..." He strolled casually around the mage, eying his body as if deciding where to start.

"Your preoccupation with that man's death is going to be your undoing," Sordith warned softly.

"Fret not, Sordith. As long as my feet are planted on this isle, my death is not going to occur anytime soon, so quit hoping." Aorun finally looked at Sordith and winked. "I know how I die and it won't be by some half-breed's hand."

Sordith just shook his head and slipped from the room. Aorun watched him go. Few men had the assurance that he had concerning the manner of their death. As long as he avoided setting up the situation in the first place, he did not fear death. He got one of the buckets of seawater that were kept here and threw it into Maxis' face, watching with satisfaction as the man sputtered awake.

"As you can see, you will be doing what needs to be done today. You will writhe here, a victim of your own arrogance." Aorun went to the table where his tools were kept and picked up a nine-tailed whip. He snapped it a couple times. "I really do not tolerate failure well." His cold snarl was as cutting as the knife he often wielded. Aorun moved around to the mage's back. "Let us count out your failures, shall we?"

He snapped the whip, watching as the nine lines of crystal-imbedded leather tore into the man's back. "One, you disobeyed my orders." Aorun twisted the grip as he jerked it back, letting the crystals dig in and tear , taking delight in the muffled tortured scream .

He didn't lash again immediately: he'd learned that if the blows came too fast, a man could quickly numb his mind to the pain. So Aorun waited for that gasp of breath that came with the body's acceptance of the first level of agony, then snapped the whip out again.

"Two, having chosen to disobey my orders, you failed to kill him." Aorun smiled as Maxis tried to move. He was bound too securely: served up to provide Aorun with perverse pleasure. The Trench Lord walked away, coiling the whip, to where he had a mug and bottle stashed. He poured himself a splash of smalgut and downed it before walking back, stopping to look Maxis in the eyes.

"It is a pity that I can't let others watch, but I can't have the entire Black Guard down on me, wanting to avenge one of their own." Aorun reached up and gently wiped a tear from Maxis' cheek. "Now, now. No tears. You earned this…"

Aorun's tone was sickly sweet. "We were counting the reasons why, remember?" He snapped the whip a few times as he walked around to the man's back again. Maxis' body braced at each snap, and then shuddered when there was no pain to accompany the snap, bringing a smile of delicious anticipation to Aorun's face.

"Let's see… where was I? Ah yes." He snapped the lash out again; this time the angle crossed the other lines, leaving a trail of bleeding, crossed marks. "Three, you let a black mage know, or confirmed for him, who you work for. This will have alerted my young foe to my plans."

The thought made Aorun angry and he struck the man again. Not finding sufficient release from his fury, he brought his whip down six more times, watching in a paroxysm of pleasure as the helpless body writhed and screamed and bled with increasing profusion.

Blood pooled around Maxis' feet. Aorun stopped at six only because the mage had passed out and sagged forward. Aorun tossed the bloodied whip aside and got another bucket of seawater, throwing half of it into Maxis' face.

Even as he regained consciousness, blinking in confusion, his eyes stinging from salt water he could not wipe from his sodden hair, Aorun tossed the rest of the bucket onto the man's back to assess his handy work.

The salt-filled water washed across the open marks, drawing another scream of agony from Maxis' gagged mouth. Aorun walked around to face him. "As you can see, failure to serve the Trench Lord is not taken lightly, my dear Maxis." Aorun's tone was one of a disappointed father, entirely inappropriate for what he was doing to the man before him.

Maxis was sobbing now; words begging for mercy could be made out even through the gag. Aorun went for another shot of liquor. The torture of this helpless fool wasn't assuaging that black need within him. He knew deep down that the only thing that would bring him the release he needed was to have Alador, and now he would have to wait.

He would have to bide his time and wait because of this arrogant idiot. Aorun wanted Maxis to die slowly, in as much pain as he could contrive. He wanted him conscious throughout the deliciously agonizing process. He considered a moment, tapping the glass against his lips.

Aorun put the glass down. He went to the table and carefully chose a blade – a knife with a deadly point and a convex blade. He touched the tip and smiled as a small bead of blood formed on his finger. Yes, this would do nicely for what he had in mind. He moved once again behind the whimpering man.

"I would tell you this is not going to hurt, but alas, I would be lying," he said, his soft voice just below Maxis' ear. A moment later, he smelled the sharp stench of urine.

Aorun plunged the blade into Maxis, just above the pelvis and next to his spine. The damage to the nerves quickly paralyzed Maxis' left leg. Aorun waited for the man to quit screaming before he spoke.

"You felt that, didn't you? Even if I were to stop here, you would be paralyzed for life in that leg. While you can feel where my blade is…" Aorun took a dagger from his belt and plunged into the man's left leg, "…you can't feel anything below it."

He peered around and looked up at horrified expression on Maxis' face as he stared down at the dagger in his leg. He really enjoyed watching the abject terror and excruciating pain in the man's eyes.

With an agonizingly slow upward motion, Aorun dragged the knife piercing first a kidney and then gouging into other vital organs. Maxis' screams were loud, despite the gag, as the pain flooded through him. Aorun took delight in cutting his way slowly up to the mage's diaphragm.

"I am going to go a little higher now. It will stop you from being able to get air. You will live a short time, all the while fighting for breath. Of all the ways a man can die, I find this one most interesting to watch."

Aorun pulled up one more time and pierced the man's diaphragm, abruptly cutting off the man's muffled screams. Maxis hung there, still alive and trying to breathe, his eyes dazed with pain.

Aorun moved around front of Maxis again, tossing the knife aside and picking up his bottle without the glass. After retrieving his dagger from Maxis' leg, he sat on a barrel, drinking and watching as the writhing and gurgling gradually diminished and the light flickered and faded from the guardsman's dying eyes.

Only when Aorun was truly sure that Maxis was dead did he upend the bottle and head out to the whorehouse. There was more than one way to forget a bad day.

Chapter Eighteen

Life quickly took on a routine inside The Blackguard caves. Alador would get up in the morning and check under the pillow, but the scroll case was never there. Mesiande had not written him back since his last letter.

He could only guess that she'd decided that his writing of magic and dragons was just too much, but he didn't stop hoping. He had asked Keelee if she had seen it, but the girl had just looked at him in confusion.

Alador had warned her that should she find such a tube, she was not to move it. He missed Mesiande, and he still intended to be at the circle next year. He could only hope that she had just decided not to write and that nothing had happened to her.

Each morning, Keelee would have Alador's things laid out for him. He felt more secure in the armor he'd been provided, though it had taken some getting used to. Then he'd hurry off to breakfast with Flame, and then to his classes.

Alador had studied hard on offensive spells, but he hadn't seen Maxis again since that first day on the fields. He didn't know if the man was avoiding him, or if he'd left the caverns. Alador was always relieved to see Jon appear at the end of his time in the practice fields.

The worst part of his day was the repetition in his magic classes. He could quickly learn simple spells, but his classes still forced him to cast them over and over again. Patience was not Alador's strong suit; this monotonous repetition of spells was boring and seemed like a waste of his time.

Dinner was his favorite time. Alador had found that Jon was extremely knowledgeable, and they'd often return to the fields after dinner to practice, study, or just talk. Jon was scheduled to be assigned before the next summer and seemed pleased enough about this. Alador, however, was worried – he had a good idea of what a commander would do with the skills that his friend possessed.

Another reason he liked dinner was that everyone gave him a wide berth when he was with the death mage. He didn't have to worry about questions about Keelee or his uncle, which sat just fine with Alador, considering how exhausted he usually was by dinner.

During the rest of the day, it was commonplace for his classmates to ask him about his uncle. Everyone seemed relieved that Luthian had not visited since he'd joined *The Blackguard*. When he'd asked Jon about this, the death mage told him Luthian used to come weekly to the caverns, and sometimes people were severely punished. He didn't go into details, and Alador didn't ask.

His half-days with Luthian became a game of cat and mouse. His uncle would teach him things he wanted Alador to know; Alador would constantly try to find out things his uncle tried to keep hidden. In the same game, Alador sidestepped more personal questions about his own desires and goals for fear of giving his uncle something he could use over him.

Despite the tension in this strange dance, Alador rather liked his visits with his uncle. Luthian made sure he met members of council and the upper tiers. As a result, Alador was becoming more comfortable at dinners and political appearances.

He still felt like Luthian's new favorite possession, however. His uncle had chosen a wardrobe and always had a servant lay out robes that would coordinate with his own. Alador hadn't failed to notice that he always seemed to be shadowed by his uncle. It reminded him of the backdrops in his brother Tentret's drawings.

Alador enjoyed spending his half-days with his father, though. They would discuss strategy, or learn magic that Alador knew his uncle didn't want him to know. He had learned spells like creating a field of magic around him that lesser spells could not penetrate. He had learned how to turn back a spell on the other caster and even how to make himself invulnerable to magic for a short time, though the drawback was he couldn't cast as long as he used this kind of protection. He still planned to talk to that dragon, so knowing how to protect against Keensight's breath weapon was going to be important.

Henrick was also teaching Alador how to enchant items: something Alador had specifically asked to learn. If he could leave *The Blackguard*, Alador hoped to start a life as a traveling enchanter like his father. He loved these spells and had enchanted his own blade and arrows. He'd even made a point of including both Flame's and Jon's: so that they'd have an edge if Maxis and his friends should ever become so bold again.

The only thing that bothered Alador on his half-days was the sense that he was being followed. He'd attempted to backtrack and catch his shadow, but had failed every time. He'd even taken some unusual routes, but never felt like he had shaken this set of unseen eyes. He had mentioned it to his father, but Henrick hadn't had much to offer in the way of advice. He'd thought it likely that Luthian had some sort of mage's eyes on him through a scrying pool or some similar device.

Keelee would go visit her father during these half-days - apparently he was a merchant of some sort on the second tier. Why Keelee could not return to her father instead of the trenches was something Alador didn't understand. It seemed to him that, as a father, he wouldn't want his daughter to be a body servant.

Keelee had shrugged Alador off the day he'd mentioned she might go home and, when he had attempted to press the matter, had taken on a full-out pout. Alador found himself unwilling to make the woman unhappy. She asked little from him and made life easier by keeping his room clean and his belongings organized. She warmed his bed, and often sought his attentions rather than him seeking hers.

Flame had taken to escorting Keelee on her half-days. Alador felt no sense of jealousy; he had meant it when he'd told her that her body was hers. She had made a point of telling him that Flame was always a perfect gentleman. Given Flame's reputation throughout the caverns, Alador doubted that he was ever a perfect gentleman.

He saw them sometimes, heads close together and laughing at some private joke, but Alador let them go about their time together without questions; he didn't really care to know. It gave him time alone, which was a luxury in the caverns.

She still slept in his bed every night, and had truly become his body servant. Alador had fought twinges of guilt for the first few weeks, but as time stretched on with no word from Mesiande, he'd become more accepting of her attentions. He continued to rationalize that she was earning her keep and since he did not force her, there was no harm.

He still dreamed about the dragons, usually a repeat of the dream from the magic pool or the one of Renamaum and Keensight above the bloodmine valley. He always woke up feeling like he was missing something crucial, but he couldn't quite put his finger on it.

Fall had drifted in with the fog, and with it more rain would come in off the sea. The caverns were often damp, but Alador was usually able to keep his room completely dry with his growing mastery of water. The caverns did not seem to change in temperature much, but the dampness made it feel chilly when compared to the heat of late summer.

It was on such a fall day that Alador was spending one of his half-days to visit his uncle. As usual, robes were laid out. The one time that Alador had come down in something less formal, Luthian had just spelled him with the outfit he had chosen in the first place. Rather than get into a war over his clothing, Alador had given in. He had gotten used to the robes over time and now did not find them nearly as uncomfortable.

Luthian had been teaching Alador Draconic. Most higher level spells, he had learned, were written in this complex language. Last half-day, Luthian had sent him home with a book: to practise. It had been a book on the use of storms in magic: how to call lightning, create windstorms and even snowstorms.

The spells for an actual storm were complex and required the presence of the individual components . The type of storm desired each had variations in the components required. Alador's growing understanding of the Draconic language had increased throughout the week as he was fascinated with this book. His favorite spell was the one that called "Lightning". It felt natural to feel the sparks of light dancing in his hands.

So far, Luthian had not shown up but that was not unusual. Alador was working in the practice room on the creation of a small whirlwind. He laughed with delight as his robes whipped around him sending the small swirling mass around the room at his direction. He had not heard the door open so when the voice spoke, he lost concentration and the dust in the wind fell to the ground slowly as the spiral died down.

"Very impressive in just a week." Luthian clapped his hands together slowly as he shut the door and walked further into the room. "I am impressed. I had expected you still to be struggling with the translation a bit."

Alador had not wanted his uncle to discern how much he had picked up and was rather frustrated that he had not been more careful. "I find the language fascinating uncle; but I fear I have not got much past the chapter on wind." It was a lie, but one that now slipped off his tongue quite easily. Lying to his uncle had become normal to him.

"I see. Well, impressive none the less." Luthian walked over to the cupboard to pull out some items as he spoke further.

"Uncle, why is this language not taught to *The Blackguard*?" He asked as he moved to take a few items from Luthian to carry to the table.

"There are two reasons. First, if a spell is attempted without the proper amount of power in the mage, the results can be disastrous. The second reason is a matter of loyalty: I do not trust most of *The Blackguard* to remain truly loyal - were they to have more power than they are currently allowed."

"However, some have been found to have motivations that support Lerdenia and have shown unusual levels of ability. Those are taught privately the language and the spells that will support both *The Blackguard* and the mage in question."

Carefully, Luthian set a large spellbook on the table. It was a book that he had not let Alador look through, though he had shown him appropriate pages during practice. Alador wanted that book more than anything he had seen in his uncle's mansion. "You are trusting me with this knowledge," he pointed out.

"You are family." Luthian conceded. "I cannot have a nephew of mine who is poorly trained. It just wouldn't look right."

Alador tipped his head to look at his uncle in disbelief. "You don't strike me as someone who sets any store by what others think?"

"Usually I don't." Luthian admitted. "However, I have been unable to produce a child, and that makes you heir to our line."

Alador had not considered this. His father had mentioned no other children, and now that he thought about it, neither one had housemates. His father often had some beautiful woman in his home for a short time, and his uncle had them everywhere. Yet, there was no consistency in the women who attended either man. "Why do you not take a mate?"

"I find that a woman changes once you are paired. I have watched many women remove their own mates from their path to gain power. I prefer to sleep safely at night." Luthian shared this observation in a matter-of-fact way.

"What exactly am I inheriting?" He knew that the place on the tiers was earned by each mage's merit: that you could only live in the household of a higher mage by his grace and goodwill.

"Your father and I are hardly without means. I would not see the Guldalian line die with us both, and I doubt there will ever be a more suitable heir to our power and knowledge." Luthian smiled warmly at Alador.

"But, I am a half-breed. They cannot rise above the third tier," Alador pointed out with a frown. "Do you not want an heir that is of full blood?" Luthian was quiet for a moment as he leafed through the thick book in front of him.

"That would be the most desirable option, but… at this time, you are what I have." In spite of the warmth in his recent smile, Luthian soft, cold tones seemed to make it clear that Alador would not have been his ideal choice when it came to an heir.

"And if either of you should have a pure-bred Lerdenian child, what then?" Alador asked watching his uncle closely.

"Then you will have benefited greatly at no loss to me: for you are still family and will make a powerful ally." Luthian looked at Alador blandly.

Alador was frustrated that he could not read behind his uncle's mask. The man could lie so easily, giving no indication of it in tone or facial expression. It was a skill he was learning to copy. He made sure to tell half-truths now and then in a way Luthian would catch so he would not look too closely at the things Alador was attempting to keep hidden. He had taken his father's warning of Luthian's ill-intent quite seriously.

Before Alador could respond, Luthian beckoned him over. "See if you can make this out." He pointed to a short spell on the page he had finally found in his searching.

Alador moved beside him and with much difficulty began to decipher the Draconic words.

"Ekess vehafor vi zkhaaneth, ir zklaen tepoha vi yoweth montu de svaklar ir shilta focus. nurti rechan nomeno tija de vi … lae coi geou qe ….. irsa wer ….. di wer tharm."

He looked up at Luthian. "A maelstrom, like spinning water?" He looked back down at the instructions: trying to second-guess the meaning of the words he did not recognize.

"Very good. This is what we will practise today. Memorize the words and then we will go on a short walk to a bathing pool for you to attempt it," Luthian instructed firmly.

Alador took his time, despite the impatient sighing of his uncle. He wasn't just memorizing the words his uncle had pointed at; he took the time also to commit to memory the adjoining page on the control of currents. To buy a little more time, he looked up at Luthian.

"I am sorry uncle, the words are in some sort of rhyme that I am having trouble keeping in rhythm in my head. What is this word?" He looked up helplessly at Luthian.

Luthian sighed with exasperation and looked to where he pointed. "Churn, that word is churn."

"Ah yes. I almost have it." He kept his finger on the spell that Luthian was seeking. He already had it committed to memory as he swiftly repeated the two spells back to back in his mind until he was sure he had them both. When he got back to his room, he would transcribe them into his personal spellbook.

Luthian was pacing as Alador worked to memorize the spell. He kept glancing over at Alador. Alador had a hard time not grinning as he would occasionally sigh in frustration just to solidify his struggles with the spell.

"Come Alador, it is not that complicated of a spell in its actual words." Luthian finally moved to his side once more.

"I am sorry. I do not memorize well when pressured and well, your pacing is not helping." Alador looked up at Luthian innocently. "However, I think I have it."

"It's about time." Luthian stated, not apologizing for his impatience. "Come, we will go see if you can do this." He picked up the book and shoved it back into the cupboard, locking it securely before he led Alador outside.

Alador knew this was one of those spells that his father had encouraged him to falter. Luthian wanted him to learn it and seemed almost desperate to see it performed. He considered the wording and what he could do to thwart his success without creating harm or being too obvious. He spent the entire time they were walking thinking on how to do this.

Fortunately, Luthian's impatience precluded conversation as they moved through the mansion and outside. His uncle's long legs had Alador moving swiftly to keep up.

Luthian led him to a pool at the center of the mansion's impressive gardens. Alador was so lost in thought that he barely acknowledged where they were. He looked around when they reached the pool. It was a beautiful sight, the pool was completely surrounded by foliage. The one day he had been able to wander the gardens, he had never seen it. It was protected from curious eyes and the water looked warm and inviting.

"I wish to see you form the spell here." Luthian commanded. He moved to a chair and sat down, he waved Alador to the pool.

Alador looked at the pool and drew himself up proudly. He circled his hands as was described but faltered the rhyme. Of course, nothing happened. He had chosen words that would not set a different spell off, fearing the consequences of such a failing.

"Churn Alador. I told you that the word was churn. Try again." Luthian seemed on edge as he leaned forward from his chair watching.

"Oh yes. Sorry uncle." Alador attempted to look quite contrite. This time, he did not use the hand motions but recited the spell perfectly. He was careful not to touch his center of power.

Luthian jumped up in exasperation. "You are being deliberately obtuse, Alador. You know the spell requires motion." Luthian looked at Alador suspiciously.

"Uncle, you have never been so demanding of a spell. You are making me nervous." Alador defended dropping his eyes in purposeful deference.

Luthian took a breath and clasped his hands behind. "You are right. I am excited to see your potential. I apologize. Try it again, but this time use words and motions. Focus on the pool's center."

"Could you show me once?" Alador asked innocently. "It would be easier if you could show me."

"If I could do that blooming spell then I wouldn't ne..." Luthian bit his words off and looked at Alador suspiciously.

"Wouldn't need what, uncle?" Alador's eyes were firmly fixed on Luthian. He suspected his uncle had been about to say 'wouldn't need you.' What was this spell for, that his uncle needed him to learn it so desperately?

"I wouldn't need to wait forever for you to memorize it. We would have already been out here practising it." Luthian's swift words were a smooth counter, but Alador did not believe his response.

He dipped his head as he spoke. "I am sorry, uncle. I keep forgetting that because your strength is in fire, that spells of water and weather are beyond you." Though his words were innocently spoken, he knew full well that Luthian was frustrated that he had not been able to master water despite the many bloodstones he had absorbed.

"Try it again." Luthian growled out, plopping down in the chair without his usual grace.

Alador repeated the spell but barely touched his center. He managed to get the water swirling ever so slightly. He held his face as if he was pulling greatly, purposefully holding a grimace.

Luthian had stood back up and moved to the pool's edge watching the very slow movement of the pool. "Well, at least it is a circle." Luthian glanced at Alador. "Are you sure you are using all your power?"

When Alador looked over at his uncle, he purposefully dropped the spell. "Well, I was till you asked me a question." He looked back at the water. "I am hungry. Can we stop to eat?" He looked at back to Luthian.

Luthian threw up his hands in defeat. "I will have something sent out to you. Keep practising and join me for dinner." He turned on his heel and strode off, disappearing into the foliage.

Alador chuckled softly and peeled off his clothes. He slipped into the pool with a sigh of pleasure. He spent the rest of his afternoon swimming, eating and enjoying the warm rays of fall.

Chapter Nineteen

Alador received word a couple weeks later that his father would be leaving Silverport after Alador's next half-day. Henrick was overdue for his rounds in the Daezun villages, and had also promised to stop and speak to the dragon about Pruatra and her possible whereabouts.

Alador would much rather approach Renamaum's mate than the red dragon he'd managed to repel from Smallbrook by shooting it in the throat. He couldn't imagine any way the dragon would forgive him for that. If he had to approach Keensight, he'd likely just be blasted with flames.

When the half-day came around, Alador headed out of the caverns. He stopped by the ledge to watch the port below. It was raining again, but he still stood there staring at the high masts of the ships. Every once in a while, Alador had been assigned guard duty at the entrance to the cave; it was one of his favorite duties. When he stood guard, he could watch the ships. They fascinated him, and he'd sometimes daydream about what lay beyond the great isle. One day, he hoped to find out.

"You are a hard man to catch alone," a soft voice whispered just behind him.

Alador jumped when he heard the man speak, spinning with his sword half-drawn. A man in a dark grey robe stood before him, the raised cowl of his matching cloak obscuring most of his features. The man's hands were out and showed no weapons.

Alador was not in his armor: he was dressed instead in simple pants and a dark blue shirt. His black cloak was his only concession to his place in the guard, and he'd only worn that because of the rain.

"I find it unsafe to spend much time away from the company of others," he told the grey-cloaked stranger. He glanced to his right and saw that the guards by the opening were watching him closely; Alador nodded to one that he knew and received a slight nod back. He slowly slid his sword back into its scabbard. "Who are you and what do you want?"

"I am Sordith, and what I want, well… It's a little difficult to explain." He dropped his hands and stepped forward cautiously. "I wonder if you would consider having a drink with me. I assure you that I will pick an inn where there are many eyes, if you feel unsafe."

Even though they were both now more relaxed, The man kept his hands where Alador could see them. Alador looked about. They weren't far from where the path to the caverns joined the busy streets of the third tier; it was true that there were few places to be caught alone.

"I'm failing to find a reason why I should take time out of my day to drink with a man who seems to know me, despite the fact that I don't know him." Alador wondered if these were the eyes he'd often felt on him.

"Let's just say I've a feeling we may need one another," Sordith answered. "Your call. I'm going to walk away now. I'll make for *The Boar's Head* and take a table in the back corner. Either you're interested in what I have to say or you're not. I will tell you, though, that I'll not approach you a second time."

The man spun and strode towards the main tier causeway: a place still busy with the midday markets. Alador watched Sordith stride off for a long moment, considering; but his curiosity got the better of him.

He knew the tavern that the man had spoken about – once in a while a few of *The Blackguard* would slip out in their free time to have a drink there. It was the closest place to the Cavern with ale and without the watchful eyes of those that held rank or instructed them.

Alador slipped in not far behind the mysterious man and worked his way through the crowded tap room to a table in the back. He had to wonder, as busy as it was, how this man had a private table. It was set back in an alcove, with three short walls about it that offered a little privacy.

Alador slipped out of his cloak and hung it on a nearby hook , then slipped into a seat across from the man. Sordith had a very relaxed manner, but his eyes moved constantly, as someone who was used to watching, and he had his back to the wall – easy in this particular location.

"All right. You have my curiosity," Alador told him. What's this about?"

"The Trench Lord," Sordith said softly. " Since your arrival, his mind has not been on business. He follows your every move, and he neglects the matters he should be attending to. As a result, profits are slipping, and that sits ill with my pockets…"

He fell silent as a barmaid slipped two mugs before them. Sordith took a drink from one then passed it to Alador, "…in case you're worried I'm out to poison you."

Alador blinked in surprise. Even as the woman sat the mugs down, he'd already decided he would not be drinking anything the man offered. He pulled the mug towards him with a nod of thanks.

"How do you know that Aorun is following my every move?" he asked softly, absently swirling the contents of his mug. The title 'Trench Lord' always made him cautious, like he was sensing the presence of Trelmar all over again.

"Because I'm one of the ones he sends to follow you," Sordith answered with a shrug. "I follow you on your half-days to see where you go and who you meet . In all honesty, I have to tell you you're really boring." Sordith grinned and took a deep pull from his mug, his eyes darting around the room again as he set it back on the table.

Alador held his mug between his hands. "I knew someone was following me." He looked up from the mug to Sordith. "Did I even come close to spotting you?"

"Couple times. You gave me the slip once, but you sort of stand out amongst most of the fourth and fifth tier mages." Sordith sat back watching Alador.

"Have we met? You look oddly familiar." Alador looked at Sordith with just as much scrutiny. The man had black hair and his eyes were a strange copper color. He was clearly not Daezun, but he looked familiar. Alador pushed the mug away slightly as he eyed Sordith.

"Not on purpose. If you've spotted me, you didn't let on and I attempted to blend."

"Maybe that's it. You just remind me of someone." Alador tried to picture all the mages on the tiers he had met, but no one seemed quite right.

"I have a rather common face, I am told." Sordith shrugged. "Let's talk bluntly. I swore my loyalty to Aorun as the Trench Lord. However, his time in power may be coming to an end, and if it does, I plan to pick those I choose to work with carefully."

He leaned forward, subjecting Alador to a piercing gaze. "You keep your word and you don't appear to play the typical backstabbing games of those seeking to augment their power.

No one in *The Blackguard* has anything unkind to say about you other than your peculiar friendship with a death mage. You have good taste in women and you treat them well. As such, I think there are some things that you can help me with and I suspect that soon you might have need of my skills."

Alador was surprised at this man's assessment of him. He really didn't have much to say about himself, and when he did, it usually wasn't nice. To hear another speak of him so well was like hearing about a totally different person. "I fail to see how I can be of any help to you, and the only help I can think of needing is a warning should Aorun finally try to kill me on his own."

Sordith grinned. "Yes, I heard that Maxis failed quite miserably to kill you in the desired manner. You need not worry about him: Aorun doesn't suffer failure lightly and, well, let's just say that the man's last report came to rather an abrupt end."

Sordith eyed Alador. "Aorun will come for you when he feels his time is right. I'm not sure what he's waiting for, to be honest, unless he's trying to decide how to get round the fact a death mage is now involved, thanks to Maxis' bungling. This is the longest I have ever seen him take in removing someone he has decided to hate so vehemently."

"Why are you telling me all this? If you have sworn an oath, you are clearly breaking it now," Alador pointed out. He was uncomfortable with this discussion and its implications. He shifted about, looking for others, wondering if this was a trap.

"Aorun promised to keep me out of certain business he was in, and, for the most part, he has done so. However, I recently learned he has been selling Lerdenian women into slavery."

Sordith put up a hand as Alador opened his mouth. "Now, before you say that you're not Lerdenian and it's not your problem, he sells your people too. I don't like slavery. The ones that end up in *The Blackguard*, well, their lot is not a bad one. However, I've been digging around, and the pure-blooded Daezun and Lerdenians have a very different fate." Sordith's expression was grim.

Alador's eyes widened at the idea that someone could sell another being. He knew slavery existed – for all intents and purposes, Keelee wasn't much more than a slave, herself, but at least she had a choice. He felt something rise up in him, cold and dangerous, at the thought of anyone being forced to serve another. The same thing was happening to the dragons: tied down and forced to a life that was not natural to them.

Alador leaned forward. "You have my attention," he growled out. His hands wrapped around the base of his mug.

Sordith had been watching him closely. "I see you like the idea about as much as I do. I need your help. If you cannot, then all I ask is that you forget that this conversation happened."

"What do you need?" Alador's tone was cold. His vision swam with the images of staked-out dragons, and he was hard-pressed to keep the pressure of Renamaum's rage in check. He absently turned the mug in his hands.

"I thought maybe you could get us in, and I would go as your bodyguard. I'm sure the Stable Lord would be proud to show the High Minister's nephew how successful he is, and that will give us both means and access to kill him."

His eyes narrowed. "Me being there will legitimize your visit – I have stood with the Trench Lord as he made these transactions. The stable lord will assume you and Aorun have a business connection." Sordith's answer was confident.

"A stable lord?" Alador asked with confusion. "I don't understand. What does a stable lord have to do with selling people?"

"It is a *breeding* stable, Alador: a breeding stable for people. They're making half-breeds for the High Minister's special army." Sordith's lip curled at the thought.

Alador was stunned by this news. His mind raced over questions... Did his uncle know? Was he really aware what this Stable Lord was doing? He had to be. There was little in the city that was going on that Luthian did not know.

Sordith drowned the last of his drink and set his cup down. "I should warn you that there is another small matter you will need to deal with."

"What is that?" Alador was reserving judgement on Sordith's proposal until he had the full story.

"The Stable Lord, Veaneth, has some ability to take away the will of another. I thought with your training in magic, you might be able to protect us somehow. I have no skills in magic; mine are in a swift dagger and a sharp eye." Sordith kept his voice low so that only the two of them could hear.

"What about other guards?" Alador was taking to his lessons well, and his father had given him a further edge in their private sessions. He knew that Sordith was right about gaining entry to the stable lord's domain. If this was happening with his uncle's approval, Alador would probably be able to waltz right in - unless Veaneth had been directed to refuse him entry

"Never more than ten that I've been able to count. If everything goes according to plan, we can have Veaneth down before any of them is even aware there's any danger. If we really get it right, we could kill him and be out before anyone notices anything wrong." Sordith was using the table as a vague floor plan.

"One problem…," Alador mused thoughtfully.

"What is that?" Sordith eyed Alador. He was clearly not a man to disregard another's views.

"We're not leaving those who've been enslaved behind; they'll just put someone new in charge," Alador pointed out. "We couldn't get them all out unnoticed, and ten guards might be a bit much for just two of us."

Sordith frowned. "I can take out maybe six after we drop Veaneth. Surely with your recent training and magic you could manage three or four?"

"I have a better idea," Alador told him softly.

"Oh? What do you have in mind?"

"We bring a death mage." He grinned slowly. "I happen to know he's rather good at silencing anyone who might set off an alarm."

"Do you think he'd come? Do you trust him?" Sordith sat back, considering. "I mean, I know for a fact that Aorun has men in *The Blackguard*."

"I know this, too, but Jon is not one of them." Alador was certain of this.

"All right then." Sordith slowly nodded. "When do you want to put this dog down?" He asked softly.

"During my next half-day - when I'm supposed to be visiting my father. He'll be out of the area, but I haven't told my afternoon instructors that."

He'd had every intention of keeping to his weekly visiting pattern unless those with power over his schedule found out that his father was out of the city. He'd been looking forward to having a night alone: no Keelee, no merrymaking classmates and no homework; just a day where he could relax or read from his father's fantastic library.

"So, in a week? That will give me time to put into some additional surveillance and see what the optimum time of day would be to hit him. Where should I meet you?" Sordith seemed already to be calculating.

"Do you know where the mage Henrick, my father, lives?" Alador asked, also making plans. He had much to do if he was going to try to use his magic in battle – not least to ask his father to teach him how to protect against this power Veaneth apparently had.

"I follow you every week. So yes, I know where he lives." Sordith grinned, his eyes strangely warm considering his position as one of Aorun's men.

Alador sighed. "Yes, don't remind me. I'll meet you there, then. It will give our visit more legitimacy if the Trench Lord's man comes properly and not scooting about like some ghost." Alador eyed the man. His copper eyes were a little unnerving.

"Ghost... I like that term." Sordith stood up. "Best we not be seen too long together. I can explain away a short encounter if I'm called upon to do so. I will see you in a week."

Alador nodded pushing away his mug. He rose to his feet. "I had best make my way to my father's before he becomes concerned."

Sordith looked from mug to Alador, and then back. "You going to drink that?"

Alador shook his head. "I'm not much of a drinker, truth be told."

Sordith frowned, grabbed the mug, and upended it. He slammed it down on the table. "Never waste a pint, my dear fellow: it's bad luck." He turned and headed through the crowd. Alador was still shaking his head as the man slid out the door. He pulled on his cloak and followed suit.

Alador arrived at his father's lost in thought. He didn't knock anymore: it was his home, too. Actually, it was the only home he knew now, other than the small room in the caverns.

Alador delighted in these times away, though he was also glad to be taught at *The Blackguard* headquarters. The things he'd been learning were important, and his instructors were good at what they taught. He knew his mastery of magic was tenfold what it has been upon his arrival. Alador had a lot to learn and a long way to go, but he was motivated.

However, this afternoon his thoughts were on Sordith's words. Was this a trap? The man had seemed sincere, and deep inside Alador felt like he could trust him, though he couldn't explain that to anyone. He wasn't quite sure himself as he made his way to his father's study. As usual, the room was warmer than the rest of the house.

His father sat by the fire his pipe in hand and was reading. He looked up as Alador entered and put down his book. "You are late."

"I had some business to attend to." Alador liked the way his father stated the obvious so simplistically.

Henrick eyed him and frowned. "Everything all right? I can wait to go east if you wish. I know your mother will be disappointed, but I can make it up to her."

"No, no, you go ahead and go. Besides, I want you to check and make sure that everyone is all right." Alador didn't add that he was looking forward to sometime in the house by himself. Even the servants would be away a great deal: visiting their own families.

Henrick paused to puff on his pipe, clearly considering. "She still has not written?" Henrick eyed his son with genuine concern.

"No. Almost ten weeks, and still nothing." Alador plopped down into the chair dejectedly.

"I am sure she is fine. You knew your magic might come between you." Henrick moved over to the fire to tap out his pipe. He returned to his seat to repack it, pulling out a bag of tobacco.

"I know. I guess I just thought... that it wouldn't matter. Maybe I shared too much, too fast." Alador leaned forward, putting his face in his hands. "I am so tired."

"You know, if you wanted to send that body servant my way so you could get some sleep..." Henrick trailed off and grinned, looking at his son, his tone teasing as he lit his pipe again.

"I am not sharing a woman with my father. That's just...wrong." Alador looked over at Henrick though his head was still in his hands.

Henrick just smirked in response. "What do you want to do today?" he asked, "We could play a game of stones or just talk."

"No, I really need to learn one thing before you go. There's a kind of magic we haven't talked about yet, and I think that I might have encountered it. This person doesn't really like me, and I'd like to know how to counter it."

Alador sat back up, having come to the realization that he was going to help Sordith. "I think this man can change someone's will."

Henrick looked at him for a long moment. "Someone in the guard uses such magic?" he asked, his tone soft and deadly.

"Not exactly." Alador didn't want to tell his father of his plans in case he was aware of this slavery. Besides, if his father was away, he could deny any responsibility or involvement should Alador and Sordith fail.

"Alador, such magic is forbidden even by the Lerdenians. Taking the will of another uses dark magic that even the dragons frown upon." Henrick sat his pipe down in a bowl and looked at his son. "If what you say is true, I need to know who."

"Wait, what? My magic can kill. A death mage's magic is designed to kill. How is this considered dark magic when magic actually used for killing isn't? That doesn't make sense." Alador did not understand this at all.

"A man who carries a sword is not necessarily a killer. It is the heart of the man that determines his nature, not the weapon he carries. A sword cannot kill unless it is drawn and used, whereas a man who acquires deadly poison normally has but one intent, and that is to commit murder with it."

Henrick's gaze was steady as he searched his son's face. "So it is with magic; it is the heart of the mage that determines his nature, not his gifts of sphere. This Jon you've spoken of could kill quite easily, but does he?" Henrick dropped into that tone of teaching he used on their half-days. He rose from his chair to stare into the fire.

"No," Alador replied, at least not that I am aware of. I've never seen him hurt anyone around him, though I'm quite aware that he's capable of doing so." He watched his father, trying to wrap his head around this new information. He'd always heard whispers of dark magic; but to him, any kind of magic you could kill with was dark.

"Like an assassin who has figured out how to harness nature to create a deadly poison, some mages figure out ways to twist their gifts with only one purpose: to harm or enslave another. To take the will of a person away is to take away their ability to defend themselves, and that is against the laws of nature," Henrick answered, running a finger along the marble mantle.

Alador considered this very carefully. "So magic that steals the will of another is in the class of dark magic. What else falls into this category?" He was weighing his father's words very carefully.

"Blood-based magic is one. While a mage cannot absorb the powers of another mage as they can those of a dragon, they can use fresh blood to cast or enhance a deadly spell. Mages are put down the moment they are discovered using blood." Henrick's tone had hardened appreciatively.

"Anything else I should be on the watch for that falls into this category of forbidden magic?" Alador eyed his father intently. Henrick obviously had some experience with confronting such a mage: his tense posture made that clear enough.

"Any spell that can twist the heart of a man against his own nature, Alador. I have heard of dark spells that could make a man take his own life. I have heard of dark, hidden spells that, in the right situation, will set off a series of spells and create a killer out of a simple servant."

Henrick turned to look at Alador with an intensity that made Alador lean back in his chair. "You have avoided my first question long enough. Who is using such spells?"

"I don't know yet. I'd hate to accuse a mage without proof... It's just a rumor," Alador murmured. "But if it turns out not to be, I will come to you immediately. Until then, how can I defend myself against such a spell?"

"One's will to do the opposite of what the mage wishes will work if the desire is strong enough. In addition, if you know such a spell is coming, a simple mage shield will work. The problem is: few know that such a spell is coming. It's often put into a simple item that draws the focus of the victim, something harmless or beautiful."

Henrick looked totally disgusted. "I expect you to come to me if such a mage exists. I will drag his rotten carcass before The High Council itself."

"What if it's someone connected to Luthian?" Alador asked softly. "What if he's involved?"

Henrick paused at that question. "Then the matter is not so simple. I would have to be sure my evidence was incontrovertible, or else remove the mage in question and attempt to leave no trace. But Luthian would not cross this line…" Henrick appeared certain. However, he hesitated just enough to reveal some doubt.

"Well, let's hope this rumor is wrong. I still need to know more of this dark magic and how to defend against it," Alador reminded his father softly. He still had no doubt that if the mage Sordith spoke of could use such spells, then his uncle knew about it.

"Then let us retire to my casting room." Henrick turned and headed for the door. Like Luthian, he'd had a room built specifically to protect the rest of the house from whatever happened inside. If a spell misfired, the room would contain it. That was where they usually worked on Alador's spells, as he had a tendency to pull more power than he intended.

They spent the rest of the afternoon in practice: Henrick throwing up different variations of spells and forcing Alador to defend against them. He used spells that might resemble the ones they'd spoken about - not an exact representation, but close enough that Alador got the basic idea. By dinner, they were both exhausted and ravenous; between them, they ate a whole roast, a bowl of mashed tubers, some sort of salad of vegetables and warm dressing, and an entire pie.

Chapter Twenty

Alador spent the next two days practising the different deflections his father had taught him. He had learned that, as with a sword, sometimes the easiest defense was not to meet the spell head on, but to let it slide around him. It took less power and less time to create a wedge that let a spell envelope around him, but not touch him.

Keelee was unusually attentive over the last two days. Not that she wasn't normally attentive to his every need and seemed to know how to predict it, but this was different. Alador decided to confront her with it the morning of his next half-day to Luthian's. He dressed in the clothes she'd laid out and as she gathered up yesterday's and headed out to wash them, Alador gently reached for Keelee's arm before she could leave, ensuring his grip was firm.

"We need to talk." Alador's voice was kind and his grip, though firm, was also gentle. "Set those down for a moment. You can go while I am on duty." He had guard post this morning and was excused from his classes.

"Oh, if you wish," Keelee murmured. She set the clothes down and moved her body close to him, her palms immediately trailing up Alador's thighs. "You should have thought of that before you dressed," she murmured against his neck.

Alador sighed and moved her back away from him. "I mean actually have a conversation, Keelee." He turned and led her to sit on the bed, pressing her gently down and then sat down beside her. "You've been... different the last few days. What's wrong?"

Keelee fell silent. The wringing of her hands in her lap made it clear that, as Alador had suspected, something was amiss. She didn't respond, her hair creating a curtain of black, silken strands around her bowed head. Her body was tense beside him.

Alador reached in past that curtain to tip her chin up to look at him, and frowned when he saw tears in Keelee's eyes. "Talk to me. You may be my assigned body servant, but I thought we were friends. You need to talk to me."

"You would not understand," she whispered.

"I have had to deal with some pretty strange things in the last four months. I think you can trust me at least to be open-minded," he offered. His thumb gently caressed her bottom lip. She was so beautiful and, in so many ways, seemed so fragile to him. She was a stark contrast to Mesiande.

"I sometimes dream things, things that come true," she murmured slowly, raising her eyes to him. There was real fear in them and a tear slid down her cheek. "I dreamed that because of me, something horrible is going to happen to you," she whispered choking back a sob.

Alador tucked her raven hair behind her ear. "I'd be the last one to judge someone because of their dreams. Do they always come true?" His tone was gentle and he wiped away a lone tear.

Keelee slowly shook her head. "I can change them sometimes," she admitted; "but they usually come true." Her eyes were so full of tears, he wondered how they didn't spill over.

Alador gently tried to reassure her. "Well then, we're forewarned and we'll be careful. Do you know what it is that you do that causes this horrible thing to happen, or what this horrible thing is?" He reached over and pulled her against him to reassure and comfort her, kissing the top of her head gently and running his hand up and down her back.

"No. I only know because of me you will be horribly hurt," she whispers. "I don't want to cause you pain, Alador. This is the happiest I have been since I came of an age where my father's tier was no longer my home."

"About that. I would have thought your father could choose to have you live on his tier. Doesn't he want you to?" Alador frowned, wondering how anyone could send Keelee away.

She was quiet for a moment and turned her

face into his shirt. Her soft words were barely audible. "He does. Very much so. But to be honest, it was safer for me to work in the High Minister's house than to remain on the second tier. Not everyone seeking a mate does so kindly, and I did not wish to put my father's business in harm's way."

She gave a soft sigh. "I have found no one I would want to set up a home with," Keelee admitted, "except, perhaps, for Flame. I do rather like him..."

She smiled , twisting her hair between her fingers absently, and Alador felt a strange twinge of possessiveness, despite having given them his blessing to spend time together. His arms tightened around her reflexively. "If you want to move in with him, Keelee, I wouldn't stop you."

"Maybe one day. Unfortunately, Flame doesn't seem the type to settle on one woman." Keelee sighed against his shoulder. She looked up at him, those eyes catching him as usual.

Alador considered Flame's reputation. "No, you're probably right. At least, not yet." He kissed the top of her head again and slowly let her go. "I had best get going. Since you know something's coming that's going to cause me pain, let's see if we can minimize that. I don't want you to go out of the caverns without me or Flame."

Alador slowly set her upright as he considered. "I can't think of what you could do that would cause me pain, unless you were hurt. So, let's make sure you stay safe, all right?" He tapped her nose gently and forced a smile. The truth was, he was a bit concerned about her dream, but he couldn't stand to see her so upset.

Keelee smiled back up at him uncertainly. She wiped her eyes on the back of her hands. "All right. I hope your day is restful. I will get this laundry done and go see my father. He likes it when I come to cook for him." She rose, ever the example of grace, scooping up the laundry she'd dropped.

Alador watched her go with a concerned gaze. He couldn't think of anything she could do that would cause him harm. He'd seen her practising spells, but most of her abilities lay in simple cantrips. Keelee had never shared dreams before, but with Renamaum haunting his own quite regularly, Alador was hardly going to discount hers.

Of all the duties he was given, standing outside the cavern to *The Blackguard* stronghold was the most boring. Few came to the gaping cavern opening and those that did were there on business. Most of the day was spent staring down to the corner of the tier. If he were lucky, he would get the harbor side of the opening. At least then he could watch the docks as well.

After Alador had finished guard duty, he scooped up his cloak and headed out of the caverns. He'd made sure his council pass was visible before he even left the water sphere halls. He was in a fair mood: his uncle had promised a night without feasts or entertaining.

Alador had known for some time that his uncle was showing him favor because there was something he either needed or wanted. He didn't know what this secret desire was, but he knew it had something to do with the whirlpool spell. The way Luthian had spoken on Alador's last half-day, suggesting they speak privately at his next visit, made Alador fairly sure that tonight was the night he'd find out.

Alador spent the entire walk up to the top tier lost in thought. Between what his uncle wanted from him and the thought of having to take out Luthian's stable lord, Alador had a lot on his mind. He had no doubt now that he was going to help shut that stable down, but he didn't know where that would leave him with his uncle.

He hoped he and Sordith could manage it in a way that his uncle would never know it was him, but that would mean killing anyone that would dare speak of it, and Alador struggled with that thought. Another part of him didn't care if Luthian found out. With each passing week, he had come to admire his uncle's skill with politics and subterfuge, but he hated him for the foul creature that he truly was under all that snakelike charm.

The door was opened for Alador before he ever reached it. The guardsmen were all *Black*

Guard, but he didn't recognize any of them. He supposed that only those who had graduated to an assignment were allowed to guard the High Minister.

Alador made his way to his room that he had been allocated for when he visited. As usual, a robe was laid out waiting for him. He quickly divested himself of his armor and washed up. He had been on duty at the port gate earlier that day, so the wash was needed. His uncle didn't like him wearing weapons, but Alador still kept a boot knife on him at all times regardless. He didn't trust his uncle, and even if he had, Luthian had many enemies who would gladly supplant him if they could.

Alador slipped on a light blue robe. Of the colors his uncle chose for him, he found he liked blue best; he'd always liked it by the water, but now with the powers of a large sea dragon, Alador found himself even more partial to things that reminded him of any body of water.

He checked himself in the mirror. He'd started growing his hair out at his uncle's request; now it was at an irritating length - unruly and always in his eyes. Last week, he'd given up and used magic to make it long enough to pull back to the nape of his neck. Alador took out the hair tie and slicked his hair back with a little water, attempting to tame the unruly locks.

Satisfied that he looked like a proper mage, Alador set out for the practice room. He was met by a young woman who whispered swiftly that Luthian was waiting for him in the library. This was unusual; usually Luthian joined him at his studies. He nodded to the young woman and turned to set off in the direction of the library.

It never boded well to keep Luthian waiting as it seemed that he ran his life on a strict timetable. When he reached the library, he knocked on the door, as was his uncle's preference, and waited for one of the guards inside to open the door for him.

When he entered, Luthian was sitting before a warm fire with a small table loaded with food set between the two chairs. Alador bowed low before Luthian. "Uncle, ever a pleasure to see you." Alador smiled with the same oily charm his uncle often used.

Luthian smirked into his glass of wine. "Liar."

Alador smiled and slid into a chair. "I learn only from the best, sir."

"How goes your training this week?" Luthian asked, as was his custom. His tone and casual manner had become commonplace.

"Nothing new this week. I've been practising the maelstrom and learning the spells of lightning and combining that energy with water. I love working with the elements of a thunderstorm – I find them most intriguing." Alador poured himself a cup of tea.

"Can you create a storm yet?" Luthian

asked watching the young man before him.

"No. I've not even been able to form a small raincloud yet. I am still at an elementary level in my studies, Uncle. I pray to the gods you would not expect me to master that in less than a season?" Alador looked up at him curiously. "I was quite excited to master the whirlpool."

"I suppose I am impatient," Luthian admitted. A tight smile graced his lips, but not his eyes. "I have plans, and I need a strong storm mage to make them come to fruition."

So this was it – he had need of Alador's powers for something specific. "What plans? Perhaps if I understood what you were seeking, I could focus my learning to help you meet your goal." He presented himself as the 'ever-willing-to-please' pupil but deep down he suspected that Luthian knew it was as much an act as his doting uncle routine was.

Luthian set down his wine glass and sat back in his chair. His fingers tapped together; the man was clearly considering what to share with Alador. "There is a country in the Otherlands that has a large fleet capable of bringing a large invading force to our shores. It is my suspicion that a recently lost trader vessel was not lost to the ocean, but to their fleet."

He looked at Alador with such intensity that Alador's cup stilled in his hand. Luthian's voice quieted and he stared past his nephew, as if imagining the immensity of the storm he sought. "If a mage could conjure a storm of sufficient strength, he could protect those shores and drive this fleet onto the rocks. You would be a valuable protector of our isle, Alador. Or, should we decide to stretch our own wings beyond this isle, a valuable person to have at my side, were we to encounter any resistance over water."

Alador sat for a time, watching his uncle, forcing himself to take a drink of his tea. He did not miss the look of greed in his uncle's eyes, nor the licking of his lips as he finished speaking of resistance.

"Surely, you have other storm mages?" He asked the question with a boy's simple curiosity. However, his eyes were locked on his uncle with a far more discerning gaze than the tone of his voice implied.

"None that can manifest a strong enough storm to crush an attacking fleet. It is my hope, nephew, that this large stone of yours has given you enough power to protect this isle before the enemy can ever set foot upon it." Luthian had not moved from his relaxed position, confident in his words as his fingers tapped together.

"What of your own vast power, Uncle?" Alador flashed him a look of admiration.

Luthian's eyes darted to him. "Do not think I am too weak to mount a ferocious attack – that is not the problem. A fire mage like me could bring fire down upon such a fleet and yes, he could wreak much havoc." Luthian put a hand out, palm up, and it filled with a ball of dancing fire. "But if their ships have mages, they could shield against such fire just as easily."

He closed his hands dramatically, snuffing the fire. "But a storm? Few would suspect there was a mage behind a storm. There have only been a few in history who could draw such power from the elements."

Alador carefully set his teacup down and picked up a bit of cheese, tossing it into his mouth and chewing before speaking. The tension between them was thick. "Such a mage could also destroy Daezun crops, drive them into the ground with pelting hail, and flood them from their riverside villages." He picked up a cake and sat back to watch his uncle.

"Why, I had not thought of that." Luthian eyes moved to Alador as if surprised. His hands stilled and he put the two index fingers to his lips.

"Liar," Alador fired the accusation right back at his uncle. He knew damned well that before his uncle could turn his eyes to outside conquests, he had to bring his own isle under a single rule. It was hidden and hinted at through every history and tactical lesson he had received so far inside the caverns.

Luthian reached over to pick up the bottle and refill his glass. "It seems our truce of honesty has ended in both directions." He picked up his glass and toasted Alador. "All right, yes, this had occurred to me." He took a sip, letting the tension build in the room. "If the Daezun were forced to turn to Lerdenia for help from the weather's unrelenting onslaught, a war could be avoided."

"So many people would die before that happened. The villages would turn to one another for assistance, first... The Daezun would have to be desperate before they turned to Lerdenia for help," Alador pointed out coldly. His eyes narrowed as he watched his uncle.

"Alador, shall we be frank with each other?" Luthian shifted his posture – he was no longer the doting uncle, but the ruler of the Lerdenian people. He crossed his legs, very relaxed in his revelations. "I *will* rule this isle." He took another sip of wine before continuing. "I will do it regardless of whether or not you help. You have the power within you to ensure that this happens with the least amount of loss to your people. People, I will remind you, that cast you out, and yet you still seem to harbor a kindness towards. If you decide to not help me in this task, well then..."

He paused, swirling the wine in his glass, "I fear a war like no other will be fought upon this isle. You have seen what *The Blackguard* can do. I am willing to wait until enough are trained to ensure that the Daezun fall. I am a patient man; I can and will wait for the right time."

"You have maybe three hundred *Black*

Guard. That's hardly enough for an invasion," Alador pointed out, working hard to look casual despite what he was learning from his uncle.

Do you think you are alone, Alador? Do you think your father spawned the only bastard in a Daezun village? Why do you think Lerdenians travel at the time of your ridiculous mating circle? You are but the first of the crop now coming into my keeping."

He eyed his nephew with cold calculation. "I assure you that there is no love for you in your father's heart." Luthian's tone contained some mockery and a hint of sadness, like he pitied Alador for not being able to see this. "You are but the first of the army I created, the first of the half-breeds that, as they come into power, will be cast from Daezun arms and into my own."

He spread both arms wide, his wine glass sloshing slightly. You are further proof of my patience." Luthian let this harsh realization wash over Alador. "Every mage out at circle uses a spell of enchantment to ensure they are chosen as often as they can endure throughout those nights –nights like the one your father spent your age and nine months or so ago in Smallbrook."

Alador's cake had been halfway to his mouth as Luthian's cold, calculated words washed over him. He set it down, no longer hungry. He felt the blood drain from his face. Alador had always feared this, always suspected that his father had used some sort of spell on his mother. She always became giddy as a middlin when Henrick was around. "My father knew of your plan to breed this army of castoffs...?" Alador asked in an almost deadly whisper.

"Of course he knew. Henrick likes his women and was more than happy to have a good excuse to bed as many as he could. I am quite sure he has a woman in every village. You have seen him with women. Did you think he held your mother in some special regard?"

Luthian snorted in contempt and sipped his wine casually. "He detests the simple village life the Daezun insist on clinging to." Luthian swirled his wine, watching his nephew squirm with a cold smile. "He used to whine every time I sent him out on a good will mission, or to check on you. Once he even went as far as to complain because he wouldn't be able to wear a new robe to a ball."

"You're lying." Alador stood slowly. Anger began to course through him as he looked down at his totally calm uncle.

Luthian shrugged. "Ask him, Alador. Ask him, yourself, if he knew what I was doing. Ask him if he loved your mother all those times he crawled into her bed. Ask him how many siblings you actually have. I doubt he truly knows."

"You bastard," Alador hissed angrily. "Why tell me this? Why break the trust I was building here?"

Luthian didn't answer immediately. He picked up a small sandwich and took a bite, looking at it as if to appreciate its fine flavor. "First, you are the only bastard in this room. My parents were properly bonded." He looked up at Alador. "Secondly, you deserve the truth. We did promise that when we first met. Lastly, you seem to be forgetting that your only truly safe place is within the confines of my good will." The man's tone held a deadly edge of confidence as Alador stood over him, hands clenched.

Luthian slowly set his wine down and picked up a cake. "Go ahead, Alador: strike out at me if you can. I know that you want to." He didn't even bother to look at his nephew; he merely sat there with an imperious grin.

Alador wanted to. He wanted to take every offensive spell he knew at that moment and send them crashing down to wipe that smile from his uncle's face. He wanted to leave nothing in that chair for anyone to identify.

But he knew that his uncle would not have shared this – would not simply sit there calmly – if he did not have some plan. Not to mention that any spell Alador could cast would likely be nothing more than a flea-bite in the face of the power Luthian held.

It was then that Alador realized that two members of *The Blackguard* were *in* the room, facing him, standing on either side of the door.

Usually they stepped out of the library during Luthian's meetings with Alador. He didn't look directly at them, but he could see both of them tense and ready. He knew that look: he'd seen it a hundred times in practice.

"Well played, Uncle." Alador answered softly. "I will not give you that satisfaction. If you want me to grovel, you will have to act first. I will not raise my hand to you."

Luthian popped a cake in his mouth with a satisfied smile. "Smart man. However, I do not want you to grovel. Wait!" He put up one hand and shook his head. "I promised honesty – so I admit it would be nice, but it's not necessary."

Luthian grinned up at Alador as he dusted off his hands. "I want you to learn what is needed to bring the storms. I know you have enough power to do it. I have received reports of how easily simple spells come to you."

Luthian's calculating gaze brought a skip to Alador's heart. "I found these reports disturbing since you always seemed to struggle with the simplest of tasks I have given you. This tells me that you are also becoming more skilful at the game of power..."

His uncle continued triumphantly. "I know about your skill with a bow. A little weak with a sword still, but progressing. I really have no need of you at a battlefront, so that small flaw does not worry me."

Alador stood there for a moment, trying to regain some kind of center. His hands clenched and unclenched, and he could feel his face flushing with the anger that coursed through him. His mind was racing.

He had already known that his uncle was conniving and cold: his father — no, his uncle's brother — had warned him. Henrick had failed to mention, however, how much involvement he'd had in the plans for Luthian's manipulations.

Had all these lessons been the result of this attempt to bring forth the power Luthian wanted? Were the reports from his instructors in the guard, from Keelee or from Henrick himself? How long had Luthian known that Alador had been deliberately disguising the true extent of his power?

"I find myself suddenly quite tired and no longer hungry, High Minister. With your permission, I will withdraw for the evening. You have given me much to think about." Alador bit out the words tersely.

"Of course, Alador. I am sure you have much to consider." Luthian held up one finger. "One thing before you go." He waited until he was sure he had Alador's attention.

"You will perform this spell for me to the utmost of your ability. That is not a request: it's an order. If I catch you downplaying your skill or power again, I will cut my losses and kill you. Do you understand?"

His voice was quiet, but hard, and brooked no argument. Luthian did not bother rising as he usually did when Alador left . He sipped his wine, watching his nephew.

Alador stared at him for a long moment. He could hear the shifting of the two *Black Guard* soldiers behind him. "Yes, I understand." He turned on his heel and headed for the door. The guardsman opened it as he approached.

Alador stopped and turned back. "One thing of my own, *uncle.*" He twisted the word with sarcasm.

"Yes, nephew?" Luthian rose with his glass of wine in hand.

"I will *never* use it on the Daezun." Alador's tone held an edge of promise as he turned and strode off, not bothering to hear if his uncle had a parting comment.

Chapter Twenty-One

Alador had been unable to sleep that night; the conflicting, distressing information he'd had just learned from Luthian had swirled around in his head incessantly, keeping him awake. He left the High Minister's home before Luthian had even risen for the day, lost in thought.

On some level, Alador had known that Henrick must have somehow been a part of all this, or the man wouldn't have been able to warn him about *The Blackguard* and Luthian's plans. But the way his uncle had just laid the information out there had shocked Alador.

He wanted to believe in his father, but much of what Luthian had said rang with honesty. There was some comfort in knowing that the best lies were told with truth mixed in, but Alador couldn't confront Henrick about it until the man returned from his rounds, and he wasn't due back for some time.

Alador made his way slowly down to the third tier, his mind whirling. He was so lost in thought that he had to set a poor old woman upright after almost knocking her to the ground. "Sorry," he murmured, already falling back into his thoughts. The morning was still new, so the streets were quiet and nearly empty. Aside from stray people like the old lady going about their business, the only traffic was the refuse carts that were still hauling garbage off the tiers in the faint, early morning light. The shopkeepers weren't even out yet: to set up their shops for the day.

Alador was glad for the quiet streets as he made his way back to the caverns – it allowed him to think. There was one thing he did not doubt: his uncle was not his friend. Luthian had made it clear that his role of doting uncle had come to an end. For a man who claimed to have such patience, he hadn't lasted long in the part of a loving family member. Alador had wanted to kill Luthian. By the gods, he still wanted to kill him. Thanks to Luthian, Alador felt like he'd been cast adrift yet again, feeling totally alone and questioning everything around him.

Alador returned to the caverns in a foul mood. Keelee wouldn't be back until after his first classes, but that was for the best – Alador didn't want to take his anger out on her. He threw himself into his studies to take his mind off Luthian and Henrick, particularly when it was time for weapons practice. Alador had advanced to the second ring since his arrival, having mastered basic skills.

Seeing his mood, his instructor, Toman, had chosen to pair off with him today rather than assign Alador to another student. At least he wouldn't be forced to soften his blows. Near the end of the class, the instructor had just decided to let Alador spar rather than practice a particular skill.

"I don't know where your head is, but it's clear you have something you need to vent." Toman saluted Alador and dropped down into a readied stance. "Come on, show me your best and see if you can disarm me."

Alador, still seething with the anger he'd been unable to resolve, didn't need to be asked twice. He danced forward daringly to strike out at the man before him. Steel clashed against steel with far more force than the ring usually heard echoing loudly about them. Those who were in the same ring paused their eyes drawn to Alador and Toman.

The instructor eyed Alador with surprise as the two spun from one another, readying for the next blow. "Anger is any swordsman's downfall, Alador. You know this." He barely had the words out before Alador had once again leapt forward, moving swiftly with three alternating blows. Toman blocked them each with practised efficiency, though the effort would have left any other lagging behind in the face of Alador's fervor.

Alador's next strike sliced the air with an audible hiss before it met with Toman's blade in another sharp clang. The swords continued to connect again and again, bringing all other practices to a stop around them. Soon a silent ring had formed around their circle. Alador would not relent, his anger fueling blow after blow. He was aware of only one thing, and that was the man before him. The fact they were using practice blades would be little consolation if any of his blows connected.

Toman was a renowned fighter in *The Blackguard*, and few had bested him. To see him fight in more than coaching practices was a rare event, and as the two battled on, more and more joined the circle to watch.

Toman's skill was being tested in the face of Alador's seemingly unflagging energy. His vehement blows struck again and again against Toman's blade in a frenzied tempest of whirling and slashing metal. The wiser, more experienced man kept waiting for Alador to tire and lower his weapon, yet still Alador pressed on.

Twice, Toman tried to lift a hand to end the duel, but each time he'd been forced to defend himself before he could stop the fight. Alador was lost in his rage – he wanted to kill something, and this man before him had allowed him to release that rage he'd been holding since leaving Smallbrook.

The two men circled around each other, Toman sweating with the effort as he sought a way to disarm his pupil. His expression was one of pure concentration as he tried a questing blow at the lad's hand or a swirling riposte to leverage the sword away. Neither man spoke nor did they seem to notice the growing throng of students around them. They had eyes for each other only.

Alador lunged in an attempt to plunge his sword deep into his adversary; Toman barely stepped out of the way, bringing his sword up from underneath and forcing it farther from his side. He immediately countered trying to knock Alador in the head with the flat of the blade.

Alador ducked and backpedaled, bringing his sword back up to the ready. His eyes were sharp with anger, hurt, and the desire to kill. Toman must have recognized the look – his stance changed in response: he was no longer defending against the possibility of a broken bone; he was defending his life.

Alador came hard and fast. His sword flashed left and right, and the swords rang out with each cut. The blades resounded as the two spun about one another. Toman pivoted right and tried again to knock out the man standing before him, but Alador was ready for him. His sword caught Toman's, and he twisted so that its dull point raked across the older fighter's bracer, turning Toman's similar attempt to disarm Alador earlier against him.

The instructor's sword slipped from his grip and slid across the sand with a hiss. Silence reigned at that moment, the crowd catching their breath in the unnatural stillness. Time seemed to slow. Toman dove for his sword, but Alador beat him to it; his foot was on the hilt just as Toman reached it. Alador raised his sword to drive it into the man's heart when a large figure flung itself toward him, tackling him over.

"Stop! Stop, it's just practice! Recover your senses, you idiot!" Flame yelled as they went crashing to the ground. Alador was so stunned by the intervention of this third person that, for a moment, he acted on pure instinct, reflexively grappling with Flame, who'd grabbed Alador's sword hand. Flame was joined almost immediately by Jon, and with some difficulty the two of them managed to hold Alador down.

"Alador, damn it man, it's me, Jon," he hissed. "Snap out of it!" Alador's struggling eased a little, and Jon looked at Flame. "What did you say to piss him off this badly?"

Alador stopped moving, staring up in confusion at the two men sitting on his chest who seemed to be arguing. He blinked at them, panting from the exertion of the fight.

"Me?" Flame looked over in surprise, both his hands now holding down Alador's sword hand. "They were already like that when I came around."

"Get off me," Alador hissed. "It's got nothing to do with either of you. I just... lost my temper for a moment."

Flame eyed Jon who nodded and the two of them slowly let Alador go. "Remind me never to make you angry," Flame muttered, and for once, his tone lacked its usual playful banter.

Alador pushed himself to his feet, sheathing his sword, and looked around for his instructor. Toman had retrieved his sword sometime after Alador had been tackled, and stood facing him. Alador immediately saluted him. "I apologize – you're right. My temper is my downfall." He waited unsure of what would befall him for attempting to kill his mentor.

Toman just saluted him back with a look of pride. "Tomorrow, you are to report to the advanced ring." Then he pivoted and strode away, the silent ring of men about them parting to make way for the weapon-master.

Alador watched him go, unsure whether he'd just been praised or punished. He suspected that, without anger, he was going to be soundly beaten for quite a while. Then again, he had just disarmed one of the best fighters on the fields. The uproar slowly built around them as a flood of guards surrounded him, congratulating him and commenting on the fight. Alador was overwhelmed by slaps and calls.

When the crowd began to dissipate, Flame came up and slapped him on the back. "Well, that ended better than I expected. Well fought. I honestly thought for a moment that you meant to kill him. I would have stayed out of it otherwise." Flame nudged him in the ribs. "Can't have my richest friend getting strung up or put to the sword."

Jon glanced coldly at Flame. "He was trying to kill him, you fool. It's a good thing you tackled him, or he would have. I wasn't close enough to reach him in time."

Alador glanced at Jon, not answering. He knew that if Flame hadn't interrupted him, Alador would have badly injured or killed Toman, even though he'd been using a practice blade. Flame looked at Alador for a long moment. "I hope you aren't that stupid?"

"I was angry," Alador conceded, liking that thought better than stupid.

"If I decided to kill whenever I was angry," Jon stated solemnly, "there would be a trail of bodies."

Alador glanced at Jon. "Somehow, I don't doubt that." The last few spectators were still approaching and slapping him on the back as a way of congratulation before moving on to dinner. "Flame, can you go check that Keelee made it back safely? She was full of strange fears before half-day, and I need to speak to Jon."

Flame's face immediately brightened as he put a reassuring hand on Alador's shoulder. "I'll do one better; I'll take her to dinner." Flame sauntered off while Jon just shook his head.

"Given the amount of time he spends with your body servant, I hope you're charging him for a share of her services." He watched the flamboyant guardsman push and banter his way into the caverns.

"Charge him? What do you mean?" Alador sat down on a bench and wiped his face with a rag before pulling out his sword: he'd nicked it some, and needed to take off the jagged edges before they caused undue injury.

"You know, to pay part of what she costs you." Jon sat down beside him.

Alador looked from the sword to his friend. "I don't pay her," Alador answered. "I... she just asked to come here with me." He eyed Jon in confusion.

"Body servants don't just come with you – they're paid companions. If you aren't paying her, then someone else is," Jon pointed out logically.

Alador's eyes narrowed. Maybe she was spying on him for his uncle. Had the plea to be saved from his uncle's designs been just an act? "I've told Flame and Keelee that what they choose to do together is their business. " he delivered that sentence a little more brusquely than he'd intended.

"Yes, I can see you are totally unaffected," Jon conceded sarcastically.

Alador flashed him a cold look as he drove his sword back into the sheath. "I still haven't quite calmed down from that fight," he pointed out. "Be nice."

"I *am* being nice: you're still alive," Jon fired back.

Alador cracked a grin on that answer. "All right, point taken. I didn't ask you to stay back so we could talk about Keelee." He glanced about. The fields were almost empty now, and the bench he'd chosen wasn't near any cover that might have concealed an eavesdropper, so he felt safe to speak.

"Jon, what are your thoughts on people being sold by one person to another for... whatever purpose?" Alador looked at him. "Not like Keelee, who chose that life, but against their will?"

"You mean slavery?" Jon asked curiously. "I'm against it. If you need to have a man do a task, there are plenty willing to work just for a roof or some food. No need to take away their freedom."

"I have recently learned that there's a... slavery racket on the third tier, and I want to put an end to it. I was wondering if you'd be interested in giving me a hand?"

Alador phrased the thought as a question, realising that if he couldn't trust Jon, who in this world could he trust? After his confrontation with Luthian, Alador was running out of people he could turn to for help.

"When do we leave?" Jon asked with utmost seriousness.

Alador cracked another smile. "I was hoping you'd say that. I want to use my next extra half-day, but there's a problem with that – it's not your half-day."

"I have a couple earned passes. I can use one," Jon answered. "I never had a use for them before, so I've just been storing them up."

"Don't you have anyone out in the city that you like to visit?" Alador didn't get earned passes; he already had two half-days. He did earn kitchen duty every now and then, but usually that was for tardiness.

"Nope. I don't make friends," Jon pointed out. "Well, except you, but you're strange."

"Well, thanks," Alador said sarcastically. "I will get you a pass to the fourth tier for dinner. My father left some for me in case I ever wanted to bring someone with me. I think it only fair to warn you that taking out this den of slavery will be an act of aggression against the High Minister himself."

Jon gave this revelation several seconds' consideration. "You mean you're moving against your own uncle?" Jon looked over at Alador.

"I do," Alador answered quietly. "I mean to see him unseated one day." His eyes were unfocused for a moment, realizing that he really did plan to one day see his uncle off the tiers.

Jon stared at Alador for another long moment, then stuck out his hand. "I'm in."

The rest of the week went uneventfully. Alador didn't want to find out if Keelee was being paid by Luthian to keep an eye on him, so he'd been avoiding her, using his hurt and anger as a shield. He knew it was likely that his uncle was bending her to his will, so he didn't share much, even though she was obviously hurt by his rebuffs.

He'd had even slapped her questing hands one night, making it clear that her services were not desired and telling her that he'd let her know when they were. Her intake of breath behind him had made him cringe, but she had rolled away and left him alone, which was what he wanted.

When at last Alador could escape the caverns for his father's home, he left both excited and fearful. He was finally going to have a taste of freedom, but he also intended to kill a man tonight. He'd been raised to believe that killing was wrong. All his life he'd had to fight the urge to take Trelmar's life until the day he'd finally given in.

But Alador hadn't planned that – he'd been angry and vengeful. Today he wouldn't be acting in anger or vengeance but in the pursuit of justice. A part of Alador had come to believe that sometimes you just couldn't reform or correct evil; sometimes you just had to kill it.

The fact that he was okay with this concerned him. He wondered for a brief moment what Mesiande would think of him now, and decided that this was something he'd never tell her… That is if she ever spoke to him again. The thought twisted in him and he forced himself to focus on this evening.

Jon had told Alador that he needed to see to a few things first and that he'd meet Alador later. Alador, meanwhile, wondered how wise it was for the three of them to go waltzing into this breeding den of Luthian's; but the very thought of women being forced to bear children against their will was against everything he believed about creating and looking after small ones. They should have lives of happiness and joy while they were young. Alador doubted that anything connected to Luthian had any sort of happiness or joy.

Alador arrived at his father's house and spoke the words of entry; the door unlocked for him and he slipped inside. His father had spoken the truth about the house shutting down while he was away; Alador's boots echoed loudly as he moved down the hall toward the library. Even the furniture had been covered with large sheets of linen.

He moved into the library and started a fire using flint and tinder; he couldn't use magic to do it. Flame had teased him about it, pointing out that his special affinity with water "just puts that spark right out." Alador could hear the words in Flame's jubilant tone of voice. He smiled as the spark caught tinder and began to spread. He sat back on his heels, watching the flames.

He'd thought about asking Flame to join them, but he wanted Keelee safe, and Flame was apparently very good at keeping the others from bothering her. And, if Keelee was to be believed, his friend always treated her like a proper lady. Alador couldn't tell if that were actually true or if Keelee were just trying to spare any feelings he might have. He put another log in the fire absent-mindedly.

"Intending to make sure everyone knows you're here?" Sordith spoke softly behind Alador.

Alador had been edgy since his fight with Toman and shot up with his boot dagger in his hand. Sordith caught that hand even as Alador spun about. "Easy, lad. It's just me."

"Sordith, you can't sneak up on people like that. It'll get you killed," Alador spat out in frustration.

Sordith just grinned at Alador, letting go of his hand. "It usually gets others killed," he pointed out.

Alador took a deep breath. "Still, don't do it around me." He sheathed his dagger, moving to the table and pouring them both a short drink. "Are we still on for tonight?" He asked handing a glass over.

Sordith took the glass filled with fine smalgut and sniffed it. "Yes, though…" Sordith paused and pointed to the glass in Alador's hand. "Wait, I thought you didn't drink?" He took the shot, winced at the burn, and smiled with satisfaction. "That's the stuff."

"I used to not do a lot of things," Alador answered softly and tipped the glass back. The burning sensation was somehow calming. He set the glass back down.

"Is your death-mage friend joining us?" Sordith asked curiously as he refilled his glass.

"Yes. He seemed as offended as I was about what's happening. And before you ask, yes, he knows that it means taking on the High Minister." Alador flopped down on a linen covered chair.

"And the Trench Lord…," Sordith pointed out, glancing round to find a chair of his own.

"I might not have mentioned the Trench Lord," Alador answered, resting his forearm across his eyes.

"You'd think any man would have the right to a trifling detail like that, Alador," Sordith said, removing the cover from another chair and settling into it.

"Yes, but you're close to the Trench Lord, and you'll know if he's one of the Trench Lord's men. I didn't mention it specifically so that you could set eyes on him. If he *is* one of the Trench Lord's men, then we kill him. I'm really hoping he isn't: I rather like him, and he did save me from one of the Trench Lord's assassins." Alador spoke without looking at Sordith, and kept his tone even.

"Growing up quickly, aren't you lad?" Sordith's tone was soft and tinged with sadness, but he nodded in approval of Alador's foresight.

"Seems like I don't have much of a choice in this city," Alador replied.

The sound of footsteps echoed in the hall, drawing their attention. "You could put five families in the front hall," Jon stated matter-of-factly as he entered.

That was my first thought." Alador smiled at Jon. "Jon, may I introduce Sordith. Sordith, this is Jon: the mage I spoke about."

Sordith rose to his feet, and both men assessed each other, neither moving to acknowledge the other. Alador sighed. "Do you know him Sordith?"

"Nope," Sordith answered evenly. "He has a determined cut. I like that."

"Why should he know me?" Jon's eyes flashed to Alador. "You said nothing about working with some back-alley rogue."

Sordith bristled at that insult. "You will find I am several cuts above a back-alley rogue."

Alador stepped between them. "This is one of the Trench Lord's right-hand men. However, he's decided that in certain matters, honor is more important than slips…" Alador began.

"Whoa, whoa, whoa! I never said that," Sordith sputtered, waving his hands in denial. "I said I didn't like being involved in certain dealings. Slips, well that is a whole other matter."

Alador rolled his eyes. "Fine… He doesn't like slavery either. Better?"

"Much…" Sordith relaxed a little.

"You can't trust him," Jon said flatly.

"People told me that about you, Jon," Alador pointed out.

"They were right – you can't trust me either." Jon's eyes were still on Sordith.

"How about this? After this last week, I don't trust anyone; but that doesn't mean we can't go kill this bastard together. Think you two can put your egos down long enough to go kill a slave trader who uses dark magic?" Alador was ready to smack their heads together. And people usually thought he was childish.

Jon considered this for a long moment then nodded once. "I think I can manage that."

Sordith grinned. "The pleasure of killing such a bastard comes close to owning a sackful of slips," he offered, his chest swelling at the thought.

Alador took a deep breath. He was still trying to come to terms with the fact that he was going to commit murder tonight. Taking a life in anger had somehow been different; but Alador couldn't get the niggling thought out of his head that killing was still wrong, even if the cause were right. "Okay, Sordith. What's the plan?"

Sordith led them both over to the table, tossing the linen aside. He laid out a crude sketch of the compound. "These are the holdings on the far side of *The Blackguard* Caverns. He pointed to the gate to the street. "There are two guards outside and two in the compound beyond."

Alador looked at the map carefully. "So there won't be a problem going in – it'll be getting out..." He looked from the map to Sordith.

Sordith nodded; Jon was silent. "There's a guard at each entry to the house. None of the windows open, except the long ones looking out over Veaneth's veranda. There are three guards that wander the halls and, as far as I can tell, another two that stay close to Veaneth himself."

He moved his gaze from Alador to Jon. "He's running it much like a brothel. Anyone with slips can come visit the Daezun. The Daezun men, although drugged, don't appear to be that unwilling, and have a fairly regular stream of women visiting, plus they can choose to lie whenever they wish with the Lerdenian women that are forced into the house. The Daezun women are pretty much chained to their beds, so if you really mean to release them, we will need to get the keys from Veaneth."

Jon eyed the map. "I foresee another problem."

Both Alador and Sordith looked at him expectantly. When Jon didn't volunteer the answer, Alador prompted him. "Which is…?"

"Once you free them, where will they go?" Jon asked. "If they return to the trenches, the Trench Lord will just round them up again. They cannot remain on the tiers."

Alador hadn't considered that. "Is that true? If they return to the trenches, will they be easily found?" He looked at Sordith with concern.

Sordith nodded. "Daezun stand out there. They're either killed out of revenge for Lerdenians injured or lost in the wars, or rounded up by Aorun's men. If you really mean to save them, we'll have to get them out of the city."

Sordith sighed at that thought. Alador's desire to save the slaves had added a further complication to the whole affair.

Alador put both hands on the table, considering. "The refuse wagons leave first thing in the morning and travel down the bridge. I saw them a couple of days ago when leaving my uncle's early in the morning. We take them out that way. Sordith, can you get me four such wagons? We can hide some inside with garbage on top and the others can leave as collectors."

"It'll take some slips, but I can make it happen," Sordith answered. "The best time of night will be to hit them just before day break anyway. The stream of customers will have dried up by that point, and all will be quiet."

"Except that we need to be in the house before then, or what would I be calling for?" Alador pointed out.

"It's run as a brothel," Jon calmly reminded Alador. "You don't go to inspect it - you go to enjoy its pleasures."

Alador's nose wrinkled at the thought. "I can't force a woman to see to my needs," he pointed out. "That's what we're supposed to be rescuing them from, remember?"

Sordith chuckled. "So sit and have a drink with them, and gag them if they won't shush till we're ready to act. I like this plan, Jon. I knew I liked the cut of you."

"I still don't trust you," Jon answered stoically.

Alador sighed. "I'd best go change, then. I will have to change into some robes – and Jon, you too. Sordith is known – he won't raise a brow armored. I have robes in my room we can wear."

Jon brought his hands up in a flourish. "I don't see any advantage in that. I'm not going in there without my sword and armor." A shadow swirled about him, and his armour and weaponry were magically transformed into black robes with no embellishments.

"We're going to buy ourselves three women for the night. Live it up Jon, pick vestments with a bit color," Sordith chided.

"I like black," Jon answered, his voice devoid of emotion as his eyes moved to Sordith. Sordith just nodded at the death mage. "Right then, black it is." He saw no point in pressing the matter.

Alador had well remembered his father's lesson so stringently taught: about how magically empowered clothes were easily dispelled. He'd therefore gotten used to just dressing. He considered Jon's point. If he changed his armor into robes, it would be a simple matter to change them back. He concentrated, remembering the many different robes of the high council, and found in his mind's eye a dark blue robe trimmed with the same silver as his eyes.

Sordith nodded. "I can tell who's been around money. That's more like it." His hands emphasised the comparison between the two mages.

"Wait here," Alador told them. "I'll get some slips. I'll be back in a moment,". He headed for the door. "Try not to insult each other too much while I'm gone."

He hurried up to his room to fill a belt pouch, moving quickly. Jon really didn't seem to like Sordith, and the last thing he needed was for the death mage to kill the man. On his way back down, he grabbed two of his father's fine cloaks: one black with red lining, and the other one he hadn't seen before, but it matched his robes well: it had a silver lining and an

embossed dragon on its back. He hoped Henrick wouldn't mind.

When he entered the library, both men were standing at the table, neither speaking to each other. Alador tossed the red trimmed cloak to Jon, who caught it deftly. "Ready?"

Sordith actually looked relieved to see Alador reappear and led the way out of the library. As they were headed out behind Sordith, Alador glanced at Jon, who seemed quite pleased with himself. "What happened while I was gone?"

"I made it clear what would happen to him if this were a trap," Jon answered.

Alador glanced at Sordith's back as he slipped out the front door, and shuddered slightly. He decided he didn't want to know how Jon had made his point.

Chapter Twenty-Two

By the time, they'd arrived at the stables, laughing and joking as if under the influence of strong drink, Sordith had arranged for the four wagons to be left by the gate just before sunrise tomorrow. They'd have to have the slaves freed just as the wagons arrived if they wanted to keep them safe.

Sordith saluted the stone-faced Lerdenian guards that stood at the gate. Alador was relieved to find that they weren't *Black Guard* – he couldn't fathom how even half-Daezun could condone what happened here, nor did he want to kill his own brothers-in-arms.

"Good evening, fine sirs! We've come to buy a couple hours with a lass or two." Sordith winked to the guards.

"Did you make prior arrangements, sir?" one of the guards asked formally.

"Surely the High Minister's own nephew does not need an appointment to spend time with a comely lass. I assure you he is quite generous with his slips." To make his point, Sordith palmed a slip into the man's hands.

"The High Minister's nephew?" The guardsman looked Alador over; Alador drew himself up fully and let the silver of his cloak glimmer in the evening light. "I expect Veaneth will be proud to welcome such a patron." The man nodded to his fellow guard, who opened the gate.

They entered the courtyard breezily, and though they blustered like the drunken patrons of the upper tiers that all three had seen at one time or another, each of them kept a sharp eyes on their surroundings. The door was opened for them and they all stepped into a warm hall, where a beautiful woman with long, blonde hair came to take their cloaks. Her dress left little to the imagination, her physical attributes boldly on display as she carefully hung them on pegs before ushering them into a private parlor.

After she had closed the door, Sordith stepped up to the small bar. "Step one accomplished – we're in." Sordith breathed out with a wink at the other two. "I wouldn't drink anything on offer here."

He surveyed the bar and beckoned them close, speaking his warning in whispers. "They lace the drinks with a drug that makes the customers part more readily with amounts of money they hadn't intended to spend. We will need our wits sharp."

They looked about the room, and Alador felt eyes assessing him. Before either could respond to Sordith's words of warning a corpulent man with a balding head stepped into the room. "By the gods, it is true! The High

Minister's nephew himself. I assure you, milord, that all is in order in my establishment." The man skipped forward, bowing ingratiatingly and grabbing hold of Alador's hands to lay a fleshy kiss on the back of it.

Alador snatched his hand away in disgust: the man's hand had been cold and sweaty. Unconsciously he wiped it on his robe. "I want a full tour first - that I may report as instructed to my uncle, after which my two friends and I here will take three of your finest for the entire night. Separate rooms, of course," he demanded, mimicking Luthian's cold, hard voice.

"Any... *preferences*, m'lords?" Veaneth asked rubbing his hands together in anticipation. His face was greasy from too much food and his nose was red from other excesses.

All three answered at once. Alador and Sordith both snapped out "female", while Jon requested "male". Both Alador and Sordith looked at Jon simultaneously in surprise, but as usual Jon's face was bland and blanks.

"And race?" Veaneth asked, apparently not fazed by Jon's response.

"I would like to spend some time with a full Daezun, as they never once let me in their circles," Alador stated coldly. "I think I deserve to know what I have missed." He crossed his arms as he stared at Veaneth.

"I don't care," Sordith paused with a grin and mimicked the feminine shape with his hands, "as long as she is comely."

"Nor I," Jon answered, staring in disgust at Sordith.

Veaneth nodded and gestured grandly towards the bar. "I will have those rooms prepared, and then I will return personally to give you the tour. Why don't you all have a drink while you wait?"

Alador had hated this man the moment he laid eyes on him. Veaneth was the personification of excess and greed, and that whining subservience in his voice didn't fool him for a second. Still, Alador said nothing, choosing instead to nod that the man's offer was agreeable. Veaneth hurried off.

Jon looked at Alador. "Why didn't we just kill him there and then – without all this... subterfuge?"

"We need to know how big this place is, and how many we'll have to sneak out," Alador pointed out. "We need a tour. I don't want to blunder about trying to free people that might not want to leave, or come across people who'd prefer to sheathe their daggers in my gut."

Sordith nodded. "Best to get the lie of the land and know what we're up against."

"Fair enough," Jon answered simply. Maybe being a death mage made life simpler in certain respects...

It wasn't long before Veaneth returned and took them on a tour of the whole area. Now that he was closer, Alador noted that the man smelled of wine and sour sweat. He was hard-pressed to walk alongside Veaneth and look properly impressed. He kept his hands clasped behind him as they walked.

Keeping his horror hidden at what was happening here was difficult for Alador. He strove to keep up the appearance of an assessing lord. The room where those soon to bear small ones were kept was easily the most appalling part of the tour; there must have been twenty or more pregnant woman there.

"I was under the assumption that those here were prisoners, but I see they are well cared for." Alador looked to Veaneth for an explanation.

"The High Minister wants the children to be grateful to him for their care in childhood. We do all that we can to ensure that those with magic are given the finest care." Veaneth preened at the praise.

"I see. And those without magic?" He asked his chin rising slightly.

"We put those down," Veaneth answered casually, as he unlocked the door.

It was all that Alador could do to school the shock from his face before looking at Veaneth again. "I have it on good authority that many half-breeds do not come into their powers until adulthood. It seems premature to kill them before their powers can truly be known. Explain."

"The eyes, My Lord," Veaneth explained matter-of-factly. "One can tell by the pigmentation of the eyes. Those that have the potential for magic are allowed to reach adulthood; but those without, well, what would be the point? That's why we weed them out at birth" He spoke as casually as someone might of sorting one set of seeds from another, rather than of murdering babies because of the color of their eyes. He opened the door.

This room had small ones of varying ages, all of them half-breeds. Although the door to the room had been locked, at least the small ones inside seemed well cared for and fed. There were toys, and the rooms were clean.

Alador stopped for a moment, staring at the curious children that had stopped their play to examine their visitors. Every child had Lerdenian eyes. Not a single child had the plain brown eyes of the full-blooded Daezun. Alador knew his own eyes were silver; Sordith's behind him were copper. Faces flashed before him, and of those with power, not a single one had plain brown eyes. "Has there ever been any of power with Daezun eyes?"

"Not that I know of," Veaneth answered. "In fact it was I who brought this to the High Minister's attention as a way of distinguishing those who will come into power from those who will not." He beamed proudly as he looked about, offering sweets to the children that had clustered about him.

Alador wanted to kill him right there. It took everything he had to stay his hand; but he didn't want the small ones to suffer the trauma of witnessing this foul creature's death. "And what of the ones that reach the age of testing and don't manifest?" Alador managed to keep his voice even, though with great difficulty. He glanced at Jon, but as usual, couldn't tell what the man was feeling.

"We send them to the mines or the brothels. If they don't come into power, well, they can still be used for rebreeding. That latent talent is still in there. Anyone who has bred animals knows this: you weed out those with the qualities you don't want and you rebreed those with the qualities you do."

Veaneth was quite proud of the children displayed before him. "Of course, this is the first batch so a bit of guesswork is involved at the moment."

Sordith walked up, intent on drawing the focus from Alador's hardening face. Alador was losing his ability to hide his disgust and rage. "And acquire quite a few extra slips in the process, eh Master Veaneth?" Sordith dug an elbow into the man's fleshy side as if to tease and play, though the force of the blow belied the playfulness of the gesture.

Veaneth exhaled a rush of air at the elbow's contact and, rubbing his side, moved towards the door a little ruefully. "Yes, well there is no harm in earning a little extra to cover expenses and in recompense for the expertise I am developing in the field..." When they were all out, he locked it again, and Alador noted which pocket he slipped that set of keys into.

"Now, to those rooms you ordered, shall we?" Veaneth lead them back upstairs.

As they walked up the stairs, Sordith dropped back beside Alador, using Jon as a buffer between them. "Rein in your temper or you'll give us away," he hissed.

Alador took a few deep breaths and nodded. "I am most impressed, Master Veaneth," he announced, once they were back up into the main hall. "Assuming our satisfaction with the performance of your choices tonight, I assure you that my uncle will soon be fully informed of my opinions concerning this process." His double-edged meaning was lost to the man who smiled with pleasure.

"Of course, milord. I have picked a special lady for you. She has some spirit and a ready tongue, so if that bothers you... well, just leave her gagged or fill her mouth with something that stops her talking." Veaneth's dark chuckle made his meaning clear, and Sordith laughed with him.

"I like this man. Knows the proper way to treat a woman – keep her on her back and

schooled to satisfy my every whim." Sordith
clapped him hard on the back once more.

Veaneth winced under the blow. Seeming
to be in a hurry to get rid of this more affable
but overly physical rogue, he hurried them
down the hall to their appointed rooms, making
sure Sordith's was opened first. Jon's was across
the hall from both Sordith and Alador. Veaneth
opened each door with a flourish, saving
Alador's for the last.

Alador entered his room as the door shut
behind him. He pushed back the curtain
between the door and the rest of the small
room, and was appalled to see a young Daezun,
not much older than Sofie, chained to the bed
by all four limbs. She was naked and clearly
splayed for him. He took a folded blanket and
gently covered her while she glared at him.

"I'm not here to hurt you in any way. I'm
going to take the gag out of your mouth so we
can talk, but I need you to be quiet,
understood?" Alador asked gently. He reached
up after a moment and pulled the gag out of her
mouth.

"You're all filthy pigs! When I get loose,
I'm going to kill every one of you!" the girl spat
at him.

Alador sighed and put the gag back into
her mouth forcibly. "All right. Let's try this one
more time, and if you can't behave, then I'll just
have to leave you here like this. My name is
Alador, and I'm here to help you escape – you

and anyone else who wishes to go. However, if you continue to snarl and spit then I will leave you here till everyone else is gone and you are the last. Do you understand? Nod once." Alador's tone was firm, but gentle.

Very slowly, the woman nodded once. Alador smiled and removed the gag again, though he was more cautious this time. The girl didn't curse or spit at him, but she did watch him with clear distrust. "What's your name?" Alador asked softly.

"Tarea," she answered. Her eyes looked over him. "Are you really going to get me out?" Alador could see the glimmer of hope amongst the doubt.

"Or die trying..." He grinned at Tarea, trying to put her at ease. "I'm hoping for 'out' over 'dying,' but I could use some help." He looked around and saw the key to the chains hanging on the wall. "If I let you go, are you still going to try to kill me?"

"Unless it's some trick, then I won't kill you. Touch me and I will rip a piece of you off and shove it where it doesn't belong," Tarea promised with hateful vehemence.

"Well, we can't have that." Alador laughed softly and moved to fetch the key. He decided he was safer starting at her feet; Tarea could probably do some serious damage through sheer hate alone if she were totally freed. He wondered if Jon or Sordith were having any luck with their 'purchases' for the night.

Carefully, Alador freed her feet and then one hand. Tarea watched him warily as he moved around the bed to free the other. When she was free, she scooted back hard up against the headboard, holding the blanket tight around her. Alador looked about but saw no clothing. "Where are your clothes?" he asked softly, knowing that loud voices or sudden movement might set her off. She had that same hurt, betrayed look he'd seen in Mesiande's eyes, and it was tearing him apart.

"The Master…" She spat at the mention of 'Master,' "says we don't need clothes till we are filled with a small one."

"How long have you been here?" Alador asked, making sure to give the bed a wide berth as he carefully poured a drink. He started to take a sip from it, but decided against it at the last moment – he remembered Sordith's warning that the drinks might be spiked. Dulling the woman's senses down, however, probably wouldn't hurt with her as tense as she was. He offered Tarea the glass instead.

She took the drink from him gratefully, staring into it for a moment before drinking deeply with obvious thirst. "I guess maybe three months," Tarea answered after she'd finished. "I've lost count of days. Sometimes men only come for a couple hours." Her hands began to shake as they held the goblet.

Rage tore through Alador. He wanted so much to see Veaneth drained of life. He wanted to move through the halls and rip out the throat of everyone that helped chain these women down. And men… If Jon had gotten what he asked for, then there was a man chained down in his quarters. There were men here forced to service the carnal desires of other men…"

Alador shuddered at that thought, then realized that Tarea was watching his face, and forced himself back to the task at hand. "If I can get you out of the city and give you some slips, is there somewhere you can go?" She looked to be full-Daezun, so maybe she wasn't an outcast.

"Yes. I can return home," Tarea whispered. She still clutched the blanket to her chest with one hand, and her eyes reminded Alador of a cornered fawn.

He decided to keep her talking, partly for information and partly hoping to see her terror fade. "How did you get here to start with?" he asked. There was peace, so how was it that women were being taken this way, he wondered?

"My mate was a half-breed that came into his magic. He was forced out, so I came here with him. We thought to make a home with him in the *Guard* he'd heard about." Tarea's voice broke. "He died when they came to take me from him. They just killed him for no reason. He wasn't even armed ." The vehemence and ferocity she'd shown when Alador had first walked into the room had disappeared. She was a bereft young woman, mourning the murder of her love.

Alador took the goblet from her and refilled it before pressing it firmly back into Tarea's shaking hand and urging her to drink. He hoped, for her sake, that it was drugged. He didn't know what to make of her story; part of him was glad now that he hadn't brought Mesiande with him.

Would this have been her fate? Would she have been wrenched from him, or would his uncle have used her as leverage for control? Alador realized if Luthian ever found out about Mesiande, that is exactly what would happen. He was grateful that the only ones that knew about her were Henrick and Keelee.

He hoped Keelee hadn't said anything to his uncle about his love for Mesiande. He was suddenly certain that Luthian would use Mesiande to get anything he wanted out of Alador; and at that moment, Alador realized that there wasn't much he wouldn't do to protect her.

They sat and talked for a while about where Tarea had come from, and about her mate, Jayte. It wasn't long before Alador realized that Sordith had been right: the wine was drugged. He took the goblet from the woman and urged her to lie down. Tarea sleepily did Alador's bidding without complaint. He tucked the blanket about her and returned the goblet to the decanter.

For an hour, Alador paced the room, anger seething within him. As much as he wanted to be with Mesiande, regardless of what his father told him he'd found out about her feelings for him while he was in Smallbrook, he simply could not be with her. As long as Luthian was in power, he could not reveal his feelings for her or for anyone else in his home village. He could see now the true depths of depravity that his uncle was capable of, and he had no doubt that if Luthian ever learned about Mesiande, he would use her as a lever to bend him to his will.

His rage at the injustice of the situation mounted ever higher, reaching a level of intensity that was dragon-like. As had happened during the fight with his instructor, his fury burned beyond the point of reason and self-control. Had Remamaum infected him with more than a dragon's geas...?

He strove to control it: to keep a grip on the plan that had the best chance of success, but finally he could contain his rage no longer, and tore out of the room. "VEANETH! SOMEONE GET ME THAT BASTARD...!"

He moved down the corridor towards the main hall and grabbed a guard by his tabard. "Take me to your Master's room. How DARE he try to drug me!?" Alador was raging and the guard's eyes flew open wide. He didn't even try to intervene to calm, but instead took Alador down to Veaneth's quarters.

Sordith and Jon had heard Alador's outraged bellowing and were right behind him as he came face-to-face with Veaneth. Veaneth must have heard the commotion: he came stumbling out into the hall while still belting his robe shut, his fleshy, naked body quivering both with haste and with alarm.

Behind Alador, Sordith was hissing: "Not the plan, not the plan…"

"CHANGED…!" Alador yelled. He grabbed Veaneth's robe and jerked him forward to his nose. "You tried to DRUG me!" he hissed. "You tried to drug the nephew of the High Minister himself, you underhanded, disgusting mountain of sniveling FILTH…!"

"I assure you sir that the wines contain only that which relaxes inhibitions and empowers the senses. The effect would have worn off long before you had decided to leave." Veaneth had paled and his hand slipped into his robe pocket.

"Yes, that will be why the woman chained to that bed - to whom I gave a drink to make her more willing - is now nothing more than a drugged and biddable child. Did you plan to make a biddable child of ME, Master Veaneth, before robbing me of my every slip?"

Alador drew the man's face close so they were nose to nose, his performance convincingly that of an angry patron, eyes blazing.

"Of course not, milord! I would never cheat or harm a guest, much less one so closely related to the High Minister," he whined, not quite meeting Alador's gaze. "Here, a gift! Let me make it up to you..."

Veaneth pulled a beautiful glowing emerald from his pocket. "I offer you this as my apology." He held the stone up, and Alador felt his gaze drawn to it by some power overwhelming his will. He knew immediately that it had been imbued by the Black Arts charm his father had warned him about.

Even so, despite his foreknowledge, it was all he could do to get a magical barrier in place - something he still wasn't good at. As it went up, he heard Jon curse and knew that his friend had shielded as well. He stepped back a little, still holding Veaneth's robe.

Sordith was apparently not so lucky. He stepped forward, eyeing the stone. "I think we should take his offer and go, Alador," he murmured.

Veaneth grinned in triumph. "Protect me! They plan to take it from you!" he screamed at Sordith, pointing at Alador. Almost like an automaton, Sordith jerked and drew his blades, spinning as if to slash them across Alador's midsection. In that same moment, Alador dragged Veaneth round by his robe —so that instead the blades carved wide wounds across the slavetrader's back.

Veaneth screamed and fell to his knees, his emerald falling to the ground. Alador brought his heel down hard on it, but it didn't break – instead it rolled under the sagging stomach of its overweight master, who was now a dead weight in Alador's hands. Alador staggered backwards, releasing him.

Jon, in the meantime, had turned to face the guard who had brought them down the hall. His robe disappeared and his armor reformed even as the guard's sword cleared its sheath. Jon's hand flashed up, a black arrow already formed; he sent it flying through the heart of the guard as if propelled by a powerful crossbow. The man had barely taken his second step .

Behind him Alador heard the rasp of a sword leaving its sheath . He spun round, still trying to change his robes back into armor, and was caught between Sordith and the other guard. The guard leapt at him, his bare sword poised over his right shoulder, its handle tightly gripped in both his hands: clearly intending to separate Alador's head from his shoulders with one savage sweep of its cutting edge.

Alador dove to the ground next to Veaneth, feeling the sword-wind whistle through his hair. He kicked out at the guard's legs in an attempt to knock him off his feet, but only managed to make him stumble towards the wall. Alador turned to regain his footing and stand up, but Sordith was already bearing down on him with both of his lethal weapons.

There was no time for him to deflect the incoming blades; he threw up his hands in pitiful defense, but by then Sordith had leapt right over him and disemboweled the guard.

Alador rolled back up to his feet, hearing the sound of heavy, metal-capped boots approaching down the corridor. "Are you back?" he asked Sordith as he spun about, looking for Jon.

"Wasn't gone," Sordith answered as he ran back into the corridor. Alador glanced after him in disbelief, and saw that Jon was already out there battling the first of the hall guards to arrive on the scene. Sordith met the charge of the second one head-on.

Alador drew on the power he needed to shift back into armor and pulled his sword. He buried his foot in Veaneth's massive midriff and discovered he wasn't dead; instead his podgy fingers were scrabbling frantically for his emerald, but in his haste he had knocked it beyond his reach.

Alador struck the glowing stone with his blade, shattering it. Veaneth cried out weakly and started to mouth something: maybe a plea for his miserable life, or maybe an evil charm… Alador raised his shining blade and with a strength he hadn't known he had, drove it through Veanth's back and through his heart and into the floor.

He knelt, and rifled Veaneth's pockets for the keys: finding them quickly, feeling their warmth from proximity to their owner's sweaty skin. He stood up, and finally re-engaged his brain. Sordith and Jon were both still engaged with the guards outside the room; they were proving harder to handle than expected.

Alador took a moment to center himself and find that well of power within him. He focused on the energy of an electric storm: until he felt his hands tingling with its power...

"DOWN!" he yelled. Both Sordith and Jon dropped instantly, and Alador fired a bolt of lightning from each hand. The two guards twitched violently inside the flash of bright white light before they too dropped to the ground. Jon and Sordith stood back up and swiftly dispatched them.

Alador grasped the handle of his sword and pulled it out of the floor and the grotesque carcase now leaking fluids from every orifice. "Ideas...?" he asked as strode past them and headed for the main hall.

"Can you make fog?" Jon asked, moving forward to stride beside him. Alador nodded. "Then you and I can take the four outside. That leaves at least another two we know of to your tender mercies, rogue; can you handle that?" Jon snapped at Sordith.

"On it." Sordith turned in the opposite direction when they reached the center entryway, leaving Jon and Alador approaching the main door stealthily. If there were any other patrons still enjoying the bawdy house's facilities, they were sensibly keeping their heads down out of the way. Jon knelt down and gestured to Alador that he should feed his fog under the door.

It took Alador a few moments to sense a water source he felt safe pulling from, and then considerably more to turn it into fog. He felt like he was taking far too long, and the pounding of his heart seemed to emphasize the seconds as they passed. He found fog hard to envision: it was elusive and shifting as. The water vapor seemed to form in snake-like tendrils from his fingers.

He shut his eyes, not wanting to know what Jon intended for fear it would break his concentration. He went on pulling the water and feeding it through his hands into the dense fog he was imagining... Then he felt Jon's hand on him.

"That's enough," Jon whispered. Alador opened his eyes and shook his hands – they were as cold as ice. He stood, looking at Jon, who lifted his hand to sign that they should wait...

On the other side of the door came the clang of a dropping sword and the thud of a falling body. Alador moved to open it, but Jon caught his hand. "Not yet. Let the air clear," he warned softly.

"What did you do?" Alador asked just as quietly. He wanted to look, but trusted Jon enough to know that he should do as he was told.

"Laced it with a poison to put him to sleep," Jon answered. Alador nodded and the two waited. The house was quiet now except for the sounds of their breathing. No outcry from Sordith: Alador decided to take that as a good sign.

Finally, Jon nodded and they both eased out the door. Alador knelt to check the first guard, only to find that the man was obviously dead. "I thought you said it would put him to sleep?"

Jon just shrugged. "Getting the strength of the dose right is not my strong suit," he admitted.

Alador grinned. He'd planned to kill the guards anyway: they couldn't risk leaving witnesses who might be able to identify them as members of *The Blackguard*. He rose and headed for the gates, on the look-out for any other guards that Sordith may not have noted. "Again?" Alador mouthed. Jon just nodded.

The fog was easier this time as it was already forming in the streets, rolling in from the harbor. He could simply take it and pull it slowly together until it formed a mass in front of him. Alador concentrated, keeping it steady, and watched in fascination as Jon turned it green.

On Jon's signal, Alador carefully fed the fog through the close-set bars of the gate. Both men dropped. Jon mimicked holding his breath and dragging them in. Alador nodded he understood.

They opened the gate and swiftly brought the bodies in - away from any prying eyes that might be in the street. One was still alive, but not for long: Jon slid his long, thin dagger neatly through the man's ribs and into his heart.

Alador turned and headed back into the house. He was confident now, his mind focused on releasing all the slaves. Jon followed a little ways behind him, his movements warier...

But neither of them saw or heard the guard behind the door. Alador felt a sharp pain, cold as ice, driving into his back. His eyes widened in shock as he looked down to see a sword point sticking out from just beneath his ribs. He dropped to his knees, clutching his chest as the sword was pulled back out, ready for the fatal second thrust.

He was dimly aware of two knives flying over his head: Sordith had arrived a fraction too late. Time seemed to stretch as Alador fell forward, the floor approaching slowly as he sank into blackness.

Chapter Twenty-Three

Renamaum looked down at the small blue dragon. It lay battered, broken and floundering on the rocks of the shore. The tide was coming in – it would clearly die if it stayed where it was, but it was too large for Renamaum to move it to safer ground.

The small dragon looked up at him, waiting for death. "What were you thinking?" Renamaum growled down at it. "Did you think that battle was a game? - that there are rules?"

"I thought the danger had passed: our foe was defeated and had left the field to the victor," the small dragon croaked out, thrashing helplessly, its injuries too great for flight.

"NEVER assume that a foe is defeated. The best ploy is to let your enemy think he has won." The large dragon nuzzled his smaller

flight mate. "Remember this when next you go into battle."

"I think I have fought my last..." The small dragon laid back against the rocks, its breaths coming in great gasps, too exhausted to keep trying to escape.

"So you will just give up and let the ocean's waves drown you?" Renaumam scoffed. "You fought so bravely for what is right, only to lie back and die now? I thought more highly of you than that."

The little dragon's eyes flashed with anger. "What would you have me do? You cannot save me and I cannot fly," it hissed in defeated vehemence. "When the waves come, I will flounder till I am beaten to death against the rocks."

"If that is what you choose, then that is what will happen." Ranaumam shook his head and looked down at the dragon. "I will leave you to wallow in your defeat; but first, allow me to give you one word of advice."

"Advice when I am about to die...?" the smaller dragon growled in frustration. "What possible advice could you give me that would be of any use?"

"When you cannot fly, my dear fledgling...." The dragon leapt into the air as he called down, "...you swim."

The sound of voices blended fuzzily in Alador's ears, like an obnoxious buzz. He shifted and felt an unfamiliar stab of pain in his ribs. Slowly, he opened his eyes for a brief moment... then quickly shut them against his too-bright surroundings.

"Mistress Vera, I think he's waking up!" a voice called.

"Don't shout," groaned Alador, moving a hand to his aching head. It felt like it thumped along with his heart.

"Yup he's awake." That annoyingly cheerful voice could only belong to Flame with. "Close one, there, Alador. A couple times I was sure you were a goner."

"What happened?" he croaked out, his throat dry and aching. He was trying – and failing – to piece together how he'd ended up... wherever he was now.

"Jon brought you in. Said the two of you got jumped. He didn't have a scratch on him, of course. Figures... Why couldn't they have stabbed HIM...?" Flame grumbled.

"Flame, no offense, but go away," growled Alador. The man's loud voice was competing with the booming of his heart.

"Fine thanks I get for sitting with you. He's all yours, Mistress Vera. Woke up grumping..." Flame's boots sounded off across the floor.

A soft, feminine hand moved Alador's hand away from his head to rest a warm cloth on his head. It felt wonderful. "The potion we gave you to keep you still has a kick to the head when you wake. Lie completely still and give yourself time – it will subside." The voice was kind.

Alador put his hand back over the cloth, glad for its warmth. "Is Jon really okay?" he asked, beginning to recall the evening. He had no idea what had happened. Had they failed? Had they accomplished nothing?

No: Alador knew for a fact that that scumbag Veaneth had died, at least. There was satisfaction in that alone. But he couldn't ask any questions, not now. Flame must have stayed to ensure that Alador stuck to the story of getting jumped. Did Flame know the truth? Alador really needed to talk to Jon.

"Jon is fine. As your friend said, the mage seemed to have escaped without a scratch. I'm afraid you lost whatever slips you were carrying, though. Jon said he gave the man what you both had to stop him from doing any further harm... You should have just given the man your slips to start with. Life is far more precious than a few slips of medure," she scolded softly.

Alador groaned, his hand going back over the compress. It figured that Jon and Sordith had cast him in the role of stubborn refuser to do what a stronger opponent had demanded. But then again, everyone knew Alador had a temper, so he supposed that fit.

His head hurt too much and he had too little information to speak, so he just nodded – and immediately regretted the motion. The sharp intake of his breath must have given him away.

"Lie STILL I said," Vera scolded. "It will pass. I'll return regularly to change the compress until you can manage without it."

Alador slipped in and out of sleep, waking when Mistress Vera changed the compress, slipping back under with its comforting warmth. He had no idea how much time had passed when he was finally able to open his eyes and smile at the woman who was putting the compress back into a pail of steaming water.

"Feeling better?" she asked.

"Yes. How long have I been here?" Alador asked. He looked around, taking in his surroundings.

"Three days," Vera answered. She must have read the alarm on his face – her hands moved to hold his shoulders down before Alador could even try to sit up. "Not yet," she scolded.

"Three days? I've been here three days?" he squeaked in frustration, his voice rising an octave.

"You almost died, Alador. I would think that thanking the gods would be of a higher priority than squealing about a few days lost to sleep," Vera chided him firmly. She let Alador go when it was clear he would remain still. "I don't know what it is with you people in *The Guard*: you'd think you'd be grateful for a couple days without lessons."

Alador put his hand to his chest. The memory of the point piercing it was now as sharp as the sword itself. The area was tender, but he felt no bandages. "I thought I was pierced," he whispered, looking back up to the healer.

"You were. In fact, the damage was so bad that we had to send for a mage of the golden sphere. Fortunately for you, a few of them were still around. They tend to be sent out on active duty quickly, once they graduate. He was able to bring you back from Dethera's door in the nick of time, though it was nearly beyond his skill. The blade barely missed your heart. What kind of man stabs another in the back?"

Alador didn't volunteer what he was sure was the right answer: a desperate one. If the guard had seen any of the bodies they'd left lying around, he'd certainly been desperate. Alador watched Vera leave, then tried to piece the fragments together...

Slowly, he was able to remember everything right up to when he'd seen Sordith throw the two knives over his head. He closed his eyes, trying to remember anything after that, but nothing came. It looked like he was going to have to wait until Jon came to see him, or until he was released from this healer's temporary prison.

It must have been several hours later when Alador woke up to find Jon sitting by his bed. Jon looked at him with disdain. "I think it quite unfair that I have to continue my studies while you lie on your back taking an enforced leave of absence."

"I DID nearly die…," Alador pointed out. He managed a weak grin as he put his hand over his chest.

Jon offered him a large tankard of water. "Yes. Thankfully, you didn't – I would have found that much more difficult to explain." Alador took it gratefully.

"Were we…? I mean, did they…? You know…" Alador looked about to see if anyone could hear them.

"All those that wanted to were loaded into the wagons, along with all the slips you had, and sent out of the city with the dawn refuse wagons. We let the children be – they were happy, and the mothers willing to stay will take good care of them," Jon answered.

"How many left the city?" Alador asked softly. He realized he was thirsty and downed the water.

"All but ten," Jon answered with a shrug. "For those ten, that was a better life, believe it or not."

"But then... won't they know who attacked the stables?" Alador frowned. "My uncle will find out."

"Oh. Your rogue took care of that," Jon stated cryptically.

Alador looked confused. "How, pray tell, did Sordith 'take care' of that?" He eyed Jon curiously and warily, though he felt a huge weight lift off his shoulders as he realized that their plan had freed so many.

"He told them Aorun sent us." Jon grinned wickedly.

"That's going to land the Trench Lord in a heap of trouble with my uncle; or Sordith in a heap of trouble with Aorun if he's ever identified." Alador was alarmed for the safety of his new-found friend.

"Sordith said that he doubted anyone would put the pieces together. He left behind a heap of slips, and there was a lot of laced wine being guzzled free of charge. He was pretty sure no one would have a clear memory of the night's events." Jon shrugged. "I think he's right."

"My cloak? If it's still there, the High Minister will think it was my father." Alador panicked and sat up, wincing at the pain in his chest.

"Faith, my friend, faith... It has been safely returned to your father's home, and the house is once again sealed." Jon finally smiled. "Your friend Sordith made sure we left no clues behind."

"I thought you didn't like him," Alador pointed out, lying back once again.

"I don't." Jon shrugged. "But it's his neck within the Trench Lord's easy reach. In this matter at least, he has a vested interest in concealing our involvement in the 'crime'."

Alador sighed with relief. "Any rumors on the streets or in the halls?" he asked.

"Not that I've heard. I have permission to take you back to your rooms." Jon tossed simple black robe onto the bed. "You might want something to wear. Your armor has already been repaired and sent to your room ."

Alador was stiff, but he got the robe over his head with minimal discomfort. He'd been in bed for three days, so he supposed his wobbliness was normal. Jon brought him his boots, and soon they was ready to leave.

It took some effort to move. Alador was weak, but slowly they made their way from the healers' hall. Alador didn't see Vera anywhere, but he made a note to come back and thank her later.

"I expected to wake up to a distraught Keelee, but I don't remember seeing her,"

Alador remarked as they made their way slowly through the halls. Jon nodded, but didn't answer. Alador picked up on his friend's silence and glanced sideways at him. "What's wrong?" he asked. "What are you not telling me?"

"I think your body servant has decided to give her services elsewhere," Jon answered softly.

"Unless she's moved in with Flame, I very much doubt that." Alador said, stopping in the hall.

"He said she hasn't come back from her half-day..." Jon's answer was factual, with no inflection. "It seemed like the most plausible explanation."

"She hasn't been here for three days? Not even a word to Flame?" Alador asked with concern. He started moving again, this time with more purpose.

"Slow down. You nearly died, remember?" Jon picked up his pace in order to keep up .

"Yes, and in the meantime, Keelee might be in trouble. She warned me that something was about to happen... What if she left to try to stop whatever it is?" Alador snapped out.

"What is it with you and wanting to save everyone?" Jon rolled his eyes as he kept up their fast walking pace. "You are one man. Maybe some people don't want saving, like those that got left behind in the stable. Ever think of that?"

"At least we gave them a choice, Jon," Alador snarled. "People should be able to choose who they want to be and how they live their lives, as long as their choices don't infringe the rights of others."

"You're an idealist, do you know that?" Jon was finally showing something resembling anger.

"Someone has to be in this god-forsaken city. There is little else to redeem it in the eyes of beast or mortal." Alador was too tired to argue and focused on walking and breathing. His chest burned with each intake of breath.

Jon also fell silent at Alador's words. They reached his room, and Alador flung open the door hoping to see Keelee there... But she was nowhere to be found in the small room. Her hairbrush was still on the desk. Alador moved to the wardrobe and threw it open. It was still full of her dresses.

"She hasn't taken another." Alador sat down on the bed, tired and concerned. "She wouldn't leave what little she owns behind." He sat and thought for a long moment. "Jon, can you get me Flame? I have never been to her father's. I doubt anyone expects me for duty, so I'm going to check on her... If Flame has a pass, maybe he can take me."

Jon nodded. "If he doesn't, I have an extra I can give him." Jon turned on his heel and strode from the room.

Alador forced himself back onto his feet and began to search his desk for any note or warning she might have left. He hoped to find some clue to what had caused her agitation...

Finding nothing, he moved to the wardrobe. At the back of a drawer, he glimpsed a glimmer of silver; he reached in, grabbed hold and pulled it out. It was the silver tube that Henrick had given him to write back and forth to Mesiande.

Alador's mind raced. Why did Keelee have it? Slowly he made his way back to the bed, where he sat and stared at it. How long had she had it? Did it ever send? Was his own letter still within? His heart racing, Alador slowly opened the case and shook out a letter in Mesiande's hand.

Alador,

I know that it took me a while to write this letter back to you. I hope you can forgive me for the pain it must have caused you to wait for it. I had a lot to think about. I have come to realize that even if you had not killed Trelmar, you would have had to leave anyway and that the village would have seen to his hanging. So really, things are as they would have been even if he had not died at your hand.

I have been thinking a lot about magic lately. I know that the Daezun hate the Lerdenians for their magic, but I do not think that is the truth of it. We were all one people once, if the stories are to be believed, so the Daezun must hate the Lerdenians for how they got their magic. Otherwise, they would hate dragons too.

I think that if anyone were going to see to freeing dragons, it would have to be a half-breed – someone with Daezun beliefs to see the task through, and with Lerdenian magic so they can actually pull it off. So I am glad if this is truly why you have these dreams. Just so as you know: I would hate to hear that a dragon had eaten you. It's never a good thing to have one's future mate eaten by a dragon.

Dorien says to tell you that the device you spoke of is a bolt-thrower. It is used to take out large animals that cross a set path or it can be set up on a harbor wall to defend against ships. He said to tell you that, much like a bow, if you disable the drawback mechanism, it will not fire.

I am very proud that you are going to use your powers to save a dragon. I know you worry about me leaving or not wanting to be with you because of your magic. I worry that you will find me dull without any. I hope that I did not take too long in writing this back. If you don't write me back, I guess I will know that you have decided I took too long.

I have to go to the celebration of Sofie's naming day tomorrow. It will be sad to have it without you here this year. Gregor continues to dote upon her, and I am sure they will housemate. Gregor is going to circle next year. I don't think the Gods gave Sofie a child this last circle, but I suspect Gregor will see that matter taken care of at the next circle.

I miss you so very much. I miss the way you would look at the stars as if you could see something there that I couldn't. I miss the way you would watch out for the small ones and teach them things. I miss *the fact that, until you found your stone, I could outshoot you. I miss your hugs and I miss your kiss. I love you, Alador, and I do not want anyone else to be my mate. I am going to next year's circle. Please! Write me back and tell me you will be there.*

Mesi ♡

Alador stared at the pages. If Mesiande had written this and sent it the night before Sofie's naming day, then she'd written back to him about six weeks ago. She must have been completely heartbroken, thinking that Alador had changed his mind.

He wanted to dash to the table and write to her right that moment to make things right. He also wanted to find Keelee so he could choke the life out of her. She had known that he was looking for this, and she'd kept it from him. Now, he wanted to find her to ask her why.

He sat heartbroken, staring at the letter. His uncle had hinted about the things he'd known. Now, more than ever, Alador suspected that Keelee was in his uncle's employ, and as more than just his body servant. Had she told

Luthian about this magic tube? Henrick had said that no one but Alador and Mesiande would be able to read anything inside it, but he doubted that applied to his uncle.

Alador buried his face in his hands, letter still clasped in one as he rocked back and forth in misery. He could not be with Mesiande as long as Luthian lived.

He knew what his uncle wanted from him, and he had no doubt that he lacked the power needed to confront him. He doubted that he could cause more than a minor irritation to the most powerful mage on the isle. He'd almost died at the hand of a mere guard! He was no match for the High Minister. His only trustworthy friends were a flamboyant fire mage, a sullen death mage, and the right hand of the Trench Lord. A fine group they made.

The door opened and two of those trustworthy people came in. Flame looked around. "She still didn't come back?" he asked with a frown.

Alador looked up in misery. "No. And now I need to speak to her about lying to me. Can you take me to her father's store? She had some dream that something bad was going to happen. I should have listened to her..." Alador was already exhausted.

"Of course. I have a pass; I can get us out," Flame answered. "It's not your half-day, but Jon said he'd give you one of his earned passes."

Flame looked across at the death mage, and Jon handed Alador his pass. "Want me to come, too?" he asked with concern, eyeing Alador, who looked deathly pale.

"No, I'm just going to ask her father where she might have run off to. I hope she's just hiding there for some reason." Alador put the letter on the table and changed from his borrowed robe to the soft linen that he wore beneath his *Black Guard* uniform. Then he started buckling on pieces of armor.

"Do you feel well enough to do this, Alador? I'm a little concerned," Jon murmured.

"Careful Jon, I might think you have feelings," Alador teased, grinning over at Jon to ease his mind. Truthfully, Alador just wanted to crawl into his bed

"I'll deny it with my dying breath," Jon answered. "I can be concerned for a friend's well-being without having feelings."

"Concern is a feeling," Flame offered brightly, grinning with mischief.

"Shut up," Jon answered. He turned on his heel and strode out, shutting the door behind him.

Alador just chuckled and finished dressing. He strapped on his sword, already feeling more comfortable with the familiar weight at his waist. There was no sign of where he'd been stabbed, though he caressed the spot on his armor. The repair was flawless.

"You sure you're up to this? I can go check without you," Flame offered with unusual care. "You look kind of done-in, to be honest."

"It's a walk. I have been in bed for three days. It will do my muscles some good, and we don't have to hurry," Alador pointed out. He forced a smile to his face, though he didn't feel like smiling. He had to know if Keelee was working for his uncle, and he had to hear from her own lips why she'd kept the case from him.

"Good point." Flame nodded. When Alador was ready, Flame led the way through the halls and out the of the cavern entrance to the third tier. It had come on to rain quite heavily, and the wind whipped in off the sea. They gathered their cloaks about them and neither of them spoke much. Breathing the cold, damp air was like breathing fire in Alador's left side; speaking was not high on his list of priorities.

He and Flame traveled down to the second tier, and finally Flame ducked out of the wind and up to a shop front. The door was locked and the windows were dark, but he knocked loudly anyway while Alador looked around. Hardly anyone moved about the streets, even though it was only just past midday – the driving rain was probably keeping most people at home. A stream of water ran down the center of the angled street.

"No one is in." Flame shrugged and looked back at Alador.

Alador peeked in the window as he spoke. "Isn't that unusual for a merchant?"

"A bit," admitted Flame. He looked about them.

Alador put his hand to the window, trying to see inside. "Things look broken up in there. We need to get in," Alador said, more anxious now. He couldn't see much, despite his frantic efforts.

Flame shrugged. "Easy enough." He turned and kicked the door hard a few times; it didn't take long before it flew open. Both Flame and Alador pulled their swords, and Alador took the lead, stepping inside. There had clearly been a fight here – everything was in shambles, and it looked like the place had been thoroughly searched .

He made his way to the back rooms beyond the shop front. They were just as bad: in the dim light Alador could see few things that hadn't been turned over or smashed.

"Looks like they were robbed." Flame frowned. "I don't see anyone anywhere…"

Alador walked down the last hall and opened the door on the end. A man's body lay on the floor, face down – Alador moved quickly to his side and turned him over. He was alive, but barely. It was amazing that the man had lived at all – his entrails were spilling out of the wound in his stomach.

"Where's Keelee?" Alador asked urgently. The older man groaned, and Alador slapped his face lightly, trying to bring him closer to consciousness. "Where is Keelee?" he asked again.

The man wheezed out only one word, but it was a word that stilled Alador's heart. "Trench…"

"I would offer to run and fetch a healer… but he isn't going to make it," Flame pointed out softly.

"I know," Alador answered, sighing in defeat. "Get a pillow from the bed," he ordered.

Flame did as he was told, and Alador carefully laid the man's head on it, careful to move him as little as possible. He put a cover over the dying man and took his hand. "I promise you," Alador swore, "I will find her." His voice held cold determination, though it was gentle.

The man on the floor looked at him and nodded, then closed his eyes. It was as if he knew that finally he could let go. His next rasping breath was his last, and the hand Alador clutched went limp.

"Where are you going to look for her, Alador? The trenches are huge, and who knows what low-life swooped her up as a prize?" Flame looked down at him incredulously. "You're in no shape to go traipsing about the trenches."

"We won't have to traipse. I know where she is. You just need to show me where the

Trench Lord lives," Alador stated coldly as he struggled to his feet.

"The Trench Lord? You plan to march on the King of Thieves? And do what? Demand he hand her over?" Flame's sarcasm was not veiled. "You've gone mad. That wound must've gotten more than just your gut. And may I also point out that you are in no shape to do this?"

"I plan to demand that he give her back ." Alador pulled his hood up and headed for the door, his anger fueling his leaden limbs with new-found energy.

"Woah, woah, Alador. You can't just go in and demand anything from the Trench Lord. He's...he's like a king." Flame scampered after Alador and grabbed hold of his arm.

Alador wrenched free. "Show me his home, and then you can return to the caverns, Flame. I don't expect anyone to come with me. This is between me and Aorun." Alador's voice was hard, and his eyes danced with anger as they met Flame's.

Flame stared at Alador for a long moment, then shook his head. "I ain't missing this. If I live, it'll be a story to buy me drinks for, well..." - Flame paused, considering - "ever."

Alador had already headed out the wrecked shop door. Flame followed him out into the rain. "If we live, Flame, I will buy those drinks forever," Alador promised softly.

He was tired of bullies. He was tired of men who didn't play by rules that were fair. He was tired of those who preyed on the weak because they could, not because had no other choice. Alador had heard once that even animals never killed for pleasure – that it was a mortal failing.

Tonight, one man was going to get that pleasure. He just wasn't sure which one.

Chapter Twenty-Four

Alador strode up the long staircase to the Trench Lord's hall, so angry that his exhaustion seemed like a memory. He looked around as he climbed the stairs, taking in the impressive walkway filled with statues carved in various acts of depravity and death.

They were probably meant to cause trepidation in any who would dare to walk here, but Alador did not feel fear – not now. He was resigned to the fact that he would likely die here today; but at least he would die honorably, in a manner of his own choosing.

His death would not be because of his uncle's manipulations or at the hand of the Trench Lord's henchmen. If they wanted him dead, one of them was going to have to do the deed himself. Alador had decided to make the rules.

He stepped into the hall boldly and was met by a large oaf of a guardsman.

"What do you want?" The man eyed Alador and Flame curiously.

"I am here to see the Trench Lord," Alador stated.

"Yes, yes, leave your card and I will see

that he gets it." The man laughed softly. "Wise up, friend. You don't just waltz in here and ask to see the Trench Lord. You only come here when he tells you to; and you'd better pray you're never that unlucky."

"He will see me," Alador insisted.

"Oh, REALLY? And who are you, who's so important that the Trench Lord will drop everything he's doing, just to see *you*?" The man's hand was now on the hilt of his sword, sarcasm dripping from his every word.

"Tell him the High Minister's nephew, Alador Guldalian, *demands* an audience. I'm sure he'll make the time," Alador answered imperiously.

Alador's name must have rung a bell in the guard's streetwise brain – or else the family connection carried some clout – because he dropped the attitude and glanced at Flame.

"Yup, that's him," Flame said, his voice tinged with pride.

The oaf lumbered off through a door and was gone for some time. When he came back, he was smirking but polite. "The Trench Lord has been able to rearrange his schedule, and will see you now. Your man can wait here with me." He jerked a thumb towards a nearby chair.

Flame shook his head. "By the gods, I'm not missing this. I go where he goes."

The guardsman just shrugged and led the way through the impressive halls. They were almost, but not quite, as large as the hallways in

Luthian's home. When at last Alador and Flame were shown into the Trench Lord's office, Aorun sat behind a rather large red desk. His booted feet were kicked up on the dark red wood and, unlike Flame and Alador, he wore no armor. He looked to have on a dressing robe and a pair of black leather pants.

"I fear you caught me in bed, gentlemen. Whenever I have a lady visitor, I consider it impolite not to take time from my busy schedule to attend to her... needs."

Aorun drew deeply from the flask in his hand, watching Alador. "So what can I do for the High Minister's... nephew?" He didn't seem at all concerned to see the mage.

Alador stepped forward, his manner formal and his back stiff. "I have come to retrieve my body servant. It appears that you took her after I gave her permission to visit her father. It is time you gave her back," he demanded with all the authority he could muster.

"Body servant... Body servant..." Aorun tapped the flask to his lips. "Oh, do you mean the lass I took into my protection after her father had that most fearsome accident?" Aorun was clearly enjoying the moment; his voice was full of amusement, and he grinned triumphantly at Alador.

"An accident at the end of your blade," Alador growled out. He could feel the dark anger rising in him, mingling with the dragon's rage. "You murdered that man."

"Bad things are known to happen to those who don't pay for the protection of the Trench Lord." Aorun shrugged. "It's a dangerous tier to work in without it."

Aorun hoisted his booted feet from his desk and placed them on the floor. He looked at Alador, and his face had lost its smile. Now his eyes held hatred. "But now you come to my home with no protection, making demands. A lone guardsman, out in the trenches... Hardly wise, when accidents are so common around here.." He rose to his feet, setting the flask on the desk.

"I am hardly alone, and both of us are mage-trained," Alador snarled.

"Odd. I thought the Daezun taught their young to count, right Jayson?" Aorun drawled out.

Alador began to turn to see who this Jayson was when pain filled his head and lights flashed in his eyes. There was no one else in the room but Flame. It was Alador's last thought as he sunk to the floor, where someone's boot connected with his temple.

Alador awoke to the feel of water in his face. He came to, sputtering, his eyes burning from the salt. Seawater filled his mouth as a second wave washed over him, and he blinked rapidly, trying to clear the dripping salt water from his eyes.

His side ached from being pulled tight, and he realized that his hands were caught in some sort of metal gloves, stretched above him on the ceiling. They were so tight around his wrists that Alador could barely feel his fingers; they tingled from the restriction in the flow of blood.

His feet were bound tightly to the ground by metal clasps around his ankles, allowing him to stand, but not move. In fact, as stretched out as he was, Alador could barely move at all. He noticed blearily, shivering in the cool room, that he was naked.

Finally, his vision cleared enough for him to see Aorun. They were alone in what appeared to be a wine cellar. Alador's heart filled with fear when he saw the number of tools on the table – Aorun wasn't just going to kill him. He was going to torture him. Alador tried to speak, only to realize that he'd been gagged with a mass of rounded leather. Unable to curse Aorun properly, Alador growled out his anger. He couldn't see the Trench Lord, but he could sense him in there with him.

"Ah, good, you are awake." Aorun sounded eager.

A whip snapped behind him, and Alador's body tensed despite himself. Aorun just laughed. "Do you know how long I have been dreaming of the time we would spend here together? All the ways I would make you beg for death?" He grinned at Alador as he came around in front of him, whip uncoiled in one hand. "The many ways I would make you pay for my mother's death?"

Alador wanted to scream at him that he hadn't even been born when that had happened, but Aorun was clearly mad. Even if he could speak, there was no way he could get the man to see reason. Aorun stepped back behind Alador, and this time the crack of his whip brought the pain Alador had expected. Fire lanced across his back as the crystal-embedded leather dug into exposed flesh. Alador moaned despite his determination not to give this man the pleasure of hearing his pain.

Alador forced his thoughts to things that would make him angry; he was always able to cast better when he could use his anger as a focus. He thought about Flame, who must have been the one to betray Alador and Keelee, giving her to Aorun. He thought about all the secrets he'd entrusted to the light-hearted redhead. Alador wondered if Sordith had betrayed him, too.

Maybe he'd been set up to die in the brothel. He kept these thoughts between the searing cracks of the whip, drawing on its anger to see him through, but even that didn't help him contain the cries of pain that only the gag muffled. Eventually, Alador lost count of the cracks – and lost track of his thoughts – and slipped into oblivion.

A searing, cold wash of water snapped

Alador back into consciousness as water drained down his back and legs, the salt inflaming the open wounds on his back. He whimpered – he couldn't help it. Aorun walked easily around Alador and set the empty bucket next to five others, three of which were still filled with water. It was going to be a long night, Alador realized. Aorun obviously did not intend to kill him quickly.

"Ready for death yet?" Aorun asked, his tone eager, clearly hoping Alador was not.

Alador could think of a few things he wanted to offer the leering man before him, but satisfaction was not one of them. He shook his head no, hatred radiating from his eyes and in the tension of his body.

Aorun moved to the door and called out loudly. "I was hoping you would say that. Jayson, bring her in."

The man Alador had known as Flame dragged Keelee in by her tied hands and tossed her to the floor in front of Alador. The past three days had obviously not been kind to her; Keelee's hair was matted, and one side of her face was bruised in the definitive shape of a man's hand. She looked up at Alador and he looked down at her with sorrow; the tears were streaming down her face.

"I tried to warn you," she sobbed up to Alador. She tried to move to him, her simple shift doing little to cover her. Flame stood behind her, arms folded.

The warning Keelee had given him washed over Alador – that, because of her, he would be horribly hurt. Now he wondered... which hurt? This? Or the fact that she'd hidden Mesiande's letter? In some ways, her betrayal in regards to the silver case was worse than Aorun's torture. Alador could only look down at her and nod sadly.

Aorun moved from where he leaned against the table and jerked her up by the hair. She squeaked in pain. "Tell him you have decided that we will be properly bonded." He held Keelee before Alador. "Tell him how much you hated being bedded by some low half-breed."

Alador wanted to yell at her, tell her to say the words, to buy herself some mercy from the Trench Lord, but he couldn't do anything except pull angrily at his wrists.

Keelee growled out in pain and fear, "I would rather bed a korpen than bond with you!"

Aorun's mouth was near her ear when he hissed, "Fine by me." He dragged her by her hair and tossed her to Flame. "Jayson, you wanted her so badly, take her."

Flame grinned brightly as he caught her, grabbing her by the bound hands and clearly intending to take her back out of the cellar. "Yes, milord!"

"No! Here! In front of him." Aorun grinned coldly, pointing to the floor across from Alador. "Let him see his little slut being used, while I bring him the pain his people deserve."

Flame looked a bit uncertain but then tossed Keelee over to one of large wine casks. "I've wanted to do this since I first saw you." He began to unbuckle his weapon belt.

Rage flooded through Alador: Flame's betrayal, Alador's helplessness, the realization that what happened to Mesiande was going to happen to Keelee, and he couldn't stop it. He thrashed at his bindings furiously. He could hear Keelee sobbing.

The dragon's voice – Renamaum's voice – sang through Alador, so loud and commanding that it was like someone shouting into his ear.

If you can't fly... you swim.

Alador stood in shock, grasping onto that thought. He had to do something before Flame could violate Keelee, but he didn't have his hands, so half the spells he could work were out. He didn't know how to focus them without words and movement. His body relaxed as the answer came to him, the pain of his back fading away slightly as he turned his eyes to Flame – not Aorun, who was at his table of tools, picking his next toy. It was so simple. Alador watched as Flame tossed his sword aside, but his mind was on a particular memory.

"I could kill someone creating water?" Alador asked, alarmed.

"Not likely, but with the powers of water granted by a blue dragon, you can kill by pulling water from them," Henrick said bluntly. *"It would be a frightful death."*

Alador had practised that spell so often that he didn't need excessive power to do it anymore – and he certainly didn't need his hands or words. His eyes slowly moved to the empty bucket, and he began to pull the water from Flame – and only Flame. Time seemed to lose all meaning as Alador stared into the bucket.

He heard the choking sounds coming from where Flame had been kneeling to violate Keelee, but he didn't stop the spell. He didn't stop when he heard Keelee scream. The bucket began to overflow, and still he didn't stop. Something twisted inside Alador, sending wracking pain through his body – and still, he did not stop.

At first, Aorun assumed that the strange sounds were being made by Jayson doing what he'd been told. But when when he turned, it was to stare open-mouthed at what he saw. Jayson was on his knees before the wench, but holding his hands out in front of him. They were wrinkling, the flesh sinking as if aging before his eyes...

Jayson's flesh was withering, falling in on itself. His eyes shrank into hard dried peas as his body crumbled to skeleton and skin. In seconds the dessicated bones were falling in a parchment-covered pile. Keelee screamed and scrambled away in horror.

"By the gods…" Aorun whispered. Fear pounded through him. His eyes flew to the man he'd stretched from the ceiling to floor; the gloves that should have prevented him from casting were still secure. Aorun didn't move till he heard Sordith speak, though he hadn't heard his right-hand man enter.

Sordith put a hand on the terrified woman and pulled her up, leading her to the door and slicing the ropes that bound her hands. "Keelee, get out." His calm words sent the wench scurrying out, and he shut the door firmly behind her.

"By the gods, Sordith, did you see that? I have never seen anything like that before," Aorun whispered. His eyes returned to what was left of Jayson – a pile of ash that lay like a cremation on the floor.

"I think you may have taken on more than you should have, Aorun." Sordith leaned back against a barrel and crossed his arms as he looked from Alador to the Trench Lord.

"I will just kill him now." Aorun moved to grab a knife to finish the half-breed mage.

"I wouldn't do that," Sordith warned him firmly, standing back up.

"Well, we can't let him go, not after that; and I am not letting him turn ME into dust." Aorun moved towards Alador with the knife…

The Trench Lord saw the hilt of the throwing knife, quivering from his side, before he felt the pain of it. He turned to look at Sordith in shock. "WHY…?" Aorun's hand went to the dagger in confusion, pain searing through the wound.

Sordith held a second knife in readiness. "Because I will not let you kill my brother," he stated in his usual, matter of fact way.

"Your *brother*…?" Fear shot through Aorun as he remembered the prophecy. He glanced frantically from Sordith to Alador.

"The sea shall rise up in a bond of betrayal and rip all that you have gained from your hand. From your blood, dragons will rise up free and hungry. Your death will unite brothers that shall one day seize the thrones of Gods."

Aorun was not in the ocean though, so he could not die here. He reassured himself – he was not at sea. He smiled coldly, wrenched the dagger loose, and launched himself at Sordith, sending them both tumbling over a wine barrel.

Aorun came up slashing with both weapons, intent on disarming the younger man. He had trained Sordith – he knew how he fought. "I should have known something was off about you," Aorun hissed, slashing at

Sordith's midriff. "Always with that damn honor crap..."

Sordith barely arched his stomach away in time to avoid Aorun's slash. He spun around with one leg, attempting to trip his deadly adversary. He didn't bother with conversation: he had one goal, it seemed, and that was to kill the Trench Lord.

Aorun hit the ground, splashing as he came down hard on the bucket's overflow. He barely managed to roll up and out of the way as Sordith brought his dagger up under his chin. The blade cut Aorun's jaw but missed the targeted jugular. Aorun slashed out in return, gouging Sordith's forearm, and smiled with satisfaction on hearing Sordith curse.

Sordith launched himself at Aorun, and this time the two landed in water deep enough to cover them. For a moment, as salt water filled his mouth and eyes, Aorun couldn't understand why so much water was even there. He rolled over onto Sordith, forcing the man's face under the water with one hand, his knee on Sordith's dagger hand. Only then did Aorun see the three buckets, filled to overflowing with seawater that spilled out onto the floor. Aorun's eyes flashed up to Alador with true fear as he realized that those buckets were exactly where Alador was looking.

Aorun reached down with the hand that had been holding Sordith underwater and grabbed a throwing knife from his belt, sending it hissing through the air toward the strung-up mage. The knife thudded home in Alador's side, but the mage didn't seem to notice.

Aorun felt Sordith take advantage of his release beneath him, but by then it was too late to do anything: Sordith had already used his free hand to drive a second dagger into Aorun's stomach. When Aorun tried to wrench the dagger free, they rolled once more and Aorun found himself on the bottom, looking up at the wavering face of Sordith through a film of bloody sea water. No amount of thrashing could free him from Sordith's grip. Aorun's last thought was an ironic one: all his life he had feared the sea, only to drown indoors.

Alador looked over to see Flame's body crumble forward as it withered, but only for a brief moment. He flicked his gaze back to the buckets again once he was sure that Flame was no more. This time, when he fixated on the buckets of seawater, he simply thought of filling them from the inexhaustible sea. The lancing pain in his side only fueled the well of anger he was drawing from to keep the spell going.

If Alador was going to die here, that bastard was going to die with him. He would go on filling this underground cellar till his last dying breath. He wasn't aware of someone unlocking the shackles that bound his ankles – his gaze never left where the buckets sat beneath the water. He couldn't see them anymore, but he still knew where they were.

"Alador, stop! It's over!"

Sordith's voice seemed far away. Alador didn't believe anyone anymore. They all lied – all of them. Henrick had lied; Keelee had lied; Flame had lied; his uncle had lied. Sordith had lied: he hadn't come to the rescue like he'd promised, and Alador was going to die because of it. They ALL lied. NONE of them could be trusted. Lerdenians all deserved to die.

Hatred consumed him as tears laced his cheeks and saltwater burned his wounds. Sordith grabbed Alador's face, trying to get his attention. His eyes met Sordith's, filled with all the hurt and betrayal he felt, then Alador closed them, not caring anymore. A part of his mind still focused on the spell that had taken on a life of its own. They all deserved to die...

But then his thoughts shifted to Mesiande. Mesiande had not lied. She was pure and sweet. Alador could see her pulling back the bowstring, glancing back at him and laughing. He saw her sitting by the river, the sun making her brown hair glisten with strands of gold as she smiled at him.

He felt her warm body pressed against his as they sat by the river and talked. He remembered the way she would blow in his ear to make him miss a shot with his bow; and the glances she gave him when they were mining. He heard her laughter when she danced around the fire on the day he sold his bloodstone. Only this mattered – everything else was a lie.

Alador felt the water, cold and final, lapping at his chin. Mesiande loved him; that was all that mattered. And finally, words from beyond him swam through the frenzied waters of his brain.

"BROTHER... PLEASE! I beg you... Stop!"

Excerpt from
The Bloodmine
Book 3

Alador's lexital landed roughly beside his father's. The flight had been exhilarating and terrifying all at the same time. Fortunately, the lexital was a gentle one and more inclined to follow its mate. He had not had to have more than the few minutes of instruction. Alador unbuckled the saddle harness and slipped shakily to the ground eyeing the great bird with amazement. He held the reins in his hand petting the lexital as if thanking it for flying kindly.

"A bit unnerving the first time, as I said." Henrick spoke softly. He had learned not to startle Alador since his encounter with the Trench Lord. He came around wide to make sure Alador could see him.

"Yes, a bit. However, I see why you like flying. The view was indescribable." Alador was still caressing the lexital's head, the bird was happily letting him loosen shafts on her crest's pin feathers.

Henrick smiled. "I do love the feel of the wind on my face. However, note that the higher you fly, the colder that wind." Henrick held his hand out for the reins. "Here, let me tether them. They will not fly any closer to Keensight's cave. The times I have tried, they have panicked every time."

Alador handed him the reins and stepped back from the bid. "So we walk from here?" He looked about. They were in Daezun land to judge by the terrain. It was the familiar rock and scrub brush he knew so well. To the east of him, hills rose up covered in rocks that seemed like the gods had just tossed them down randomly. Some were larger than a dragon.

Henrick was tying the two birds to a larger bush with a solid base. "*You* walk from here." He stated glancing over at Alador.

"You are not coming?" Alador looked at him in surprise. "You said you would take me to him."

"I have brought you to him." Henrick gestured up at the hills rising up beside them. "However, he said if I joined you at the cave he would finally eat me and this time I do not think he was playing." Henrick looked at Alador. "You don't have to do this. We are only an hour's flight south of Smallbrook. We could fly up there and I could bring Mesiande to you and you can make things right." Henrick offered. "I am not sure you are well enough for this, son."

"I told you not to call me that." Alador glared at him, his response snarled in an almost feral manner.

"I am not going to stop calling you son just because you have some fool idea that I lied to you. I will say it one more time. I have never lied to you." Henrick sighed in defeat. "Maybe Keensight can knock some sense into that thick skull of yours."

"I know you used a spell on my mother." Alador's accusation seemed to be solely centered around this one statement.

"I have never said I didn't." Henrick stated. "It doesn't mean I don't care for her or enjoy her company. It doesn't mean I don't give a damn what happens to the result of that union." He glared back at Alador.

"It was a use of dark magic, a magic may I remind you, that you said was a violation of all the rules of magic." Alador glared at him.

Henrick dropped his head in defeat. "I don't want to fight with you when I may never see you again. Please. What is done is done. You exist because of that night. You should be grateful."

"Grateful that I am the result of a dark magic used in violation of a sacred trust from the dragons themselves. That might make the damn dragon eat me in itself." Alador looked up at the hill. "Which way do I go?" He demanded.

"Alador, a spell of glamour is not changing the will of another. It merely makes one a little more appealing. Your mother was free to choose as she wished. I did not compel her choice." Henrick's tone implored Alador to understand.

"As you said, what is done is done. Which way do I go?" Alador repeated the question not looking at Henrick.

Henrick watched his son for a long moment before turning to get a pack off his own lexital. "There is a path just across the stream near that large tree next to the cliff face. It will take you up the hills and into a hidden valley. Within that valley there is a stream. Follow the stream to its head and you will see the cave. The stream swells from the ground and out the door of Keensight's cave." Henrick brought him the pack. "It is about an hour's hike to the valley. Maybe another hour to the cave."

Alador had been listening intently to Henrick's instructions. He eyed the indicated tree as he took the pack. "Will you be here when I am done?"

Henrick nodded. "I will wait here for three days. If you are not back by then, I will come looking."

Alador nodded and strode off, headed for the tree. He was determined to speak to

Keensight now more than ever. He needed the dragon's help and it was the only one that either he or Henrick knew how to find. He only hoped the dragon had not decided to take off for a couple of weeks. As he moved to part the brush, to head out of the small clearing they had landed in, he heard his father call after him.

May the gods be with you and for once, watch that tongue of yours." Henrick's tone held true care and concern.

Alador just smiled coldly as he moved on, not looking back. He was done watching his tongue. If those that crossed his path didn't want to hear what he had to say, they had best not ask.

ABOUT THE AUTHOR

Cheryl Matthynssens is a mother of four and a grandmother of three. She graduated from Western Washington University as an English Education Major with a minor in Psychology. She later went back and received certification as a Chemical Dependency Counselor.

Combined with a love of helping others has remained a strong passion for all things fantasy. An avid reader, RPG player, and as her family calls her, a computer nerd, Cheryl has never given up her writing or desire to share her art with others. Book one of this series, *Outcast*, was released in 2013. In addition to these novels, she has also published two Children's Books: *How the Dragon's Got Their Colors* and *Not an Egg?!* Now available in e-format, hard copy and audio. *Once Upon a...Wait!* Is due out later this year.

Cheryl also has a blog and website. You

can contact her through those sites at dragonsgeas.blogspot.com or http://dragonologists.com/

Made in the USA
Charleston, SC
07 December 2014